Tales from the Kingdoms

Tales from the Kingdoms

Sarah Pinborough

GOLLANCZ

LONDON

Omnibus copyright © Sarah Pinborough 2016
Interior illustrations copyright © Les Edwards 2013
All rights reserved

Poison copyright © Sarah Pinborough 2013
Charm copyright © Sarah Pinborough 2013
Beauty copyright © Sarah Pinborough 2013

The right of Sarah Pinborough to be identified as the author
of this work has been asserted by her in accordance with
the Copyright, Designs and Patents Act 1988.

First published in Great Britain in 2016
by Gollancz
An imprint of the Orion Publishing Group
Carmelite House, 50 Victoria Embankment,
London EC4Y 0DZ
An Hachette UK Company

A CIP catalogue record for this book
is available from the British Library.

ISBN 978 1 473 20233 7

1 3 5 7 9 10 8 6 4 2

Typeset by Input Data Services Ltd, Bridgwater, Somerset

Printed in Great Britain by Clays Ltd, St Ives plc

The Orion Publishing Group's policy is to use papers that
are natural, renewable and recyclable products and made
from wood grown in sustainable forests. The logging and
manufacturing processes are expected to conform to the
environmental regulations of the country of origin.

www.sarahpinborough.com
www.orionbooks.co.uk
www.gollancz.co.uk

Contents

Poison

Sarah Pinborough

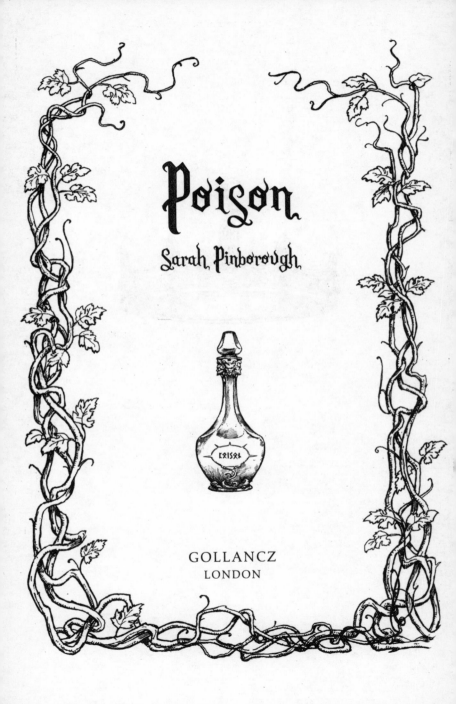

GOLLANCZ
LONDON

1

'Air and earth, Light and dark'

'She's too old for that nickname,' the queen said. She was standing at the window of the royal bedchamber and looking down at the courtyard below. Morning sun beat on the ground, but the air was still chilly. She shivered. 'She needs to start behaving like a lady. A princess.'

'She's young. There's time enough for that yet. And anyway,' the king laughed – a throaty sound that could have been born in the bowels of the earth or in the mud of the battlefield. 'You gave it to her.' He hauled himself out of bed and his footsteps were heavy. *He* was heavy. Getting heavier too. She'd married a glutton.

'She's not that young. Only four years younger than me,' the queen muttered. From behind her came the sound of liquid hitting ceramic and for the thousandth time she wished he'd have the good grace to at least piss in a different room. 'It was simply a passing remark that she was pale. It wasn't a compliment. It was meant to be a joke.' Her quiet words went unheard as her husband continued noisily with his bodily functions. 'And it was a long time ago,' she whispered, bitterly.

She watched as, far below, the young woman dismounted from her horse. She wore brown breeches and rode with her long legs astride the beast like a man. Her shirt was loose but, as the light breeze touched it, it clung to her slim form, flowing over the curve of her full breasts onto her flat stomach. Her thick raven hair fell around her shoulders and as she handed the reins of her stallion to the stable boy she tossed the dark mane to one side and the sunlight shone on it. She smiled and touched the boy's arm, and they shared a joke that made her laugh out loud. Cherry red lips. Pale skin with just a touch of dusky rose on her cheeks. Sparkling violet eyes. A living swirl of clichés. So free. So *care*free.

The queen's mouth tightened. 'She shouldn't ride in the forest so early. It isn't safe. And she shouldn't ride anywhere dressed like a common boy.'

'Everyone in the kingdom knows who Snow is,' the king said. 'No one would dare harm her. No one would want to. She's like her mother; everyone loves her.'

There was no reproach in his voice. The barb was unintended but it stung all the same. The saintly dead wife. The glorified beautiful daughter. The queen's mouth twisted slightly. 'She should be thinking about marriage. Finding a decent match for the kingdom.'

Below, Snow White slapped the horse affectionately on the rear as the boy led him away, and then turned to head into the castle. With the sudden awareness a mouse might get as an owl swoops above it she glanced up, her eyes meeting her step-mother's. Her smile wavered nervously for a second and then she raised her hand in a gesture of hello. The queen did not return it. Snow White dropped her hand.

How did she look from down there, the queen wondered. Did her own blonde hair shine in the sunlight? Or was she merely a resentful ghost – a shadow against the glass? She clenched her delicate jaw. The girl disappeared from view but still the queen's teeth remained gritted. They couldn't both stay in this castle for much longer. She couldn't stand it. She stayed where she was, gazing out of the window, and after a few moments the king came and stood behind her.

'It's still early,' he said, his thick body pressed hard against her back. He wrapped his arms around her waist and pulled her closer before one hand slid between the ribbons of her nightdress, seeking out her breast. His fingers were rough against her soft skin; a soldier's touch. She let him caress her.

'We should go back to bed,' he whispered hot in her ear. 'You know I go to war again tomorrow.' He pulled her back from the window, one hand inside her clothes as the other tugged at the bows that held it together. 'Show me how much you'll miss me.'

Finally, she turned away from the window and faced him. His eyes were glazed already and that made her smile. It took so very little from her to make him this way. His dead wife might have been well-loved, but she had never had this power. She had never realised her husband was a glutton for everything, or that all men wanted more than just good food on the table and excitement on the battlefield. They wanted excitement in the bedroom too.

She pushed the king back onto the bed and then finished the work he'd started on her shift. It slipped to the floor and she stood naked before him. She smiled and stepped forward, brushing his lips with hers, teasing him, before lowering onto her knees. She met his gaze – hers wanton and challenging, his powerless and full of need. The knot in her stomach unfurled. He was her puppet. His dead wife might have been loved more than she, but love was irrelevant. She didn't care how much he loved her, it was more important that he *wanted* her. And as much as his attentions were rough and coarse, she had learned how to please him beyond any other he had ever had, her dead predecessor included. He called her his water witch – because if there had ever been a lady of the Lake then she must have looked like her, his new queen who had so enchanted him. And even though he was old enough to be her father, she understood the power that gave her. Men were base. They were manageable. The king was her puppet and she would keep it that way. She hardened her heart and ran her slim fingers across his thighs so her red nails scored his skin slightly.

He flinched. She leaned forward and teased the tip of him with her tongue.

'You are so beautiful,' the king murmured.

Yes, the queen thought. *Yes, I am.* Snow White's face rose unbidden in her mind, and she pushed it angrily away as she took him in her mouth.

The king and his men left the next day in a glorious parade of pomp and ceremony. The queen watched from the battlements as he went off to wage his war against the neighbouring kingdoms. Although it was summer rain fell in a fine mist. Courtiers said that the sky was crying to see their king leave and risk his life for their safety and their kingdom's strength. Lilith, the queen, his water witch, knew better. Rain was just rain, and the king fought for his own ambition, not for his kingdom. It was the one quality she liked about him. The one she could understand.

As the gates opened, he turned and waved up at her and she nodded her farewell, the eyes of the city beyond straining to see her. They waited for her to cry, to show some emotion from behind her icy beauty, but she would not oblige them. She was a queen. She did not perform for the populace. They did not matter to her; they weren't *her* people.

A cheer went up, and the crowd turned their collective gaze from her as if she had been but a momentary distraction. The king's horse stopped as a figure ran towards it; a girl in blue, holding up her dress so the hems didn't get ruined, but still running with the joy of a child who has yet to be corseted instead of cosseted. Snow White. Of course. Above them all

8

the grey sky broke and a shaft of sunlight struck the castle and its grounds. Where the common people had looked at Lilith with wary fascination, they looked upon the father and daughter – especially the daughter – with fondness and love.

The queen kept her chin high. Her spine was straight from the tight stays that bound her, but it stiffened further at the crude display of emotion taking place below. Snow White reached up on her tip toes as her father leaned forward and she threw her arm around his neck, before handing him something she'd held behind her back. An apple. A bright red, perfect apple, the waxy skin catching the sudden light. The crowd cheered again as the king took the fruit, his face splitting into an enormous grin. Snow White stepped back and then curtseyed, her head bowed; once again the dutiful daughter and princess. The people went wild. Snow White, the queen of their hearts. The girl who could wow them all with something as simple as an apple. Everything was so easy for beautiful, lovable, perfect Snow White.

Lilith did not wait for the gates to close behind her husband, but turned and stormed haughtily back into the castle. The king was gone. The last time he had gone to war she had been a young bride, but now she was a woman. A queen. She was in charge and this time she'd make sure her presence was felt.

The drizzle developed into a storm and the whole castle was enveloped in a gloomy hush. The queen did not go to the formal banqueting room for dinner, but instead had a small supper sent to her room. She waited until the last minute, knowing that the cooks would have prepared several roasted meats and delicacies for her to choose from, before she sent a servant to fetch only bread and cheese and wine. The cooks would moan about the waste in a way they never would if the king did the same, but none would do it to her face and that was all that mattered. The king would be gone a long time and the sooner they learned to do as they were told the better. She had been forced to this kingdom and her marriage much against her will but she was learning to make the best of it. Her life could have been much worse.

Waiting for her bath to be filled, she gazed out at the rain and the distant glow of the foundries and the mines where the dwarves laboured. Each team worked long shifts and the fires never went out. This was a hardy land and the dwarves were the hardiest of its peoples. She wondered sometimes if they were hardy simply from years spent breaking their backs at the rock face, but when she'd mentioned it to the king he'd grown angry. He'd said that the dwarves enjoyed their work. Hadn't she heard them singing? Her words had stung him – he didn't like to be seen as unkind, even by her.

She had kept her thoughts to herself after that, but she could remember men who sang from the land of her own birth. Those men had been captured in foreign lands and brought across the seas, their dark skin so different from the milky cream of her own, and they too had sung as they'd been forced to beat at the earth and dig fresh roads. Sometimes a song was all a people had.

In its way the king's reaction, however, had amused her. What was this need to be seen as benevolent? If you were going to be cruel, then admit it. Embrace it. Anything else was just self-delusion and weakness.

The clatter of horse's hooves sung out above the rain and she opened the window to peer out into the evening. The rain was cold on her face and she squinted against it. The slim, cloaked figure on the horse was holding a heavily laden basket, and a wisp of dark hair was blowing free in the wind.

'I've changed my mind,' the queen said haughtily. 'I'd like my dinner now.'

The cooks and scullery maids kept their heads down. She could see their skin flushing from the rarity of this visit. She was the queen. She did not venture to the kitchens.

'All of it. I know the courses and I expect to see them all here.' Her words were greeted with silence. Outside, thunder rumbled. She walked carefully along the kitchen table where the platters from the dining room had been laid out. 'And yet they are not. Where is the pigeon? And the venison? There is always a haunch.' Her words were as sharp as the diamonds that covered her, shards of ice filling the air. 'Has one of you stolen it?'

'No, your Majesty.' Finally, the head cook, a fat ageing woman with warts on her chin and yet the softness of expression that told stories of a long and happy marriage and children at her ankles, spoke up. 'You know we would not do that.'

Lilith heard the slight reproach in her voice. As if she were talking to a spoilt child, rather than her queen.

'Then who did?'

'The princess. She said it was a shame for it all to go to waste. She said there were plenty that were in need of such a feast.'

'Who exactly?' Her stomach twisted in a knot of

cold snakes as it so often did when the girl was mentioned, but she remained cool. She was practised at
it. 'My husband is a generous king. To say otherwise
is treason.'

The servants' heads dipped lower, suddenly aware
that they had inadvertently trodden on dangerous
ground, but the cook simply twitched an eyebrow.

'The dwarves, your Majesty. She took the food
to the dwarves. They've been working through the
storm. She's very fond of them.'

'Why was she in the kitchens at all?' The queen
continued to move around the table, one slim pale
hand poking and touching the dishes, spoiling them
for whoever in the room might have thought to
eat them for supper. 'This is no place for the royal
family.'

'She's always come in here,' the cook said. 'Ever
since she was small and the good queen passed away.'

The *good* queen. The word didn't escape her.

'She needed some love,' the cook continued. 'It
didn't do her no harm.'

'That's debatable.' Her smile was a razor slash.
'She hardly behaves as a lady of her standing should.
I fear your interference has spoiled her.' She drew
herself up tall. 'She will not come in here again. If
she does, I shall throw whichever of you condones it

into the dungeons. You know the kind of creatures we keep down there. You would not last long.'

'The king would not—'

'The king isn't here,' Lilith cut her off. 'And I doubt he'd be impressed at his fine dinners being given to the dwarves. He won't be here for a long time, so you will do as I command.' She turned to leave, her heavy dress scratching at the floor. 'Oh, and one more thing.' Her cold eyes rested on the cook. 'You are dismissed. Get your things and leave the castle by morning. I will not have you here again.'

The gasps that rippled around the room were satisfaction enough, as was the expression on the woman's face, her mouth and eyes wide in disbelief as if she'd suddenly been slapped hard. In a way she had.

'And count yourself lucky,' the queen added. 'You've all heard the rumours about me. How I enchanted the king? How he calls me his witch? There is magic in my blood and you all know it. I have been kind, old woman. I could have turned you into a crone.'

She did not wait for their reaction but strode away from the suffocating warmth at the heart of the castle. She might not have their love. But she would have their fear.

The only place the queen truly relaxed was in the hidden room she had claimed for her own ever since she arrived. It was in the West Wing of the castle, the side that rarely caught the light and had therefore been mainly abandoned. The servants moved like ghosts through the rooms polishing the floors and ensuring everything sparkled regardless whether any but the queen ever visited.

Her sanctuary was at the back of the great library, a vast and beautiful domed room filled with row upon row of dusty books that held every story and history of this land, some true, some simply believed to be true, some that had somehow become truth as the years had passed. When they had first married the king had intended to clear the library out and turn it into a winter ballroom. What was the point of it? She had persuaded him otherwise. He had always found it hard to resist her persuasion, and when the day came that he could, then she would resort to other means to keep his interest. The rumours aside, she hadn't needed to enchant him *yet*.

Her secret room had no windows but she didn't mind that, preferring the softer light from candles and lamps as they danced on her treasures. She took a long swallow of red wine and leaned back in her chair, letting her fine blonde hair run down the mahogany back like a waterfall. Tatters of fabric were scattered across the floor and she viewed them with satisfaction. That was one mess she'd have to clean up herself. No servants were allowed in here.

Her gaze grazed the sparkling glass cabinets that housed her possessions. Some she had brought with her on her reluctant journey into marriage, others she had purchased surreptitiously, her nose always checking the wind for the scent of magic, but of late most had come from the boy she sent to search them out. Soon he'd be back again. What would he have found this time? As her great-grandmother had taught her, a wise woman could never have enough magic.

She got to her feet and tugged her black robe tighter, moving through the room and taking comfort from the items and bottled potions and poisons. It wasn't enough to own them, you had to know how and when to use them. More than that, you had to be *prepared* to use them. Her face was reflected in the glass like a ghost on water; fascinating and untouchable. She was beautiful. She had always been the most beautiful woman wherever she was. Ethereal, that's what they called her, both in her own lands and in this new one which she had been forced to take as her home.

Her mother had the same beauty and it was perhaps only that which had saved them both from burning when her father had discovered that they were cuckoos in the royal nest. When he'd found out about her great-grandmother in the woods, the crone in her candy house, where Lilith had spent childhood days learning the craft and playing with the bones of lost children. When he'd realised a witch's curse ran through their blood, he'd locked them both away for days. But her mother was no fool. She'd used her beauty against him. Lilith had been banished into marriage and her father, the king, had declared that cottage and part of the forest out of bounds. Men would do a lot for beauty, that's what Lilith learned in that time. Beauty had a magic all of its own.

'I know you're in there!' The words were accompanied by a pummelling fist on the door. The queen jumped, her reverie broken. She looked down at the mess on the floor again.

Snow White.

'I know you're in there! Open the door!'

How did she know about this room? No one knew

about this room! The king might have, once, but he'd have long ago forgotten. His interest in his wife didn't extend very far. She stared at the thick wood and remained silent. The fists beat out another angry round on the other side.

'You fired Maddy! You sent her home! I'm not going anywhere until you open this door. I'll wait until you come out. You can't hide from me forever!'

The queen heard the first hint of tears in the girl's voice, and only then did she pull back the bolts that separated them. She stood in the doorway blocking her possessions from view. Not that it mattered. All of Snow White's attention was on her step-mother. Tears spilled from her eyes, but her skin wasn't blotchy. Her thick dark hair was like a wild mane around her shoulders. If Lilith's beauty was ethereal then Snow's was earthy. Raw and sensual. Standing there, anger and upset making her whole body tremble while her eyes were wild and full of rage, Lilith thought Snow had taken on the spirit of one of the magnificent horses she so loved to ride.

But horses were breakable. They *had* to be broken. That was the way of things. Snow White would be no different in the end.

Lilith remained impassive, a wall of cool ice before the pacing animal. Air and earth. Light and dark.

'What are you doing here?' she asked, eventually, pleased with the mild irritation in her tone. 'This is a private place.'

'This is where you hide,' Snow said. 'I've known about it for ages. Why did you fire Maddy? She's been here since I was a child. You can't fire her; you just can't! I took the food to the forest, not her. It's my fault. If anyone should be punished it's me. And I'm really sorry. I didn't mean to upset you.' She paused. 'I never mean to upset you, although I seem to do it all the time.'

Now that they were face to face, her fire was dying. Snow White had never learned to harness her anger as Lilith had. The queen had watched her over the past three years, since marriage had made them family. The girl was quick to anger, just as quick to forget. Always thinking the best of people. Always wanting everyone to be happy. There were only four years between them but it felt like a lifetime. Lilith was a woman. She'd had to grow up fast. Snow White? She was still a foolish girl.

'She was insolent,' the queen said. 'Not that I have to explain myself to you.'

'You can't dismiss her. My father would hate it.'

Lilith raised an eyebrow and smiled slightly. 'Your father isn't here. I think you'll find I'm in charge.

And as for your punishment,' she swung the door open slightly revealing the scraps of cloth on the floor, 'you will no longer go out riding in breeches.'

Snow White's perfect mouth dropped open. 'You cut up my clothes?' Her voice had softened. The anger was fading into something else. 'Why would you do something like that?'

'It's time for you to stop behaving like a child. This will be better for you in the long run. You can't be wild forever, the world won't let you. It doesn't work like that. Trust me.'

'Trust you?' The tears were flowing free now, clear warm streams on the gentle curves of her face. 'Why should I trust you? You hate me! I don't even know why you hate me!' Snow's hands had balled into fists of frustration, and it seemed as if even the dust on the books that surrounded them scuttled away to hide from her anger. 'Are you jealous that my father loves me so much, is that it? Do you want him all for yourself?'

The queen was so surprised she burst into a fit of unexpected laughter. She saw it hit Snow like a punch. Laughter didn't come easily to Lilith – her great-grandmother had taught her to hide her emotions where possible – and she doubted she'd had a belly laugh like this in all the three years of her marriage.

'Oh, that's priceless,' she wiped a tear from her own eye, a laughing mockery of Snow's own, 'truly, it is.' She gasped again as another wave of giggles threatened to overwhelm her. Snow was so wrong it was funny. She thought of the children's bones her great-grandmother used to rap her knuckles with, took two deep breaths to contain her laughter and let the icy mantle that shielded her from the world settle over her once more.

'I don't love your father,' she whispered, the sound somewhere between a hiss and a snarl. 'I loathe him. He repulses me. He's a stupid, fat, arrogant man.' She stepped forward; a precise deadly movement. Snow White didn't move.

'You can't mean that. You can't. You *married* him.'

'You foolish spoilt little princess. Is that what you think? It's all about *true love*? Love and marriage have nothing to do with each other.'

'But he loves you,' Snow said. 'He always says he loves you.'

'He wants me. That's different.' Lilith smiled. 'And I want his power. Men take it so much for granted. You need to learn that the only way to wield it in the kingdoms is by making a great match.' She leaned forward slightly. 'Now he's gone to war and I have it. I will train you to be a lady. I will find you a husband. Then you'll be gone from here and I will have some *peace*.' She spat the last words out before turning back into her room. She slammed the door in the dark beauty's face and shot the bolts across.

Beneath her milky complexion her face was burning and she rested her forehead against the cool wood for a moment. Only the sound of her own ragged breath filled her ears. No fists beat from the other side. Eventually, she straightened up and poured another glass of wine. Snow White had gone. No doubt crying on her bed already, mourning her dead mother and wishing her father had never married again.

The candlelight was softly comforting and she lost herself in its dance on the crimson surface. Her thoughts were as dark as the liquid she swirled in the glass and she was drowning in them, the here and now forgotten. In the corner, hidden in the shadows, a black cabinet hung on the wall. The imp who'd sold it to her, long ago, had said it was made from the bones of burned saints from the barbaric lands across the sea, that the glass the cabinet housed came from the blood of mermaids, and the magic bound in it came from the Far Mountain itself.

For a long while she'd tried to ignore it. As the door creaked open, she took a deep drink from the glass. Her head would hurt in the morning.

'*She truly is the fairest in the land.*'

Lilith looked up. She saw the familiar face in the glass, hung on the inside of the door, was surrounded by inlaid precious jewels. The emeralds sparkled green.

'Shut up,' she said.

She should have smashed that mirror. It had belonged to an emperor in the East, the imp claimed, stolen as he lay dying after a hundred year reign. The story went that he had opened the cabinet every day for every one of those years and listened to its words. She didn't believe it. The lands were filled with stories, most of which were just inventions. She didn't think anyone could bear the enchanted mirror day after day.

'*And so graceful.*' In the mirror the face was frozen but the words came anyway, from some endless place behind the glass that could never be understood. It was a soft voice full of warmth, but still every syllable stung the queen. Her jaw tightened.

'I said, shut up.'

'*Everyone loves her, don't they? And it's so easy to see why. Beauty and kindness and yet still wild and free. She will have her pick of the princes to fall in love with. Yes, she truly is the fairest in the land. Isn't she? Isn't she beautiful?* '

Poison

Cold, bitter fire burned in the queen's heart and it erupted in a screech as she launched her goblet at the glass. The door slammed shut and the liquid splatted like blood across the gargoyle faces which decorated it. She stared as it trickled across their open eyes and dripped to the floor.

'Good,' she hissed. 'If she wants a prince then I shall find her one. One who will take her far, far away.'

She trembled and magic tingled on her skin. She spun round, leaving the spilt wine to drip red over the shredded fabric, the wind from her robe snuffing out the candle, and she stormed out into the dark.

One way or another, Snow White had to go.

2
'A giant from the Far Mountains'

By the time the king had been gone a month, things had changed significantly in the castle and the land beyond. It was astounding how much could be done in so short a time when you put your mind to it. The king, although bluff enough by nature and deed, had never given much thought to his subjects who lived beyond the castle walls. They loved him, they always had, and they paid their taxes which allowed him to go on his wars. In turn he made sure they had enough food to be the right side of starving, but not too much that they would become greedy and consider rebellion. The king took them for granted, in a way that only one born to a throne really can. They got on with their business and he got on with his and they cheered when he passed on his horse and that was generally enough.

There were no statues or portraits of him in public places. He hadn't seen the need. Having narrowly escaped the flames in the land of her birth, the queen, more than most understood the power of public perception. She did not have their love or their natural fealty, but she knew how to get their fear and respect.

She wanted the people to feel she was watching them at all times. The busts and paintings in every hall and market took care of that, along with, for a brief time at least, a network of spies who ensured she knew enough to make the people believe that she could see all of their secrets. She dealt a very visible and unpleasant justice to a few merchants who had been less than honest with their taxes, and the rumours of the queen's sharp eye and iron grip subsequently spread like fire through the kingdom. Her spies added a few stories of dark magic and soon all cheered loudly when she passed but none would meet her eyes.

People were so easy.

Life in the castle had changed as well, especially for Snow White. The stable boys had been ordered to only saddle the gentle mares should she wish to ride, and she'd been instructed – under pain of punishment falling on her maids – to dress according to her station at all times. The queen had ordered a selection of dresses to be sent from her own kingdom for her step-daughter. They came with stiffer corsets and stronger binding than they made here, and if she wore them for a month or two she'd realise what a blessing her normal dresses were. Perhaps then she wouldn't fight wearing them so much. Maybe then she'd see there was no point in fighting any of it.

On top of this, Snow White was no longer allowed to find refuge in the servants' quarters, and although she still roamed the forest – even the queen could not imprison her in the castle – and visited her beloved dwarves out by the mines, her visits were less frequent and always reported. A little magic here, a curse here and there, was all it took to gain the loyalty of the forest folk. Her great-grandmother had taught her well.

No one would dare defy the queen's orders, how-ever much they hated seeing their beloved princess so unhappy. And she was *desperately* unhappy but that, after all, the queen reminded herself, was the point. Why would Snow White agree to a marriage if she was happy at home? The queen wanted her gone. She *needed* her gone. And if there was one thing she'd learned in her lifetime it was that noth-ing was ever achieved without a little pain.

She swept out into the busy courtyard her black dress, glittering with precious black rubies that dwarves had died to find, at odds with the brightly coloured ribbons and bunting that were being hung from the walls and posts. Doves cooed in boxes. Merchants dragged carts filled with all manner of foods and the finest wines towards the heavy doors that led to the store rooms and kitchens. The preparations were well under way. Even though she prided herself on quelling her emotions, Lilith felt a small tingle of excitement run through her veins. By the following evening her plans would have come to fruition.

It was the queen's twenty-fourth birthday and she was having the most magnificent ball. All the finest ladies and gentlemen of the city would be there and she had invited handsome princes and noblemen from all of the allied kingdoms as well. Her jaw tightened. Snow White would be, as the saying went, like a pig in shit amongst them.

She snapped unnecessary orders and then retreated inside. She kept her head high, ignoring the sharp glances from the women scrubbing the floor. The corridor was one hundred feet long and the two ageing women had reached approximately half-way. Their knees would be raw and bruised and no doubt their lower bodies would ache and cramp for the rest of the day when they were done. She'd learned as a child in her great-grandmother's cottage that scrubbing floors could be back-breaking work. She reached the far end and then paused and turned.

'Not good enough,' she said. 'Start again.' This time they did look up, eyes wide in their tired, sagging faces. The queen tightened her lips, accentuating the sharp angles of her delicate beauty, each one like a knife's blade. 'Right from the door.'

She watched as the two women hauled themselves to their feet, picked up their buckets and brushes and hobbled, broken, back to where they had started hours before. They didn't argue and Lilith allowed herself a small smile. The old queen and her daughter had the people's love. She would have their fear. It was a hardier emotion. As she turned away she felt a small twinge in her chest and wondered idly if it was a small part of her own heart turning black and hardening. Good, she thought. The sooner the better.

'Come on,' Snow White said as she wiped her tears of laughter away. 'Let's try again.' She took a sip from the beer tankard, sighed, hitched out another laugh, and then passed the mug along to the first of the dwarves who were picking themselves up on the grass.

'It's never going to work,' Dreamy said. 'And I'm not sure the beer is helping.' He was sitting beside the princess on the wooden table, having taken and caused enough bruises during the previous attempts to get himself removed from the proceedings for all their safety.

'Beer helps everything.' She winked. 'It will relax them.' She clapped and laughed. 'Try again. Grouchy, you on the bottom. I think you're the hardiest!'

There were exclamations of protest as each of the dwarves wanted to be the strongest in Snow White's eyes, even though they knew in their hearts that she loved them all equally. Grouchy, squinting in the warm sunshine, steadied himself and then Feisty clambered onto his shoulders. When he was steady the next climbed the rickety ladder to perch on his shoulders.

'Keep going! It's amazing!' Snow White said, smiling. 'We can do this! You can do this!'

'It'll go wrong at the top. It's the coat. It unbalances them.' Dreamy took a swallow of beer from the mug.

'Hmmm,' Snow White frowned, looking at Bolshy, drowning in the overcoat designed to cover them all and with his shoulders padded out with quilted coat hangers to make him ridiculously broad. 'You might have a point. Maybe Grouchy needs to be at the top.'

A few moments, and another tumble to the grass later and she was proved right. Luckily although the dwarves weren't good at balancing, they were good at landing. The mines weren't safe and tunnels often gave way, dropping them great heights to the rocks below. If they didn't know how to land, they didn't live long. The grass might as well have been cushions for what they were used to and so after more giggles, more beer and a dusting down, they began again, this time with Grouchy draped in the coat and going up last.

'Are you sure this is a good idea?' Dreamy asked. He'd been wondering it for a while, but had been caught up in the fun of it with the rest of them, and when Snow White was enthusiastic about something it was hard not to get swept along. But now that he was sitting out and watching, doubts niggled at him.

'What do you mean? It'll be funny.'

'I'm sure it *could* be funny,' he said, slightly hesitant. 'But I'm not sure your step-mother has a sense of humour.'

'That's where you're wrong.' Snow White smiled and squeezed his knee. 'She used to have one. When she first got here. I remember we used to laugh a lot. She laughed yesterday.' She looked away from him. 'She's just lost her reasons to have fun, that's all. Maybe that's what being married does to you.' Snow took the mug from Dreamy. 'I'm getting it now. She just doesn't like being married very much. And that must make someone quite unhappy.'

'She's not unhappy,' Dreamy muttered. 'She's plain mean.'

'Well, maybe unhappiness makes people mean.' Her eyes sparkled as she looked at the tower of small men which looked like it might actually stay together for more than thirty seconds. 'But my father's gone to war again, for a long time this time, I think, so we need to make her smile. It's her birthday, she'll love it.'

'You think too well of people, Snow White.'

'Someone's got to, Dreamy.'

The precarious tower took a few hesitant steps towards her.

'Yes!' Snow White leapt from the table and almost jumped with glee. 'We've got it! You've done it!' She looked over her shoulder at Dreamy, her grin enticing and wicked. 'This is going to be amazing!'

It was a magnificent affair. The chandeliers sparkled and filled the vast space with light. Musicians in every corner created a magical symphony in perfect time with each other although so far apart. Masked servants circled the room with platters of the most exquisite canapés and wines each served at their perfect temperature. Every invited guest was in attendance, and the gowns worn by the ladies transformed even the plainest of them.

The queen surveyed the room from her throne. It was a sea of pastel colours, as was the tradition of such events. She'd chosen to wear red, the same colour on her lips. Even those who hated her, and their number was growing fast, had to admire her beauty. Her blonde hair hung long and straight down her back, the colour of the far off winter lands. And her heart, she'd heard them whispering, was just as hard.

She smiled but she did not join them, although she commanded the music and watched the timeless dance between the sexes begin. A glance that lingered too long. A smile behind a fan. Eyes that peeked up playfully from a bow. It was always the same. She wondered how many ever ended happily ever after? Her mother had wanted that. It hadn't lasted.

After the first round of dancing came the entertainment as her guests ate and drank some more.

There were the tumblers, the piper and his dancing rats, the fire eaters and the dancers, and soon the music would begin again. The queen clenched her teeth. The ball was in full swing and Snow White had yet to appear. She snapped her fingers. A footman scurried over and bowed.

'Send someone to the princess's rooms. Tell her she must come at once. I will not have her keeping my guests waiting longer.' Enough was enough. There was lateness and then there was arrogance. 'This delay is clearly the fault of her maids.' Lilith smiled. 'Make sure the princess knows that I shall punish them for embarrassing her if she does not arrive within five minutes.' She gestured for music, sat as far back in her throne as the stiff upright chair would allow and focused on her annoyance rather than how easily the threats came from her these days, or on the knowledge that she would follow through on them if she had to.

The footman, however, had barely turned to leave when the trumpet sounded and the doors at the far end opened wide. The orchestras stopped, trickling away to nothing as the performers forgot their notes and their bows hung in mid-air above the strings. Even the queen was breathless for a second at the sight of Snow White's beauty. Gasps punctuated the stillness. Snow White stepped through the doors and paused at the top of the three marble steps that led down to the ballroom. She wore a pure white dress, strapless and fitted, so different to the full-skirted style that the ladies of the court preferred, and it was decorated with small purple jewels. The same gems sparkled in her dark hair, swept high and tousled on her head, and they served to highlight the violet of her eyes.

All attention on her, she smiled and curtseyed, a more sensuous movement than all the years of training had ever given Lilith. The queen dragged her eyes away from the beautiful girl and got to her feet, scanning the ballroom. Every prince was staring, their pretty dancing partners completely forgotten, as if they were simply shadows. Snow White could have her pick of them, that was clear. A shard of envy pierced her hardening heart, and her face ached with the effort of maintaining her smile. Still. That didn't matter. Snow White would be gone, out of the kingdom forever, and then maybe she would be able to relax.

'I'm so sorry I'm late,' Snow said, addressing the room. If Lilith was ice then Snow White was warm honey, and the mischievous twinkle as she smiled only enhanced her beauty. 'But I was waiting for my companion.' She held out one hand and curtseyed again as a man, thus far out of sight, came through the open doorway and joined her on the steps.

The queen, always so controlled, could not contain her gasp. He stood eight feet or more tall and wore a bright purple suit with a silver trim, the colour almost an exact match to the gems adorning the princess. A painted mask covered most of his face.

'May I introduce Agard, Prince of the Far Mountains, home of the Giants.' She smiled again and took the enormous man's hand, leading him into the party. Dresses rustled as men and women pulled away from them creating a path, not entirely out of politeness. The queen wasn't the only one who was shocked. No one had been near the Far Mountains for as long as she'd been alive, and probably not in the generation before either. How could Snow possibly have … ?

'We've been communicating by dove since I found one injured in the forest with a message attached to its leg and restored it to health. The prince wanted to reach out to distant people, and he found me.'

The strange couple moved further and further into the room, taking remarkably short steps given the man's height, the queen noticed. Was he compensating for Snow White? How could he possibly have got into the castle without one of her spies telling her? And how could she have possibly fallen in love with this giant, as it seemed clear she had?

Her eyes fixed on their progress, Lilith tried to relax. It didn't matter which man Snow White chose. In fact, this creature might be a blessing in disguise. The king would surely disapprove of their union – what monstrous children would they create, for one thing? – and it was unlikely that Snow White would ever be allowed to return from the Far Mountains. The girl was embarrassing herself, but she was also doing all of Lilith's work for her. She needn't have wasted time and money inviting all the princes to a grand ball. Perhaps she should have just called for a circus or a freak show and given her step-daughter more to choose from.

As they approached, she walked forward to meet them and then curtseyed deeply at the giant's feet. Snow's curtsey might have been sensuous but the queen's was elegant and flawless, her back remaining perfectly straight. She made the gesture seem so effortless, but hours of training and tears had gone into it when she was four years old. The backs of her knees had been bruised and bleeding from the thwacks of the ruler her instructress used to inflict if she didn't do it perfectly. Her father, the king, would

not accept less than a perfect princess for a daughter.
She had become one for him, despite herself. Even if
magic ran in her veins as well as royal blood. It was
a man's world and she had learned to play the game.
What else could a woman with beauty and brains do?

'Your highness,' the queen said. 'Welcome to our
home. We are honoured to be the first of the kingdoms to receive a visit from the people of the Far
Mountains, and I hope it shall not be your last.
We have heard so much of your strength and generosity of spirit.' Her words were clear and humble
although most of what she'd heard of the giants was
that they were clumsy, stupid and greedy and spent
most of their time fighting each other. Legend said
that whenever rocks fell in the low lands, a giant in
the Far Mountains was stamping his feet because he
couldn't get his own way. But she was a queen and
she would behave like one.

'Thank you, your Majesty.' The giant's voice was
gruff but not as resonant as she expected. But then
what did she really know of them? Nothing. Their
guest began to lean forward to bow. The movement
started well and then suddenly he wobbled, losing
his balance and tilting dangerously sideways. The
queen stepped backwards as two courtiers rushed
forward and took the giant's hands to stabilise him.

It was only then the queen noticed how small the hand was. How could a giant … ?

Before she could finish her thought, the giant's middle section began to erupt. Buttons flew from the purple suit. Somewhere amongst the guests an idiot girl shrieked and another fainted. From within the giant came several exclamations before the body finally collapsed into a small pile of moving pieces.

For a moment there was silence and then Snow White burst into warm laughter. 'I knew they couldn't balance for long, but I was hoping for a first dance at least.' She turned to the assembled guests. 'A giant from the Far Mountains? Oh, come, come. You really fell for that? Anyway, my companions are far more impressive than any giant.'

The bundle of dwarves slowly pulled themselves to their feet. Lilith stepped backwards, icy cold anger running through her pumping heart. She had curt-seyed to them, these strange rough mining men. She had addressed them as royals, and worse than all of that was that they had tricked her.

The little men lined up alongside Snow White and bowed. The gathered guests laughed and applauded as did Snow herself. They blushed and muttered to each other, but their bashful joy at being part of this humiliating game was obvious. Snow White leaned down and kissed their heads and two of the little faces turned almost the colour of their princess's jewels.

Snow stood alongside the queen and faced the guests. 'It is so lovely to see so many visitors from other kingdoms here,' she nodded and smiled at several of the princes. 'Some of you I have not seen since childhood when I would beat you all to the top of the trees.' Again, there was a round of laughter. Black crept into the corner of Lilith's vision as she raged inside. This was uncalled for. Women did not make speeches at balls. Even she hadn't and the purpose of the occasion was *her* birthday. Kings and princes made speeches. That was the protocol in all the allied kingdoms. What was Snow White doing? Why were all the guests so enamoured of her that they didn't care? Why was it all so *easy* for her?

'I am so very fond of you all,' Snow White continued, apparently unaware of the waves of hatred coming from the slim figure in red beside her. 'But if you have come here to seek my hand in marriage, then let me put you at ease so we can all just enjoy this wonderful party. I have no desire to be betrothed to any of you. You will not find marriage with me.' She raised a dark eyebrow. 'Although perhaps you might with some of the lovely ladies you're already dancing with.' Around the room couples blushed and moved closer together. Lilith felt sick, the few morsels of food she'd eaten curdling in her stomach. The princess was making a fool of her. Was she supposed to just smile through this embarrassment? Was she doing it on purpose ... some act of revenge in front of princes from all the kingdoms?

'You are all handsome and charming men,' Snow White continued. 'But I will only ever surrender myself to true love.' She glanced at the queen and smiled, and from behind her own smile all Lilith wanted to do was choke the triumphant expression from the girl's face.

'Until then,' Snow finished, 'I shall make do with the company of my friends.' She looked down once again at the dwarves who bowed in unison, first to Snow White, then to the queen and then to the guests, who gave another round of spontaneous applause.

The musicians returned their bows to their instruments and the air was filled with music. The party began again, but this time there was a belle for their ball; the wonderful, unique Snow White. She led the dancing with the princes and the dwarves, so unlike the icy queen who oversaw the revelry from her throne. Within fifteen minutes Lilith, for all her great beauty, had been forgotten and she gladly slipped away, forcing herself to maintain a steady pace instead of bursting into a run as soon as she was through the doors.

The corridor echoed with laughter that chased her until she was sure she was the cause of it. They were all laughing at her. Of course they were. She fled through the castle, a whirlwind of blazing fury, until at last there was only the silence of her forgotten library and the dry books which were as unloved as she was. Her pace slowed but still books fell from the shelves as she passed, her rage and hurt slamming them to the ground.

Finally, there was the comfort of the room beyond. Her room. Her things. Her power was here. Her honesty was here. This was who she was. The candles and lamps lit as she glanced at them. Her magic was always stronger in anger and high emotion. Her mother's magic had been weak, she hadn't exercised it. Lilith had no intention of that happening to hers. She would no longer be ashamed of it.

She poured warm red wine from the silver decanter that never emptied, and drank the first glass quickly. Her hand was still trembling when she poured the second. Her eyes were glittering diamonds in the candlelight. How could they have humiliated her like that? How could she have let them? Her insides twisted; a ball of snakes trapped by the fires of her emotions. She wanted to cry. She wanted to scream. She wanted to shout at the girl and shake her until she understood that the world *expected* things of her.

Behind glass, her crystal ball glowed red and green and then a rainbow of colours. With her glass refilled she sat in her chair and stared at it, letting the colours entrance and calm her. She drank quickly until her vision was hazy and her angry thoughts could no longer keep their sharp edges, and then she put the goblet down. She allowed herself to be lost in the colours and her memories of the past. Of happier times. Of being free.

'Why did you leave?'

The words, cutting the silence, made her jump and she turned to see the door open and Snow White, in all her beautiful finery, standing at the threshold. In her anger she hadn't locked herself in. She cursed under her breath.

'It's your birthday ball. You should be there.'

The queen rose to her feet, happy to find her legs steady. It took more than a heady wine to take her steel.

'You humiliated me,' she hissed. 'And at my own birthday. I suppose you thought that was funny.'

'It was supposed to be a joke,' Snow White said,

her eyes wide with innocence and hurt. 'I thought you'd like it. I thought you'd *get* it.'

Lilith wondered how much practice went into that look. The king and the courtiers might be fooled by it, but the queen would not be.

'So, now you're calling me stupid? A little girl like you who wants to play with dwarves thinks she can laugh at me?' Where the candlelight accentuated each of Snow's soft curves and full features, the queen knew it hardened her sharp cheekbones and cast shadows under her eyes. She wondered how she must look. Still the great beauty of the North, or a harpy? She found she did not much care. 'Or do you really want to marry one? Maybe you'd like to marry all seven of your friends? It could be arranged. They'd tire you out soon enough.'

'Why do you have to be so horrible?' Snow White reeled slightly, and stepped backwards. 'What happened to you? Why must you always be so mean?'

Lilith opened her mouth to laugh and then Snow White's gaze shifted from her to something behind them in the dark shadows of the room. The familiar creak of the cabinet. The queen's eyes widened.

'*She is so beautiful. Snow White, the fairest in all the lands.*'

'What is that?' Snow said, curiosity replacing her

hurt. 'Have you got someone in here with you? Their voice is ... strange.'

'It's nothing.' The queen flashed a look behind her, seeing the mirror glint slightly in the dark. 'Nothing for you to—'

'None can compare, none shall ever compare, to Snow White.'

'Is that a talking *cupboard*?' Snow White tried to push past, but Lilith blocked her way. 'One of your crazy magic things the servants talk about?'

'I said it was—' The queen shoved her backwards.

'Such a beauty. Such a heart. So easy to love. Snow White. Unbearably beautiful, isn't she?'

The cabinet slammed shut and silent with the ferocity of the queen's glare.

'It was talking about me,' Snow White said. Her eyes came back to the queen's. *'The fairest in the land.* You have a cupboard that *talks* about me?' She laughed suddenly, a short, shocked burst of emotion. 'What is *wrong* with you?'

'Shut up,' the queen said. 'Shut up and get out.'

'You *are* jealous of me,' Snow said. 'Not of my father loving me, but of everyone else. It's not that hard, you know, to have people like you. You just have to be *nice*.'

'I said get out!' She spat the words at the girl, her

47

fists balled. 'You know nothing. You're stupid and blind and I hate you.'

Snow White's jaw clenched. 'Well, your cabinet doesn't. Maybe I should take it back to the party instead.'

The queen could see the mockery clearly in the princess's eyes. She took a deep breath and drew herself up tall. 'You'll regret this. All of it. I promise you.'

'Look, why can't we—'

'Go back to the party. Enjoy it. Tomorrow your dwarves are banished from the palace grounds. On pain of death.'

'You can't—'

The slamming door cut off the rest of Snow White's shocked sentence, and this time the queen remembered to pull the bolt across. Her breathing filled the room but this time it was slow and calm. A chill bloomed inside her. She looked back at the crystal ball. A black mist swirled inside it. So be it, the queen thought grimly. So be it.

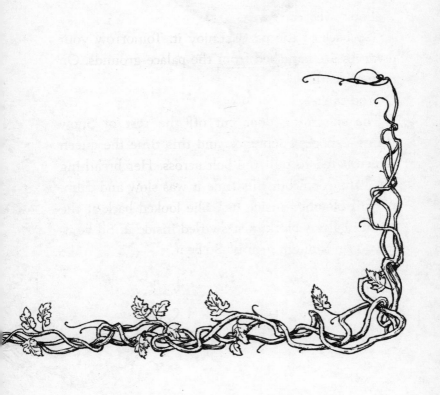

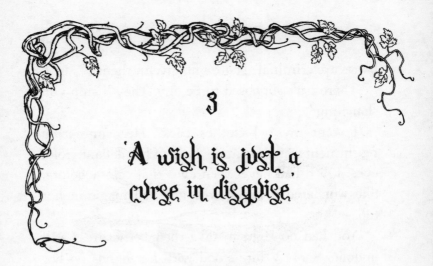

3

'A wish is just a curse in disguise'

he new dresses arrived two days after the ball.
The atmosphere had remained frosty, the
queen had avoided Snow White and it seemed
the princess had been doing the same because it was
only now, as they both stood in the princess's rooms,
that they were face to face since their argument.
That suited Lilith.

'Are you sure they'll fit?' one of Snow White's
handmaids said. She was a small, mousy thing who
could probably come somewhere close to pretty if
she straightened her shoulders and put some curls
in her hair but, as things stood, she erred on the side
of plain.

'Of course they'll fit,' she said.

'It'll break me in half to wear this,' Snow White
had pulled on the blue dress closest to her. 'These

bones are criminal. There's no give in them.'

'There isn't supposed to be any. They'll stop you slouching.'

'I want my old clothes back.' Her simmering resentment was clear in the flash of her defiant violet eyes. Lilith had never seen eyes that colour before. She wondered if maybe the girl had magic in her too.

'You had no right to take them.' The dress still undone, Snow White stood with her hands on her hips, her hair falling loose over her shoulders. 'No right at all.'

'I had every right,' Lilith snapped, aware that the two maids had drawn close together and were no doubt memorising every word of this confrontation to take down to the servants' quarters and relay as soon as they could. 'You're twenty years old. You need to be preparing for marriage.'

'I don't want to get married,' Snow White said, looking squarely at her. 'I'm not seeing the appeal.'

Lilith ignored her and, with her teeth gritted, grabbed the laces at the back of the dress. Beneath them, Snow White's skin was white and soft, used to freedom. By tonight, if she did as she was told and stayed in the garment, it would be sore where the bindings had been. The laces shone beautifully but were coarse and rough, woven from looms housed in the attics of castles far away. There was no comfort in the court dresses of her own kingdom. She'd forgotten how unforgiving they were. Still, it would do Snow White good to wear them for a while. To feel what it was like to be so trapped by something that you felt you couldn't breathe.

She pulled tighter, the laces burning her cold fingers like rope and Snow White gasped.

'Not too tight, your Majesty,' the other maid stepped forward. This one was bolder. Older perhaps, and her eyes met the queen's. 'I can do it.'

'You will stay silent,' Lilith spat, and the girl, whatever bravery she might have had, slunk back a few steps like a scolded cat.

'It is really tight,' Snow White said, her voice small. 'I'm not sure I can breathe properly.'

'That's how it should be.' The stays secured, the queen stepped back. Her fingers flashed white against pink and burned where she'd pulled the laces so tight. 'There. Now you look like a proper princess. Of course you won't be able to ride like that. And if you have hidden some *other* clothes somewhere ...' The darting glance from Snow White confirmed that was the case, '... then don't even think about changing into them.'

'I'll ride anyway,' Snow White said. Her faced had paled.

'Don't be so ridiculous,' Lilith said. 'You can't.'

'You can't stop me!' The girl pushed past her and stormed out into the corridor. 'I'll do what I want!'

Lilith stared at the door. There was no way she could go riding, not in that dress. She was just having a tantrum. Always the child. Always so child-like.

'I'm surprised she hasn't broken a rib,' one of the servants muttered. 'Far too tight.'

Lilith ignored them both and strode out of the room. The boy was due back at any moment and she had more to think about than the disapproval of a pair of foolish maids. Her fingertips still felt numb from working on the rough stays. She thought of Snow White's soft skin that would be rubbed by the bone and pinched by the tightness of the bindings.

Good, she thought bitterly. *Good.*

The queen was never fooled by Aladdin. He always returned full of simpering smiles and obsequious comments but she knew that, underneath them all, he hated her. No, he *loathed* her. Of course he did. No one ever liked anyone they were beholden to, or who controlled them. That was the nature of people; more than that, Aladdin simply wasn't a very pleasant child. Even by Lilith's standards.

He was standing in front of her, perhaps thirteen years old, as he always would be, wearing the same clothes he wore on any of these trips – the only clothes he could possibly wear, and his dark eyes danced in that Arabian face which was made to be the subject of tales in market places where snakes danced to tunes played by weathered men. He bowed.

She waved him up, but kept her distance. Their whole relationship was based on a lie, but she felt no guilt about that. After all, Aladdin had murdered a great magician to get the lamp in the first place, and then he'd murdered his own father when he'd tried to sell the lamp. Greed could be a terrible thing, but greed combined with the wickedness of this small boy's heart was a terrible combination.

The boy, however, had never learned the secret of the lamp. The curse of it. How could he have? The genie hadn't been about to tell him and Aladdin was too arrogant to realise that with magic there was always a catch. Ten wishes. That was all you got. Although technically it was nine, because once you breathed your tenth wish the genie was free – and you took their place. You became the slave to the next owner of the lamp. The genie Aladdin had freed had been wise to sell it to her – he'd had enough of magic, and he was perceptive enough to know the boy was a psychopath. When he eventually regained his freedom he would hunt the old genie down. He did not want that sword hanging over his head. Lilith had promised him that while she would make the boy hers to command, she would never make a single wish. It suited her anyway. Her grandmother had taught her early on that a wish was just a curse disguised.

Lilith had used the powers of the lamp more wisely than for wishes and whims. She would let the boy out for two weeks at a time to go and search for magical items for her. He was a slave of the lamp and had to do her bidding. If he returned empty-handed then she made the delay before his next release much longer. She had quickly learned that Aladdin did not like being caged. But then, who did? She'd promised him that one day she'd give the lamp to an enemy to make his ten wishes and then the boy would be free. That would never happen. She'd heard the reports of unsettling, sadistic murders that always occurred when he was abroad from the lamp, and she was sure that not even a queen would be safe from him.

The room was as ever lit by flickering candles and as he handed over the small silver comb, it glittered in the glow. Two unicorns were carved into it, their heads bowed at each other. It was a pretty trinket, that was for sure, but in itself it held no interest for her.

'It brings the wearer happiness. Great happiness,' Aladdin said. He smiled, his small teeth white and sharp. He had blood under his fingernails. She didn't want to ask about that.

'Happiness?' she said, sharply. Too sharply. The word had stung her – could he sense her unhappiness? Was that it?

'That is, after all, the only thing some people desire, isn't it?' His dark eyes watched her carefully. 'To be happy?'

She stared at him, trying to read something in his cold, dead eyes. 'Well, then they are fools,' she said eventually and then snapped her fingers and said the word and enjoyed the moment of pain and anger that flashed across his face as the tarnished lamp on the table sucked him back in through the spout.

She looked at the comb again. Happiness. For a moment she was almost tempted to slide it into her blonde hair, but instead she put it in the glass cabinet, before carefully placing the lamp beside it. False happiness was probably no happiness at all.

Snow White was barely breathing when Grouchy and Dreamy found her. Her face was pale and her horse was whinnying and pawing at the ground in distress beside her.

'Can't ... breathe ...' she finally whispered, her lips almost blue and her violet eyes watery with fear. Dreamy stared at her in horror. Had the horse thrown her? Had she fallen? 'My ... dress ...'

'Quickly!' Grouchy snapped. 'Get your knife!' He was already rolling the limp girl over and pulling at the cords tied so tightly at her back. Dreamy, with trembling hands, scrabbled at his belt, pulling the small blade free and almost dropping it before Grouchy snatched it away from him, forcing the blade under the rough thick strings and tearing through them. One by one they broke, and Snow White's breath came deep and fast and desperate as she sucked the air into her starved lungs. She coughed and sat up, the dress gaping open at the back to reveal purple bruises in lines across her pale back. Her whole body trembled and she struggled to her feet.

'No,' Dreamy said. 'Sit down.'

'It's fine,' Snow White said, the words more wheeze than sound. 'Really, I'm ...'

And with that, she fainted.

The queen knew what they were saying about her. That she'd known Snow White would go riding, if only to spite her, and she'd laced the stays too tight on purpose. That she'd known the exertion would suffocate the princess and she'd die in the forest somewhere.

It had been a day and a half since she'd come back, wrapped in a dwarf blanket, her back and ribs as violet as her eyes with bruising. The queen had tried to apologise but Snow White hadn't even paused, just gone into her rooms and locked the doors. Lilith had questioned her maids of course, and they told her the princess had simply had a long bath and then slept. The queen ordered them to remove all the new dresses and have them burned. She'd supervised their destruction herself. She'd hoped it would go part way to an apology but it had dawned on her, as she caught the looks flashing between the kitchen staff as each of the new garments was thrust into the

59

oven, that they thought she might just be disposing of the evidence.

Her heart thumped hard as she stood in her room of treasures. Her face was flushed. She poured wine with a shaking hand and swallowed half the glass in one go. It was too early to drink but she needed to calm herself. What had she done? The glimpse of the bruises on Snow White's body haunted her. She'd gone too far. How could she take it back? How could she make it better? It was one thing to be feared, and quite another to have the entire castle thinking she'd tried to murder the princess. Had messages been sent to the king already? She needed to get more spies abroad. She needed eyes everywhere.

She drank more wine and tried to breathe deeply, finally calming. There were images she couldn't shift though. The bruises. The glare of the old dwarf who'd defied her ruling to bring the princess back safely. And more than all of that, Snow White's face as she walked past Lilith in the corridor as if she wasn't there. Her eyes watering still. Her shoulders slumped. She'd looked defeated. All her natural fire had gone. She'd looked so desperately unhappy.

Unhappy.

Lilith stared into the glass cabinet, her reflection like a sad watery ghost trapped on the other side.

She stared so long her breath misted the surface. But still, on its velvet cushion, the small silver hair comb shone in the candlelight. She'd tried to apologise but just couldn't get the words out. She'd never get the right words out, not now. She thought of the corsets. She thought of her own unhappy marriage and her relief when the king had gone to war again. She tried to imagine Snow White, so wild and free, confined in a marriage like hers. No tight corset could prepare you for that. Her head was giddy with wine and her heart was heavy with things she didn't understand.

In a moment of impetuousness, the kind she hadn't felt since she'd been a child running through the forest around her great-grandmother's house, she grabbed the hair comb from the cabinet and thrust it into a small box. She didn't pause. She didn't hesitate. She didn't want to change her mind. She ran out through the empty library, one hand holding her skirt up while her hair flew out behind her like a bridal train. Maybe she could make things better, after all. Maybe false happiness wouldn't be so bad if the person didn't know. Surely the happiness was all that counted?

By the time she arrived at Snow White's rooms she was flushed and out of breath. It had been a long time since she'd moved with such abandon, and she paused and smoothed her dress and stood tall before opening the door. She could do this. She could apologise.

The two maids were tidying the room and changing the water in the jug on the table. Lilith stared at the large bed that was now neatly made and empty.

'Where's Snow White?' she asked. 'I thought she was recuperating?'

'She's gone out,' the prettier of the two answered. 'Don't worry, she's not gone riding. She's still too bruised for that.'

The barb in the remarks stung but Lilith kept her chin up. She might owe Snow White an apology, but not these girls.

'Where is she?'

'She went walking,' the drab-looking thing said, eager not to be entirely outdone by her peer. 'Not sure where though. Maybe to the market.'

Lilith didn't pause. She knew if she hesitated then she'd change her mind and the moment would be lost. She thrust the box at the more confident girl. 'Here. It's a gift for her.'

The servant took it cautiously.

'It's for Snow White alone. No one else is to touch it. Do you understand?' She was glad to hear her voice returning to normal. To the icy cool that had

become normal at any rate. 'There will be grave consequences if you disobey me.'

'Yes, your Majesty.' The girl's eyes dropped. She
knew her place. 'Of course, your Majesty.'

'Tell her I want . . .' Lilith stopped and her voice softened, 'Tell her I would like her to wear it to dinner
this evening.'

'Yes, your Majesty.'

'Good.' She turned and left them, and she felt
better than she had in a long time. Perhaps it was
just the wine.

he girl died two hours later.
    She hadn't been pretty to start with but in
death her face was left frozen in the agony in which
she'd died. No longer mousy and hunched, her body
was contorted and her hair matted and red where
her scalp had bled from contact with the poison. It
was Snow White who had found her, and after the
doctors had been called and the body removed from
the hushed castle, it was Snow White who now stood
trembling with anger, her violet eyes flecked with
red from crying, in front of her.

'The comb was poisoned,' she said, eventually,

once she'd got her breathing under control. 'It killed Tillie, but it was meant for me. *You* gave it to me. She only tried it on because she wanted to look pretty. Like a princess!'

'It wasn't like that,' Lilith said. Her haughtiness had left her and her stomach was a watery pit of fear. The stays being too tight had been one thing. But this, this to all and sundry, looked like attempted murder. What would the whispers be saying now? How far would they travel? 'I didn't know.'

'You didn't know?' Snow White almost laughed. Her nose was running and she wiped it with the back of her hand. 'You know everything!'

'I thought it was simply enchanted.' Tears pricked at her and she did her best to swallow them down, but one broke free, cutting a sparkling track down the angles of her face. 'That's all. Why would I poison you? And if I wanted to poison you why would I do it so *obviously*?' Her fear was turning to aggression, just as it always had, even when she was a little girl. 'I was *trying* to say sorry.'

'Enchanted?' Snow White stared at her. 'What do you mean?'

'It doesn't matter.' Around them, the unused library had settled into silence as if listening to their story so as to bind it and add it to their shelves later.

'It was supposed to bring you happiness. I almost used it myself.'

'I don't trust your magic,' Snow White said. Her voice was calmer and her eyes, although still hurt, were now confused. It was a gift and a blessing, this trait she had of wanting to believe the best in everyone.

'I didn't know it was poisoned,' Lilith repeated. The dark beauty stared at her for a long time, and the queen knew that if there was ever a moment for all the secrets she hid, this was the time to share them. They choked in her throat, though. She couldn't bring herself to set them free.

'I believe you,' the princess said eventually. 'But stay away from me.' She turned and walked away and didn't look back. The queen didn't blame her, but she also knew that things had changed. How could this be kept a secret? A girl had been killed by her gift and Snow White no longer trusted her. The king would hear about it. Her tears threatened her again and she cursed the day she'd ever laid eyes on the beautiful princess.

By nightfall her fear had hardened. She would take control of the city. It was the only option she had. The people needed to fear their queen as much as they loved and respected their absent king. She'd already sent her most loyal soldiers – some of whom were no doubt more than a little in love with her – to track down any messages that might have been sent from the castle. The king would not hear about this yet. He would not at all, if she could help it. She hadn't been through all of this to stumble now.

She went to her small room at the back of the library and locked the door. She placed several pieces of her gold jewellery into a small cast iron pot; trinkets and gifts from visiting ambassadors. From one of the cabinets she took a small vial and tipped some of the dust on top. Within seconds the gold began to melt and bubble. She smiled. She sipped her wine, enjoying the moment, and then carefully took the battered lamp from its place. She had a score to settle.

'Good try, Aladdin,' she whispered, leaning so close her face almost touched the surface and she could smell the tang of a thousand sweaty palms. 'Good try.'

She picked up a paintbrush and carefully painted the liquid gold across the surface of the lamp, covering every centimetre. No one would ever rub the magic bronze again. When she was finished she took what was left of the melted gold and poured it over the spout. Just in case. It cooled instantly, sealing the dangerous little boy in forever.

The queen was sure she could hear the tiniest echo of his frustrated scream.

It made her feel better.

4
'I want her heart'

It was a warm day in the forest and even though it made the hair on his chest tickle with sweat as he moved through the trees, that pleased the huntsman. Heat slowed animals as much as men and although his skills were such he'd had no doubt meat would roast over the fire tonight, the task was going to be easier than he'd expected. He could counter the laziness that came with the sun and force himself to be alert. It was unlikely to be the same for the animals in this dense woodland. So far, apart from an old crone scurrying between the trees just before he'd spied the stag, he'd seen little sign of human habitation and he'd heard no horn blowing for a royal hunt. It was wild here. He liked that.

These woods were new to him, but he tracked the white beast easily enough, moving silently perhaps twenty feet or so behind it, his eyes scanning for the simplest of landmarks and storing them to memory. Following the animal would not be the problem. In his home land the men born to the hunt could track even the lightest footed doe by the time they were ten. It was a matter of pride. Finding the kill was easy. Finding your way home afterwards could be harder. He'd spent one night lost in the forest when he was six and although that was now twenty years ago it was an experience that would stay with him until his dying day. He shook away the memory of those long hours of darkness and the unnatural wolf – a beast that still haunted his dreams – and moved steadily forward, sunlight cutting jagged hot paths through the heavy-laden branches. The air was sweet with the fresh scent of unfamiliar greenery; citrus and leathery and sweet. He had no idea which of the kingdoms he was now in, whether they were friend or foe, but he was far from home, that was for certain.

His bag sat awkwardly on his back alongside his bow and arrows, and perhaps he should have left it at the camp site, but he'd learned a long time ago to keep the rewards of your hunts close. Man was the wiliest of creatures and very few could be trusted. Huntsmen grew up fast and he'd earned what he carried. The shoes he'd taken as a prize would stay with him.

The ground flattened for a while as the beast led him near a rough-edged track, beaten out by years of pounding hooves finding their way through the forest until it had become a lane of its own, but it didn't linger there long and turned back to its relative safety amidst the greenery.

The huntsman didn't hurry, instead allowing the creature to take in the beauty of this day in ignorance that there would be no more. Finally the trees thinned and opened out into a natural clearing with a narrow stream running through it.

Ahead the white stag, a rare beast, fine and noble, paused to drink. The huntsman dropped silently to the ground, stretching his body long against the earth. He pulled his bow free. His brown eyes narrowed as they studied the creature, small lines wrinkling his forehead and joining those that had sprung there early, the result of a life spent outdoors that was leaving him tanned and rugged before thirty. His heart beat fast against the ground and for a moment, as was always the case in these seconds before the kill, he felt everything in nature connect as one; him, the forest, the earth, and the stag itself. He watched as its thick neck lowered, its antlers dipping into the cool water, before it raised its head and shook the drops all over its glorious hide.

Without taking his eyes from the creature he shifted position, one arm tugging back the arrow until it was fighting him to spring free. White stags were rare and magical and notoriously difficult to track. They were protected from hunting, and belonged – if they could belong at all to anyone – to the royal houses of the kingdoms. It was treason to take something which belonged to your king. Even with this thought, the huntsman's hand didn't waver. He was a stranger in this land. He had his own prince to honour. But more than that, he did not believe that any one life was more precious than another. Each creature that breathed was unique, so each death was equal. He respected them all.

He silently wished the animal safe passage. He wished it happiness in its moment of death. He closed his eyes and let the arrow fly true.

The stag fell without a sound. Its legs twitched momentarily and then it was still. The huntsman got to his feet, pleased with his work. It had been a clean kill and the animal had been unaware that death was coming. They should all have such a death.

He was so intent on skinning the stag, with the hunt now over and his senses no longer alert, that by the time he heard the soldiers crashing through the forest it was too late. He was surrounded.

'Put your knife down!'

The huntsman weighed up his options and it was clear he only had the one. He put the knife, thick with the animal's hot blood, on the ground next to the carcass. The black stallions, whose colour matched the black tabards and helmets of the men who rode them, pawed at the earth, excited by the proximity of death. It was an unnatural reaction, the huntsman thought. Horses, noble and beautiful as they might be, were natural prey, just like the stag. The blood should make them nervous.

'To kill a white stag is treason, you thieving bastard,' the captain said. 'The queen will want to deal with you herself!'

'The queen?' the huntsman asked. The tabards they wore were marked in blood-red with a lion and serpent bound together. Was the queen the serpent? And in what land did a queen ever wield power?

'Not from round here, then?' a second soldier, one with a rougher accent, growled. 'That won't save you. The queen takes her magic very seriously. White stags are guardians of magic. You killed yourself when you killed it, boy.' The circle of men drew closer.

'An animal is just an animal,' the huntsman said, standing tall, his shoulders wide and with his dark eyes burning. 'I don't hold with superstition.'

The blow to the side of his head came hard and he fell to his knees, reeling and dazed, black spots filling the corners of his eyes. The men around him laughed, and he forced himself back to his feet.

'Shall we finish him off?' one voice said.

'No, tie him up,' the captain's eyes were cold through the gaps in his heavy helmet. 'We'll drag him back and let the queen deal with him. We're the Queen's Guard, after all.'

Two men leapt down from their horses and the huntsman's jaw clenched as rough rope burned his skin as they tugged it tight around his arms.

'And bring his things.'

'What about the stag?'

'You two. Take it up to Ender's Pit and throw it in. Even the dwarves won't be able to get it out of there.'

As the soldiers dragged him out of the clearing, tugging the rope this way and that to shake him off balance, the huntsman tried not to think of the beast that he had now killed for nothing. To take any life was a serious business, that was the first lesson of the hunters. A death before its time must have value, whether it be to provide food or safety or shelter. The

stag's now pointless death left a stain on the huntsman's soul. He would have his revenge for that,
one way or another. He kept his feet solidly on the
ground despite the men's attempts to topple him, but
when they reached the track and the horses picked
up their pace no man could have stayed upright. He
did not scream though, even as the ground tore at his
clothes and skin. He would not give them that.

The world spun by in a kaleidoscope of trees and
light and sandy stones until they reached the edge of
the forest where finally the track widened and lev-
elled into a well-used thoroughfare. It was no kinder
to his battered body and the huntsman fought to keep
his face twisted away from the ground. As blue sky
replaced the wooded canopy, the shape of the kingdom laid itself out around him, strangely vast and
oppressive when seen from the ground. He bit down
on the inside of his mouth and tried to focus on anything but the searing pain through his shoulders as
they threatened to pop free of their sockets. The land
was the hunter's friend and knowing its layout could
help him. A huntsman never gave up and at least the
agony of his body was proof that, for now at least, he
was still very much alive.

In the distance to the right was the Far Mountain
which sat on the skyline of all the kingdoms, but here

it was fringed with a range of jagged hills punctuated with dark patches from which black smoke rose
in clouds. Mines, they had to be. And mines meant
a dwarf land. He had never seen a dwarf although
the tales of their small stature, long lives and hardy
spirits had reached his own kingdom. To be so small
forever was a strange concept to the hunter. How different the world must look.

A small rock was kicked up by a horse's hoof and
caught his cheek, slicing it open slightly. He gasped
and fought the urge to cry out. He would not give
them the satisfaction of showing his weakness. Pain,
like all things, his father had told him, passes. The
few people who had come to the road from the patchy
villages they passed, took a cursory glance at him
and then scurried away. He caught a flash of pity on
a few faces he was dragged by, but their glances all
remained downcast and none came too close.

The Queen's Guard finally came to a halt outside
the castle walls, and as the huntsman rolled carefully onto his back and panted out his exhaustion he
saw that different soldiers guarded the gates. These
were dressed in a rich blue decorated with a gold lion
on their chests. He recognised this uniform – and
it wasn't of his own kingdom's alliance. They wore
silver helmets that, unlike the Queen's Guard, did

not cover their faces. Why were the Queen's Guard hiding their identities, he wondered. Were they unpopular or did the anonymity guarantee them more fear from the populace? Both were likely, judging by the bristling of both sets of soldiers' horses, reflecting the tension between the men who rode them.

The soldiers were certainly eyeing the Queen's Guard with a healthy dislike. The huntsman lay back and breathed hard into the dirt, happy just to have a moment of respite after being dragged so far.

Shadows fell across him and he looked up to see one of the soldiers in blue – an old dog with battle scars cutting across his weather-beaten face – standing over him. He reached down and, with one strong tug, pulled the huntsman to his feet. The world spun madly for a moment as the agony in his arms became almost sweet in its exquisiteness, but as it faded to an excruciating throb he was pleased that, although he was swaying, his trembling legs hadn't failed him. It wasn't just dwarves who were hardy. The men of the hunt were born tough too and he would not let them down while so far from the forests of home.

'He killed a white stag. He deserved the ground,' the captain snarled. 'He's the queen's prisoner. One of ours. You have no right to touch him.'

'He may well be a traitor, and if so, then I'm sure he'll pay the price.' The second soldier remained where he was at the huntsman's side, defying any of the soldiers in black to knock the prisoner back down again. 'But our king, the Commander of *all* the guards, queen's and otherwise, respects bravery in all. This man hasn't screamed on the road. Not once. We'd have heard him.' He turned his head and spat into the dusty ground. 'We normally do. The king would allow him to face his fate on his feet.'

'The king isn't here, or haven't you noticed?'

'But he will be back. And I still outrank you, little brother.'

'So you do, Jeremiah, so you do.'

The huntsman looked from one to the other. Even though the captain's face was mostly covered by the lines of his helmet, he could see the two men had the same eyes. The same chin.

Although the captain still looked defiant, the huntsman knew he would stay on his feet for the rest of the journey. As the gates opened and they left the king's guard behind, he nodded slightly to Jeremiah. The soldier didn't respond and the huntsman hadn't expected him to, but thanks had still been required. He now owed the man a debt, just as he owed the white stag a life.

The city was full of life and energy, as were all the kingdoms this close to their castles. Merchants hurried this way and that with carts laden with cloths and fruit, from side streets came the clang of metal as blacksmiths worked on the ore from the mines and children ran between adults, ignoring the shouted reprimands and laughing as they chased each other. It seemed the city of his kingdom's enemy was not so very different in spirit to the city of his own. No wonder his father always shook his head and laughed quietly when they heard new stories of war. Their kings might have their battles, but a huntsman could talk to a huntsman and a baker could talk to a baker happily enough no matter what flag they served under.

He walked wearily forward as the small entourage took the centre of the road, no matter if there was someone already in their path or not. As quickly as the pedestrians cleared out of their way, so laughter died as they passed. One man spat in his face as he walked by, the warm thick liquid, rancid with tobacco, stinging the cut on his cheek, even though the man couldn't know what crime, if any, the huntsman was being dragged in for. As he stepped back the man looked to the guards for approval and then glanced upwards. A small twitch at the corner of his mouth betrayed his fear.

The ravens perched so still on the rooftops were out of place against the brightness of the wealthy city, filled as it was with ornate buildings and shiny clear glass windows. This kingdom was winning its skirmishes and it had the mines, and therefore plenty of strong metal which so many of the kingdoms lacked. No doubt much of the metal scraped from the heart of the earth made its way to his own alliance. Traders didn't let wars get in the way of business and kings didn't let wars get in the way of revenue. There was affluence here. The market squares were lined with pale sandstone and the closer they drew to the white castle at the core of the city, the richer the stones became, glinting with shards of crystal in the sunshine.

He let his hair fall across his face to shade his eyes as he studied the ravens above them. There were too many of them, perched every twenty yards or so on a turret or chimney. They made no noise and their eyes, shining like the tiniest black pearls from the Meridian Sea, darted this way and that. They were watching the activity on the streets below. One met the huntsman's gaze as he walked beneath it and the bird stared back, coldly fixated. Despite the events of the past months the huntsman still didn't really understand the politics of cities and princes, but he did know wildlife. This behaviour wasn't natural. He had no fear of ravens – they had done nothing to deserve their reputation as a bad omen. It was just a bird of a differing feather to a dove. This bird's feathers though, were decidedly unruffled.

The huntsman dropped his gaze, having seen all he needed. The ravens were enchanted. He was sure of it.

It felt like they marched up hundreds of stairs before they reached the highest tower of the castle, where the queen was waiting. The huntsman had lost count by the time they got to the top, but as the soldiers' boots echoed on the black marble floor all the huntsman could see through the arched windows was the sky. A cool breeze, much sharper than the warm wind below, caught him and he shivered. Were they so high they were almost among the clouds? And why would the queen of such a rich land have her throne room so far above her people?

Finally they reached a vast circular room high in the tower. The walls here were as black as the stone beneath their feet, but the solid colour was broken up by patterns and streaks of crimson red, the decoration sharp and jagged like winter branches that had stretched up through the floor, far from wherever their roots might be in the castle below. It looked like unnatural veins on black skin to the huntsman.

In the centre of the room was a solitary throne made of cast black ore and lined with luxurious red velvet cushioning. The huntsman took in a deep breath. Everything here was new. Opulent and impressive as it all was, these had not been the queen's rooms for long. There were no scents in the crisp and brittle air as if even the summer outside didn't dare venture in.

At the back, an ornate archway led to a smaller room and as the guards threw him to the floor and he slid forward a few feet, he caught a glimpse of strange objects laid on soft cushions and locked in sparkling glass cases. A shadow fell across his line of sight and behind him the guards stood to attention. The queen had arrived.

Her footsteps were delicate and her stride short as her heeled feet tapped over to stop before him. The huntsman's dark eyes rose from the cold floor and for a moment his aches and pains were forgotten. She was beautiful. Her hair was like the ice on the sheer walls of the Far Mountain. Her lips were pink hearts from the highest branches of the blossom tree and her eyes were so blue and cold they stung him to look into them. He'd seen winter wolves who looked like that just as spring began to ease the rest of nature's suffering but start their own. Pure defiance, even though they knew their time to chase the frost to a different kingdom or die had likely come. Winter wolves, so much smaller and more ethereal than their grey rough brothers, were beautiful, delicate and dangerous. This queen was no different.

'I see you're still taking orders from your big brother,' she said, her eyes on the captain.

'I had to, your Majesty. He's the senior ranking officer. What else could I do?'

'You'd do well to remember that the king will not be returning home soon. I'm told his campaign is doing well and he's pushing towards the sea. He says he might not be back for another two years.' The soldier shuffled awkwardly under the intensity of her icy gaze.

'That's a long time. Terrible things can happen to people – or their families – in that time. The dwarves always need ore sorters, and sadly, as we all know, only dwarves' lungs can cope with the dust for very long. If you feel uncomfortable serving in my guard then I'm sure I can find a use for you elsewhere,

Captain Cricket. And remember, in his absence, I am the voice of the king himself.'

'It won't happen again, your Majesty.' The captain quickly tugged open the huntsman's rough hemp bag. 'The prisoner had these on him. I thought you might want them.'

The diamond slippers. Of course. The huntsman watched as the queen's irritation with her servant vanished at the sight of the sparkling shoes. As the light hit them and refracted, all the colours in the rainbow dazzled in their surfaces. The queen's beautiful eyes widened and her mouth opened slightly. He knew why. The slippers were warm to the touch. They tingled with charm and charisma. He'd felt it when he'd taken them from that very different kingdom, and he'd heard their story since. There was more than precious stones in their making.

'Slippers for a ball,' the queen whispered. 'And with such magic in them.' She looked down at the huntsman again, this time with far more curiosity. 'And he killed a white stag?'

'In the heart of the forest. I ordered my men to throw it into Ender's Pit.'

'Not a fitting burial for such a beast. But at least no peasant will eat it.'

The huntsman could smell the relief in the sharp

tang of the captain's sweat, but it was overwhelmed by the warmth radiating from the queen's skin. How could someone so cold on the surface have so much heat inside her? His own heart beat faster. He was a huntsman, after all, and proximity to danger always excited him. How old was she, this queen? Younger than him, for sure. He met her gaze.

'You can leave us,' she said, still not looking up at her men. They didn't protest, and the huntsman wondered what kind of weapons this delicate beauty had in her arsenal that made her men sure they could leave her with a killer and she'd be safe. Magic, it had to be. He'd learned a lot about magic in the past few weeks – it was more powerful than any blade. Not that he had a blade. Even if he did, he'd find it hard to use on this exquisite creature.

As the soldiers left he got to his feet, regardless of a lack of permission. The queen didn't comment, merely studied him as he rose. He stood several inches taller than her but she didn't step back. She was not afraid of him, that was for sure.

'Where did you get these?' She held up the slippers and the sunshine they reflected danced across her flawless face.

'I earned them.' It was the truth in a way. She was watching him thoughtfully and he examined her in turn. She was even younger than he'd thought, a second wife to the king perhaps. How did she like that? Was it the cause of the hardness in her eyes?

'The words of many a thief. They have magic in them. Did you know that?'

'I don't hold with magic.'

'I can see that. If you did you wouldn't have killed my stag.'

'It was the forest's stag, not yours,' the huntsman said. 'We're all just beasts. We all breathe. No one creature is more valuable than another.' He paused, the memory of the stag still fresh. 'And no death must be wasted.'

'All life is equal,' she finished, stealing his un-spoken words from him. 'All death is equal.' She smiled at his surprise, her white teeth small and perfect. 'We had tribes of huntsmen like you in my homeland. Men who lived by the code.' She took a step closer to him and his heart beat faster. Could she sense his rising excitement? What game was she playing with him?

'What about your own life?' she asked, looking up at him and standing so near that he could feel her warm breath on his skin. 'Are you so casual about that?'

'That one,' he smiled, 'I have to say, I am more careful with than others'.'

'That tends to be the case.' She held up the slippers. 'I shall keep these for now.'

'The words of many a thief.' The atmosphere between them was charged and the huntsman's blood rushed hot through his body. The ache in his muscles was almost forgotten.

'You should watch your mouth.'

'If I'm going to die I'm not sure what difference my words could make.'

'I was going to offer you a deal.' This time she did take a step back and he saw the slightest shift in her posture as her spine stiffened. She was the queen again. What was she hiding? Why were there so many layers of defences around the queen in the clouds?

'What kind of deal?'

'The kind where you do as you're told and you get to keep your life.' Her mouth twisted; tight with bitterness. 'But it does involve taking another one. Something you seem to be adept at.'

'But you have a whole guard for that.'

'There are some lengths,' she turned away from him and moved towards the window, 'that I wouldn't ask my men to go to. For some tasks, you need an outsider. I also want it done cleanly and with respect.' She didn't look at him as she spoke, her voice dropping until he had to strain to hear her.

'She hasn't been in the castle much. Not for a while. Not since I banished the dwarves from the inner city and replaced her maids with some of my own. Now she comes in late at night and goes out in the early morning. I hear whispers about her, though. Helping the poor, riding through the streets and distributing her father's alms. The kindest, the most gracious, fairest princess in all the kingdoms. That's what they say. They're running out of superlatives.'

The huntsman wondered how much she was talking to him and how much to herself. She was lost in her own thoughts, and as the light caught her face for a moment he thought he saw another animal beneath her cool surface. A rare creature, one who had been hidden so long that perhaps she'd forgotten that she even existed. He felt himself stir despite his torn muscles and aching body.

'She'll be in the forest somewhere. I hear that's where she spends her days.'

'You seem to hear a lot for someone who prefers the top of a tower to having the warm grass beneath her feet.' He moved closer until he was standing only a foot or so behind her.

I want her heart

'I have eyes everywhere,' she said. He thought of the ravens sitting so still on the rooftops. Ethereally beautiful she might be, but she was damaged and dangerous. He wanted her, he couldn't deny that, but this would be no conquest. There would be no love in it. Not from her.

'How will I recognise her?' he asked.

'Oh, there is no one quite like Snow White. You'll know when you've found her.' She turned to face him. 'But just in case ...' She tilted her head back, her neck as slim and pale and strong as the swans' on the great lake, and opened up a locket at her throat. He leaned closer, to both look and also to feel her heat again. He had been on the road a long time and there had been plenty of danger and little earthly pleasure. He tore his eyes away from her pale skin and looked at the pictures. On one side was the image of a middle-aged man; thick-set and piggy eyed. If this image was a flattering likeness then the huntsman was not surprised the queen was so unhappy. The other frame held the image of a full-lipped dark-haired beauty whose eyes, even trapped by an artist's pen, danced with merriment and joy at life.

'I want her heart,' the queen said softly, before snapping the locket shut. 'You will bring it to me or I will cut yours out myself.' From within the folds of her delicate gown, she pulled out a hunting knife. 'Finest dwarf silver and steel. It will make it quick. And don't even think about running. The forest is deep but my guards will find you.'

She didn't hand him the knife but instead stepped closer, tugged at his belt and holstered it there. He looked down at the swell of her breasts trapped tightly in the bones of her dress. He was hardening and her hands were so close he wondered if she was aware of it.

He was still covered in dirt and sweat and both the stag's dried blood and his own, and her fingers drifted across the stains on his clothes as if fascinated by them. Finally she looked up at him and he could see in the endless lakes of her eyes, where good and bad and everything in between darted like fish in their icy depths, that she knew exactly what effect she was having on him.

'Why are you so sad?' he asked.

She pulled back slightly, shocked. 'Why would you say that?'

He moved fast, reaching in and taking her face in his hands. His mouth was on hers, soft and sweet and so far from the taste of the forest, before she could stop him. His tongue pushed against her protesting one for a long moment and then she broke free. She stared at him, panting slightly, and for the first time she looked like a young woman rather than a queen.

'I can taste it on you,' he said.

'Bullshit.'

'Not exactly royal language.' He laughed aloud, unable to stop himself. 'Dragged up in the streets, were you, before the king found you?'

'You know nothing about me,' she spat at him. 'Nothing.'

'Except that you are filled with sadness.' He grabbed her arms and she struggled against him, but he held her firmly as he pulled her close. She wasn't really fighting him, he knew that. She was fighting herself. She had magic. If she wanted to stop him, she could no doubt kill him where he stood. He'd be helpless against her. That excited him further. Danger had always been his Achilles' heel. He leaned forward to kiss her again.

'You revolt me,' she said.

'You prefer your fat, old king?' he whispered. He kissed her again, tenderly this time, and the tension eased in her arms. Her hard shell was cracking. Her hot mouth tasted of fresh orchard apples. This was not love, he knew, not even a hint of it in the meeting of their lips, but it was a release they both needed. His body ached. He was tired. And he wasn't out of the woods yet. This woman, this strange queen would strike him dead if she wanted to.

He broke away to breathe, blood pumping loud in his ears. She was not trustworthy, but she was beautiful and sensuous and aloof. She was different to him in many ways, that was true, but they were both predators. He watched her for a moment, her head tilted slightly backwards, her pale breasts rising and falling fast within the constraints of her dress. Her eyes were shut, and he was surprised to see a tear squeeze out and run like a winter stream down her pale face. He wiped it away with his rough fingers.

'Just make her go away,' the queen whispered, as his hands reached for her corset laces and freed her hot skin. 'Just make her go away. I have no choice anymore.' With her eyes firmly shut, she kissed him back and pulled him to the ground. For a while, the stag and his past adventures, and the killing to come, were entirely forgotten.

It didn't take him long to track Snow White. People were creatures of habit and her horse's hooves had scored their mark in the paths leading into the thickest part of the forest at the base of the mountain. Even without them to guide him he'd have searched that way. The dwarves were her friends and the dwarves lived at the base of the mountain within whose guts they toiled for such long hours. She came this way each morning and left each night to head back to the castle. Animal tracks never lied.

The sun was hot as it cut through the canopy and he glanced up occasionally to scour the branches for ravens, but he hadn't seen a single one since he'd left the city walls behind, hidden on the back of a merchant's cart. Perhaps the queen's control over the birds had a physical limit. Still, he didn't relax. There would be soldiers behind him before long and there was no doubt she'd have doubled the patrols on the borders of the kingdom. Whatever moment they'd shared – and she'd been so cold about it when they were done that he'd almost thought it was a dream – no trust had come with it.

There had been no affection in what they'd done. The strange beauty had kept her eyes closed from start to finish, murmuring words he couldn't quite make out as he explored her body and took his satis- faction from it. It was the huntsman's way until true love found them, but this time he was the one who came away feeling awkward afterwards. They had used each other – there was no denying that – but he knew that she had used him *more*. If she'd had any respect for him beforehand, there was none in evidence when she finally sent him on his way. Maybe he had been foolish, but there had been too much wickedness around him of late and nothing shook that away like the pleasures of the body, whether they be taken with a queen or a serving girl.

He concentrated on the task she'd set him. He was a straightforward man, but he was learning the wiles of the wealthy. It seemed that no matter how much he wished for a quiet life, fate had drawn him into royal games once again, and this one would have a twist in it before it was done. There was still a debt that needed paying and he wouldn't forget it.

Ahead, just out of sight, a horse whinnied and pawed at the leafy ground. His skin prickled and he edged silently forward, ignoring the tiny insects which hovered and darted around his head in the muggy heat. The air so close to the base of the mountain carried a tang of minerals from the mines, and as he peered through the low branches to the pool beyond, it grew stronger. A thick mist coated the surface of the water, thinning into steam as if the water was warmer than the air. Perhaps it was. There were no mines in his homeland and who knew how the metals in the earth changed its nature.

From somewhere in the haze came splashing, light and free, and as he was sure that he couldn't see her then he believed the reverse must also be true; he slipped between the trees until he was in the clearing beside a fine horse with royal colours in its reins. He patted the thick black neck and calmed it, impressed by its size and strength; not the steed he expected for a princess. Dark eyes full of fire watched him warily. This was no prancing pony, this was a stallion fit for a fighting king. What was it about the women in this royal family that made them so strange? An ice queen in a tower and a princess with a knight's horse who swam – he took the pair of riding breeches and white shirt from the horse's back to find her underclothes there too – naked in the forest? There was nothing normal about this – but then, with his adventures of late, normality was becoming a rarity. He hid behind the thickest willow trunk and waited.

She emerged from the water not long after, standing on the bank and tipping her head back to squeeze the water from her black hair, as naked as the day of her birth and brazenly comfortable with it. Suddenly, he understood the horse. Where the queen chose to hide in her tower, this princess was earthy, a creature of nature. Her slim legs were long and firm and she moved with the grace of the finest white stag. This was no delicate animal; no skittish forest deer. She was beautiful without a doubt, but not fragile. She was fuller figured and rounder featured than her step-mother – generosity made flesh. Her stride was confident and sunlight glittered on the drops of water that clung to her skin like jewels. She paused and stretched, smiling at the mix of warm air and cool liquid on her drying body.

That was what was so wrong with the queen, he realised as he watched the girl so comfortable in her nudity. She was equally beautiful but with none of the freedom or calm of this princess she hated. She was harder. One day she'd harden so much the pressure would shatter her.

Snow White paused and frowned, and before she had time to realise she wasn't alone, the huntsman stepped out in front of her. He held up her clothes.

'Looking for these?'

She crouched slightly, making ready to fight, but made no effort to cover her glorious nakedness and her eyes darted here and there searching for a potential weapon. He liked her more already.

'I'm not here to harm you,' he said. 'Well, technically I'm here to kill you, but she owes me a life in exchange for one she wasted, and so I choose to spare yours.' This girl's life for the stag's would be a good payment. One creature of nature for another. He held out her clothes but instead of reaching for them, she'd been distracted by something else. Her eyes widened as she spotted the elegant knife tucked into his belt.

'That's a royal blade,' she said. Her voice was as rich and sweet as her curves. 'Where did you get it, thief? And if you're looking for riches,' she raised her arms and one eyebrow, 'as you can see, I'm not hiding any.'

'That's the second time a beautiful woman has called me a thief today and neither time has it been true.'

'I don't believe you.' She snatched her shirt and glared at him while tugging it over her still damp skin. He could see from the saddle that she rode like a man, the horse firmly clamped between her thighs, and his eyes fell to examining the taut muscles. He wondered how it would feel to be gripped by them. 'There's only one person who could have given you that knife and that's my ...' She fell silent as the truth dawned on her. '... my step-mother.' She stood and stared at him for a moment as if willing him to deny it, but he said nothing. Eventually, she came towards him and searched his face. '*She* sent you? To kill me?' She looked down at the knife again. 'But why? Why would she … ? I thought … it was all a misunderstanding so why would she … ?' Tears welled up in her eyes. 'She hates me,' she whispered. 'She really hates me.'

'You can't go back to the castle,' the huntsman said. Heat rose under his collar. Women's tears were something he didn't understand. In fact women, beyond their physical aspects, were something he didn't understand, and nothing he'd seen in the past few weeks had done anything to change that. 'Go somewhere you can hide for a while. Until your father returns from his campaigns. Do you have people you can trust?'

'It was all a lie. Everything she said. She *was* trying to kill me. Why would she want to kill me?' She was lost in her own thoughts, and he dropped the rest of her clothes in order to grab her arms and shake her slightly. There was no time for this. Her skin was warm and supple.

'Listen to me! Do you have people you can trust?'

It took a moment for her to focus, but finally she nodded. Her tears were still falling and she sniffed hard. 'Yes. Yes, I do.'

'Good,' he said. 'I'll take a deer's heart back instead.'

'She wants my heart?' She laughed and then choked on the fresh tears. 'My *heart*?'

'I'll have to take your horse,' the huntsman said. 'It will make it more believable. She doesn't trust me.' This brought a fresh wave of tears and he wondered if she was listening to him at all, but she patted the horse's neck and then pressed her face into it. Finally, she looked up at him. 'Thank you,' she said.

'She owed me a life,' he answered, simply. The queen, who claimed to know the huntsman's code, had not realised how closely he lived by it. Regardless of the danger it might place him in, the stag's wasted life demanded the balance was restored. The weeping princess threw her arms around his neck and hugged him tight, a sudden gesture he had no time to pull back from. Her body was warm through his clothes, her nipples pressing into him through his thin shirt. His arms folded around her, his hands on the taut curve of her back, fighting the urge to slip them down to the rise of her buttocks.

'Thank you,' she repeated. After a moment, she stiffened in his arms. 'I can smell her on you,' she said, pulling back slightly before pushing her face into his neck and breathing deeply. She looked up at him. 'It's her. You've *been* with her.' Between her body pressed against his and her breath on his skin, the huntsman couldn't stop himself responding. She could feel it, he was sure. What was going on today?

'If you tell your father,' he said, roughly, 'it won't just be her head he takes. It will be mine too. He tried to step back, but she kept her arms around him. They were strong and he could feel the lean muscles beneath her skin.

'What did you do with her?' she asked, her eyes drifting half-shut, tears still falling. 'Touch me like you touched her. Touch me like she touched you.' The huntsman said nothing, once again feeling like a pawn in a game he hadn't signed up to play. Soldiers would be coming to find him if he didn't return soon. And this girl was a princess, not a wicked queen. She should not be touched by any man before her wedding day. Not even by the man saving her life. He felt the strands of the web he was trapped in tightening around him as she pressed her body into his and lifted her lips. 'Kiss me like she kissed you,' she whispered, all hot breath and warm skin. 'Please.'

And, cursing his own nature, he did.

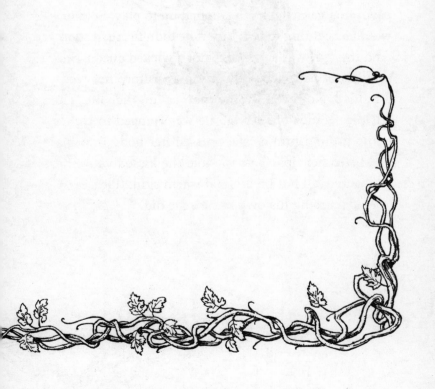

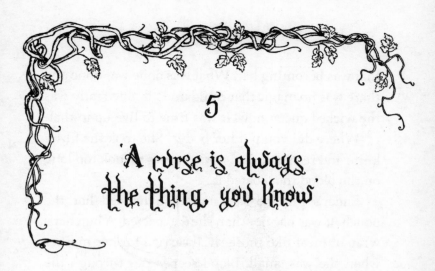

5

'A curse is always the thing you know'

The first thing the queen did was take her knife from him. The blade was still bloody and sticky to the touch. For a moment she felt faint and swayed on her feet. Flashes of imagined scenes hit her in a wave; Snow White bleeding to death in the forest, her eyes widening as the metal cut into her chest, the huntsman's hand pulling her warm, dead flesh apart to find the trophy that would secure his own freedom.

She stared at the weapon. What had she done? The stark reality of it was like ice in her veins and she tightened her grip on the hilt to stop her hand trembling so obviously. 'Did she suffer?'

'No,' the huntsman answered levelly. He looked so calm. Was he as much of a monster as she? She drew herself up tall and haughty; playing the part that was becoming her. What was done was done and there was no magic that could undo it. She really was the wicked queen now. It was time to live up to that.

'Where did you put her body?' She took the filthy knife and resheathed it, not wanting to look too long on the blood that coated it.

'Ender's Pit,' he said and then handed her the pouch. It was heavier than she'd expected. A butcher's wrap of meat like those she'd carried for her mother when she was small. Blood seeped out through the roughly sewn edges. She didn't open it. She didn't want to see.

'And now if I can have my slippers I'll be on my way. A deal's a deal and I have unfinished business elsewhere.' He didn't let his eyes, deep and un-fathomable, drop from hers. He was rough and handsome and arrogant, this travelling stranger, and she detested him. She wanted to sink the knife into his neck and be done with the whole damned business.

'Of course.' Around them, the walls blackened further and the red jagged lines sprouted new crim-son branches. This room was her forest of magic and as her heart hardened, her power grew stronger. Her lips tightened into a smile that was as sharp as the murderous blade. It was for the best. All of it was.

'Are these what he wants, dear?' The familiar voice cracked like dry forest twigs under children's running feet. 'They're very pretty. In fact, I'm very impressed with your entire collection. You've done well.'

Lilith didn't look round as the old woman shuffled out from the back room. Her great-grandmother had arrived unannounced only an hour earlier and she hadn't had time to process it yet. The day had been surreal enough without her. As far as Lilith knew or remembered the old woman had never left her candy cottage, and yet here she was. She had trekked across kingdoms and turned up as if she'd been just passing. She was also doing that hunched over, helpless little old lady thing that she slipped into whenever she had an agenda. The huntsman's face crinkled in disgust at the sight of her and Lilith felt a surge of pride in her bloodline. Women put too much store in beauty as a power to wield over men. There were other powers which were just as valuable. She was learning that.

'Yes. They're his. He can have them back.'

'No need to be hasty.' The crone placed the shoes on the floor beside the wide cushioned throne, out of reach of the huntsman. 'You were always in such a hurry. Even as a child.' She took the pouch from

Lilith's hands and her gnarled hands pulled on the drawstrings.

'You don't need to look in there.' Her heart raced slightly and she flushed, just as she'd done as a child when she'd been caught peeling a strip of liquorice from the walls, black juice smeared around her mouth. There was no need for her great-grandmother to know what she'd done. She didn't want anyone to know what she'd done.

'Oh, you should always check the goods before you pay, my dear.' She tipped the heart into her hand. Glistening meat. The queen felt sick.

'Oh my,' the old woman said, turning it over in her hands until they were covered in redness. 'I see.' She slid it back into the sopping cloth and then licked her fingers, savouring the taste. Her lips smacked together and her eyes twinkled. 'But those shoes? For a deer's heart? It's not much of a trade.'

'What? It's not ... ?' Lilith stared at her and then at the huntsman, whose eyes darted from the pouch to the old woman and then to the queen again.

'Did you think it was a human heart?'

'I ...' Heat burned her from the inside. 'But ...'

'I know the taste, dear,' the old woman said, 'and this is not to my taste.' She tutted at the huntsman. 'I fear you've been a little deceptive, young man.'

'Where is she?' Blood rushed to the queen's face and she seized the knife and stepped forward, jabbing it towards him. 'You let her go?' A whirl of emotions gripped her and for the first time she saw fear in the huntsman's face. She liked it. 'Was it her beauty? Is that what stopped you? Was her beauty worth your own precious life?' He stepped backwards slightly and her angry glare darted at the vast doors beyond which slammed immediately shut.

'Very nice, Lilith dear,' her great-grandmother said, approvingly.

'You wouldn't understand,' he said.

'Why?' The dark snakes in her soul writhed. 'Because I don't have her charm? Her beauty? Because I'm filled with poison?' Her words were the dry hiss of a trapped animal. Fear was eating at her anger. If Snow White was still alive then where was she? Already sending messages to her father? Was the executioner's block all her own future now held? The people wouldn't mourn their cold, unfriendly queen. Would the king call her a witch for real and burn her? Were the flames that haunted her finally going to claim her?

'Did she give herself to you to set her free?'

A nerve twitched in his cheek as the arrow of truth in her words struck home. Her anger burned brighter, a white heat that could turn a city to dust.

'You think you're such a righteous man,' she sneered, not caring that it made her ugly. 'You're not. You're nothing but a mouse.' She spat the last word out and a jolt of energy shot through her arm.

The huntsman vanished.

For a moment she couldn't understand what had happened, and then, as her great-grandmother cackled and clapped applause, she heard the tiniest of squeaks. A small brown field mouse was scurrying across the floor.

'Much better!' the crone said. 'A mouse. Very good. A fitting punishment for a double-crossing huntsman. Let's see how he survives the forest now.' She snapped her fingers and the mouse was gone. Lilith stared at the empty patch of floor and then looked over at her great-grandmother. The old woman was smiling.

'Don't worry, dear. He'll be back one day.' She patted the throne. 'Have a sit down.' Lilith did as she was told and the old woman looked into the pouch once again. 'Cutting out a heart. I do sympathise with the sentiment, but death is so ...' she paused. 'Final. No magic can change it.'

Lilith looked at her great-grandmother and

thought of all the small bones that littered her garden. 'And you should know.'

'I only want what's best for you, dear. Don't be irritable. It doesn't suit you.'

'What am I going to do?' She just wanted to cry.

'A curse is always the thing, you know.' Her great-grandmother nudged her along the seat and squeezed her bony hips into the throne to share it. 'Death is a last resort. Curses, well, they give you power.'

'Then I'd like to curse her to sleep forever,' Lilith said. She was aware that her voice had taken on the slightly surly tone of her youth.

'Forever is a long time,' her great-grandmother said. 'Aside from death, the only thing that lasts forever is true love.' She rummaged in the folds of her raggedy clothes and pulled out a rosy apple. 'Eat this. They're good for you.'

Lilith took it and bit in, chewing the crisp, sweet flesh, hoping it could cleanse the bitter remnants of hate that filled her mouth. 'Then I want her to sleep until true love's kiss wakes her.'

'Now you're getting the hang of it.' The old lady nodded approvingly. 'That one's always a winner.'

Lilith leaned her head on the bony shoulder beside her. It was good to be with someone who loved her.

'Leave it with me.' Her great-grandmother patted

her leg affectionately. 'I'll take care of it on my way home. It'll all work out in the end. I'm like your fairy godmother, eh?'

Lilith shut her eyes and let the old woman soothe her. 'It's good to see you, Granny,' she said, quietly. 'It really is.'

6

'No good can come from a crone'

They didn't speak much as they came down the mountain from the mine. Despite the hardiness that came from their nature and a lifetime of working underground, it still took a while to recover any energy after a full shift. Even as they reached the edge of the forest the three dwarves didn't sing as the hot metal in their lungs was cooled by the fresh open air. Their minds were occupied with the secret they shared and as soon as their feet marched in steady rhythm onto the soft grass, their eyes were darting this way and that for evidence of soldiers. They had a princess to protect. Dwarf honour was second to none – as was so often the way with people so long subjugated – and they had vowed to keep their friend safe. If they failed in their promise, a terrible fate would befall them. Dwarves never broke an oath.

It was a warm day, but the swarms of tiny flies that filled the damp air stayed clear of them as they made their way past the hot pool and towards the path home, hovering high above the short-statured dwarves. The rest of the team would follow soon, but these three, whose real names hadn't been used in so long they'd almost forgotten what they were, had earned themselves an early finish. Grouchy took the lead, Dreamy behind him, and Stumpy, his nickname earned after he'd been pulled screaming from beneath a rock slide, his crushed hand missing, followed behind them. They were lost in their own thoughts for most of the journey until they reached the crossroads. Dreamy paused, his feet breaking their marching rhythm and his companions stopped beside him.

A figure was shuffling along the worn path. Even with her head bowed the glaring warts that covered her nose and chin were visible and her hair hung in grey strings. Her dress, a mixture of worn rags cobbled together into some kind of shroud-like garment had perhaps once been black but was long faded to grey. 'A crone,' Dreamy muttered, his eyes narrowing. 'No good can come from a crone.'

The old woman raised a hand in greeting and

hobbled closer. She smiled and Dreamy shivered at the blackness in the gaps where so many missing teeth should have been. 'Travel safely, ma'am.' Grouchy nodded to her, tipping his hat as if he were a gentleman of the court rather than a dwarf with black mine dust so ingrained on his skin that he could no longer scrub it off.

'I thank you, young man.' The words were weak and came out in a hiss of air that whistled through her gums. She was carrying a basket and under the checked cloth, Dreamy could just make out a large, perfectly red and waxy apple. His mouth watered slightly. She started to hobble away from them and then paused, her wizened head creaking round on her brittle shoulders until she'd fixed them with one watery eye.

'I saw a thing,' she said, 'that might be useful to you. A deer. Dead a little way back in the shade of a great willow. Straight from here as the crow flies. Looked fresh.' She paused. 'You look hungry.'

'We have to get back to our cottage,' Dreamy said. His skin tingled warily even though she was an old woman and he was a hardy dwarf with thirty years mining under his belt and an axe hanging across his back.

'Fair enough. Something in the forest will have it.

Fresh meat rarely goes to waste.' He raised a hand to say farewell, but she'd already turned and continued her slow shuffle along the path. The dwarves didn't move.

'A deer.' Stumpy licked his lips loudly. 'A fresh one.' Dreamy knew how he felt. His stomach had rumbled at the mention of the animal. Tonight, all seven dwarves would be home and most of what they'd eat would be boiled potatoes and cabbage, flavoured with a few herbs and the juice of a boiled scrawny rabbit carcass all the meat of which had been eaten days before. Now they also had Snow White to feed – a royal princess. The small forest animals who weakened at the mountain's edge were not good enough for her, no matter how she protested that their generosity in hiding her was banquet enough.

As Grouchy and Stumpy muttered between themselves, Dreamy watched the old woman slowly making her way along the path that they should have been taking home instead of lingering here. 'No good comes from a crone,' he repeated.

'You can't judge a book by its cover,' Grouchy snorted with mild amusement. 'She might just be an old grandmother visiting nearby.'

'What would you know about books?' Dreamy said. 'You've never even read one.'

Grouchy was their unofficial leader, his rank in the mine granting him the same authority in the cottage and it was rare for any of them to snap at him, least of all Dreamy, the gentlest of them all. But there was something about this crone that unsettled him.

Snow White had brought Dreamy books, slim volumes of adventures that she'd sneaked out of the vast library in the castle. They had changed Dreamy's world and he would always love her for that alone.

'Don't need to read one to see how they've addled your brain,' Grouchy said. 'But then, your head's always been in the clouds.'

'The stories keep me sane while my body is in the mines,' Dreamy said. The old woman was almost out of sight now.

'Music should do that,' Stumpy said. 'Music is the dwarf way.' He spat on the ground. 'We should at least look for that deer. I'm fucking starving.'

Dreamy didn't argue. Two to one said they should try, and his own stomach was turning against him in the argument. Venison was a strong meat. A delicious meat. And a whole deer would last them a while.

They found the carcass barely ten minutes along the path the old woman had been following and she hadn't lied. It lay beneath a willow tree on cool ground. The meat was in good condition. More than that, with its heart cut out, it was clearly the deer the huntsman had killed to trick the queen. 'We have to take it,' Grouchy said. 'It's evidence that Snow White is still alive. We can't have the Queen's Guard finding it, and find it they will before long.' They roped its legs with vines and Dreamy used his axe to hack down a long branch from a tree which they could strap it to. When the dead animal was secured, Grouchy took one end and Dreamy the other, leaving Stumpy to carry their tools as best he could, and by the time they were back at the crossroads and heading home Dreamy's misgivings about the crone had passed. She'd been a blessing as it turned out. They would all eat well and the princess's survival would stay secret. He smiled and even joined in as the other two began to hum a working tune.

Finally a thin, barely visible line of worn ground branched off from the main path and the dwarves turned on to it. Their cottage was only twenty feet or so away but was still completely invisible to the naked eye. Even if the crone had been of wicked intent she'd have walked right past it. He shook his

head slightly and laughed at his own nervousness.
No one ever found dwarf cottages, and theirs had
become considerably better protected in the past
twenty-four hours. The forest had a tendency to
wrap itself around dwarf cottages. Bushes and trees
were thicker and heavy roots broke the ground's
surface ready to trip any passer-by who came too
close. Branches hung so low that anyone taller than
a young child would have to duck to find their way
through, and Snow White aside – because everyone, even the forest, could see the goodness in her
– would then find themselves tangled in and stabbed
at by errant twigs they hadn't noticed were there.
Brambles would creep out and dig into skin until
finally any curiosity would be overwhelmed and the
interloper would back away, no longer interested in
the hints of life they'd spotted through the bushes.
It wasn't that the dwarves wanted to hide, it was
just that they liked what little privacy they had, and
nature respected that. Nature was a magic in itself. It
took care of those who loved it.

As they passed under the last of the thick branches,
the clearing opened up in front of them and their
cottage, bathed in golden sunshine, came into view.
Dreamy smiled. Grouchy had been right. He was
too caught up in his world of stories. Snow White,

dressed in her riding breeches and shirt, was sitting on the heavy wooden table where they all ate outside in the summer. A bowl of peeled potatoes was to her right and a tankard sat to her left. Dwarf ale, of course. She could drink the heady mix with the best of them and sing along until dawn when the occasion arose, her beautiful face shining with earthy joy. The thought stabbed at his insides.

He wished she could shake this terrible sadness that was on her. She'd refused to send a message to her father. She'd cried. A lot. They hadn't really known what to do about that. Dwarves didn't cry that much and as far as they'd known neither did Snow White. They'd brought her drink and forced her to eat something and left her to work it out of her system. That had been Dreamy's suggestion. There were lots of women in the stories he'd been reading and he'd learned that sometimes they just needed to be left alone to think. More of the stories would have turned out better if the men had seen that as clearly as Dreamy did.

At least today she was up and keeping busy. Maybe it would all work out all right. He grinned and waved and she gave them a soft smile in return before raising something to her mouth. Dreamy froze as he saw what it was. An apple; large and impossibly red and waxy. He tried to cry out – to stop her taking a bite – but the words choked in his throat.

No good can come of a crone.

Her eyes widened as she took the first crisp bite and as the dwarves dropped the deer and started to run, she was on her feet and clawing at her neck. Her legs buckled and, with the rest of the apple still gripped tightly in her hand, she fell lifeless to the forest floor.

With shattered hearts they searched the forest for the crone but there was no sign of her. She had vanished, leaving them no outlet for their anger. When the other four marched back to the cottage and discovered the awful events, the dwarves mourned, singing low songs into the moonlight and through until dawn. The deer began to rot where it had been dropped, a symbol of their stupidity that they taunted themselves with.

They pushed their small beds together and laid Snow White out across them, the apple still gripped in her cold fingers. They lit candles around her. They sang some more. They discovered that dwarves could cry. Over the next few days they worked long, dangerous shifts for extra gold and then Dreamy spent everything they had saved on a beautiful pink and white dress, bought from a passing merchant on his way to the fine ladies of the city.

In the clearing the deer stank and mouldered in the heat, but Snow White neither breathed nor rotted. Grouchy worked through the night forging a glass coffin, and on the third day they washed and gently redressed her, curling her long hair and rouging her lips and cheeks. When she was ready, they carried the coffin to the mound on the other side of the thicket where it was rare for anyone but a dwarf to pass. Bluebells grew on the banks and the sun caught the space all year round. They would not put her underground. They knew better than any how harsh and brutal the earth's grip could be. She would lie in the sun, just as she had loved to do.

Some of the dwarves thought that perhaps she should have been dressed in the breeches she'd loved too but Dreamy was so distraught that they let him make a proper princess of her. She *was* a princess, after all. They would guard her until her father returned, and then perhaps one day a cure for the curse would be found.

They sat with her when their long, bone-tiring

shifts were done, but it was always Dreamy who stayed with her the longest. Her sadness was over — his had begun.

Dreamy was sitting alone, tossing small pieces of old cheese to a small brown field mouse, when the prince stumbled through the trees that guided him up onto the mound. Dreamy should have been in the mines. He should have been there all week, but Grouchy had told the supervisor that he had lungflu and no one had questioned it. He wasn't getting paid, but then they'd all lost their appetites and less food was required. Why bother trying to cook something tasty when it felt as if all the joy had been drained from the world? They were grieving and weighed down with guilt, but it was generally acknowledged that Dreamy, so much more sensitive than the average dwarf, was suffering the most.

He was so lost in his thoughts that he didn't hear the young man until he had staggered up the other side of the mound and was almost beside the coffin. The mouse scurried into the bushes. Dreamy reached for his knife. The stranger was tall and broad and framed in late-afternoon sunshine that danced on his dirty blond hair. He was handsome. He was also injured. Dreamy got to his feet, and moved forward quickly to catch his arm as he fell.

'Thank you,' the stranger mumbled, as Dreamy lowered him carefully to the ground. He wasn't a soldier, not from this land at any rate, and although his clothes were dirty they were made from fine fabrics. Both the hilt of his sword and his red cloak carried the same insignia. A lit torch shining through a golden crown. He was royal this one; a prince perhaps. But not of this kingdom.

'Here. Drink.' He handed over his flask and the prince drank greedily from it, not caring that it was heady beer and not water. His pale skin glistened with sweat; a thick sheen that had nothing to do with the warm summer's day.

'I must find my companion,' he said, eventually. 'He's been gone for days. I think.' He frowned. 'I'm losing track of time.'

'You're injured,' Dreamy said. It was clear the man had a fever. His eyes were brilliant blue, but flecked with red and his whole body trembled. Dreamy pulled the cloak back slightly and the young man winced. A bandage of sorts was wrapped around his middle but blood had leaked through and dried, mixed with mud, on the once-white linen shirt. Whatever injury lay beneath was festering. It would need attention or the dwarves would have a second lifeless royal body on their hands.

'You should come back to my cottage,' he said. 'We can—'

'What is this?' The prince's eyes narrowed as he pulled away from the dwarf and leaned over towards the glass coffin containing Snow White's perfect form. 'She's beautiful,' he said. His voice was as dry as whispering baked autumn leaves and, hearing a strange nervousness in his tone, Dreamy wondered when he'd last drunk or eaten properly. Had he lost his way to the river? How long had he been wandering?

The prince's face was so close to the glass that his sickly breath condensed on it and Snow's beautiful face was almost lost from view. He frowned again.

'Yes, she is,' Dreamy said, simply. 'She was cursed by a crone. She seems to be neither completely dead nor alive.' His heart broke all over again saying the words aloud.

'Cursed?' The prince's head darted round. Why did he look so wary? 'In what way, cursed?'

'The apple,' Dreamy nodded at the perfect fruit still gripped tightly in her small palm. 'She ate the apple.' They both stared at the frozen girl a little longer, lost in their individual thoughts.

'What was she like before?' the prince asked. 'Did you know her?'

'She was beautiful,' Dreamy said. He could barely get the words out. 'And always kind.' He wasn't ready to talk about her yet; her wild charm, her skill on horseback, the way she swam free and naked in the lake. Those were his memories. They'd be razor blades on his tongue if he spoke of them so soon.

'She was a princess,' he said. That much he could be truthful about. There were many princesses in the stories he'd read. Maybe none quite like Snow White, but many he could draw on. 'A pure girl with a kind and delicate disposition. She excelled at dancing and music. She sewed the most ornate tapestries with silk threads. Her laugh was like sunlight on dappled water.' He choked a little at that. It was almost true. Her laugh was richer though; molten ore in the heart of the rocks they battled daily. But her smile, her smile was all nature and sunlight, and when he remembered it she was always splashing in the pond, gently mocking them for not coming in.

'She sounds perfect.' The prince had laid down alongside the coffin, staring in. 'A true beauty.'

'She was.' Dreamy wiped away his tears and then dipped into his fictions to tell more stories of the beautiful princess who'd been cursed for her kindness. The sun slowly set, but he didn't stop. The prince didn't interrupt him, but it was only when he began to twitch and mutter that Dreamy snapped back to reality and realised how much time had passed. The stranger had fallen into a fever, no doubt caused by his wound and, collapsed on the grass, he tossed and turned in the grip of a nightmare, his eyes moving rapidly behind their lids. Dreamy tried to wake him and pull him to his feet, but he was too far gone and too heavy.

'Beauty,' the prince mumbled urgently, the rest of his sentence lost in hot breath and half-words. 'Beauty.'

'A princess is
missing'

The dwarves made him a makeshift bed beside the coffin. The cottage was too cramped and they decided the fresh, warm air would be good for him. Stumpy built him a fire and they dressed his wounds and fed him broth as the fever slowly broke. It wasn't just him who slowly recovered; the dwarves did too. They had someone to care for, someone to mend, and in doing so their hearts too mended a little as the days passed into weeks.

The prince made his home by the glass coffin and the dwarves returned to work. Each day they came back and brought bread and stew up to the mound and would sit in the dying light and talk and sometimes even sing. They would sing to Snow White and the prince would join in. Every day he grew stronger, and after a while they'd come back to find he'd fetched wood and water and caught animals in the forest for them to eat. He never left the mound for long though, and hardy as the dwarves were, they could see that he was falling in love with their frozen princess.

He talked to her. They heard him sometimes, his voice low and full of good humour, recounting stories of battles and jousts and balls and a glittering castle of light. He smiled and touched the glass, as if hoping she would lift her own hand and touch his from the other side. Sometimes Dreamy would just watch from the trees. The handsome prince regaling the frozen beauty with his stories, or just sitting quietly beside her and looking at her. He willed her to breathe, just as they all did. But her eyes remained lifeless and staring skywards. As the world turned and the days passed, she did not change.

'You're nearly recovered,' Dreamy said, one evening as the fire embers died down and the dwarves headed back to their cottages. 'You'll be able to return to your land soon. You must be pleased.'

'I'm not quite well enough yet,' the young prince replied, and Dreamy thought he'd never seen such a sad and handsome face as that upon which the fading firelight danced. His own heart felt heavy. Perhaps they should have made his bed inside the small cottage. Perhaps giving him so much time with their cursed princess had been stupid. Now there was more heartache ahead when the young man would have to leave her.

He didn't read before sleeping that night. There was too much tragedy and romance already surrounding them. Instead, he lay awake on the wooden table outside the cottage and stared at the stars and wished for happy endings.

It was perhaps a week later, as the cool breath of autumn swept through the forest, that they first noticed the ravens. They were sitting on the fences at the bottom of the mountain on the Dwarf Path.

'Ravens don't come out here,' Stumpy said. He didn't break his pace, but his eyes darted upwards and his voice was low. Dreamy remembered when Stumpy had been a merrier soul who'd laughed and chatted as they'd worked, but four hours stuck beneath a rock slide, his hand crushed beside him and the dead bodies of four dwarves around him in the dark had changed him. Dreamy had been part of the rescue team. It was a day he would never forget. Stumpy had been screaming for at least an hour before he passed out. When he'd woken up, he was not the same. There were some things that changed you. This was as true as a first breath and a last, and that day had killed the dwarf who had been Dreamy's best friend, even if he still walked, and talked, and mined. Perhaps one day the old Stumpy would return, but those shadows would never be entirely shaken free. Just as Dreamy would never shake off the sound of his screams.

'What are they doing here?' Stumpy kept his voice low. They were on the mountain now, and the guard would be watching. There was no love lost between those who mined and those who supervised. The men were nearly all there on punishment duties and they envied the dwarves their good health amid the dust.

'Queen's birds,' a voice came from a team marching beside them. Dreamy looked round. The leader was rough-skinned and his face had a long scar running down one side. Belcher, Dreamy thought his name was. He'd been a warrior dwarf, a city dwarf. His songs were different to theirs and his team never smiled or broke ranks when they dug. Belcher's team would not have got separated and allowed one of their own to lose a hand. Had the words come from any dwarf but him, Dreamy would have laughed them off. Instead, his guts chilled.

'How do you know?' Stumpy asked. Dreamy stayed quiet. Belcher respected Stumpy. He respected how he'd changed. Dreamy wondered what Belcher might have been like decades ago before the wars and then the mines changed him.

'I hear talk. I still have friends among the soldiers. Those are charmed birds.' His mouth barely moved as he grunted out the words and all of them kept their eyes ahead. 'She *sees* through them. Watches the city. They've never left its limits before.'

'What's she looking for, do you reckon?' Dreamy was impressed with Stumpy's casual tone. He gripped his axe hard to stop his hands trembling. There was only one thing – one person – the queen could be looking for, and that was Snow White.

'You tell me, Stumpy lad,' Belcher said, wryly. 'You tell me.'

Their shift passed interminably slowly. Dreamy found a moment to tell Grouchy what had been said, but it was nothing that could be talked about in the hot, close confines they worked in. Ears were everywhere and Dreamy didn't know if it was his imagination or not, but it seemed as if here and there hooded eyes turned his team's way. Was their secret safe? Snow White had been friends to all the dwarves, but it was their cottage she had come to when the drinking and singing was done. Would the other teams pass that information on to the soldiers if asked? How strong was dwarf honour – and what would happen to them if Snow White was discovered? He fought the rising panic. He would take whatever fate passed their way. They had vowed to protect the princess. They had failed once – they would not fail again.

There were no ravens in the forest; that much at least was a relief. Rain was pouring heavily through the trees as they trudged home and the drops were cold and had no summer scent as they turned their faces upwards into it and scanned the branches for silent birds.

The prince had a fire lit for them and a fresh rabbit was roasting on a spit, but as the water dripped from the dwarves to the cottage floor, the meaty scent did nothing to entice them to eat.

They sat in silence for a while, sipping beer.

'Maybe it's nothing to do with us,' Breezy said. 'Maybe she just wants to make sure we're all working?'

Grouchy barely snorted in response.

'A princess is missing,' Stumpy said. 'Even if the queen thinks she's dead, she's got to make a show of looking for her. We didn't think of that.'

'Is there anything I can do?' The prince had stayed out of their conversation, but he'd been listening from the fireside.

'You should go,' Grouchy said. 'Your land needs its prince and these are our troubles. Plus, winter is coming. You can't sleep out there forever.'

Dreamy's heart stung at the words, and the thought of Snow White out on the mound in the dark in her glass coffin, the rain hammering on it. At least the prince stayed with her. At least while he was here she was rarely alone.

'Maybe in a day or two.' He turned back to the fire. 'I still need to rest.' His jaw locked and although no one would argue with Grouchy, and he was right, they knew what really kept the handsome prince in their poor cottage and up on the mound.

'A day or two longer,' Grouchy said. 'And then, my friend, you must leave. I will not have more on my conscience.'

The prince nodded and as something unspoken passed between the two, a thought dawned on Dreamy that hadn't occurred to him before. This prince's land might not be one of the allied kingdoms. Dwarves and politics did not mix, but had Grouchy recognised the prince's crest? Would he become a prisoner, if the queen knew about him? Would they all end up in the dungeons for harbouring him? Suddenly it was all clear. And suddenly their present danger increased tenfold.

Eventually, they filled their plates with food and forced themselves to eat, but every mouthful of meat made Dreamy want to be sick. He wished he was braver. He'd always imagined himself as the hero in the adventures he'd read, but he was starting to realise that adventures in real life were far more fear than excitement. The wicked queen was coming.

And come she did.

It was as if the weather could sense the dark magic that was spreading across the forest. The temperature had dropped overnight and rain hung in half-frozen droplets across the branches. Autumn had been crushed by an early winter, the browning leaves killed by the sudden cold.

Dreamy was alone when he heard the heavy wheels of a carriage on the other side of the thick trees and bushes, followed by the sharp shouts of soldiers coming to a halt. He had been building the fire so it would last all day, and was about to race to catch the others up when he stopped, his stomach turning to water, in the clearing. The prince had gone up to the mound only minutes before, a pot of hot stew to keep him warm during his vigil, and Dreamy willed him to stay away. He stared at the trees. Maybe they wouldn't find the cottage – maybe they—

'It's here somewhere.' A woman's voice; quiet but commanding. 'Cut your way through. I will speak to them *all*.' It was *her*. The queen. Snow White's step-mother.

More shouted commands and axes and swords cut into the veins of the forest, determined to clear a pathway to the cottage door. Dreamy wanted to cry. Why was he the last one here? Why not Grouchy? Or Stumpy? They were braver. They would not be so afraid. He looked around at the small tracks leading to the pond and the mound. He wanted to run. His short, thick legs trembled with the urgency. He could make it, he was sure, and be clear and at the mine before the soldiers found their way to the Dwarf Path. The soldiers would never know the ways through the forest like the dwarves did and fear concentrated the mind.

And his mind concentrated as the axes beat out a steady rhythm towards him, branches creaking as they were torn free. He *could* run. But what would happen then? They'd search the cottage. He tried to remember if there was anything incriminating in there? Something of Snow's from times gone by? Her breeches were kept somewhere. Maybe they'd

find them. Chances were they'd then search the surrounding areas. The mound was well-hidden but
nowhere near well enough to escape a determined
queen. He thought of the ravens. How much did she
know already?

Ahead of him, a gap formed in the butchered
trees and he glimpsed the soldiers coming forward.
The Queen's Guard. He couldn't run. He knew that
much. He was the only one who could save himself
and his friends.

'Hello?' he called, and stepped forward, his voice
innocent and wary. 'Who's there?'

'Her Majesty the Queen!' a soldier barked.

Dreamy fell to one knee and bowed his head. He
waited. Finally the axes fell silent and there was only
the cool breeze rustling in the trees and the clank of
soldiers' metal.

'Get up, dwarf.'

'Your Majesty.' He paused for a moment in defer-
ence before standing with his head bowed. 'What an
honour. What can I do for you? I live to serve.' He'd
been worried that, not being a natural liar, his face
would give his guilt away; but instead, as he finally
glanced up, his mouth dropped open and all thought
was momentarily gone. He wasn't sure what he'd
been expecting. A monster? A crone?

She was beautiful. He'd *heard* she was beautiful, of course. Snow White had said as much and the soldiers at the mines made plenty of lewd jokes about the old king's luck, but Dreamy hadn't been part of the birthday ball joke – his balance hadn't been good enough to stand on another's shoulders without causing them all to collapse – so he had never seen her for himself. He hadn't thought that there could ever be anyone as beautiful as Snow White, but here was proof otherwise.

Where Snow's hair was dark and thick, the queen's was white-blonde and like a sheet of silk down her back. Her eyes angled upwards like a cat's. He noticed that beneath them were dark shadows. He felt terrified and full of pity all at once. Guilt could drive a person mad, he was sure of it.

'The princess is missing,' she said curtly. 'I know how much she likes to socialise with you ... people.' She looked at the cottage and its surrounds as if the idea of spending any time in such a place was her idea of hell. 'If any of you have caused her any harm, then we will find out.'

'No dwarf would hurt her!' Dreamy exclaimed. 'We love the princess. Your Majesty knows that. But we haven't seen her for days. We thought perhaps she was caught up in business at the castle, and we're no longer allowed in the castle ... so ...' He let the sentence drift off to a natural end. It was this queen who had banished them, after all.

'Please,' he dropped his bag and ran to the cottage door, pulling it open – he hoped not too dramatically. 'Search our house. Please. Dwarf honour is at stake. Search the house and then I will help you hunt for her anywhere you ask. As will my brothers.'

She stared at him for a long moment and his heart was in his mouth. If they *did* search the cottage then Snow White's breeches would be found and they would be done for. But if he hadn't offered this woman would have insisted. It was a dangerous bluff, but it was also all he had.

'You've heard none of the other dwarves talking about her?' the queen asked.

'No, your Majesty. But I will listen harder, I promise you.'

'Make sure you do. My ravens will travel further into the forest soon.' She looked at the trees around them as if they were an army standing against her. 'Then we'll find her, however well she's hidden.'

Dreamy said nothing, not sure he could trust himself to speak, but the queen was lost in her own thoughts.

'I just need to know,' she said softly, to the trees

and the breeze perhaps, but not to man or dwarf. 'I'll go mad if I never *know*.'

She turned and walked back along the new path to her carriage and after a second or two snapped her fingers. The Queen's Guard gave Dreamy one more suspicious glare and then followed her. The trees and bushes were already knotting themselves back together and the dwarf was pleased to hear one small exclamation of pain as a bramble caught on a passing soldier's cheek.

'To the next one!' The queen commanded, her voice carrying easily to the clearing. 'And then to the mines.'

Dreamy waited until the horses had been spurred on, and the roll of the carriage's wheels was no longer audible, before he allowed his legs to give way beneath him. He sat trembling on a tree stump, his breathing ragged and harsh. For a while he thought perhaps that they might come back – that this was an elaborate ruse to lull him into a sense of calm only to return, declare him a traitor and drag him to the dungeons – but no wheels or horses returned and as his panic finally left him and his skin cooled, Dreamy knew what he had to do. There was no time to wait for the others. Their shift wouldn't be finished for many long hours yet, and by then anything could have happened. The ravens might spy Snow White from above or – and although it was a terrible thought he knew it was possible – one of their own kind might betray them. They'd kept Snow White a secret, but all the dwarves knew that his team were her favourites.

As soon as his legs were steady he went up to the mound, fighting the urge to run and instead moving cautiously, checking around him for signs of soldiers or spies. The dense forest, however, was empty and each of his own footsteps was too loud as he made his way along the familiar route and up to the sunny peak.

The prince was sitting with his head bowed as Dreamy arrived. He didn't look over, but continued to stare at the beautiful face within the glass coffin.

'I know you all want me to go,' he said. 'And I should go. For all your sakes. But I can't. I can't leave her.' A single tear trickled down his perfect face. 'I think it would kill me.'

'You have to take her with you,' Dreamy said. 'You have to take her back to your kingdom.'

'What?' The prince looked up.

'I'll come with you to the border. She's not safe here.'

'But your kingdom and mine ...'

'I know,' Dreamy said. There was a war between them. Of course. He had been naïve. Not anymore. Dreamy was growing up fast today. 'But you must keep her safe until her father returns. Until we can figure out what the curse is and how to lift it.'

'And then I will marry her and our two kingdoms will be unified at last.' The prince's shoulders were straightening already.

'I'll prepare the cart,' Dreamy said. 'The Queen's Guard are searching the dwarf cottages. If we move now and stay away from those paths then we have a chance of getting out of the forest and away from the clutches of the castle by nightfall. But we have to move now.'

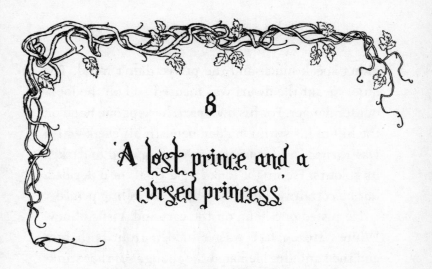

8
'A lost prince and a cursed princess'

They had worked quickly, and were on the road within an hour. Dreamy had cleared the evidence from the cottage and then they lifted the coffin onto the back of the dusty wooden cart and covered it with an old blanket before surrounding it with firewood and bags of potatoes and old vegetables in the hope that it would pass at least a brief inspection. They'd harnessed the dwarves' old, tired pony, that had done no more than the occasional trip to market for years, and the forest had let them through.

The first half an hour had been a tense affair until they were away from the main tracks and onto rockier, less well-used terrain. The dwarf led them, the pony responding best to his familiar clicks and tugs on the rein, and the prince brought up the rear. They didn't speak much and the prince didn't mind. The quiet meant the dwarf was focused and on the look-out for danger. For his own part, he kept one hand on the hilt of his sword, hidden beneath his cloak which was turned inside out and covered in mud to darken its colours. He might look like a thief, he'd decided, but he certainly didn't look like a travelling prince.

He rested one hand on the cart and wished Snow White's frozen face wasn't hidden from both him and the sunlight. He hated the thought of that stinking blanket covering her like a shroud. She was too beautiful and tragic and perfect for that. Dreamy was right, she was safer this way, but he didn't have to like it. There was nothing noble or regal about being transported in fear, on the back of a dirty cart. Maybe when he got back to the castle he'd change the story. For her sake, as much as his. He remembered his injury and all that came *before* he'd wandered and found the dwarves. He shuddered. There would be a few stories that would have to be changed. But still, the dwarves had saved his life and brought him *this* sleeping beauty, and for that he would forever be grateful. When he was home he would send riches back to them as a reward.

In the absence of his missing companion the prince might never have found his way out of this kingdom and back to his own, but the little dwarf up ahead seemed never to be lost, instead steadily picking his way along the narrow paths and choosing between two or three at a crossroads with a confident ease. The prince was glad. Now that he had secured his princess he couldn't wait to get home. He'd had enough of adventures. The castle of light, jousts and dancing; that's all he wanted. His prince's life again. He shivered with pleasure at the thought. This mining kingdom was rough and brutal compared to his own, where courtly manners and beautiful things were treasured, and music and society balls filled the evenings. His heart ached to be there with his exquisite princess by his side. He would have his father scour the land for the finest magicians there were, to undo whatever curse had been laid upon her. He would save her and she would love him as he loved her and they would live happily ever after.

His feet trudged on in pace with the pony that might not have been swift but was at least steady, and after a few hours, Dreamy began to hum. Although the tune was coarse and clumsy compared to the minuets they played at home, he'd grown used to the dwarf songs, and he joined in. Maybe there were parts of the dwarf life he would miss. The brother-hood. The unspoken friendships and loyalties. Both things that were so hard to find when born of royal blood.

'You're not singing it right.'

The gruff voice came from behind them, and the prince turned fast, drawing his sword.

'You could take a man's eye out with that,' Grouchy said, emerging from the bushes and onto the rocky track. 'A taller man's eye, admittedly.'

'What are you doing here?' Dreamy asked as he rushed towards the older dwarf. 'Are you angry? I couldn't wait. I'm sorry. I thought this was for the best. There was no time to—'

'Stop babbling.' Grouchy swatted at the air as if Dreamy's words were irritating flies. 'You did the right thing. We heard about the queen's hunt at the mines when the next shift came in, and as you hadn't showed up I came looking for you. Saw your note in the chimney.' He slapped Dreamy on the shoulder. 'That was good thinking. Where Snow White used to leave us messages.' He nodded at the prince. 'But I thought I'd come and keep you company. Dwarves aren't solitary creatures and it'll be a long walk back when these two are safe.'

'Thank you, Grouchy.' Dreamy looked as if he might burst into tears of relief, and the prince wondered at how little he really knew these hardy men.

A fear of walking alone was not one he'd imagined in someone who was finding his way so well through the forest. 'It's good to have you along,' he said, and smiled. 'Now teach us how to sing it properly.'

They sang quietly together, the prince daydreaming of home and Snow White dancing at his side, and day slowly shifted into afternoon and then into the strange grey of dusk. Finally, they fell silent and walked by the flame of a single torch. They were tired and their legs ached, but they would walk through the night if that's what it took to get to the edge of the forest. To be far enough from the castle to be safe.

As it turned out that was what it took. The prince was sure that he dozed as he walked for a while, suddenly jolted out of his reverie by either Dreamy or Grouchy handing him some water and a piece of hard bread to chew on. The hours were endless and the uneven ground beneath his boots meant he stumbled painfully as much as he walked. The hardy pony should have been dead hours ago but it maintained the same steady pace, forcing them all to keep up. The night was relentless. The prince began to wonder if they were all cursed on a journey that would never end. He tried to focus on thoughts of home or Snow White's perfect beauty but his mind kept being dragged down into other, darker memories which played out like nightmares. Running through a different forest in fear for his life. A couple of times he cried out, and Grouchy took his arm, gruffly waking him, but it was hard to tell where the boundary between fantasy and reality lay.

At last the pitch darkness that gripped them fractured with shards of grey and then yellow and orange as dawn broke. The prince could have cried with relief. Exhaustion had taken them all prisoner and was torturing their every step, but the trees were definitely thinning and the track widening into a proper road. They were near the edge of the forest. They would have rest soon. He was about to burst into a laugh of relief when the pony suddenly started and reared up, whinnying in terror and sending the cart tilting up and the contents spilling out onto the road.

The prince felt as if he was moving through sludge as he grabbed for the cart, missing completely and falling sideways to find himself attacked by tumbling vegetables. The dwarves tugged at the pony's reins trying to calm her and then finally, there was a quiet stillness.

'What the fuck happened?' Grouchy said.

'It's just a mouse.' Dreamy was crouched in the

road. 'Look.' The prince hauled himself to his aching feet and limped over. A small field mouse, a scar cutting down its back, was merrily cleaning itself in the middle of their path. It paused and looked up curiously at them, completely unafraid. Dreamy laughed a little. 'It's just a mouse.'

'Look at the mess. I'm sure that wheel isn't sitting right. This is going to—'

'What's that sound?' The prince frowned.

'What sound? Dreamy looked round, suddenly peering through the gaps in the trees, no doubt for the arrival of soldiers.

'Listen.' The prince turned back towards the broken cart. It had come from that direction. He heard it again. A cough. 'That.'

The little mouse scurried between their legs and over to the glass coffin which lay, half-spilled, still covered with the dirty blanket, on the road. They all turned and watched as he sniffed around a little and then nibbled on a fallen potato. The cough came again. Light and feminine.

'The coffin,' the prince whispered. 'It's coming from the coffin.'

The prince reached it first, the dwarves right behind him and between the three of them they carefully laid it out on the road and pulled the blanket away. From inside, Snow White looked blearily up at them, the small piece of apple that had been trapped in her throat now lying on her chest.

'The crash dislodged it!' Dreamy cried. 'She hadn't swallowed it! It was stuck half-way!'

'Get her out of there,' Grouchy grumbled. 'The clasps on the side. Undo them.'

The prince was already working at them. Was this a dream? Were they still walking through the night and this was just an illusion that would shatter at any moment? Could she really be awake? He'd wished for this moment since he'd first laid eyes on her, and now here it was, out of the blue.

The glass lid came away, and he leaned forward.

'Who are you?' Her voice was husky and cracked a little.

'Shh,' he said, and before he could stop himself, he leaned down and kissed her. Her lips were every bit as soft and sweet as he'd imagined them to be. He lingered for a few seconds enjoying the feel of her body heat rising from the confines of the glass, and then he pulled back. She looked up at him, breathless.

'I'm the man you're going to marry.'

She sat up suddenly and looked down at her dress and then at the apple in her hand. 'Um ... what's going on?'

'It's a long story,' Dreamy said. 'Let's get a fire going and we'll tell you. First,' he leaned in towards the apple, 'we should throw that away.'

Out of nowhere, the little brown mouse scurried up Dreamy's arm and onto the edge of the glass side, standing on his rear legs, with his whiskers twitching. He leaned towards the fruit.

'No, no,' Snow White said. 'We need to put it somewhere safe. Otherwise the animals will eat it.' She looked at the prince. 'Have you got a pouch or something?'

'Of course.' He took the apple and the small bite she'd coughed up and put them in his money bag. She was beautiful and also kind. The dwarves had been right. This was magical. It was love. It had to be.

They made camp in a small clearing at the side of the road and in the glow of the fire, the two dwarves and the prince told her all that had happened since the crone gave her the apple. The prince let Dreamy tell her of his vigil and how he'd sat beside her as she lay there somewhere between life and death, through all the days and nights. When they were done, she turned and looked up at him. 'You were going to keep me safe?' she asked.

'I'm still going to keep you safe,' he said, wrapping one arm around her and pulling her close. On the other side of the fire, the two dwarves beamed with happiness. 'Marry me and come back to my kingdom. You will be the brightest jewel in the crown of my palace of light. You will never want for anything, I promise you.'

She looked into the fire and his heart raced with his love for her. 'Please be my wife,' he said. 'I've been searching for you all my life. This is true love. I knew it when I first laid eyes on you.' He could feel heat rising on his face; embarrassment and excitement. She had to say yes. She had to. Surely she must feel something for him too.

'A lost prince and a cursed princess,' Dreamy said. 'It's so romantic. Like something from one of the story books you gave me.'

'The queen tried to kill me,' she said softly.

'And she'll try again if she gets the chance,' Grouchy said. 'She's wicked, that one.'

The seconds passed like hours as she continued gazing into the crackling flames, the light from which licked at her face as if it too wanted to touch her beauty. What was she thinking? Her expression was as unreadable as it had been while she was frozen. He was rushing her, he knew, but what else could he do? If he took her back unmarried his father would probably try and put a stop to it. He wanted to arrange his son's marriage himself. He'd *seen* some of the women his father would choose and they weren't for him. But to return already married, to a royal princess, was something he wouldn't be able to put aside. And once he'd calmed down, he'd realise that the warring could end and a new alliance could be made. Snow White's kingdom had mines and metal. His father would want both.

'Yes,' she said. The first time she said the word so quietly it was almost lost in the crackle of the fire.

'What?'

'Yes.' She looked up at him. 'Yes, I will marry you. Why not?'

The dwarves were on their feet and hugging the breath from Snow White before her answer had sunk in, and then his hand was being shaken so hard by Grouchy that he could barely speak.

'Enough, enough!' She broke away, laughing. 'Let's do it straight away. Tomorrow. Why wait?' Her face was shining with a wild excitement and he leaned forward to kiss her again. Her lips brushed his and then she pulled back. 'Not until our wedding night,' she said. 'I'm a princess, after all.'

The prince's heart almost burst. Beautiful, kind and demure. Exactly what he'd always wanted. A perfect princess. After everything that had happened *before* his injury he'd lost faith that such a creature existed, but after all his trials, the loss of his companion and the days of nightmarish delirium, here she was.

'Tomorrow,' he said, grinning like a child. 'We'll wed tomorrow!'

9
'Let's get married'

Dreamy and Grouchy had mended the cart and reloaded it as the young couple slept. The dwarves hadn't slept much, guarding the fire and their precious human company throughout the night, but they were both happy in their work. 'Sometimes things happen for a reason,' Grouchy said. 'If the crone hadn't given her the apple, who knows if these two would have found each other.'

'Have you been reading one of my story books?' Dreamy teased as they harnessed the pony. 'You're sounding almost romantic.'

'Fuck off with you,' Grouchy said, but a small blush crept across his gnarly face. Dreamy smiled. It was a happy ending. They'd be able to leave tonight knowing she was finally safe. The weight of their guilt had been lifted. There would be no awful fate awaiting them for not being able to keep their word.

'I'll miss her though,' he added. It was true. Snow White was a light in their otherwise dull lives, and as the kingdom was sinking into the dark mire of the queen's magic, there would be very little pleasure to see them through the winter and to the king's eventual return. She had always been there for them, and now she would become part of another kingdom.

'She'll be back,' Grouchy said. 'I've got a feeling in my bones about it.'

'At least she'll be safe and happy.'

They smiled at each other and finally woke the sleeping beauties.

After the chill of the dawn the day broke into sunshine; a final war cry of summer, or perhaps just that the queen's winter hadn't stretched this far out into the kingdom yet. Either way, the sun was warm on their backs as they finally broke free of the forest.

'Look,' the prince said. Ahead, where the land dipped into a valley, a higgledy piggeldy town was visible, smoke rising from chimneys as the day started. The royal crest flew from the top of the town hall, the bright colours standing proud against the white stone of the buildings and the blue sky above. Next to the pennant was a smaller one, and although none of them could make it out exactly they knew it was the queen's mark.

'Not short of ambition then, your step-mother.' Grouchy muttered as the road widened beneath them.

'No,' Snow said. 'She's certainly unique.' She was holding Dreamy's hand and he gave it a squeeze.

'Well, she can't hurt you now,' he said. 'You're safe from her.'

'I suppose I am.' Her voice was soft but sadness gave it weight.

'We can't be sure of that until you're across the border,' Grouchy added.

'There's a chapel,' the prince cried. 'There! I can see the steeple!' He smiled down at Snow White. 'Let's get married.'

Dreamy was as close to tears as dwarves got before Grouchy had even started to walk Snow White down the aisle. It hadn't taken them long to find the priest, and even though he'd raised his eyebrows at the young couple's urgency to marry – no doubt suspecting it a sudden necessity rather than a romantic act – it had only taken a couple of the prince's gold coins to persuade him to get dressed and meet them at the chapel. It was still quite early and the streets were relatively quiet. Dreamy had picked the last of summer's wild flowers and threaded them together into a headband for Snow White, the pinks and reds picking out the lilac hue of her beautiful eyes. The prince had beaten at the door of a dressmaker's until they too had opened up and their initial anger evaporated when they sold a fine white dress to the beautiful girl and her beau.

Snow hadn't stopped laughing all morning; a wild carefree sound that Dreamy normally associated with some crazy adventure or prank, but as she went with Grouchy to get rooms at the inn and change into her dress she became calmer. It was her wedding day, after all. It needed to be taken seriously. Even by one so wild as Snow White.

Dreamy went to the chapel with the prince and they waited quietly with the priest for her to arrive. It was no ornate royal church, but the small building had a charm of its own. The high arched windows were clear of decoration. The cool air sang with the scent of the lilies that filled huge vases on either side of the small altar. The wooden pews were plain but well-varnished. It was a peaceful place, Dreamy decided. A good place. He couldn't imagine a royal wedding, with all its sumptuous glory, could be more meaningful.

He remembered the parades and processions when the king married his ice queen. The kingdom had been filled with pageantry for days, and what did that marriage have? A man in thrall to a beautiful woman, perhaps, but that was not a union of love. No woman became that wicked when she'd fallen in love. But then, his knowledge of these things was limited. Dwarf women were rare and always died in child-birth, producing at least five small babies at once. No dwarf ever knew their mother. Waiting in the chapel he said a quiet prayer for his own lost mother. He didn't believe in any of the gods, but neither did he know what else to do with his sudden maudlin thoughts. This was a happy day. Snow White would be blessed with children and she would know them and love them. Her life would be perfect. It *had* to be.

Finally, the doors opened and Grouchy and Snow White began the walk to the altar. There was no organ, but Grouchy was singing a dwarf song, a slow end of the day marching tune. His deep voice echoed and Dreamy's throat tightened as he watched them pass him. Like a true princess, Snow White kept her head up and focused on her waiting husband ahead, and Dreamy thought that dressed in the simple white shift, and with her dark hair flowing free around her shoulders beneath the crown of flowers, he'd never seen her looking so beautiful.

Sunlight cut through the church, dust dancing in it like fireflies, and framed the pair as they quietly took their vows. The prince, so tall and handsome, didn't take his eyes from the princess throughout the whole ceremony, and when the priest finally declared that he could kiss the bride, even he smiled happily as the young couple did as they were bid. There was something special in the moment, something magical, and outside birds began to sing.

They were man and wife. Prince and princess. And they would live happily ever after.

'I think we should keep it,' the prince said. 'As a souvenir of how we met.' He stroked the glass coffin on the back of the cart.

'Technically, we didn't meet that way,' Snow White said. 'I wasn't exactly there. But if it has sentimental value to you then why not. I love that the dwarves made it for me. That they didn't bury me.' She smiled at Grouchy. 'You saved me, really.'

The day was getting hotter and after a quick

wedding breakfast at the inn, the dwarves were getting ready to say their farewells and head back into the forest. Dreamy wasn't looking forward to it. It had all happened so fast and now Snow White was heading off to live in a completely different kingdom. It was for her own good, he knew, but he wished he and Grouchy could stay too. Not that it was possible. Dwarves belonged in the mines, and if they didn't return the rest of their team would suffer.

'Here,' the prince reached into his money pouch and pulled out several gold coins. 'To replace your cart and pony. If you don't mind us taking them.' He stroked the pony's mane. 'She's worked hard. She deserves a good retirement.'

'Then you take her,' Grouchy said. 'You'll give her a better life than we can.' The prince pressed the coins into Dreamy's protesting hands. He could smell sweet apples on the metal from where they'd shared space with the crone's cursed gift to Snow. Was this now poisoned money, he wondered. Why did that thought give him such a chill? He shook it away. Grouchy was right. He spent far too much time with his head in books. His imagination was getting too able to carry him away.

'But we should buy ourselves some horses to ride home on,' the prince said. 'I can't walk back into the castle. I need a proper horse and mine is lost.'

'Let me get changed first,' Snow White said. 'I want my normal clothes on.' She reached up and kissed her husband on his nose. 'Wait here.' The prince blushed and Dreamy felt better. Money could be washed. There was nothing tainted here.

The prince had bought her several fine dresses from the seamstress, but when she emerged she was wearing her riding breeches and white shirt, and her hair was pulled back in an untidy knot. Natural beauty shone from her and she took the prince's hand and dragged him to the horse merchant. The prince looked surprised at what she was wearing, but it made Dreamy smile. It was her, their princess, earthy and passionate and back with them again.

After picking out a fine steed for himself, the prince chose Snow White a grey pony with plaits in its mane and that pranced around the corral as if it were dancing. She laughed and shook her head, her hair shining in the sunlight. 'That's no horse for me. I've always ridden a stallion. Let me choose.' She pushed past him and walked along the line of stalls until she reached the furthest. Inside, a black beast pawed at the ground, eyes burning with rage at his captivity.

'This one,' she said.

'Are you sure?' Dreamy peered over the edge of the door. 'He looks a little dangerous, even for you.'

'That's no lady's horse,' the prince said.

'I'm with yer man,' the horse dealer cut in, spitting tobacco into the sawdust. 'That one won't break.'

'Let's see, shall we?' Ignoring them all, Snow White undid the gate and stepped inside the stable. The horse stamped his feet and shook his head, snorting angrily, but the slim girl stood beside him and stroked his neck, whispering quietly into the beast's ear. After a moment, she gripped the thick mane and pulled herself effortlessly onto his back.

The beast reared and snarled but she stayed on, urging him out of the confined space and into the sunlight. She laughed as he tried to throw her, her face glowing with the sheer energy of life.

'He's going to throw you!' the prince cried out. 'Get down!'

'I'm no chicken!' Snow White called back. 'Just watch me.'

And watch they did. It was all they could do as the horse and rider took to the corral and began their battle for command. Dreamy was in awe. She was so fearless; so alive in the moment. She had her father's strength and her mother's grace and beauty. She and the horse were as one.

'She rides like a man,' the prince said, as they watched her finally tame the beast to a canter, her thighs controlling him as they turned this way and that, her hair falling free from the loose bun. 'What woman rides like a man?'

'Oh, I don't think there's another woman like our Snow White in all the kingdoms,' Grouchy said, pride clear in his voice. 'You're a lucky man.'

'That horse is more powerful than mine,' the prince said. He looked a little stunned and Dreamy squeezed his arm.

'She's a force of nature. You'll get used to her.'

'I suppose I shall.'

The horse came to a halt in front of them and whinnied as Snow White dismounted. She was breathless and flushed with excitement and she flung her arms around the prince's neck. 'What an amazing ride.' Her voice was so sweet and warm that Dreamy could see the prince melting in it.

'If you want the horse, he's yours.'

'We should leave,' Grouchy said. 'You'll be safe here and the border is only a mile or so north.'

'Don't go yet.' Snow White turned, crestfallen.

'But it's your wedding day. Tonight's your wedding night. It's a time for you two to be alone.'

Dreamy blushed and kicked at the earth. Sex

wasn't something dwarves had a lot to do with.

'But that's tonight,' Snow White said. 'Leave tonight then. Today's our wedding day so celebrate with us. I know what.' She grinned. 'Let's have a beer.' She strode off ahead, and then turned, one hand on her trousered hip. 'Come on, what are you waiting for?'

The prince was staring after her, dumbfounded.

'She's probably just nervous,' Dreamy said, suddenly feeling as if he needed to make an excuse for her behaviour. He'd read that women got nervous before their wedding nights. He didn't really want to contemplate why.

'Yes, that's probably it,' the prince said, and finally they followed her.

10

What was his father going to say?

It was not quite as he'd expected. In fact, it was not at all as he'd expected. The prince felt somewhat dazed and confused by his new wife's behaviour. His head was in a whirl, although that could have been the beer. There had been a lot of beer, and as he watched his wife dancing enthusiastically with Dreamy in the middle of the tavern, he realised that not only could she outride him, she could outdrink him too.

It was hot and humid in the bar and although it had been early afternoon when they'd arrived, it was now dark outside. The day had lived up to its promise and given them the last of the summer, but it meant that men who'd spent hours sweating in the baking heat were now crammed into the small space. In the corner a fiddler was playing furiously and several couples joined the dwarf and the princess in a reel, whirling each other this way and that in a clumsy over-enthusiastic frenzy. The prince could feel his hair curling with the moisture and he took another sip of his beer. His time with the dwarves had accustomed him to the bitter taste but he longed for the fine wines of home. Elegant dinners. Polite dances.

The party had started when Snow White had drained her third beer in a drinking competition with two merchants and then demanded they both dance with her as her prize. They were, of course, delighted, and he had no recourse but to give them his nod. After that, the whole inn became infected with her energy and soon word had spread throughout the town that a celebration was in progress and more revellers poured in. That had been several hours ago, and now night had fallen outside but the dancers showed no hint of slowing down. He wished they would. He hated the way his shirt clung to his skin and, more than that, he hated the way his new bride's shirt clung to hers so every man in the room could see the lines of her body. What was she wearing a man's shirt for anyway?

'We should leave soon.'

The prince looked down to see Grouchy standing beside him.

'And you two should be getting to your bridal bed.'

'My bride doesn't seem too keen,' the prince said. 'She's more interested in dancing and drinking.'

'Well, she's always loved both of those, that's true. But she's also been through a terrible time. She seems a little wilder than normal, I can't deny it, but what can you really expect? And this is her wedding day. Wild and happy have always gone hand in hand with Snow White.' He slapped the prince's arm lightly. 'Don't you worry, she can do serene and lady-like when she has to. It just doesn't come naturally to her.'

'She's ... she's not how Dreamy described her. When she was in the box. When we'd talk about her.'

'Ha!' Grouchy snorted. 'Why do you think we call him Dreamy? He lives in story books that one. Perhaps thinking of her as she really is was too painful.' The dwarf paused. 'But she is the kindest, most beautiful person I have ever met. Look at the joy she instils in strangers. It's a rare gift, she has, the ability to make people smile. She'll make you very happy.'

The prince watched his beautiful dancing wife as the crowd applauded her. 'Yes, she will,' he said. 'Yes, she will.'

It was late by the time they said farewell to the dwarves and headed up to their bedroom. All Snow White's good humour had dampened into tears as she squeezed each of the two goodbye, and she had insisted on watching until they had long disappeared into the night. He'd taken her hand and led her up to the bedroom where he'd just held her for a while as she'd cried, and he found her tears were something of a relief. She was helpless like this, her face pressed into his chest. He felt like a prince again. The man who'd saved her from imprisonment in the box. She was his perfect princess. Her breath was hot on his neck and her full breasts were pressed into his chest. His heart beat faster and he swallowed hard as desire crept up on him, warmth flooding his body. He'd imagined this moment so many times before, and now it was finally here.

He'd had his share of serving girls and even several of the ladies of the court at home, but never had he longed for a woman as he had Snow White. He'd studied the curves of her body as she'd laid in her glass coffin and he'd dreamed of touching her and feeling her respond beneath him. His breath became more uneven and hers steadied as he stiffened against her. Finally she looked up at him.

'Don't worry,' he said. 'I won't hurt you.'

'I'll go and ...' she hesitated, 'and get myself ready. There's a washroom in the corridor.'

He put a finger over her lips, not wanting to sully the moment with talk of hygiene and human sweat. That was for base lust and servants, not for a prince and his princess. He kissed her, and despite the beer and roasted meat she'd devoured so enthusiastically throughout the evening, she still tasted sweet, and her mouth was warm, wet and inviting.

She picked up the new nightdress he'd bought her and when she left the room he quickly stripped and washed with the water in the jug and basin on the small table. It was icy cold and made him shiver but even an entire freezing ocean wouldn't be able to douse his desire. He throbbed with the thought of possessing her, his qualms about her wildness forgotten as he thought of her ripe body. There were no princesses in any of the kingdoms so beautiful. A dark memory came to him and he shook it away before it could cling to his skin and make him wilt. That adventure was done and, foul as it had been, it had led him to this happy conclusion. He was married. He would unite the kingdoms. His father would have steel in the land and keep his enemies at bay, and he and Snow White would live happily ever after and produce fit and healthy heirs. Not too soon, he hoped. He'd seen how quickly women's bodies changed after childbirth and he wanted to enjoy his wife's for as long as possible before they settled into domesticity and he went back to relieving himself with a mistress. He wasn't kidding himself that there wouldn't be other women – some of his needs were more base than others and he couldn't imagine treating Snow White that way – but she was beautiful and he wanted to make love to her for years to come.

Snow White. Purity. Perfection. He didn't even know her real name, and neither did he want to. He blew out the candles around the room, leaving only the red glow of the crackling fire that was slowly dying in the grate. He slid beneath the sheets and waited, resting on one arm, his heart thumping in anticipation.

After what seemed like an age, she finally returned. The soft, sheer fabric caught around her legs as she moved towards the bed, hinting at what was hidden beneath. Was she nervous he wondered? Her eyes were dark coals in the dim light, and they gave nothing away. Her hair hung loose and thick around her shoulders.

'Come to bed,' he said. His voice choked slightly. However strange he'd found some of her behaviour, he was in no doubt that he wanted her. He pulled the sheets back, but she didn't move. 'Don't be nervous.'

'I'm not,' she said, and her hands went to the neck of the fabric and she undid the delicate ties there. The nightdress slid from her, floating to the floor like gossamer. She swayed slightly; a flower caught in a breeze, and he realised she was still a bit drunk. Had she needed to drink because she was nervous? Maybe that was it? She stepped forward out of the shadow and into the glow of the fire. He'd expected her to get into the bed still dressed – he'd half-expected her clothing to stay tangled on her throughout, especially the first time. But instead she stood before him gloriously naked. He couldn't stop staring. Her skin was smooth and her full breasts sat high, generous dark pink nipples erect in the evening air. Generous. Despite her slim frame, it was the word that best fit her. Generous. Luxurious. Decadent. Her head fell forward slightly, her hair tumbling across her face, and she held her arms out wide and spun slowly round.

'How do you like your princess?' She looked over her shoulder at him, her full lips slightly parted, her eyes challenging him from behind her hair.

'I like her very much,' he said. Her arse was round and firm. His balls ached and he throbbed with wanting to feel her from the inside; to ride her as she'd ridden that stallion. To *tame* her. 'Now come to bed.'

'Say please,' she purred.

This wasn't how he'd expected it to be at all. Where was his nervous bride? Why did he suddenly feel as if he were the one being seduced? He was the prince, the warrior; he'd faced things no man should ever see, but he suddenly felt weak. His mouth dried as lust overwhelmed him. 'Please.' The word was barely more than a whisper.

She smiled, the cat with the cream and came onto the bed on all fours, crawling towards him. He reached for her and pulled her close, one hand in her hair, his mouth seeking hers. Her tongue danced with his, and the air was filled with their hot breathing. His hand reached for her breast, feeling the warm weight of it and rolling her nipple hard between his fingers. She moaned slightly and bit down on his lip. He gasped, and in that moment she pulled away, leaving only the night air caressing his skin.

'What are you ... ?' The question faded as her tongue ran down his chest and into the coarse hairs at the base of his belly. Her soft, dark mane trailed behind her mouth like feathers over his skin.

He couldn't stand it. He was going to explode.

Her tongue flicked over the tip of his erection and he gasped again, reaching for her hair to pull her mouth over him, but she moved on, her mouth exploring lower, running through the crevices between his thighs. What was she doing? How? Sensation flooded through his body sending electric tingles to each of his extremities and then, just as he thought his pleasure couldn't get more tantalising, she took him in her mouth.

All thought left him as he thrust deep into her hot throat, her tongue running up and down the length of him as her wet mouth embraced him. He hardened, his balls contracting. It had been too long. He wasn't going to last.

She broke free and straddled him, on her knees before him, a vision of earthy, animal beauty. She was no perfect princess, he knew that now. He didn't quite know what she was, this creature before him. He didn't understand her at all. What kind of royal family was this, where the king's treasure, his only daughter, could learn such tricks that never came until the marriage bed, and even then were more to the taste of wenches than ladies?

He grabbed her hips, wanting to pull her down on him.

'No,' she said, her voice all husky breath; a wolf in the forest. She pushed him back on the bed. 'Your turn first.'

Her tongue dipped into his mouth briefly, she flashed him a wild smile, and then she was over him, her legs either side of his head. She moaned as she pushed herself against his tongue and he was overwhelmed by the heady, musky taste of her. He looked up as she grew wetter and hotter in his mouth. One hand gripped the headboard, and the other teased one nipple of her perfect breasts. Her head was thrown back as she rode him, lost in her own imaginings. She was a stranger. Someone he didn't know. He pushed his tongue further inside her and felt her squirm, the firm muscles in her thighs tightening around him. She was panting, loud and raw, moving closer to a climax.

She was riding *him*. The thought hit him, and his passion and anger and confusion roared into one movement. He pulled her down and rolled on top of her. Her eyes, still hazy with lust, widened with surprise. He pinned her down on the bed, his arms blocking hers, and pushed hard into her, waiting for the moment of give. None came, just tight heat and wetness and an upward thrust from beneath him. He buried his head in her hair and fucked her hard, until finally he exploded inside her, crying out with the release.

They lay side by side in the growing dark as their sweat cooled on their skin. The prince didn't pull her close to him and neither did she move. There was only the sound of their slowing breathing and the flutter of wings on the windowsill outside.

'Must be an owl,' Snow White said, eventually. Her voice was soft and small. Guilty. He rolled onto his side, away from her, and stared into the gloom. His jaw tightened. What was it with women and deception? Why could they never be as they appeared?

'Look, I . . .' The bed creaked as she turned to face his back.

'It wasn't your first time.' It wasn't a question. He knew it as fact. It was obvious from everything she'd done. He'd been deceived.

'It's not like . . . there was only . . . it wasn't like you think.'

He didn't move. He didn't speak and the silence became interminable. He squeezed his eyes shut and wished sleep would come.

'I'm sorry,' she said, eventually, and rolled the other way, pulling her knees up under her chin. The air between them was cold; a few inches and yet vast as an ocean. How had it come to this so quickly? And why had that stupid dwarf not just told him the truth about her? Would he have loved her anyway if she hadn't been such a shock?

What was his father going to say?

By morning, he had made up his mind.

After a fitful hour or so's sleep he woke to find her lying on her side watching him, her dark hair spread out on the pillow behind her. As ever, for a moment, he was lost in her beauty.

'I've been thinking,' she said. She chewed her rose-bud bottom lip slightly, with her perfect white teeth. 'We could just pretend we never got married. I'd understand. I wouldn't say anything. I could go back to the dwarves. Or somewhere else. You can go back to your kingdom. No one would ever have to know. I should have said ...'

He reached a hand out and stroked her face and then leaned forward and kissed her. 'It's okay.'

'But you ... ?'

'I said it's okay.' He moved closer, pulling her ripe body next to his. 'You're so beautiful,' he whispered, as he felt himself react to the feel of her. 'So perfect. I could never let you go.'

He rolled her under him, taking control, and when she tried to speak he silenced her words with his mouth on hers. She was his princess. She was *his*. And she would stay that way.

11

Wine never solved anyone's problems

The raven had flown all night, and although it was morning the castle was still shrouded in darkness from the heavy black rain clouds that hung thick across the land. Candles flickered here and there in the gloom, and as the wind and rain from the open windows gusted in, their flames went out one by one.

Lilith was cold but she didn't care. A hot fire burned inside as she sat on her lone throne, her knees pulled up under her chin, and stared at the small mirrors which relayed all the bird had seen. She watched it over and over. Snow White and the handsome prince in bed. Alive and breathing. The wine glass was tight in her hands. If her great-grandmother had still been there she would have tutted and taken it from her. Wine in the morning was no good for kings or paupers, she'd have said. Wine never solved anyone's problems. Have some milk instead. She took another gulp and her head swam.

The wind howled outside, lashing rain across the tower's marble floor as thunder growled in the sky, and on the window sill the raven shivered. She snapped her fingers and the images stopped. The raven flew away, released from her charm for now. She'd seen enough. She'd seen far too much.

She got to her feet, her legs stiff and aching, and headed to the small room at the back. Her head was a jumble of drunken thoughts and as she thought once more of Snow White and the handsome prince being so base together in that cheap country inn, lightning flashed bright. The tower was in the eye of the storm. The queen *was* the eye of the storm.

As she touched and caressed her magical items, hoping to find some calm in them, she raged against her own stupidity. She'd been to that dwarf cottage. She recognised the little man the raven had shown her, standing at the back of the church as Snow White had wed her weak-chinned prince. He'd lied to her face and she'd believed him. She'd thought their fear of her would overwhelm their love of Snow White, but once again she'd been wrong. The diamond shoes glittered on a red velvet cushion. Where was the huntsman now, she wondered? Dead in the forest? Eaten by an owl? Had Snow White's beauty been worth the price he'd paid?

In the corner the cabinet creaked open and, hearing it, Lilith's shoulders slumped. She didn't need this. Not right now. She didn't turn to look at the face she knew would be staring back at her, but drank more wine. She was getting drunk, she knew it. But drunk was good.

'Snow White is truly the fairest in the land.'

She ignored it, listening instead to the anger of the storm and the heavy beat of the rain. So Snow White had been woken by true love's kiss. She almost laughed. Good luck to them. If she couldn't see the prince for what he was then she was as foolish as she was beautiful. He was spoiled and vain; that much had been clear from what the raven had shown her. Maybe he was exactly what Snow White deserved.

The girl was finally gone, that was all that mattered.

That was all that should matter.

She drank some more wine.

All she'd wanted was her heart.

12
If it will make you happy

It wasn't as hot as the previous day had been and there was a hint of rain in the muggy air, but it was still warm in the village and the prince had left Snow White to bathe while he fetched them some breakfast. He smiled, unable to suppress his happiness. Today, he'd get to go home. It felt as if he'd been away forever and there had been dark moments when he'd thought perhaps his life before had simply been a dream. It was supposed to have been an adventure. Something to prove to his father he was a man once and for all, but the adventure had turned into a nightmare and he'd been lucky to get away alive.

He wondered what had happened to his companion, his guide, but there was no small measure of relief that he would not be returning home with him. Alone, the prince could re-write the tales he had to tell with no shame at someone else knowing the truth. Not that his companion would ever have said – he was a man of few words – but there was an *honour* about him that would have made the prince feel ashamed of his necessary lies. The story would have to change. He was the prince, after all. And the prince was always the hero.

He wandered through the lively market and bought bread and fruit and some cold meats and then went to the inn kitchen and paid the cook, a warty but warm lady called Maddy, well to finish what he needed and then prepare them a tray. He left her with instructions to send it up to their room shortly. There was no rush. He wanted his princess to enjoy her morning.

Snow White was still in the bath when he returned; he could hear her singing as he passed the washroom. She sounded happy and he was glad about that. He wanted her to be happy. She made him happy. She was *going* to make him happy.

There were roses in the vase on the window ledge and he pulled the petals from the stems and scattered them across the floor and bed. There weren't as many as there would have been for a bride at home – the floor in the palace would have been a sea of them,

soft and scented and filling the room with perfume
– but it was better than nothing. He took the pink
and white dress the dwarves had bought her from
its hook in the wardrobe and laid it out on the bed.
It was the dress they had met in, after all, and he
wanted her to wear it when she arrived in his city.

His heart tightened with love for her and he
smiled. He couldn't help it. He waited impatiently.

At last the door opened and she came in wrapped
in a thin robe which clung to her hot, damp skin. The
dusky patches on her cheeks were shining from the
hot water, and her hair was piled up untidily on her
head. She paused, noticing the petals under her feet.

'That's very sweet,' she said. 'Thank you.'

He could see the wariness still in her eyes after his
coolness of the previous night, but that would pass
soon enough.

'I looked for more flowers at the market, but there
were none fine enough for you.'

'Oh, I'm sure that's not true.'

'Yes it is.'

She blushed slightly and then saw the dress on the
bed. 'You want me to wear this one? I thought you'd
want something finer. You know, for meeting your
father. It's pretty enough but not, I imagine, the kind
of thing the ladies of your castle wear.' She held it

up against her. 'And I didn't want to tell Dreamy, but I really hate pink. Maybe we should go back to the dressmaker? See if there's something else?' She chewed her bottom lip again. 'I just want to make a good impression.'

She was nervous of him, he knew. After the awkwardness of the previous night, he'd expected it.

'But this is what you were wearing when we met. When I first kissed you.' He smiled. 'And that is what I will tell my father, when I tell him all that has happened to you.' He stepped towards her and kissed her on her smooth, pale forehead. 'For me? Please?'

'Okay.' She smiled and shrugged. 'If it will make you happy.'

'Yes.' His heart was racing. 'Yes, it will.'

He turned his back and let her dress with her modesty intact, although she seemed to have no qualms about taking her robe off in front of him, even laughing a little at his good manners after everything they had already done together. She didn't understand, of course. He didn't want to see her like that; earthy and cheap. He wanted his princess back.

'Breakfast, sir?' The voice came from the other side of the door and he pulled it open. The kitchen help stood there, a young boy of maybe fourteen or so. He stared at Snow White, a mixture of lust and awe, but the prince's bride didn't notice how inappropriate it was and simply sent a sweet smile his way.

'Thank you,' she said. 'I'm starving.'

'Just put it on the bed.'

'Yes, sir.' The tray held one glass of juice and one plate with warm bread and jam and some sliced meat and cheese. As the boy closed the door behind him, casting one longing look back at the princess, Snow White frowned.

'Aren't you having any?'

'I ate in the market. I wanted to test it all and make sure it was good enough.'

She laughed again. 'You'll learn that I don't have very fine tastes. I like ordinary things. I always have. They're more real, aren't they?'

She pulled the laces tight on her bodice and then sat on the edge of the bed. 'This looks delicious.' She smiled at him again, her eyes merry and twinkling at last. 'Thank you for everything. For being so kind. And understanding. You didn't have to. I'll be a good wife to you. I promise.'

'It'll be perfect,' he said, and watched as she raised the glass to her lips. There must have been something in his expression; a sudden hunger or urgency, because just before the liquid slipped down her throat, her eyes widened in sudden panic and darted sideways. He knew what she was looking at. His money pouch. It sat on the bed, thin and empty. The apple was gone. Crushed up into her glass. She looked back at him, the sparkle in her violet eyes replaced with a terrible sadness, and then the cup tumbled from her hand and spilled its cursed contents onto the floorboards which sucked it up greedily. She fell backwards onto the bed.

He kicked the cup under the bed and then lowered his face close to hers. No breath came from those perfect rosebud lips. Her eyes stared upwards, at nothing and everything. He stroked her cooling face. The apple was gone. And this time there was no chunk stuck in her throat that could be dislodged. He'd made sure of that by getting the cook to make a juice of it.

'Hello again, my darling,' he whispered, tucking a stray strand of hair carefully behind her ear. 'I've missed you.'

The crowds cheered as their prince returned. Many had presumed him dead and his sudden arrival brought cheer to the kingdom and the streets were filled with music and laughter and banners flying high. The prince had waited at the city walls while a message was sent to the castle in order to give the king's men time to organise his parade. He had no intention of coming back barely noticed. Not after all he'd been through. He was a returning hero. He had the scar to prove it.

He waved at the people as he came through the streets, sitting high and proud on his new steed. Behind him, a few feet back and safely away from prying eyes, a servant followed with the old mule and cart and strict instructions not to look under the blanket. The prince would know if he had. He would see it in his eyes. He'd take care of him as he needed if that was the case. His travels had made him less squeamish. He thought of the dwarves and the reward he'd promised them. He had trusted them too easily. He swallowed the sudden anger that surged through him and leaned down to kiss a milkmaid who'd pushed her way to the front of the crowd. She nearly swooned as he pressed his lips into hers and then pulled away, and her face glowed with excitement. He looked up at the larger houses which lined the streets closer to the castle. On the balconies, finely-dressed young women waved handkerchiefs that matched their dresses at him, their eyes flirtatious above the fans that half-covered their faces.

It was good to be home. He *would* send something back to the dwarves. They had earned it. But it wouldn't be money or jewellery; it would be an assassin's blade. They had deceived him. They had given him faulty goods. All may have turned out well in the end but that was not down to any action on their part. He did not like to be made a fool of.

Up ahead the crowd roared louder, and he saw that his mother and father had come out onto the castle balcony to greet him. He raised one hand in a salute and his father returned it. The people were almost ecstatic. The prince turned and nodded at the soldier behind him to bring forward the black stallion. The beast wasn't as fully broken as its new owner had been, but that no longer mattered.

The stallion would make an excellent present for the king.

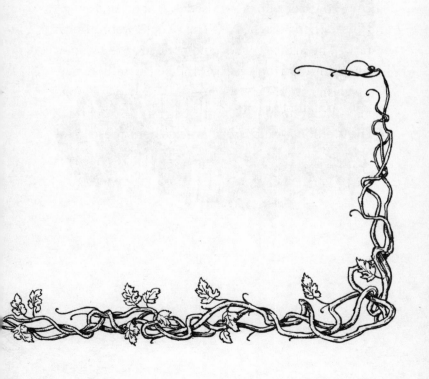

Epilogue

The mouse had lost the band of travellers in the forest. He hadn't been able to keep up no matter how fast his little legs carried him. He stood up on his hind legs and sniffed at the air, his whiskers twitching this way and that. Too many scents assailed him, and he couldn't yet tell them apart.

He scurried from bush to bush, keeping close to the ground hoping to avoid the attention of the hungry birds that filled the night skies, hooting and calling to each other as they hunted. Since claws had torn flesh from his back his first night of being cursed, he'd learned to make himself smaller, almost invisible. It was the safest way to be. Now, though, he was close to panic. He knew the edge of the forest must be close, but he was sure he was somehow going in circles. There had been too much change, too much for him to cope with, and when he'd woken under a pile of leaves near the campfire to find the dwarves and Snow White had gone, he'd almost broken. She was his salvation, he was sure of it. Only she might see past his cursed exterior. Only she could perhaps persuade the queen to reverse it.

He was tired and wanted to sleep until daylight but he pushed himself onwards. To pause would be to admit defeat and he couldn't do that. Something white glimmered suddenly on the path ahead. He trembled and moved closer, his small nose quivering. Bread. It was bread. He nibbled a corner and it was thick and fresh. His tiny dark eyes shone as he looked further ahead. He could see another piece perhaps ten feet ahead. He ran towards it, his feet silent on the forest floor. Up ahead, another. His heart lifted. A breadcrumb trail. He ran back into the safety of the falling leaves but followed the path someone had left for him which finally took him to the forest's edge. A new adventure was just beginning.

Finally back at home, the old lady soaked her feet, a mass of corns and bunions, in a bucket of warm water as she sat by the fire. It had been a long few days, but she smiled contentedly. It had been good to get out. She'd enjoyed messing in the business of the world a little. It made her feel alive again. It had been too many long years since she'd ventured beyond the forest, and it had been invigorating. And always good to see little Lilith. Lilith with the lisp as she'd been so many years ago.

She let her old bones settle and creak back into the chair and watched the flames dance. The house had been cold when she'd got back but it would soon warm up. The large oven was back on and soon her cottage would be toasty warm again. Yes, it had been good to get out, but it was always lovely to be home.

She thought of the breadcrumbs she'd left for the mouse. He'd find them. She was sure of that. She'd also dropped breadcrumbs all the way home too. She wasn't even sure why, she just had nothing else to do with the bread she supposed. Bread had never really agreed with her, she just liked the smell of it baking. Gave her wind whenever she ate it.

She dozed a little and then, just as the fire began to die down, she roused herself and got up to close the curtains.

And there they were.

Two children.

'Look! Look! This is where the bread leads!'
'Is that fence made of chocolate?'
Giggles. Whispers.

She bent her back over, made herself look frail and prepared herself for visitors. She was happy. She peered out between the gap in the curtains. A boy and a girl. Not too young but not too old. And the little boy was decidedly chubby. She smiled and her mouth watered. She'd earned a good dinner.

THE END

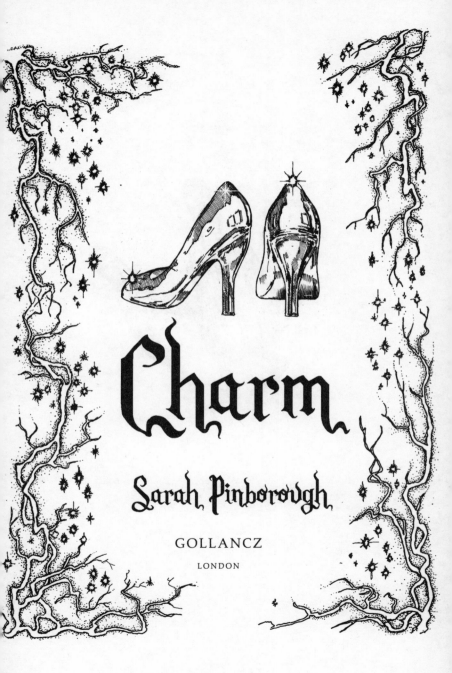

Charm

Sarah Pinborough

GOLLANCZ

LONDON

1

'Once upon a time . . .'

Winter had come early. Its fierce breath tore
the leaves from the trees before they had
even turned crisp and golden, and although
the New Year was still a month away the cityscape
had been white for several weeks. Frost sparkled on
window panes and the ground, especially at the cusp
of dawn, was slippery underfoot. Only on those days
when the sky turned clear blue, in a moment's respite from the grey that hung like a pall across the
kingdom, could the peak of the Far Mountain be
seen. But no one would really look for it until spring.
Winter had come, and its freezing grip would keep
the people's heads down until the ice melted. This
was not the season for adventure or exploration.

As was the way with all the kingdoms, the forest

lay between the city and the mountain. It was a sea of white under a canopy of snow and, beyond the grasping skeletons of the weather-beaten trees at its edge, it was still dense and dark. From time to time, on quiet nights, the cries of the winter wolves could be heard as they called to each other in the hunt.

The man kept his head down and his scarf pulled up over his nose as he moved from post to post, nailing the sheets of paper to the cold wood. It had been a particularly bitter night, and even though it was drawing close to breakfast time the air was still midnight blue. His breath poured so crystalline from his lungs that he could almost believe it was fairy dust. He hurried from one street lamp to the next eager to be done and home and by a warm fire.

He paused at the end of the street of houses and pulled a sheet of paper from the now mercifully small bundle tucked beneath his arm and began nailing it to the post. Residents would send their maids – for although these houses lacked the grandeur of those nearer the castle they were still respectably middle-class, home to the heart of the city: the merchants and traders who kept the populace employed and alive – to discover what news there might be of the ordinary people. It wouldn't be spoken of when the criers came later to share news from the court.

Although he wore woollen gloves they were cut off at the knuckles to give his fingers dexterity, but after two hours in the cold the tips of his fingers were red and raw and clumsy. With the nail between his teeth he pulled the small hammer from his pocket but it tumbled to the ground. He cursed, muttering the words under his breath, and leaned forward, his back creaking, to pick it up.

'I'll get that for you.'

He turned, startled, to find a man in a battered crimson coat standing there. He had a heavy knapsack on his back and his boots were muddy and worn. He wore no scarf, but neither did he seem particularly bothered by the cold that consumed the city, despite the chapped patches on his cheeks. As the stranger crouched, the tip of a spindle was visible poking out of the heavy bag across his back.

'Thank 'ee.'

The stranger watched as he nailed the paper down, his eyes scanning the information there.

Child missing.
Lila the Miller's daughter.
Ten years old. Blonde hair. Checked dress.
Last seen two days ago going for wood in the forest.

'That happen a lot?' The stranger's voice was light, softer than expected from his worn exterior.

'More than ought to, I suppose.' He didn't want to say too much. A city's secrets should stay its own. He sniffed. 'Easy for a child to get lost in a forest.'

'Easy for a forest to lose a child,' the stranger countered, gently. 'The forest moves when it wants, haven't you noticed? And it can spin you in a different direction and send you wherever it decides best.'

The man turned to look at the stranger again, more thoughtfully this time. The wisdom in his old bones told him that there were secrets and stories hidden in the weaver; perhaps some that never should be told, for once a story was told it could not be untold. 'If it's a man that's done it, then he'll take the Troll Road when they catch him, that's for sure.'

'The Troll Road?' The stranger's eyes narrowed. 'That doesn't sound like a good place.'

'Let's hope neither of us ever finds out.'

The barb of suspicion in the man's voice must have been clear, because the stranger smiled, his teeth so white and even they hinted at a life that was once much better than this one, and his eyes warmed. 'I did not see any children in the forest,' he said. 'If I had, I'd have sent them home.'

'Have you come far?' The man asked, putting his hammer back in his pocket.

'I'm just passing through.'

It wasn't an answer to the question, but it seemed to suffice and the two men nodded their farewells. Tired as he was, and with his nose starting to run again, he watched the stranger wander up the street with his spindle on his back. The stranger didn't look back but continued his walk at a steady, even pace as if it were a warm summer's afternoon. The man watched him until he'd disappeared around the corner and then shivered. While he'd stood still the cold had crept under his clothes like a wraith and wormed its way into his bones. He was suddenly exhausted. It was time to go home.

Around him the houses were slowly coming to life, curtains being drawn open like bleary eyelids and here and there lamps flickered on, mainly downstairs where fires were being prepared and breakfasts of hot porridge made. As if on cue, a door bolt was pulled back and a slim girl wrapped in a coat hurried out of a doorway and crouched beside the coal box with a bucket. Even in the gloom he could see that her long hair was a rich red; autumn leaves and dying sunsets caught in every curl.

The metal scraped loudly as she pulled the last

coals from the bottom, the small shovel reaching for the tiniest broken pieces that might be hiding in the corners of the scuttle. There was barely enough in that bucket for one fire, and not a big one, the man reckoned. The girl would be going to the forest to fetch wood soon enough, missing children or not.

As she got to her feet their eyes met briefly and she gave him a half-smile in return to his tug on his cap. He turned and headed on his way. He still had five notices to pin up and a smile from a pretty girl would only warm him for part way of that.

Cinderella was back in the house and clearing the ashes from the dining room fireplace when Rose came down in her thick dressing gown, her hands shoved deep in the pockets. Cinderella was dressed but she still hadn't taken her coat off. The house wasn't that much warmer than it was outside, and if they didn't start having fires in more than one room soon, she'd be spending her mornings scraping ice from the top of the milk and the morning washing bowls as well as doing all the other chores that had crept up on her over recent months, since Ivy's romance and wedding.

'It's getting colder,' Rose said. Cinderella didn't answer as her sister – her *step*-sister – pulled open the shutters and lit the lamp on the wall, keeping it down so low to preserve oil that it barely dispelled the darkness.

'So, what's the news?'

'What do you mean?' Cinderella finally looked up, her bucket of ashes full.

'I saw you reading the *Morning Post*,' Rose said, nodding towards the wooden post with the sheet of paper nailed to it and fluttering like a hooked fish in the sea of the rising winter wind.

'Another missing child. A little girl.' She got up and dusted her coat down. The new fire still needed to be laid but she'd forgotten to bring the kindling up from the kitchen with her. She'd sit for five minutes by the stove and get warm first.

'Something needs to be done about whatever's in the woods,' Rose muttered. 'We can't keep losing children. And the forest is the city's life blood. The more people fear going into it, the weaker the kingdom becomes.'

'Might just be winter wolves.'

'A sudden plague of them?' Rose's sarcasm was clear in both her tone of voice and the flashed look she sent Cinderella's way. 'It's not wolves. They can be vicious but not like this. And, without being indelicate, if it were wolves, at least some remains would be found. These children are disappearing entirely.'

'Maybe they'll turn up.' Cinderella was tired enough without having to listen to another of Rose's rants. She'd already put the porridge on, put the risen bread in the oven and after breakfast she'd have to peel the potatoes and vegetables before even having a wash.

'Of course they won't. And then we'll have a whole generation growing up scared to go into the woods and a society even more fuelled by suspicion. If the king doesn't act soon he's going to find the people losing their love for him. A visible presence of soldiers or guards at the forest's edge is what he needs. At the very least.'

Tight lines had formed around her mouth and between her eyes and Cinderella thought they made Rose look older than her twenty-five years. Rose's hair was fine and poker straight, the sort of hair that could never hold a curl for long, no matter how much lacquer was applied or how long the rollers were in, and although her features were regular enough there was nothing striking or unusual about them. She was, if the truth were to be told, a plain girl. Neither Rose nor her sister Ivy had ever been pretty. They might have come from money, but it was Cinderella who had the looks.

'Breakfast will be done in a minute.' She tucked a thick red curl behind one ear and picked up the bucket of ash. 'As soon as I've got this cleared away.'

'I'd help,' Rose said. 'But mother says I have to keep my hands soft.'

'Will take more than soft hands to get you wed,' Cinderella muttered under her breath as she headed for the door.

'What did you say?'

'A mouse!' The shriek was so loud and unexpected that Cinderella, whose arms were aching, jumped and dropped the bucket of ash, mainly down her own coat. 'There's a mouse!' her step-mother shrieked again, appearing in the doorway, her face pale and her hair still in rollers and firmly under a net from the night before. 'It's gone down to the kitchen! We can't have a mouse. Not here. Not now. Not with Ivy coming!'

'What is going on here today?' She stared in dismay at the cloud of ash that was settling across the floor and surfaces of her pride and joy, her dining room. 'Oh, Cinderella, we don't have time for this. Get it cleaned up. I want this place spotless by nine.' She turned to bustle away and then paused. 'No, I want it spotless by eight. And Rose, once you've had breakfast it's time for a facial and manicure. There's a girl coming at half-past nine. Highly recommended.'

Cinderella looked down at her own chapped hands. 'I wouldn't mind a manicure.'

'Don't be so ridiculous,' her step-mother snapped. 'Why would you need one? Rose is the daughter of an Earl. People are beginning to remember that. And anyway, they're expensive, we can only afford one. Now come on, I want everything perfect for Ivy and the Viscount.' She swept out of the room, the mouse and the ash forgotten, and Rose followed her, leaving Cinderella standing in the pile of grey dust. She was living up to her name at least, she thought as she got down on her knees once more and reached for the pan and brush.

Ivy and her Viscount arrived just after noon, in a glorious carriage driven by two perfectly matching grey ponies. Cinderella watched from the window as her step-mother ran out to greet them, loitering perhaps a little longer than necessary in the freezing weather, in order to make sure all the neighbours saw her daughter's fine winter wolf stole and the rich blue of her dress. Cinderella thought she might kill for a dress like that, or even for a single ride in that beautiful carriage. Kill she might, but she wasn't sure she would kiss the Viscount for any of it.

She watched as Ivy took her new husband's arm and walked towards the house. Her pale face was rouged and her lips were painted pink and even her hair, almost as fine as Rose's, had managed to find some lift and body. Money was making her prettier, that was certain, but no amount of luxury could turn her into a beauty. Cinderella's stomach knotted in envy. It was all wasted on Ivy.

The Viscount was a nervous young man of perhaps thirty, whose right cheek had an unfortunate tic and whose shoulders hunched over slightly as if he didn't want to be noticed. He'd met Ivy when she'd run out in front of his carriage, chasing a note of money that was being blown across the road. By the time he'd picked her up, retrieved the money and driven her home, the two had somehow found something they liked about each other. Here they were, two months later, already married.

Cinderella watched as he sat quietly, smiling as his wife talked, not so dissimilar to her own father, who spent much of his time doing the same. The Viscount must love Ivy, though, she thought, otherwise how could he sit here and pretend that this small roast beef dinner was in any way satisfactory compared to the delicious feasts they must have at home every day. There wasn't even a girl to serve them – other than Cinderella, of course – and despite the fire the room still carried a chill. She cut into her own tiny slice of beef, eating it slowly, just as her step-mother and father were doing, to try and prevent the Viscount from realising how much smaller their portions were than his or Ivy's. Thus far, it was working. He seemed perfectly content, but it was hard to know as Ivy was dominating the conversation.

'There are so many winter balls coming up, mama,' she said, her grey eyes alive with excitement and happiness. 'You've never seen anything like it.'

'Oh but I have, darling,' her mother countered. 'I remember my own coming out ball. I went to many balls as a young woman.' She smiled at the Viscount. 'I was quite the beauty then, you know.'

'Indeed you were, my dear,' Cinderella's father finally joined it. 'When I met you, you were quite breath-taking.'

His compliment earned him a sharp glance from his wife and Cinderella knew why. She didn't want the Viscount reminded of her fall from grace, not when she was so close to getting back into court society after all these years. The Viscount smiled anyway, and Cinderella noticed that the tic in his face had calmed in their company. She couldn't understand why, when their small house must be so far removed from the grandeur he was used to.

'Anyway, there is going to be one at the castle tomorrow night,' Ivy glanced at her husband and smiled, 'and George and I thought that perhaps you and Rose would like to come with us.'

The table erupted. Cinderella's step-mother was on her feet with her hand clamped over her mouth, but the shriek she was emitting behind it was loud enough to threaten their wine glasses. Ivy was smiling and laughing, and even the Viscount blushed slightly. Rose remained in her seat with her mouth half-open, and then within seconds they were all talking over each other, a babble of excited chatter and plans.

Cinderella cleared away the plates. No one was going to eat any more after that announcement, and Cinderella was never going to go to a ball.

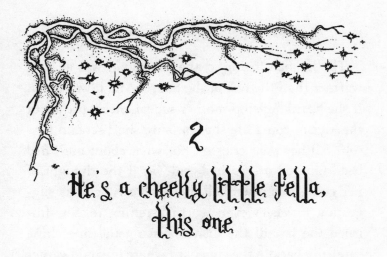

2

'He's a cheeky little fella, this one'

Once Ivy and the Viscount had left, Cinderella retreated to the kitchen and busied herself with the washing up. For once she didn't care that much about being on her own downstairs. Her step-mother's excitement was too much for her to cope with. Tailors had been sent for and the last of the family coffers were being emptied in the search for ball dresses for Rose and her mother. There wouldn't be any coal for the foreseeable future, even if her father did sell a few more articles and papers or take in some book-keeping while writing his interminable novel. Someone would have to go into the forest for wood, and that someone would no doubt be her. She shivered slightly at the thought. The forest was not the safest place to go wandering alone.

The kitchen, being in the basement, was at least warmer than the rest of the house. And it was quiet. If she heard her step-mother squeal once more about the joys of court life she was sure she'd scream herself. All her own cries of 'but what about me?' had been ignored or brushed aside, as if the thought of her going to a court ball was such a ridiculous suggestion it wasn't even worth listening to. She finished the last of the dishes, placing the fine china carefully back in the cupboard where it would gather dust until Ivy and her husband came again, and then began to sweep the floor. She didn't hurry. Today she was glad of her chores.

There was a light tapping at the back door – three small knocks and then a pause before one more – and Cinderella's mood lifted. She pulled back the bolts and opened up, still smiling even though the blast of cold that rushed in threatened the tiny amount of warmth the room was managing to contain.

'Buttons!'

'Evening, princess.' He nodded at a brown sack by his feet. 'Shall I put it straight in the scuttle on my way back?'

'You've brought coal?'

'No one will miss it. They've got more than they need.' He grinned at her, dark eyes twinkling in the night. 'And we wouldn't want your pretty nose getting frostbite, would we? Speaking of frostbite, are you going to let me in?'

She ushered him inside and closed the door as he pulled another chair close to the stove and sat down. 'This winter's a bastard.' He shivered.

'You didn't need to bring me anything,' Cinderella rummaged in the cupboards, put some bread and cheese on a plate and poured him a glass of her father's table wine. 'You're too kind to me.'

'It's not my coal, princess. Just like the half a ham I just left at Granny Parker's wasn't my ham, so don't worry.' He winked at her. 'But I like bringing you things best.'

Cinderella blushed and sat down, happy to give him a moment or two of silence while he ate. Sometimes it felt like Buttons was her only real friend in the world, and she didn't even know his real name. She called him Buttons because he'd brought her two fine pearl buttons for her torn dress when she'd first met him and then the nickname stuck. He probably had grateful nicknames in houses all over the city. The winter made times hard, but Buttons made them better.

He couldn't be more than twenty or so, she thought. Thin and wiry with a mop of black hair and sharp eyes that were always up to mischief. But what a heart he had. He had a crush on her, she knew, but she never encouraged it, no matter how extraordinary he was. She wanted more from her life. She wanted what Ivy had, but with a tall, handsome man. She longed for it so much she ached from it.

'I hope you're careful,' she said. 'If you get caught, well . . .' She didn't need to finish the sentence. They both knew what the consequences would be.

Buttons was a thief. He was also an errand boy at the castle and spent much of his time delivering messages to the great houses or doing chores in the castle itself. The latter fed into the former and Buttons was an expert at taking small but valuable items that no one would notice were gone and they would either be sold and the money given away, or he'd pass them on directly.

'I steal from the rich and give to the poor,' he'd told her once. 'It's the only way to be a happy thief. And so many people have so little while so few have so much. It's not fair.'

Buttons had made their winter easier, even if her family didn't notice. Why would they? It was Cinderella who did the day to day housekeeping and not even her step-mother had noticed they didn't have enough money for the food that was appearing on their table. But then her step-mother had never understood money – not until they'd run out of it, at any rate. She had been born in wealth and married in wealth and it was only when she'd run away with Cinderella's father she'd had to learn the cost of things. It appeared to have been a very long learning curve.

'Ah, there you are!' Buttons smiled as a small brown nose emerged from the warm gap between the oven and the tiles. He broke off a piece of cheese and held it out.

'Urgh, a mouse,' Cinderella pulled her feet up onto the chair. 'That must be the one all the fuss was about this morning.'

'He's a cheeky little fella this one,' Buttons said, as the mouse confidently ran towards him and sat up on his hind legs to take the offered chunk of cheddar. 'He's everywhere I go. Well, he was until last week. He must have followed me here and decided to stay.' The mouse didn't scurry back to his hiding place as Cinderella expected, but stayed where he was, settling down on his haunches and nibbling contentedly. 'I don't blame him,' Buttons said. 'He's a mouse with good taste.'

'It's probably not even the same mouse. Mice don't follow people around.' She smiled. Sometimes with

Charm

Buttons it was very hard to tell if he was joking or not.

'Oh, it's him. Look, he's got a little scar on his back. See?' He winked at her. 'Same mouse.'

'Well, I can't guarantee his safety if my step-mother finds him.' Cinderella slowly lowered her feet back to the ground. If it was Buttons' mouse then she was somehow less afraid of it. And there was something quite endearing about the way it was sitting between them, happily munching on the cheese.

'I think he's a hardy little fellow,' Buttons said. 'I know a survivor when I see one.'

'I hear there's a ball at the castle tomorrow night,' Cinderella suddenly blurted out. 'My step-sisters are both going. It's not fair.'

'Yes, yes there is. There are a few balls lined up I think. I've spent a lot of the day fetching polish and ordering the finest wines and foods to be delivered.'

'And the ballroom?' Cinderella asked. 'Are the chandeliers glittering? Will there be musicians?'

'You know all this,' he smiled, but his eyes were thoughtful. 'You ask me to tell you every time. But yes, it will be quite fantastic. There's a rumour that the Prince might be reaching the time when he wants to find a wife. If he does, he'll set a trend for all the

226

young noblemen to marry. Where the prince leads, they follow.'

'Oh, how wonderful,' Cinderella said, taking a sip of Buttons' wine and then leaning back in her chair. 'Imagine how that must be, to have the prince fall in love with you.' Her voice had dropped to a slightly deeper tone, and Buttons raised an eyebrow. She smiled at him. This wasn't a new game, nor was it one they played often, but she needed an escape and Buttons was good at providing it.

'Can we?' she asked. She didn't need to elaborate. He smiled at her slightly and she smiled back. She didn't analyse their actions, and nor did she feel any guilt over it, even though no doubt her step-mother and father would be furious if they were caught. They weren't doing any real harm. It was just a game, and Cinderella was not the sort of girl to feel any shame over her body.

'Whatever you want, princess,' he said. 'What are friends for?'

Cinderella smiled and closed her eyes. They weren't hurting anyone. And they were friends, after all. As Buttons began to whisper to her, his breath warm in her ear, her drab surroundings were forgotten and she was transported to the castle, full of light and heat and beauty as couples danced around her and waiters moved elegantly between them with glasses of the finest champagne. She twirled from handsome man to handsome man in a dress of emerald green with jewels to match at her slim neck. Even the footmen at the doors couldn't take their eyes from her. In her fantasy – and it was one she had often – by the end of the evening she would have three men in love with her, all three ready to duel for her, and then the prince himself would sweep her away and marry her with more haste and urgency than even the Viscount for Ivy, and both her step-sisters would watch enviously as she lived happily ever after in the castle.

Buttons spoke softly of dancing and romance and, as she imagined the prince's body pressed close to hers, his hand slid up under her dress and his mouth softly kissed her neck. Her breathing came faster as finally, after teasing the soft skin of her thighs, his fingers hit their mark, teasing her to wetness and then sliding inside. She pushed against him and panted as he told her of beauty and music until even-tually, her mind a whirl of ballrooms and the prince and music and love, she shuddered against his touch.

She sighed and lingered in her fantasy for a moment longer before opening her eyes and adjusting her dress and letting her miserable reality settle around her. 'It's so much better when you do it than me,' she said, and smiled, leaning forward and kissing Buttons' cheek.

'Oh you're a strange one, Cinderella,' Buttons' face had flushed slightly. 'There aren't many girls like you.'

'There are lots of girls worse than me,' she answered. 'It's only touching. What's wrong with that? It feels good. It's natural.'

'I'm not arguing with you,' he said. 'You're just full of contrasts.' He poured himself more wine. 'And rather me than another. I'm your friend. I'll never hurt you.'

'You're as strange as I am,' she said. Her comment didn't need an explanation, they both knew what she meant. She'd tried once, the first time they'd found themselves playing this game, to touch the boy. Not from any passion for him, but because she was curious and wanted him to feel as nice as she had, but he'd stopped her. He'd said that wasn't for him.

'That may well be true, princess.' He winked at her. 'That may well be true.'

She thought again of the castle and all its beauty and was quite envious that Buttons got to spend every day inside it.

'It must be wonderful,' she said. 'So much more wonderful than it is in my imagination. I would do anything to be part of that life. Anything at all.'

'Wonderful's one way to see it, I suppose.' Buttons finished his food and put the plate on the floor. The mouse scurried over and began sniffing for crumbs. Cinderella made a mental note to give that plate to Rose tomorrow at breakfast. Maybe it would make her sick and she wouldn't be able to go to the ball. It was a mean thought, but she couldn't help it.

'Of course it's beautiful,' Buttons continued. 'Beauty is easy with money and these people have the finest of everything.' He looked at her intently. 'But court life isn't all dancing and music and love, Cinderella. The gentle don't survive well when everyone is after power. Everyone is using other people to shuffle into a position where they have the king or the prince's ear. It's a place full of wolves in disguise. Why do you think I feel no guilt stealing from most of these people?'

Cinderella didn't say anything. She didn't care about all that and it wouldn't matter to her anyway. She had no interest in power, she just wanted beautiful clothes and music and fun. Life had been hard enough over recent years.

'Tell me again about their carriages,' she said, eagerly. 'The gold and silver ones. The king and queen's one that never leaves the castle gates because it's so encrusted with jewels they fear the ordinary people won't be able to stop themselves tearing it apart to have a piece for themselves. Tell me about that.'

She smiled at him, and this time it was his turn to sigh. 'They keep it in a converted stable at the back of the castle. It's under constant guard. At night it twinkles as though all the stars in the sky have been captured and sprinkled onto its surface . . .'

Cinderella closed her eyes and let her mind drift as the familiar words washed over her.

Buttons left an hour or so later, tipping the coal into the scuttle on his way, and taking the sack away with him to hide somewhere on his way back to the castle. The night had turned bitter, but Cinderella came up the outside stairs in just her worn shoes and with a shawl wrapped round her shoulders and watched until he'd vanished in the foggy mist that was settling over the streets like a blanket.

She didn't notice the little mouse valiantly scrabbling his way up the stairs, his fur puffed out a little as if it could somehow protect him from the grip of the icy night. By the time Cinderella had retreated back into the house and firmly bolted the door behind her, he had reached the pavement. He stood up on his hind legs and sniffed the wet air, searching for the right direction.

This time he didn't follow Buttons back to the castle, he turned away and scurried through the night towards the forest. He was glad he'd had the cheese and breadcrumbs. He had a long way to travel that night.

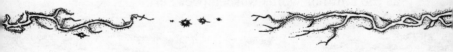

Cinderella had done her best to hide away for most of the next day – even going out for a long walk in the bitter cold – but she'd still been subjected to having to 'ooh' and 'aah' at Rose in her new blue dress. Admittedly, she did look prettier in it. Her skin looked less pasty with some rouge applied and the royal blue made her hair look darker. It was even managing to hold some curls, although Cinderella doubted they would last. Doubted and hoped not, if she was honest.

By the time Ivy's carriage arrived, she was in a foul mood. She watched through the window as a footman helped Rose and her step-mother inside, her mind a nest of squirming dark feelings that she couldn't even form into coherent thoughts. It was envy of course, she knew that. Envy and more than a touch of self-pity, but she couldn't help herself. How was she supposed to feel? It just wasn't fair. It was as if she didn't matter.

'Penny for them?'

The carriage rolled away and Cinderella let the curtain drop.

'Doesn't matter.'

'Your mother got these for you.' Her father was standing in the doorway holding up a box of choco-lates. 'It's a two-layer box. Not cheap.'

'I don't want them.' She almost stamped her foot, the way she had when she was annoyed as a small girl. How could a box of chocolates compare with going to a ball at the castle? Was she being laughed at now? It felt like salt in a wound. 'And she's not my mother.'

'She's looked after you since you were very small, Cinderella. She loves you.' He'd been carrying a chequers board under his arm and he set it down on a coffee table and drew it close to the fire Cinderella had made with some of the coal Buttons had brought. It was a good fire and neither her step-mother or step-sister would feel the benefit of it. A small victory maybe, but it was something.

'You're not writing tonight?' she asked.

'I thought we'd have some father and daughter time,' he smiled at her. 'Eat some chocolate and play a few board games. What do you think?'

'I think I'd rather be at the ball, but my *mother* didn't invite me.'

Her father sighed and in the glow of the fire she noticed, for the first time, that more of his hair was grey than brown, and wrinkles ran like a spider's web across his face. How did that happen? He was suddenly middle-aged, not the smiling, solid man who'd bounced her on his knee when her real mother was still alive.

'You have a lot to learn, Cinderella. It's not so easy as that.'

'She hates me.' She flopped down into the chair opposite him, feeling more ten than twenty. 'She always has.'

Her father burst out laughing. 'Don't be so childish!'

She glared at him – probably childishly.

'Your step-mother, well, she feels a great responsibility for what her daughters lost. For what she *lost*. You were too young to understand. When she left the old earl and married me their entire lives changed. And does she miss the trappings of her old life sometimes? Of course she does. I could never give her all the things she used to have. Things she'd had all her life.' He gazed into the flames. 'But she chose us, Cinderella. Over all of that. And she never looked back.'

'You make it sound like true love.' Cinderella snorted; it was a ridiculous thought. 'If my mother hadn't died, you wouldn't have *needed* her.'

'Oh darling,' he smiled at her softly. 'It was true love. It *is* true love. You were too young to remember it all properly. Your mother – well, she could be difficult. If she hadn't fallen sick then I would have left her for Esme, just like Esme left the Earl for me.'

Cinderella stared at him as cold crept up from the pit of her stomach and burned her cheeks like ice. He couldn't mean that. He just couldn't. 'You're lying.'

Her father shook his head. 'No. It's true. It was true love. I was just the old Earl's secretary, but she fell in love with me and I with her. If you're lucky you'll find the same thing one day.'

'Not without going to a ball, I won't!' She got to

her feet, tears stinging the back of her eyes. How could he have fallen in love with her stupid step-mother? How could he say her mother was *difficult*? True, she didn't remember her much, most of her early memories seem to just feature her father and flashes of a woman holding her close and reading her stories, but she was her *mother*. 'You're as bad as she is!'

She stormed out and stomped up the stairs, leaving the warmth of the fire and the chocolates behind her. She slammed her bedroom door and flopped down on her bed. A few moments later her father knocked on the door but she told him to just 'Go away!' before burying her face in her pillow and crying. She wasn't quite sure who she was crying for, but she knew she was completely alone. Not even her father was on her side. It wasn't fair. None of it was fair.

She must have eventually cried herself to sleep, because the next thing she knew, she was freezing cold on her bed and lights were being carried through the hallway, slivers of yellow moving and creeping under her bedroom door. There was a flurry of activity in the hallway; then feet coming up the stairs and her step-mother's laughter, loud and brash, dancing up ahead of them.

They were back.

Cinderella wrapped her shawl around her and lit the candle by her bed as if that small flame could give some heat as well as light, and then crept over to the door. She didn't want to face them and be drawn into conversation, but she did want to hear what they were saying. She hoped it had gone badly for them. After all, her step-mother had shamed the old Earl she'd wed by walking out on him, and although he'd died two years ago it was likely she still wouldn't be welcome in the court circles. Even being the daughter of a lord was no shield against scandal. The sound of merry, tired giggles, however, put paid to that hope. Cinderella looked at the clock on the wall. It was just after half-past one.

'Oh, Rose. How wonderful.' Her step-mother had reached the top of the stairs and Cinderella carefully pulled her door open a fraction to hear them more clearly. 'You danced with two Earls. Two. Can you believe it?'

'It didn't *mean* anything. It was just dancing.' Rose was quieter, still down in the hallway. 'Oh, it's good to get these shoes off. They're killing my feet.'

'And the prince kissed your hand!'

'I think he kissed everyone's hand.' Rose's voice was full of good humour. She didn't sound like Rose at all. Then her feet thumped up the stairs. *That* sounded like Rose; she didn't have an ounce of grace in her clumsy body.

'But isn't he handsome, Rose? I mean, I knew him of course, when he was a boy and he always had something about him, but well . . .'

'Yes, he's very handsome. Now, please, please, please help me get this dress off before my ribs break. I told you it was too small.'

'Men like a slim waist, Rose. And, unfortunately, you're rather too fond of food.'

Their voices faded and then there was the click of a door closing as the two women disappeared into her step-sister's room. Cinderella waited until there was only silence and then pushed her door shut. Her blood raced through her veins, the cold and her tiredness sloughed off as she absorbed what she'd heard. Two earls. And the Prince had kissed Rose's hand.

She picked up the framed print of the smiling Prince that she kept in her room – the picture Rose had once laughed at her for, even though nearly all the girls in the kingdom had one – and climbed into her bed, pulling the covers up to her chin. She stared at the handsome smiling face. How could he have kissed Rose's hand? It must have just been politeness. Yes, that was it. He'd kissed all the girls' hands, isn't that what they'd said? There was nothing special about Rose.

She blew the candle out and lay back on her pillow, the picture face down on her chest, and tried to calm down. Yes, she hated that Rose had gone to the castle when she hadn't, but maybe tonight's ball going well wasn't such a bad thing. Maybe if Rose got married off to some horrible old Earl like her mother had been, then surely their family would be respected enough for her to be invited? Just once. Just once. How she wished for it.

She closed her eyes and let her mind drift into the familiar fantasy.

She's standing in the castle and the ballroom is full of men and women dressed in their finery. As her name is announced at the top of the stairs, all eyes turn her way, and although no one knows who she is, they're dazzled by her style and beauty. She dances with the most handsome men, but all the while her eyes are locked with the Prince's until eventually he comes to claim her as his own. As they whirl around the room, they only have eyes for each other and she knows that he'll love her forever and she'll love him forever and they'll never stray. The music slows and he pulls her closer, his strong arm tight across her back. She can feel his body heat and every inch of her skin is aching for him to kiss her. Eventually, he does. His lips brush hers, teasing her until she can barely breathe and then his tongue touches hers and stars explode in her head.

Her fantasy shifted, as it always did, and it was their wedding night. The party was over, although in the streets it would continue for hours, and they had retired to their bedchamber. He was standing close to her, his lust so clear in his hazy eyes, and his hands undid the strings of her shift leaving her naked before him. Her hand slipped into her night-dress and teased her right nipple as if it was his fingers and then mouth. She gasped slightly, lost in the moment, her head filled with experiences she could only imagine. His hand in her hair as he kissed her. Her arms wrapped around his neck as he pushed her to the bed. Feeling him pressing against her as they lost themselves in their passion. Her hand moved further down, sliding between her legs and exploring the wetness there.

Her hand was his hand, and then, as her own touch moved into a rhythm, he was inside her, moving with her, his mouth on her neck, his own moans coming louder, her arms over her head and pinned down by his hand as he possessed her. They moved like frantic animals, growing rougher with each other as their needs grew more urgent until finally, in her small bed in the merchant's house, Cinderella's back arched and the stars exploded bright behind her closed eyes.

3

'A Bride Ball . . .'

'Their boy's gone missing in the woods.'

'The baker's boy? Jack?'

'They didn't send him alone, did they?'

'No, young Greta was with him. She came back. She must have had a fever though, because she was full of wild stories.'

Cinderella was on the edge of the huddle outside the tiny store where a tired, red-eyed man had just sold her a small loaf. She'd wondered why he hadn't given her a wink and a smile as normal, but she'd just put it down to the terrible cold that rushed in every time a new customer opened the door and the fact that she wasn't in the best of moods herself and maybe that showed. But now she knew and the icy wind was nothing to the cold at the pit of her stomach. Jack was a good boy. He had his father's cheerful disposition and worked hard. Nothing bad could have happened to Jack? Surely not.

She listened to the low chattering voices around her.

'What do you mean, "wild stories"?'

'Well,' the old woman leaned in closer and her friends did the same. Standing just behind them, Cinderella couldn't help but feel that the subject of their conversation was obvious to the poor grief-stricken man on the other side of the window. But still she stepped a little closer too, in order to hear them.

'It was preposterous. Obviously she just couldn't cope with whatever had really happened, but she said that they'd stayed on the normal path, just like they'd been told to and just like they'd always done, but that the woods had moved somehow – the path had changed – and then before she knew it they were lost in the dense trees. They walked through the night—'

'But that can't be right!' a thin woman with a crooked nose cut in. 'She was back within a few hours, that's what my Jeannie told me and she lives near Greta's family.'

'Like I said, she must've had a fever or something. But this is the story she *told*, and that's the one you wanted to hear. Right?'

'Well, yes . . .'

'Then be quiet and listen.' The speaker pulled her shawl tighter round her shoulders and sniffed before continuing. 'So, they walked through the night and then they found this clearing. Right in the centre of it is a house. Made of cakes and candy according to Greta.'

A few snorts of derision accompanied this but any thought of laughter died with the next words. 'There was an old lady there. She invited them inside. Greta said no, but Jack went in. When he didn't come out, Greta went round to the back of the house to see if there was a window with the curtains open that she could see through.'

'What did she see?' They might have laughed originally but, just like Cinderella, the old women were being drawn into the story.

'Nothing. She saw what was piled up at the back of the house and she turned and ran back into the woods. She said she ran and ran until somehow she found her way back to the path.'

'Don't be a tease, Gertrude. It's freezing out here. What did she see?'

'Bones,' the woman's voice had dropped to a whisper. 'Small bones. Children's bones.'

There was a long pause after that.

'Pah,' the thin woman said, eventually. 'The boy got eaten by wolves and the girl got a fever. That's what that will be.'

'They need to do something about those woods.' The words were out almost before Cinderella knew she was speaking. 'They need more soldiers guarding them. We can't have a whole generation of children growing up scared to go into the woods. We *need* the woods.' She was repeating what Rose had said even though when her step-sister had spoken, Cinderella had been bored by it. But now she knew one of the children who'd vanished and that made everything different. Rose's words, much as it irked her, made sense. The three women turned to stare at her.

'It's true,' Cinderella stammered on. 'Someone needs to talk to the king about—'

Her sentence was cut off by the thunder of horses' hooves and the burst of a herald's horn as the two men in livery clattered into the street. She stared at them. The Royal Crier? The baker's boy and his terrible fate were forgotten, and even the baker came out to join the throng who hurried to gather and hear the castle news. Royal Criers were rare in this part of the city – not enough noblemen lived here – so whatever the news was, it would be of some great importance.

Cinderella pushed her way to the front of the growing crowd.

'Hear ye! Hear ye!' The young man on the white horse was wearing a tunic of red and gold without a speck of dust on it, and his perfectly styled brown hair shone almost as brightly as the leather of his riding boots. 'His Majesty the King announces his intent to hold two Bride Balls two weeks from Saturday for his royal Highness the Prince. All young ladies of noble birth and their chaperones are invited to attend. The Prince himself will dance with each, and by the end of the two balls he will have selected his bride.'

A rush of gasps and excited babble ran through the crowd as women and children clapped their hands together excitedly and men smiled and slapped each other on the back. A royal wedding meant extra holidays and feasting and the king could be very generous when he wanted the people to celebrate with him. Pigs would roast on street corners and ale would flow. There were good times ahead.

Cinderella almost dropped the shopping she carried. The prince was having two Bride Balls and she wouldn't be invited. *She* wouldn't be, but Rose and her step-mother would. It was so awful she couldn't bear it. Worse still, she was going to have to put up with hearing about it for the next two weeks. As if reading her mood, the sky darkened, and as she reluctantly hurried home an icy rain began to fall.

*S*teps were hard to manage when you were a mouse and it took him two whole days and nights to reach the top of the castle tower. It was a long, long way up at the end of an already long journey and he was exhausted. At least the forest had been kind and given him a clear path and the leafy canopy had protected him from the cold nights. A hare had carried him part of the way, letting him sleep in the warm fur of its back as it bounded through the night and he wondered once again at magic and nature and fate and how bound together they all were in the forest.

He had been surprised by the city. The first clues that all was not well had come when he passed the mines. The songs that hummed in the air, as if the mountain itself was singing, were melancholy and ached with tiredness. The hardy dwarves were finding no pleasure in their toil. At the edge of the woods were patches of dead ground as if the bushes and trees which had grown there had simply given up and slumped into a pile of rotting mulch.

It was winter across all the kingdoms, and those in the East were always gripped harder and for longer than the rest, but he had not expected what he found here. Black ice was slick across the tracks and roads and the sky raged in grey and ragged darkness whatever the hour of the day. Ravens covered the rooftops.

He had kept close to the buildings as his tiny feet carried him, fast as they could, towards the castle at the city's core. It grew colder with each step and the wind blew harder. The castle, it soon became clear to him, was the eye of the storm. This was an unhappy city, a bitter sadness spreading like a pool of blood from the wound at its heart.

It was also a city in mourning. In each house he passed colourful drapes had been removed and replaced with the customary black, and all were pulled shut. Many shops were closed, only those selling the necessities of life allowed to trade, but still their windows had been blackened and there were no cheery greetings or hawking of wares.

The little mouse paused in his quest and squeezed

through a gap in the wall of a house, eavesdropping in the warm for a while and, as well as stealing a few breadcrumbs from the floor, he learned what had passed.

The king had died in battle. His body had not yet been returned home.

It did not come as a surprise to the mouse. Kings liked battles and brave kings often got in the midst of them. And in the midst of every battle sat death, making his camp in the melee and gorging on life until his hunger was sated. All life was equal. Kings died as easily as other men.

So now the queen and her magic were in charge, and although the woman who chattered as she sewed seemed convinced that the winter storm was just the icy queen's expression of grief for her lost husband and vanished step-daughter, the mouse thought that perhaps the rest of the city was not so kind in its judgements. They thought perhaps, as could be seen in the nervous glances up at the ravens, that the queen was not so sad her husband would no longer be returning to her bed. That the queen had what she'd always wanted; a kingdom of her own. None of the nobles would challenge her rule, even though, by the laws of the land, they had every right to. Magic and bitterness could be a terrifying combination. Kings might die in battles but politicians chose theirs more wisely. This second wife was not to be challenged lightly.

She didn't see him for a while. She was lost in her reverie, her knees pulled up under her chin, curled up in the single throne at the centre of the tower. Around her the life of the city so far below played out in the mirrors, the bewitched ravens' eyes showing her everything they saw. She wasn't looking though. Her beautiful face was dark and drawn and lost in places that belonged only to her.

He squeaked.

She jumped.

She swore under her breath, a crude word entirely out of place in one so high in society, and raised her hand. Sparks glittered at her fingertips and then she paused and frowned, leaning forward to take a closer look. He stood up on his hind legs as she loomed over him, her pale face an enormous moon against the black night of the walls that were fractured with red lightning. There were fresh lines around her eyes and her cheekbones were sharper. But then, he thought, and if a mouse could smile he would have, they'd both changed since he'd taken her on this cool marble floor.

She stared at him for quite a while and he stared

back. He was banking on her curiosity getting the better of her, rather than destroying him at her feet. His future happiness as well as his life depended on it. Finally, her fingers sparkled again and a tinkling sound filled the air as the glittering light coated him with its warmth, and the world shimmered and shook and trembled and so did his insides.

He was a man again.

He was also dressed, which came as something of a relief. For a moment he felt quite dizzy, strange to be tall in the world after such a long time, and there was a strange sensation in his gut which let him know he wasn't free of her curse but had only a temporary reprieve.

He did not waste time flirting with her. Whatever moment of lust they had once shared was long gone for both of them. Instead, she poured two glasses of wine and they sat on cushions on the floor and talked long into the night. Finally a pact was made, an agreement of sorts, and she told him how his curse could be lifted. It was the way of all curses and it came as no surprise. Until then, however, she would half-lift it so they could help each other. As deals went, it could have been worse.

It was only when morning came and he was a mouse again did he wish he'd thought to go back *down all the stairs before the change had been once again upon him.*

It was a long two weeks between the announcement and the commencement of the Bride Ball, and throughout the city there was an air of excitement, even among the common people who would never in their lifetimes get through the castle gates. All day long dressmakers hurried from one noble house to another, each trying to come up with unique designs that would guarantee to catch the prince's eye and his heart. No expenses were being spared and the tradesmen were happy. Jewellers, hairdressers and haberdashers were bringing the sinking economy back to life and butchers and bakers were also busy, as many of those who had no chance of a royal invitation planned their own parties at home. Bride Balls were a rarity and everyone wanted to enjoy the weekend of festivities.

Except perhaps Cinderella. The days dragged by endlessly as teams of experts traipsed in and out of the house. There was a woman to teach Rose deportment, there was another to manage her eating as her mother insisted she must lose several pounds if she was to shine and not look like a 'brood mare' compared to the glamorous young ladies of the court. A man came to teach her how to engage in court conversation, another how to dance all the latest fashionable reels. They arrived like an army before it was light and they often kept working her until it was very nearly midnight.

Cinderella moved quietly around the house doing her chores but all the time watching and learning. Alone in her room she'd easily manage the moves Rose found so difficult, twirling this way and that, so naturally elegant compared to the girl who spent most of her afternoons thudding across the floor, trying to dance in the heels she'd been bought especially to practise in. It wasn't fair, Cinderella would think, for the hundred thousandth time. It just wasn't fair. She almost wept with envy when the dressmaker came bearing swathes of beautiful silks for Rose to choose from. Ivy was paying for her sister's dress and cost was no object, and her mother was holding her to that.

Rose was pinched and pinned and squeezed and tutted at until two suitable designs were chosen and then the exhausted girl was sent to bed with no supper in order that she might just fit into her gowns by the night of the first ball. Cinderella heard her sobbing through the wall one night and almost knocked on the door but decided against it. What could she say? Rose knew how much Cinderella wanted that invite herself. She could hardly pity her step-sister for being the one allowed to go. But still, though she might be terribly, achingly jealous of the event, she was no longer jealous of Rose.

The preparations were endless and her step-mother had become relentless in her determination to turn her daughter into a girl to rival those of the best houses of the kingdom. Cinderella wondered if perhaps, underneath all the laughter and reminiscing of her youth, that first ball hadn't been too kind to her. Had she been the subject of a few barbed remarks she hadn't told Rose about? Did she have a few scores to settle at the castle?

For the first time Cinderella gave some proper thought to her step-mother's life *before* this one. How very different it must have been. And how very difficult it must have been to go back into that castle where so many people would remember what she'd done. It made Cinderella feel strange. She didn't want to feel sorry for either her step-mother *or* Rose, but somehow she did. Her step-mother had become obsessed with regaining her place in court life and Ivy and the Viscount weren't enough. The Viscount was a nervous man and preferred to spend his time with his new wife in the privacy of their estate rather than wrangling in court matters, and so now all her hopes were pinned on Rose to secure her position.

'If you can make the prince fall in love with you, Rose, just imagine . . .'

Cinderella had lost count of the times she'd heard those words from her step-mother by the time the night of the first ball finally drew close. There was an edge to it. A nervous anxiety. Cinderella might want to go to the ball, yes, but she was very glad she wasn't Rose. Rose was exhausted and her step-mother was on the verge of madness as far as she could see. It must be madness if she thought a man as wonderful as the prince would ever think of marrying a lump like Rose. It was impossible. And Rose, Cinderella suspected, knew it.

4

'All beauty is magic'

On the opening night of the Prince's Bride Ball the thick grey clouds that had coated the kingdom throughout winter cleared and the curious sky looked down on the magical proceedings occupying the city so far below. The stars sparkled like diamonds on a midnight blue dress and the bitter wind dropped, as if nature itself didn't wish to damage the carefully styled curls that had taken hours of primping and preparation.

The frantic atmosphere that had gripped the city for the previous two weeks finally eased into happy excitement. The dress fittings were all done. The carriages were booked. The moment the ladies of the land had been waiting for was finally here. Tonight, they would all dance with the prince, and by the end of the next Ball one of them would return home engaged. Although each girl protested aloud that *of course* he wouldn't choose them, in their hearts they hoped and hoped he would.

All the starving had worked and Rose's crimson dress fitted perfectly. Rose Red, her step-mother had called her, smiling proudly at the culmination of all her hard work. Cinderella didn't say anything, but she had to admit that Rose looked quite pretty. If not beautiful, then perhaps intriguing and elegant. Her step-mother wore a dress of chaperone brown as was the custom, but it was rich taffeta and the colour suited her. Cinderella watched them from the doorway of the sitting room as they waited in the hallway to leave, and she had never felt more like a poor secretary's daughter.

Her father, standing on the stairs, caught her eye and smiled at her, but she ignored him, and slunk past them all and down to the kitchen. Her father would say she was sulking, and perhaps she was, but he would never understand. How could he? Ever since the newspaper had been shut down, his ambitions only went as far as writing his stupid novel or stories or whatever it was he did locked away in his attic study all day. He didn't care about visiting the castle or fine clothes and dancing. How could he possibly understand how unfair all of this felt to her? But then, what did she expect? He'd already said he'd have left her poor mother for that silly cow of a step-mother if she hadn't died. He was as horrible and selfish as the rest of them. He should be on the out-side, like her, not approving of all the spending that had taken place just so Rose could go to a ball that would come to nothing and leave them all in debt.

She opened the back door and crept out onto the steps leading from the basement to the pavement level. Frost bit in the air, but without the sharp wind the night was comparatively mild, and she sat on the cold, damp stone and watched as Ivy's beautiful car-riage pulled up and Rose and her step-mother, their hands warm in fur stoles that matched the elegant wraps over their shoulders came out, laughing, and climbed aboard.

Cinderella stayed on the step long after the car-riage had carried them away to the castle, staring up at the night sky and fighting back tears. Was this how her life was going to be forever? Always in drudgery, working in the shadow of Rose and Ivy? The poor step-sister? The commoner? Maybe that was how it had to be, but all she wanted was one night. One night of feeling special. Overhead, a star shot across the dark sky. She squeezed her eyes shut.

Just one ball, she wished. If only she could go to the castle just once.

'It would appear I'm late.'

Startled, Cinderella opened her eyes, just in time to see the last of the sparkles of light disappear in the frosty air, leaving a beautiful woman in their place. Her blonde hair, so light it was almost the colour of ice, ran freely down her back and against her black dress her skin was pale. Her blue eyes were like frozen pools. She tucked the black wand she carried into a velvet bag and glanced, irritated, down at a small brown mouse who sat at the hem of her gown. 'The directions weren't the best.'

'Who are you?' Cinderella breathed. The woman had appeared out of nowhere in a flurry of what could only be magic. What was she doing here?

'I suppose,' the woman shrugged, 'if you must call me something, you can think of me as your fairy godmother. Now let's get inside. It's bloody freezing out here and I need something to drink.' She shooed the mouse away so it scurried round the corner of the building and then glared at Cinderella. 'Well, come on then. Do you want to go to this ball or not?'

Inside the warmth of the kitchen Cinderella thought her fairy godmother looked even more beautiful than she had in the moonlight. Her delicate features were catlike but there was a hardness in her poise that transformed her into something ethereal. There was also something quite unsettling about her. She hardly radiated kindness. She was yet to even smile.

'This is the best you have?' she asked Cinderella, frowning slightly as she swallowed a large mouthful of red wine.

'I'm sorry, yes. We're not . . . we don't have much—'

'It will have to do then.' The fairy godmother leaned back on the kitchen table and studied Cinderella thoughtfully as she refilled her glass. 'So, you want to go to this Prince's Ball?'

'Oh yes,' Cinderella's eyes widened and her heart thumped. 'More than anything.'

'Let me guess. You want to dance with the prince, have him fall in love with you and then live happily ever after?'

'Oh yes.' Cinderella nodded eagerly.

'That I can't promise.' She drank some more wine. 'No amount of magic can guarantee you happy ever after. I can, however, guarantee you'll get his attention. Make him want you. You'll catch your prince. After that, though, all bets are off.'

'But how? How can I go?' Cinderella's head was in

a whirl. She had dreamed so many times of going to the castle but she had never really thought it could come true. Was she dreaming? Was that it? Had she fallen asleep on the steps? 'I don't even have a dress.'

'Stop simpering.' Her fairy godmother's lips tightened. 'That part is easy.' She pulled a dark walnut from her bag and cracked it against the kitchen table before holding it up and blowing its contents carefully over Cinderella. Black dust that tasted of coal glittered around her and she was sure she heard the echo of men singing as metal clanged against rocks, and then butterflies tumbled from Cinderella's stomach and tingles like tiny wings flooded through her limbs leaving her breathless. For a moment she was in a whirlwind of sparkling stars. Her skin trembled as cold air touched her and then she gasped as something tugged hard at her waist and back; stays being tightened.

Finally, she looked down. Her dowdy house dress was gone. Now she wore a fine silver gown, pinched at the waist and sleeveless. Diamonds shone here and there in the silk and her skin glittered as if the stars that had spun around her head had settled there. She turned to look in the small mirror on the kitchen wall and almost didn't recognise herself. Her curls were styled half-up and half-down, and more jewels shone from within the deep red. Her face was painted and her lips glistened pink.

'It's magic,' she breathed, finally.

'All beauty is magical. You'll learn that,' the fairy godmother said softly. 'But it's not a magic you can control.'

'I do look beautiful though,' Cinderella said, smiling. 'The prince will surely fall in love with me.'

'Oh, you little fool.' The fairy godmother laughed, and it was like the sound of ice splintering. 'They will *all* be beautiful. It's the Prince's Bride Ball, after all. It will take more than a pretty face and a smart dress to snare him. Thankfully, you have those slippers on your feet.' Cinderella looked down. They were the most beautiful shoes she'd ever seen.

'Are they glass?'

'Don't be so ridiculous. Do you want to walk on glass? They're diamond.' She turned them this way and that so the light caught and reflected every sparkle of silver in Cinderella's dress from their surfaces. 'Diamond and something entirely of their own, too. They're charmed.' She looked at Cinderella, her clear blue eyes cold and calculating. 'They'll make you charming.'

'They fit perfectly.' The shoes were lighter than she expected and warm.

'I imagine they fit when they want to,' the fairy godmother purred.

Cinderella smiled. The high heels made her taller than the strange exquisite woman in her kitchen. She felt elegant. They were perfect. They were also soft and warm against the soles of her feet. They were shoes she could dance all night in.

'Here is a second nut,' the fairy godmother said, hiding the dark-shelled magic behind some plates on the second shelf of the dresser. 'Crack it as I did and inhale the dust tomorrow night and you will be transformed again.' The fairy godmother clapped her hands together. 'And now you're ready.'

'I can't believe you're doing this for me,' Cinderella was almost bursting with excitement. 'Thank you so much. You've made my dreams come true.' With a rush of warmth she tried to hug the fairy godmother, but instead of embracing her, the icy woman gripped her arms tightly, breaking off the gesture before it had begun. She didn't let go.

'I didn't say it wasn't without a price.'

'What do you mean?' The slim fingers were digging into her skin so tightly she was afraid they'd leave bruises.

'Nothing comes without a price.' Slowly the fairy godmother released her. 'I can do this for you, but there is something I need in return.'

Cinderella remained silent and listened. Whatever it was, she knew she'd do it. To have her wish taken from her now would break her heart.

'You will get your precious prince should you so want him. When he invites you to live in the castle with him in preparation for your glorious wedding, I want you to explore every room there. A servant of mine, the same one who is waiting outside with your carriage to take you there, will come to you every night and you will report your findings to him.'

'Every room? But there must be hundreds.'

'Castles are never quite as big as they seem from the outside.' Her eyes darkened and for a moment Cinderella thought her fairy godmother looked sad and wounded rolled into one. 'From the inside they can be quite claustrophobic,' she finished softly, lost in a world that Cinderella couldn't penetrate.

'Every room, though. You understand?'

Cinderella nodded. 'I understand.'

The fairy godmother studied her for a moment, before pulling a third walnut from the bodice of her dress. Unlike the others, the shell was so dark it was almost black and it was small and gnarled, as if dug up fossilised from the forest earth. 'This one,' she said softly, 'you break in case of emergency. But only after you've searched the castle.'

'What kind of emergency?' Cinderella asked.

'If castle life doesn't turn out quite as you planned. If you need a quiet escape.'

Cinderella thought of the castle and the handsome prince. 'I doubt I'll need that,' she said, defiantly.

'Good.' The fairy godmother smiled and stood up, picking up her bag. 'And now you shall go to the ball.' She snapped her fingers and the back door opened.

A fine silver carriage was waiting on the street. Two grey ponies with impossibly black manes pranced eagerly in the reins. A rugged man jumped down from the seat and held the delicate door open. Even in the dark, Cinderella could see that the seats were made of red velvet and lined with gold trim. The driver's hand was strong as he took hers and helped her step up. She muttered a thank you, but all her attention was on the glory of her dress and her carriage and the thought of the prince.

'Don't forget our arrangement.' Her fairy godmother stood on the pavement watching her through the open door. 'It won't go well for you if you forget.'

'I won't forget.' Cinderella heard the menace in the woman's words and shivered slightly. 'And thank you.'

'One more thing,' the fairy godmother pushed the door closed. 'Make sure you leave by midnight at the very latest. Both nights.'

'Midnight?' Inside the carriage, Cinderella's smile fell. 'But the last dances will barely have started by then. He'll dance with others. He'll forget me.'

'You have a lot to learn about men. Wind him up then leave him wanting.' She smiled but there was a touch of bitterness in it. 'That's where your real power lies.' She nodded to the driver. 'Midnight. Don't forget!'

And then the carriage was moving under her. When Cinderella peered out to the street behind them, the fairy godmother was gone. There were just the faint fireflies of sparkles left in the cold, night air.

The temperature was dropping as night took hold, but Cinderella hardly noticed the chill as she stepped down at the entrance to the castle. She could barely breathe with the beauty of it. No wonder her step-mother was so keen to get back into favour at court if it meant visiting here often. She wondered how she could have borne losing it in the first place. Built entirely from white marble, the castle rose up in elegant towers that surrounded the main building, each a different height from the rest, and each with a burning beacon at its tip.

The tales told that in the days of dragons the great beasts would sweep and circle the lights of the castle in their mating rituals before flying to the far mountain to nest. She could believe it. They looked like stars hanging low and smiling down on her sudden good fortune. Tonight it looked as if there were candles burning in every window of every tower for the ball. She ached at the sight of it.

'At the end of the day, it's just a house.'

Cinderella realised that, lost in her awe of the castle, she hadn't let go of the driver's hand after he'd helped her down. She quickly pulled it away.

'It's beautiful,' she said.

'Beauty can be over-rated.' His dark eyes seemed to be mocking her. 'And it fades.'

Her skin flushed slightly. 'Well, it will be my beauty that captures the prince,' she said, defiant. 'Wait and see.'

He laughed, his weathered face cracking into a grin, and she was surprised at what a warm sound it was.

'What's so funny?' she asked. He unsettled her. She didn't like it.

'That you think you're the hunter this evening.' He bowed slightly. 'Now run along inside and prance with all the other pretty little deer and let your shoes do their work. Just be back here by midnight. I'll be waiting.'

She lifted her chin and glared at him, before turning and making her way up the elegant stairs to the footmen waiting at the door. She didn't look back. He could laugh at her all he wanted, she didn't care. He was nobody. Nothing. Who cared what he thought?

By the time she came down the red carpeted stairs into the main ballroom, all thoughts of the rude driver were gone from her head. At one side a champagne fountain flowed over a tower of delicate glasses. Footmen were spaced out at intervals along the walls, their wigs dusted blue to match their jackets. Music played, an elegant waltz, and beyond the sea of young women and the prince's noble friends, she could see the masked band, all dressed in white and raised high on a glass stage. It was everything she'd imagined and more. She took a glass of champagne from a passing waiter and was surprised by how steady her hand was. She'd expected to be more nervous, but with the warmth tingling through her from her shoes she breezed into the room, her head held high. She would be confident and mysterious, just like her fairy godmother.

She sipped her drink, enjoying the bubbles but not so keen on the sharp taste, and scanned the room. It was a sea of colour, each of the noble women in the city wearing the finest dresses their money could afford. Her own silver dress nearly faded in comparison, but as she walked further into the vast ballroom heads turned her way as she passed, and voices dropped to a hush. The women eyed her suspiciously, but the men's glances ran the length of her body and lingered. She fought the urge to smile. She would be the belle of the ball. She really, really would. She didn't return any of the young men's smiles. There was only one man she was interested in dancing with; the prince himself.

When he came into view she stopped short and drew in a breath, her heart suddenly racing. He was the most handsome man she'd ever seen. She'd wondered if he could match the picture she kept by her bed, but now she knew that was really just a poor imitation. He was tall and broad, and was dressed all in black. His dirty blond hair was smoothly combed to one side, and his perfect face was tanned. Cinderella watched, entranced, as he danced with a short girl in a blue dress. He moved effortlessly and the girl was obviously already in love with him, but it was also obvious that however charming the prince was, he wasn't focusing much of his attention on his partner. His smile was going over her shoulder to someone just out of Cinderella's sight.

'He's still looking at her.'

'Why her? He's danced with her twice. She's the only one he's danced with twice. I mean, she's not even that pretty.'

'She's interesting looking though.'

'If you like that sort of thing.'

Cinderella wasn't sure which of the gathered girls around her was whispering and she didn't look, but she did listen hard. Someone had already seized the prince's attention? Her stomach twisted in a cold sickly knot. Who? Who was her competition? Her feet burned in her shoes.

'And you know what her mother did, don't you? She left an Earl for a secretary! How ridiculous! Maybe he just feels sorry for her.'

Cinderella leaned on a pillar to steady herself. Rose? They were talking about Rose? Surely they couldn't be? She stepped forward, suddenly having to know. It didn't take more than a moment to spot Rose standing at the edge of the circle watching the prince dance, her red dress matching the flush high in her cheeks. She was smiling at the prince and her face was transformed into something very close to beautiful. The weight she'd lost in the diet she'd been forced to undertake had made her features stronger, and for the first time Cinderella realised that her step-sister wasn't ugly at all. Unusual perhaps, but not ugly. She gritted her teeth. She wouldn't lose her prince to Rose. Not to Rose of all girls.

The music stopped and a smattering of applause ran round the room. Many of the girls were now turning their attention to the other noblemen in the room, realising that the prince's eye had already been taken but there were plenty of other good matches to be made at this Royal Bride Ball. Cinderella looked down at her shoes. They twinkled reflected silver from her dress, like moonlight on water. She took a deep breath. This was magic. And Rose couldn't fight magic.

The prince, after bowing politely to the girl who was no doubt already forgotten in his mind, but who would probably remember the feel of his hand on her back for the rest of her life, was heading back towards Rose.

Cinderella made her move. With her back to her step-sister, she crossed the room, cutting into the prince's path. Her arm brushed his and she looked up at him, her eyes wide. 'I'm so sorry, your highness.' She dropped into a curtsey. 'I should have looked where I was going.'

'No, I should have looked . . .' his eyes had been locked on Rose, but now he glanced down at Cinderella. It was enough. The end of the sentence drained away. He held his hand out to her. 'I don't believe we've danced this evening. I would have remembered.'

'We haven't.'

'Then we should rectify that.' Without taking his eyes from hers, he pulled her close, much closer than he'd danced with the last girl. His arm was strong around her waist, and every inch of her skin tingled at his touch. Her face was inches from his neck and she could smell his scented warmth. She looked up at him and their lips almost brushed.

'Who are you?' he whispered.

'I'm . . .' She thought of Rose and her step-mother somewhere close by and she thought of her father, the secretary, and in the end she said all she could think of to escape discovery. 'Names can wait until later. Just dance with me.'

'As you wish, mystery girl,' he said and when he smiled she thought that all the beauty in the world was caught up in that expression. She melted into his embrace and let him whirl her around the floor, their feet in perfect harmony against the marble. She didn't care if Rose or her step-mother saw her. She didn't even look for them. As far as Cinderella was concerned no one else existed. It was just her, her handsome prince and the music. She had no concept of time passing; she was simply caught up in a moment she wanted to last forever. Eventually, the musicians paused for a rest, and the prince led Cinderella to a seat at the side of the room, the two of them sharing a velvet bench, his courtiers ensuring the rest of the guests allowed them some privacy. Cinderella still turned her head sideways and tilted her face down in case her step-mother or Rose should stare at her too hard.

'I've dreamed of meeting you,' she said, the words blurting out before she could stop them. She blushed slightly. 'I know that sounds stupid.'

'It's uncanny,' the prince murmured. 'I feel as if I know you and I don't even know your name. From the moment I saw you, my heart, well . . .' He leaned forward and touched her hand. 'Everyone else faded . . . I just *knew*.'

His hand was warm against hers and as he stroked the back of her hand gently with his thumb, she could feel her breath getting quicker. His face was thoughtful as his eyes searched hers.

'I'd given up on love, you know. True love.' He had leaned in closer to her and their lips were almost touching as they spoke. Cinderella longed to touch his face, to feel his hands on her. Her heart thumped in her chest. This was everything she'd dreamed of since she'd been a little girl. She'd never seen such a beautiful man, and here he was, and he wanted her.

'So much isn't as it seems, don't you think?' he said. 'But this, it's magical.'

'Love at first sight,' she said. She ignored the faintly unsettled feeling the mention of magic gave her.

'Yes,' he said. 'I do believe it is.'

'Shall we dance again?' she said. She wanted to feel his body against hers and wrap her arms around his neck and move freely. Break away from the formality of the set pieces. More than anything, she wanted to kiss him.

'Your wish is my command,' he said.

She felt as if she was floating when she got to her feet, and it was only when she glanced at the clock as they passed it, that she came crashing back to earth. It was quarter past eleven. It couldn't be. Her heart raced. Leave by midnight or be home by midnight? What had the fairy godmother said? She couldn't take the chance of being late. Of having the second night stolen from her. The night when the prince would *choose*.

'Would you excuse me for a moment?' she looked up at him, and let her eyes absorb the perfection of his face, storing it in memory. 'I must . . .' she wasn't quite sure how to finish the sentence. Thankfully, he simply nodded.

'Hurry back, my love.'

She tore herself away before she lost her determination, and then scurried through the revellers towards the stairs. She didn't look back.

The carriage was waiting for her, the driver leaning against the door watching as she fled the castle.

'Did you meet your handsome prince?' he asked. Again, there was a tone in his gruff voice that hinted he was laughing at her. She glared at him, wanting him to move away from the door so she could climb in. Although broad, he wasn't as tall as the prince, and where her love was blond and beautiful, this man had dark hair that hung slightly over his eyes and rough stubble peppered his chin and cheeks. His brown eyes made her nervous. She couldn't read them.

'Yes I did,' she said. 'Now get me back home before we're both in trouble.'

He laughed a little, an earthy sound, and stepped back, pulling the door with him and giving a brief mock bow as she climbed in.

'I was born in trouble it seems,' he said. 'But at least I'm no pansy prince who can't take care of himself.'

'What do you mean?' Cinderella asked, leaning forward in her seat. He either didn't hear her or just refused to answer because suddenly the wheels were turning and they were on their way. He was jealous, she decided. Who wouldn't be? The prince had everything a woman could want. That much was obvious. And he was going to be hers. That thought made her smile and, as they raced back to the house, she lost herself in the memory of his touch on her hand and the way he'd held her close as they danced.

The magic vanished as soon as she'd stepped through the kitchen door, her hair tumbling free down her shoulders and her fine silver gown evaporating to leave her back in her house dress. Her feet cooled as her own shoes, clunky and uncomfortable in comparison, replaced the diamond slippers. She was still smiling though, and made sure the other two nuts were safely into her pocket before drinking a glass of her father's wine and dancing with a broomstick across the kitchen floor and giggling to herself.

She'd barely crept upstairs in the dark and crawled into her cold bed by the time the front door slammed and lights went on throughout the house. She could hear her step-mother shouting. She was sure Rose was crying.

'You stupid, stupid girl!'

'It wasn't my fault, I—'

'You *had* him. In the palm of your hand! All my dreams – all your dreams – shattered!'

'Look, mother, I did my best—'

'Well it wasn't good enough!'

Cinderella pulled her knees up under her chin. Her excitement and the glow of love still burned in the pit of her stomach, but hearing her step-mother screeching so hysterically was something new and it gave her a sickening twist. As did Rose's sobbing.

'I'm sorry. I'm sorry—'

'Sorry isn't good enough! You're ruined everything! Everything!'

Cinderella pulled the covers over her head and
pushed her fists into her ears. She wouldn't let them
spoil her happiness. She wouldn't. And if she did
win the prince's hand the next night then she made
a quiet promise to herself that she'd find an Earl for
Rose to marry. A handsome one.

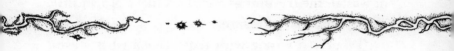

The next day passed interminably, and once her
chores were done she hid in her room avoiding
her step-mother. She veered from berating Rose to
encouraging her to make the best of the second night
to come while Cinderella wished the hours away. Finally, night came round again and she watched from
the window as Rose went off in Ivy's carriage. This
time, however, she felt no jealousy, just her own
overwhelming excitement. Once her father had gone
up to his study to work into the early hours, she ran
down to the kitchen and cracked the second nut open.

This time, her dress shone like spun gold, reflecting every shade of red from her magnificent hair.
Her feet tingled with the warmth from the slippers
and her face glowed.

'Very nice,' the driver said, as he opened the door, 'if you like that kind of thing.'

'Are you being rude to me on purpose?' Cinderella asked, frowning at him. 'If you think I'm so ugly just keep your opinions to yourself.'

He smiled again, laughing at her she was sure. 'What?' she snapped, crossly.

'It wasn't the raw product I was commenting on, it was all the trimmings. You look like a proper little court lady, that's for sure.'

'What's so wrong with that? That's what I *want* to be.'

'Nothing. It suits some. I just prefer a real woman, that's all. The type who runs free through the forest. Now, let's get you to your perfect prince, shall we?'

She didn't say another word, but pressed her lips tightly together. She could quite happily not speak to the insufferable brute for the rest of her life.

Rose was trying to talk to the prince as Cinderella swept into the ballroom, and she was glad to see that he was showing no interest in her whatsoever. If anything, he looked distracted and irritated, his glance going this way and that, scanning the room. Her heart lifted at the sight of him and she took a glass of champagne and waited until he'd fully spurned her step-sister, sending her scurrying to the sides of the ballroom in shame, before she approached him.

'Hello,' she said, simply, as his mouth dropped open.

'You! You're here! You look . . .' He stared at her and smiled. 'Perfect.'

'I'm sorry I left,' she said, as he took her in his arms and swept her onto the dance floor. Around them, couples pulled back slightly and the partnerless young women drifted into the corners to console each other. It was clear the prince had eyes for no other. He had come back to life with her arrival, his listlessness suddenly shed like a second skin.

'I thought you had left me,' he said. 'I couldn't sleep. I've thought of nothing but you.'

'I've been the same,' she said and smiled. Could he have become more handsome overnight? It seemed that way. Once again, just like the previous night, they danced and talked and revelled in each other's presence until he gave a signal and the music paused, and then the prince took her hand and led Cinderella out towards the balcony.

'Let's go somewhere more private,' he whispered

into her ear. His voice was like electricity running through her, and she simply nodded. She was breathless. Her skin was flushed. Two servants pulled the glass doors open for them and they stepped out into the night. The doors closed, sealing them off from the rest of the party. No one would join them out here, that was clear, and now that the dance had stopped Cinderella was glad to be away from the rest of the guests. Rose and her step-mother wouldn't be expecting to see her here, and certainly not dressed so glamorously, but that still wouldn't stop them recognising her if they looked for too long – and everyone's eyes had been on her by the time the music finished. Everyone thought the prince had made his choice.

At some point while they'd danced soft snow flakes had started to fall, but the balcony was covered in a silk canopy and fires burned in ornate metal stands and the air was warm. Cinderella was sure that even if it was pouring with icy rain she wouldn't notice. Ahead of them the city was spread out, an ocean of darkness with only occasional ships of light in the gloom. It was late, and while the castle was still filled with music and dancing, the ordinary people had long days ahead. As she stood at the low wall that ran around the balcony, looking out over it all, she felt a lifetime away from the grime and cold of the city's winter.

She looked up at the handsome man beside her and smiled. The prince, saying nothing, pulled her close, one arm wrapping tight around her. He lifted his other hand and traced his fingers down her face and to her neck, his eyes lingering on her skin. Her breath came more rapidly as her stomach knotted with longing. Each controlled touch sent a thousand shivers through her. His hand finally reached the curve of her breasts, which pushed upwards as the dress was designed to have them do, and she arched her back against him slightly, unable to control herself. She moaned softly as he brushed over her skin and then he lifted his gaze and his eyes met hers. He leaned forward and finally they kissed. His mouth was warm and soft, and his lips were gentle, barely touching hers at first and then pressing harder as she responded, his hands exploring her body through the confines of her dress. She touched him back, her fingers running down his chest, and then resting one hand on his thigh, his leg strong beneath the material of his trousers. Unable to stop herself, she lifted the hand higher, enjoying the heat coming from him, and the urgency of his breath. He kissed her harder, his hand pulling at her skirts and she thought of Buttons' fingers, slim and feminine and wondered how different the prince's would feel.

She barely heard the clock chimes ringing out. She was lost in the moment, fireworks exploding in her mind and sending traces of intensity throughout her body. Even in her fantasies it had never been like this. She wanted to pull his clothes free and feel his skin next to hers. She couldn't stand the longing, she was desperate for him. His hands were struggling with her underskirts and she wanted to tug them up and give him access. All childish thoughts fell away from her and she was suddenly all woman, eager to do all the things she had only heard about from Ivy and from the other, less well-behaved, girls in the town.

'It's only midnight,' he said, as the first chime echoed across the city. 'We have hours yet. We could go somewhere and—'

'Midnight?' Her head still a haze, Cinderella could barely focus, but the word cut through the heat that filled her. 'It's midnight?'

'Yes, but—'

She broke free from him so suddenly it took him

by surprise. His arms fell away, and by the time he reached for her again she was already at the doors. She had to leave by midnight, even though every inch of her wanted to stay in the prince's arms and kiss him all night. The fairy godmother's icy expression flashed behind her eyes. She had to do as she'd been told.

'I have to leave!' she called back as she yanked the door open, grasping the handle from the footman in order to get back in more quickly. 'I'm sorry. I have to leave.'

She let her eyes drink in his handsome face one more time and then she turned and fled. As she pushed her way through the dancing couples, she knew he was coming after her. She kept ahead and finally broke clear of the ballroom, running down the sweeping red staircase to the exit. She could see the carriage, door open, waiting for her, the rough driver already sitting at the reins.

'Hurry up!' he called.

'Wait!' the prince shouted, chasing her down the stairs. 'Wait! I don't even know your name!'

Cinderella ran faster still and threw herself, all dignity forgotten, into the back of the carriage that was already beginning to move away. She dragged the door closed as the horses picked up speed, and then, recovering her breath, she peered back through the window. The prince was staring after her, one hand reaching out as if he could somehow pull the carriage back to him. The cold night air gripped one foot and she looked down and the last chime rang out. One of her enchanted shoes was missing. How could it have come off? And when? They fitted so perfectly. And what would her fairy godmother say?

As it turned out, the fairy godmother was waiting for them and as Cinderella climbed out of the coach in her dull house dress with her hair loose, she didn't seem overly concerned about the diamond slipper. 'It'll find its way back, I'm sure,' she said and smiled as if she understood something that Cinderella didn't. That didn't surprise Cinderella. She thought there were probably a lot of things the fairy godmother understood that were beyond her own reach.

The night was cold and she was suddenly tired, even though her heart was racing.

'You've got your prince. Now remember your promise,' the fairy godmother said. 'Do what I asked of you or none of this will end well.'

Cinderella nodded. Not that she knew how she was ever going to get back into the castle again. The prince didn't even know her name, and she'd been in too much of a panic to shout it to him.

'And you,' the fairy godmother glanced at the driver as a flurry of stardust swallowed up both her and the glittering coach, 'Remember, it'll be morning soon.' By the time she'd finished the sentence, the echo of the words were all that was left of her. Cinderella shivered and glared at him. 'You were going to drive away without me.'

'I knew you'd make it.' He leaned on the wall. 'Did you get what you wanted? Is true love in the air?'

'What would you know about it?'

'I know a few things,' he said, leaning in closer, one hand teasing a strand of her wild red hair. Cinderella pressed herself back against the kitchen door, but she could feel his musky heat and she still throbbed from her embrace with the prince. He touched her hair. She couldn't help but shiver slightly and she couldn't decide if it was revulsion or attraction.

'I know your hair looks prettier free than trapped,' he said. 'Like most things. I also know princes are just men. Mainly not very good ones. And a castle can't give a girl like you what the woman inside will want.'

'You don't know anything.' Why did he make her feel so uncomfortable and awkward? Why couldn't he just shut up and leave?

'I know you're no court lady.' He smiled, his teeth white and even against his rugged face. 'And it would be a shame to see you turn into one.'

'The prince loves me,' she said, defiantly.

'So you say. But do you love him?'

Finally, behind her back, she found the latch to the gate and pushed it open. 'That's none of your business.' He was so arrogant. Who was he anyway? Just some lackey. She stomped down the stairs to the kitchen door. 'But yes,' she said. 'I think I do!' She closed the door behind her without looking back.

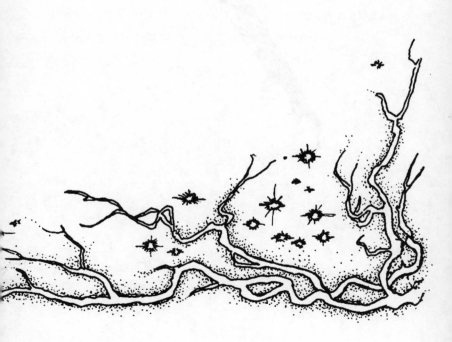

5

'Help me . . .'

Over the course of the two days after the prince's last Bride Ball a black storm raged over the city. A fierce wind blew down from the mountain so hard that they said it was the ghostly fire of the dead dragons' breath, so long cold in their graves. It blew the snow canopy from the forest into the city streets. Thunder and lightning waged a war in clouds so low that those brave enough to venture out claimed that if they stretched an arm up they could touch them. The sky was a roiling ocean and all the people could do was to huddle round their small fires and wait for it to pass.

The anger of the storm outside, however, was nothing compared to the dark atmosphere that gripped Cinderella's house. Ivy, like everyone else in the city who had heard of the strange turn of events at the second ball, braved the weather and visited her sister and mother. She didn't stay long. Cinderella hid while her step-mother railed at Ivy for not helping them more, and then launched into a bitter attack on the pathetic physicality of her noble husband. Ivy slapped her and left. The house stood in silence for a long time after that, the girls staying in their rooms to avoid being caught by a wandering lash of Esme's tongue.

Rose got everything worst. Her pale skin was constantly blotched from crying and, at every meal time, Cinderella and her father would listen to the digs and jibes and feel the stings with her. Esme was drinking too. It was as if something inside her had cracked. Finally, as she berated Rose once more for being useless and destroying all her dreams of her old life which she'd come so close to achieving, Cinderella's father finally slammed his hand down on the table and stood up.

'If this life is so bloody terrible, Esme, why did you choose it? It was love that mattered then? Don't you love me now?'

Cinderella and Rose both shrank down in their chairs. Their parents didn't argue. They didn't appear to have much in common, but they never fought.

'Don't be so ridiculous,' Wine spilled from her glass as Esme looked up. 'This isn't about love, this is about life! Ever since Ivy married that idiot Viscount—'

'He's not an idiot. If you took time to talk to him—'

'He's an idiot. He doesn't even go to court. But having been back to the castle and remembered what my life used to be like—'

'You hated it. You said it was shallow. You ran away from it, Esme, don't you remember? You were married to a man you loathed because of that life? You slept with that randy old bastard for five long years, every night of which you hated. That's what that life gave you!'

The two young women were forgotten in the heat of the fight, but Cinderella wished she could just slide down to the floor and crawl away. Worse still was the thought that this was all her fault. She still clung to her bubble of joy over her time at the castle but she'd been so focused on chasing what she'd wanted she hadn't considered the fallout.

'Yes, but if Rose had married the prince then I could have had the best of that life *and* you. I'm tired of all those people sniggering at us – at *me*. I'm tired of being poor. I'm tired of being cold. Don't you understand it?'

'I understand that. And I'm trying hard. But you can't have everything in life, it doesn't work that way. You have to decide what the important parts are.' The fight went out of Cinderella's father. 'The thing I don't understand anymore is you.' He turned his back on them and left the room. No one spoke after that.

In the morning, Rose and Cinderella cleared away the breakfast things and were doing the washing up, the two working slowly together in the relative safety of the basement room.

'Don't you have to take care of your hands?' Cinderella asked, as Rose scrubbed at a roasting tin. The other girl let out a short bitter bark of laughter.

'I don't think the softness of my skin matters anymore. Not to mother, anyway.'

'There'll be other balls.' Cinderella felt a surprising wave of affection for her step-sister. Rose had always been the practical one. The clever one. Rose did not cry or get over-emotional. Not even when they'd been children.

'You don't get it, Cinderella.' Rose sighed, tired. 'You never do. If the prince had just danced with me once, like the other girls, or not even danced with me at all, then that would have been okay. But I'm now the girl who wasn't good enough. I'm the *discarded* one.' She put the dish down and leaned on the side of the sink as if she didn't have the energy to stand. 'Even after that other girl ran off the prince didn't want anything to do with me. Mother made me try and talk to him and he brushed me off. In front of *everyone*, as if I suddenly disgusted him.'

Tears, always so close, welled up in her eyes. 'Now none of the other noblemen will come near me. I've made everything worse. All that effort mother put in to get me ready for the ball and it's come to nothing.' She sniffed hard. 'She's going through the change and I think this on top of that has driven her a bit mad. I think she's driving me mad.'

Cinderella's eyes fell away from her step-sister's. She had been so happy that night. She and the prince were meant to be, she was sure of it. Whenever she closed the door of her room and looked at his picture, she was transported back to the wonders of the ball, and his arms around her and his kiss . . . and she fantasised about him finding her and all being as her fairy godmother promised and life being wonderful. But every time she looked at Rose or her step-mother she felt bad. She wondered if maybe she should tell Rose what happened? How the other girl was her? Maybe Rose would actually be relieved, because then they could send for the prince and her step-mother would have the life she wanted and it would all be well again.

'Look, Rose—' she started, and then the back door opened and a burst of fresh cold and rain delivered Buttons into the kitchen.

'Evening, princess,' he said. 'Sorry I didn't knock. It's a bastard out there.' He pushed the door closed and then hurried over to the stove – handing Rose the small sack he carried before pressing his palms against the warm metal and shivering. 'You must be Rose,' he grinned. 'I've heard about you.'

Rose looked in the bag and then pulled out a large round of cheese, a ham and two loaves of bread. 'And you must be the boy who's been refilling our coal scuttle when it empties,' she said wryly.

'That could be me, I confess.'

Cinderella couldn't look at Rose. She'd thought no one had noticed the gifts Buttons had been bringing her, but clearly that wasn't the case. 'Thanks, Buttons.'

'No problem, princess.'

Rose visibly flinched at the use of the word, but she pulled a chair up for him and poured him a hot coffee from the pot. 'You shouldn't be out on the streets in this if you don't have to be,' she said. 'Aside from the trouble you could get into. I'm presuming you didn't buy this stuff.'

'Can't keep me from the ladies,' He winked at her and then smiled at Cinderella. 'And it won't be missed. They have plenty.' He sat down. 'Anyway, I thought you'd want all the latest gossip from the castle, princess. You never get tired of that.'

'If it's about the Bride Balls, don't bother,' Rose said, bristling slightly. 'We know all about it.'

'But do you know about the shoe?' Buttons asked. Cinderella's heart leapt and Rose frowned.

'What shoe?'

'The one the girl left behind. They found it on the stairs when the party was being cleaned up. It's beautiful apparently. Made of diamonds or something. A dainty, narrow slipper that the prince is convinced belongs to his mystery beauty. He's totally all over the place. Quite funny to see. He was moping about like a teenager until they found it.'

'Really?' Cinderella fought back her smile although inside she was dancing all over again. He loved her! He felt the same way she did.

'Anyway,' Buttons continued. 'He's sending his footman on a tour of the city to try the slipper on the

foot of every girl of the right age. When the slipper
finds its owner, he'll marry her.'

'But that's ridiculous! It's a shoe. It'll fit a lot of
girls,' Rose said. 'Surely you just look for the girl
who has the other shoe.'

'I've seen it,' Buttons said. 'There's something
funny about that slipper. And our handsome highness wants the girl who can wear it perfectly.'

'When does the search start?' Cinderella tried
to keep the excitement out of her voice, but she
wanted to sing with happiness. The slipper wouldn't
fit anyone else, no matter how logical Rose's point
was. It would be too big or too small for every lady
but her. It would make itself that way. Her stomach
fizzed. The fairy godmother's promise was going to
come true.

'Tomorrow. But even if they work all day and
night it's still going to take weeks to go through the
whole city.'

'Not necessarily,' Rose said. 'Maybe they'll find
her quickly.' There was a longing in her voice and
then she sighed. She looked up at Cinderella, her face
full of despair. 'If we could keep this from mother,
that would be good.'

Cinderella nodded. The mood dampened after
that, and Buttons, now warm and dry got up to leave.

Rose gave him an extra scarf to wrap tight around his face against the outside onslaught and both girls waved him off.

A small brown mouse ran in between their legs and sat shivering on the floor, half under the stove. Rose reached for the broom to shoo it out, but Cinderella stopped her. 'The little thing will die out in that weather. Leave it be. I think it's rather sweet.' She then broke a small chunk of the cheese off and dropped it on the floor. 'Now come on, let's go upstairs. We can't hide in here forever.'

Cinderella's step-mother had heard about the slipper by lunchtime. Everybody had. In a city that was besieged by bad weather it seemed gossip could still travel faster than the icy wind. A fevered light came on in her eyes as she gathered all the information she could about the shoe, paying money they didn't have to the servants of those whose houses had already been visited for every tiny detail. She clapped her hands together and smiled and laughed. There was still a chance for Rose – there was still a chance for *her*.

'But it's not my shoe,' Rose said. 'And he doesn't

want me.' It was a plaintive, quiet protest of one who knows they're already defeated.

'He wants whoever that shoe fits,' Esme countered. 'If it fits you, he'll marry you.'

She spent a lot of time examining Rose's feet. They were too wide for the slipper, she decided, and so she bound them so tightly in bandages that the poor girl could barely walk without crying. Cinderella's father tried to stop it, but Rose said it was fine and that it didn't hurt that much and she just wanted to make her mother happy. Every morning and every night the bandages would come off and Esme would force her poor daughter to try to squeeze her bruised foot into a shoe which was purportedly the exact size of the sparkling one that was stopping at each house in the city. It should be – Cinderella's step-mother had paid enough for it.

Rose's foot never fit. It wasn't the length that was the problem, it was the width. Rose might have lost weight but her feet were still wide. After five days of binding, Cinderella's step-mother decided more drastic action was needed. She plunged her daughter's bare feet into buckets of ice for hours at a time and then bandaged them up again.

Cinderella wasn't sure what was the most

disturbing – her actions or the soothing way she spoke to Rose as she did them. She loved her, she said. She just wanted the best for her, she said. And all the time Rose cried and the storm outside continued to rage. Cinderella just wished the prince's procession would hurry up and get to them. This madness needed to stop.

The night before it happened, the storm finally broke. The skies cleared and the wind dropped, leaving the city in an icy calm.

Rose finally broke too.

Upstairs on the top floor two middle-aged people, once brought together by true love, now shouted and sobbed at each other. Cinderella heard the words, 'menopause' and 'hormones' and then her stepmother completely lost it, attacking her husband with a barrage of insults whose targets ranged from his manhood to his wages. Cinderella had been keeping mainly to her room. No one was paying her any attention anyway, and once she'd done her chores for the day she'd go and lock herself away with her lover's picture, close her eyes and turn time back to the night of the ball. This time even that daydream couldn't block out the fighting. It was gone ten at night when she crept into the kitchen and found Rose.

At first she couldn't quite take it in. The bandages were undone and spread all over the floor. Rose, her hair free around her shoulders, was sitting on a wooden chair, one knee tucked under her chin. She was sobbing and muttering incoherently, focused intently on whatever she was trying to do. Cinderella's eyes widened. What *was* she trying to do?

Rose had gripped her little toe with one hand, separating it from the rest, and was cutting at it with a small knife. She paused, and with a bloody hand reached for the bottle of brandy on the kitchen table and took a long swallow from it. Only when she put it back down did she see Cinderella. She stared for a moment.

'Help me,' she said eventually, her words thick through the snot and sweat that covered her face. 'I can't quite cut it off.' Tears came in a sudden rush, and the awful sobs broke Cinderella's shock. She ran to her, and grabbed the knife. Blood gushed, thick and red from the wound and her stomach lurched as she saw the protruding bone. She moved quickly, grabbing a bowl and running outside. She flew up to the street, fell to her hands and knees and filled it with icy snow. Her hands burned with the cold, but she didn't feel it. How could Rose do this? How could she have done this?

Back in the kitchen, she thrust her step-sister's foot into the bowl and held her as she shrieked with the pain. Then, while Rose drank more from the brandy bottle, Cinderella gently stitched her skin back up, coated it in medicinal salves and bandaged her two smallest toes together. She felt sick. Her family was crumbling into madness. And they were her family, she knew that in her heart, however much she sometimes felt separate from them.

'There you go,' she said, softly. 'That should heal.' Rose's foot would never be pretty to look at, but hopefully she'd keep her toe. She was tired. Rose was exhausted. What a mess it had all become. 'We should tell father,' she said. 'You probably need to see a doctor.' The floor was still slick with crimson and Cinderella reached for the mop.

Rose studied her, eyes glazed. 'Your mother didn't die, you know.' She sniffed and ran the back of her hand across her nose. 'You do know that, don't you?' Cinderella turned and the blood was forgotten as she leaned on the mop to keep herself standing. The world tilted slightly beneath her.

'What?'

'She didn't die,' Rose said, simply. 'She ran away

with a travelling man. They were going to the Far Mountain to find the dragons. That's what she said.' She sighed. 'But she was a drunk. She said a lot of things, when she wasn't shouting at you or your father.'

'You're lying.' Unwanted images rose unbidden behind her eyes. Hiding behind bannisters. A woman laughing unpleasantly. Shouting.

'She used to come to my father's house and scream crazy things. She was wild, your mother. Wild and mean.'

'That's not true.'

'We didn't tell you because you were so little. We felt sorry for you.' Fresh tears filled her eyes. 'We loved you. You were like mine and Ivy's pretty little doll. My mother used to scoop you up and read you stories and stroke your hair until you slept. Why do you think you want to marry a prince so much? Who do you think told you those pretty stories of castle life?'

'No. No!' The walls of Cinderella's world crumbled, as Rose's words jarred with precious memories. 'That wasn't her! That was *my* mother. My dead mother.'

'We should have told you,' Rose was staring into space. 'We really should. Then maybe you wouldn't

'Help me . . .'

have grown up to be such a little bitch to us all the time.'

Cinderella turned and ran. She didn't look back.

6

'It finally fits!'

The sky was blue overhead and, although it remained freezing cold, the sun shone down on the street as the fanfare played and the procession of prince's men pulled up in their street. Cinderella's father refused to come downstairs. Even Esme was subdued as she and Rose waited in the sitting room, with Cinderella loitering in the background pretending to stoke up the fire. Rose, in her best dress, was sitting in an armchair. Her face was pale, no doubt she was in agony with her injured foot. Cinderella caught her eye and the two girls shared a wan smile. Esme didn't look at either of them. Cinderella wasn't sure she could bring herself to. The shouting had stopped when she'd seen what Rose had done, and there were dark circles around her eyes that no longer held fevered madness.

As the footmen swept in, the familiar diamond slipper glittering on a red cushion, for a brief moment Cinderella wished it would fit Rose so they could be done with it. Or better still, for it to fit neither of them and to pass them by.

'His royal highness has decreed that whomever this shoe fits, he shall take as his betrothed. Every young woman in the land is required to try it on.' The man looked tired and spoke the words wearily. 'Ma'am. If you would,' he said to Rose. He lowered the cushion and placed the shoe at her feet. Rose looked at it and laughed a little; a low sad sound. 'I cut the wrong foot,' she said, softly. 'How typical.'

'Ma'am?' the footman asked.

She ignored him and lifted her right foot, pushing it into the glass. Her heel hung half an inch over the back and she couldn't squeeze it in any further. Cinderella didn't think she tried very hard, and nor could she blame her.

'Well, that's that then,' Esme said. After all the hysteria of the previous two weeks, her voice was now calm and empty. 'Thank you.'

The footman picked up the shoe and brought it over to Cinderella, 'Ma'am. If you would.'

Cinderella's heart raced. She couldn't help it.

'She didn't go to the ball,' her step-mother said. 'You needn't bother with her.'

'All the ladies in the land.' The footman gave a small smile. In his exhaustion he could barely raise the corners of his mouth. 'Otherwise I'm going to have to start all over again.'

Cinderella carefully lifted her foot. She could feel the warmth from the strange diamond slipper already. Her sole had barely touched the inside when she felt it tighten gently around her, moulding itself to her shape.

There was a long moment's silence as the truth dawned on them all.

'It fits!' The footman's mouth had dropped open. 'It finally fits!'

'But that's not possible!' Esme was staring at her in disbelief. 'How did you . . . How . . . why didn't you say?'

'You.' Rose's voice was cold as she pulled herself upright painfully. 'It was you all along.'

It was Cinderella's turn to avoid their faces. Her heart raced with excitement but her stomach squirmed in shame. Still. She lifted her chin. She'd make it better for all of them. They'd see that when they calmed down. Surely they would.

There wasn't a lot of time for discussion. As soon as the footman had stepped back outside with the shoe and announced that the girl had been found to the prince's guard, a team of men arrived to start packing up their possessions ready to move them into the castle and their new royal apartments. Whatever misgivings her step-mother might have initially had evaporated as the realisation that her dreams had been achieved after all took hold. She squeezed Cinderella's cheeks and kissed her on the forehead, declaring that she'd always been the prettiest of the girls and how could she not have recognised that glorious red hair when she'd seen it at the ball.

Cinderella had wanted to point out that it was probably because ever since Ivy got married Rose had been the sole focus of her attention, and she'd been pretty much forgotten, but decided that silence on the matter might be her best option. Esme took to directing the packers who were dismantling their old life and home with alarming speed. A little over an hour later several tailors showed up with a selection of fine dresses for the women and suits for Cinderella's father. Their old clothes would not do for life at the castle.

After they had fussed over Cinderella, dressing her in an ermine-trimmed silver dress almost the same colour as the one she'd worn at the ball, she picked out several other dresses and took them upstairs. With her heart slightly in her mouth, she knocked on Rose's door. Her step-sister was sitting on the edge of her bed looking around at all her books and old toys that she'd never brought herself to throw away.

'I picked you out some dresses,' Cinderella said. 'They're very beautiful.'

Rose looked at her. 'Why didn't you just say?' She ignored the dresses and, feeling awkward, Cinderella lay them out across the mattress.

'They're all for you. I picked the prettiest ones.'

'You must have been laughing at me all this time.' Rose stared into space again. 'All this time.'

'No!' The words were like darts into Cinderella's heart. 'No, I wasn't! I just didn't know how to say . . . I didn't know what to say . . . I'm so sorry.' Tears stung her eyes.

'What did I ever do to you? You're my little sister. I've always looked after you.'

'Rose – I—'

'Just leave me alone. I'll put on one of your precious dresses. I wouldn't want to embarrass you in front of your prince.'

313

'I don't care about . . .' Cinderella couldn't finish the sentence. She *did* care about the prince. She cared that her family arrived looking as fine as they could. She cared about going to live in the castle and marrying the man all the girls wanted. She couldn't help it.

Rose smiled sadly. 'As long as you've got what you wanted, eh, Cinderella? I guess that's all that matters.'

Her face flushed, Cinderella backed out of the room and closed the door. A cold wind rushed up the stairs as men trekked in and out carrying clocks, chairs and boxes of china and cutlery that Esme deemed fit enough to take with them. Cinderella peered over the bannister. Her step-mother seemed to be taking a lot of their ordinary things. Why wouldn't she just leave them behind? There would be better things in the castle. Their possessions would just look cheap.

'I'm very disappointed in you.'

The voice made her jump, and she turned to see her father standing on the bottom step of the stairs that led up to his attic study. 'But now we're going to live in the castle,' she said. It sounded lame. It was. That wasn't what her father was talking about and she knew it.

'I can almost forgive the deception. Sneaking out to the ball – although how you did it I'll never know and I'm not sure I want to – was wrong, but I know how much you wanted to go. But this behaviour – watching everything your step-mother and Rose have been through these past few weeks—'

'She's been crazy!' Cinderella blurted out. 'That's not my fault.'

'Your step-mother is going through . . . well, there's a time of life that comes to all women. It's difficult. And times have been hard since the newspaper closed down and my work has been less regular. Your step-mother wants us to have both worlds. And if anyone can make that happen she can. We've talked about it. She thinks at court we could get the newspaper started again. We could make things better for a lot of people.' He paused and stared at Cinderella. 'But your behaviour towards your sister and the rest of us has been plain selfish. Perhaps it's our fault. We've always spoiled you. You were the favourite baby of the family.'

Spoilt? Her? Cinderella couldn't believe what she was hearing.

'I never thought I'd say this,' her father turned back to the stairs, 'but you're reminding me of your mother.'

Alone in the hallway, Cinderella's shock turned to anger and she seethed quietly. Where was the gratitude? She'd just completely changed their lives for the better! Where were the congratulations? She'd fallen in love and was going to marry the man of her dreams. Surely her own father should be happy for her? She stormed into her bedroom and slammed the door, and she didn't care if it made her sound like a child. Not even a spoilt one.

Her bad mood vanished once she stepped up into the golden carriage the prince sent for her, a silver one directly behind it for the rest of her family. The whole street came out to see them off, and Cinderella knew that at least her step-mother would be bursting with pride. Her respectability was being restored to her – in grand style – and it was all down to Cinderella. She settled back in the luxurious fur cushions and looked out of the window at all the ordinary people coming out of their houses, curious to see her as the delicate wheels carried her quickly back to the castle. It was a perfect distraction from thinking about the diamond slippers and the magic she had used to grab the prince's attention. He'd fall in love with her without them anyway. She was sure of that. He just had to get to know her.

He was waiting for her on the sweeping stairs, now coated in a red carpet, and lined with wigged courtiers. As she stepped down, the crowds who filled the streets and stretched out from their balconies to catch a glimpse of her, cheered wildly. Cinderella barely heard them. Although the rest of the city was still filthy after the storm the castle gleamed white and all the windows glinted in the winter sunshine truly making it a castle of light. It was as glorious in the daylight as it had been at night, and, Cinderella thought as she fell into a deep curtsey, so was the prince. She smiled at him and he smiled back, but there was an edge of wariness in the look. He snapped his fingers and a servant stepped forward quickly carrying the cushion with the shoe and placed it on the step in front of her.

Only when she slipped her foot into it again, lifting her leg elegantly so he could see how perfect the fit was, did the prince's smile break into a grin.

'My darling,' he said, leaning forward and kissing her. 'I'm so glad I've found you.' He looked up at the crowd. Around them the courtiers burst into cheers, and she took his arm as he led her into the castle.

Her family's apartments were quite magnificent. The living area alone was bigger than the ground floor of their old house, now locked up and forgotten, and windows ran almost from floor to ceiling, with heavy gold and silver drapes hanging to either side. Servants dashed here and there making lists of all their requirements, Esme insisting on having a writing desk and chair placed by the window with the best view of the city, where her husband could finish his novel and write his articles. Cinderella watched as her father smiled at her step-mother and she saw in that moment how much he loved her. He would not complain about this new life if it made her happy.

Rose's room was next to her own and there was an inter-connecting door between the two vast boudoirs. Cinderella wondered if they'd ever use it. She doubted it. Not that she'd be in her own room for long. Soon they would have the wedding and she'd be in the prince's bed. She remembered how his kisses had made her feel on the night of the ball and wondered if she could wait until she was married. And would it matter that much if she didn't? The world was suddenly her oyster. Perhaps Rose wouldn't be in her room too long either. She'd be a fine catch for a nobleman now, and Cinderella was determined to advocate a good match for her, if only to ease the nagging sense of guilt she couldn't quite shake off.

The royal surgeon visited Rose that evening before

dinner to examine her foot. Cinderella's new maids were dressing her when he left, but she was sure she could hear crying from the other room. Dismissing the two girls – and rather enjoying the powerful feeling that gave her – she opened the middle door a crack to hear what was being said.

'It's okay, mother,' Rose said. 'It's just a limp.'

'But needing a stick forever?' Esme was crying, one arm round her daughter. 'I'm so sorry. It was madness. It's all my fault.'

'Beauty has never been my finest feature. And *you* didn't try to cut my toe off. I did.'

'Because of me.'

'It's done now.' Rose kissed her mother's cheek. 'I love you. Now let's get ready for dinner and show the royal family we know how to play this game as well as they do.'

Cinderella closed the door and leaned against it, feeling slightly sick. How could her seizing her own happiness have caused so much unhappiness for others? It would get better. It would. She lay on her bed, careful not to mess up her freshly styled hair, and waited for dinner. She pushed all the sad thoughts from her mind and concentrated on how happy dancing with the prince had made her. She tried not to think about how the prince had been looking at Rose before she'd cut across his path that night, wearing her enchanted shoes. It made something in her stomach twist; something dark and unpleasant that made her feel like a thief.

The king was a large, gruff man whose hair was a shock of white beneath his crown and his formal robes were tight around a body that was once no doubt thick-set and muscular, but now was veering towards fat as the weight slipped from his chest and shoulders and settled around his middle. His eyes were still sharp though. When they'd been drinking champagne before dinner and the prince had introduced her, Cinderella had done her best to remember what she'd learned from eavesdropping on the lessons Rose had endured, and complimented him on his beautiful castle, and answered his questions as well as she could. But she couldn't help but be distracted by the hairs sprouting from his ears and nose and her knowledge of contemporary art and music was quite lacking.

They ate dinner without the queen, who was apparently indisposed with a chill, the delicate clinking of their silver knives and forks against the bone china echoing around the vast dining room. Cinderella sat opposite the prince, but it was Rose and Esme who sat to either side of the king himself, and Ivy and her Viscount made up the rest of the table, the group talking and leaving the young lovers with a little privacy to talk. Although the prince smiled at her often, their conversation was somewhat stilted, as if the passion they had felt two weeks previously had left them awkward in each other's company. Cinderella found herself reaching for her wine glass frequently to try and calm her nerves.

Rose, however, was having no trouble talking to the king.

'I think it's as many as fifteen children now,' she said. 'It's terrible. And they're all tradesmen's children because they can't afford to buy coal or logs from the merchants to warm their homes. So they have to go into the forest for firewood while their parents are working.'

'And no bodies are found? They're not simply being attacked by hungry wolves?'

'Who knows, your majesty. But I'm sure the people would feel much safer knowing you had soldiers in the woods protecting them.'

'Hmmm.' The king nodded.

'In fact,' Rose said, 'if your majesty's soldiers were

to gather the firewood and give it to the children, it would be a sign of the great affection you obviously have for the ordinary people.' She sipped her wine. 'Such good feeling would probably make taxes easier to collect too.' The last sentence was spoken so delicately that it was almost an afterthought, but the king's heavily-laden fork paused on its journey.

'I do love the people,' he said. 'This is true. And there are always spare soldiers.' He looked up at the prince. 'Did you know about these missing children?'

'I had heard something.' The prince shrugged, but it clearly wasn't a subject that interested him much. Cinderella thought of the baker's boy with his cheeky grin and she was proud of Rose for bringing it up.

'Why had I not heard about it?' The king frowned slightly. 'There used to be a newspaper. What happened to that?'

'It was closed down, your majesty,' Esme said. 'I believe some of your advisors worried that copies would be smuggled out of the city to your enemies who would gain a greater understanding of your kingdom.'

'Advisors,' the king snorted. 'They do get over-enthusiastic.'

'My dear Henry was the editor,' Esme touched her husband's hand. 'I'm sure he could help re-start it should you so wish. There's really nothing like reading all the news from the streets' perspective before hearing it, from perhaps somewhat protective advisors.'

The king nodded. 'Perhaps you're right.' He looked at Esme and smiled. 'I remember your first wedding you know. He was very old, the Earl, wasn't he?'

Cinderella's step-mother nodded. 'But he was a good man.'

'A randy old bugger from what I hear.' The king patted her hand. 'You were too young. Your actions are forgiven.'

Esme smiled and so did Cinderella's father, and the love between the two of them shone, infecting the old king's own smile with the warmth of the man, rather than the affection of a monarch. Cinderella looked to the prince and smiled at him hoping to see some of that same glow coming back to her, but she and the prince didn't have the years of companionship behind them – in fact, she realised, they didn't know each other at all. Her feet felt cold in her beautiful, charmless shoes.

When dinner was finally over, the king dismissed them all back to their apartments insisting that the family must be tired after their move and that Cinderella must get her beauty sleep before the preparations for the wedding began in earnest the next day. He signalled for the prince to retire with him for a nightcap.

Cinderella did not go back to her apartments. She lingered behind her family, who were intent on saying farewells to Ivy and then, as they followed her step-sister down to the courtyard where their carriage waited, Cinderella loitered in the corridor for a few minutes, then took her shoes off and crept barefoot and silent back to the drawing room. The door was open a tiny crack and she pressed her face against it. A huge fire, built with as much coal as they would be able to afford in a month, blazed in a vast grate. She heard the tinkle of liquid being poured into a glass and the heavy creak of leather as the king sat down. She could see neither her beau nor his father, but their voices drifted to her as they spoke.

'I had hoped that your recent adventures would make you grow up.' It was the king. 'But apparently not. What on earth possessed you to make a grand gesture like that? A few dances and your cock is so hard you want to marry the girl?'

'If it offends you so much father, we can call the wedding off.' The prince's voice was cold and Cinderella's heart dropped to her stomach. Surely he would fight for her? He loved her, didn't he? Surely he hadn't gone through all this searching to send her packing now? She'd be humiliated. Tears stung her eyes and she swallowed hard and willed them to pass.

'After this nonsense with that shoe, have the whole kingdom think you're a fool who can't keep his word?' The king snorted. 'No. We'll play this farce out. She's a pretty enough little thing and she'll give you heirs. I'm sure of it.' He sighed again. 'But the other one would have been a much better choice. At least she's noble. And she has a brain. She reminds me of your mother.'

'Cinderella is prettier,' the prince said. It sounded weak. From her place at the door Cinderella couldn't decide if he was defending her or himself with the statement.

'Listening at doors so early in your relationship? Where's the trust?'

A hand suddenly reached in front of her and closed the door and Cinderella jumped backwards, her heart racing. The driver, the fairy godmother's servant, leaned against the wall. He smiled but she was sure he was laughing at her. 'I didn't take you for the sort.'

'I just wanted to . . . I just . . .' She couldn't finish the sentence. 'It's none of your business anyway. And how did you get in the castle?'

'You wouldn't believe me if I told you.' Even in the gloomy corridor she could see his eyes twinkling. He folded his arms across his chest. 'So how's true love working out?'

She turned her back on him and started to walk away. She didn't have time for him now. What did he know about anything anyway? She thought he'd stayed by the door until she rounded the corner and then glanced back. She jumped again to find him right behind her.

'You're not the only one who can move silently, you know.'

Close up she could see the roughness of his tanned skin, and was struck once again by how different it was from the prince's smooth pale face. Even though she was sure he wasn't very much older than her, creases had formed on his cheeks and she wondered if they'd been made where he smiled. His dark hair flopped slightly over one eye, and she knew that, unlike his skin, it would be silky soft to the touch. He was standing so close to her she could smell him;

warm and almost musky. He reminded her of the forest and all the wild things that lived there.

'What do you want?' Her voice was cold and she stood tall. He was not going to intimidate her. The king's words still rang in her head. *She's a pretty little thing.* They stung her and she wasn't entirely sure why.

'Just reminding you of your promise. To search the castle.'

'I hadn't forgotten.' Cinderella lifted her chin. He irritated her. It was the way he spoke. The way he was so confident. He irritated her *a lot.* 'I don't need a lackey to remind me.'

'Good.' This time he was the one to turn and walk away. 'I'll meet you at the back kitchen door tomorrow night at three. Don't be late.' He didn't even look back.

Cinderella crept to her room, crawled into her bed and stared at the ceiling. It was a warmer and more comfortable bed than she'd slept in for years, but she couldn't sleep. When she finally did her dreams were plagued with nightmares of running endlessly through the castle trying to find a way out.

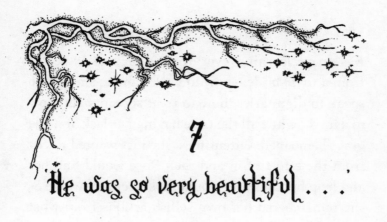

7

He was so very beautiful . . .

Over the next few days things seemed to get better. The prince began to court her properly and amidst the dress fittings and wedding preparations he lunched with her and walked her through the frozen maze gardens that were so beautiful, even in the grip of winter, that they almost took her breath away. They became more familiar with each other and while she told him stories of her childhood, the prince regaled her with tales of his adventures abroad. She would watch him and sometimes have to pinch herself that her arm was linked with his and that they were going to be married.

He kissed her often and his lips were soft on hers, but she ached to feel the passion they'd shared on the night of the Bride Ball. Much of her time though was spent learning everything that was expected from a royal bride – how to walk, how to sit, how to speak to dignitaries, how to treat servants and how to dance – while all the time having her lack of noble grace bemoaned. Oftentimes, she just wanted to cry from the effort of it, and then Rose would find her and help her and that would make her feel worse as she remembered her own selfish actions from what seemed like a lifetime ago. Her father was busy setting up the new national newspaper and her stepmother was helping him and when the two young women did see them they were full of such excited happy talk that it made the small empty space inside Cinderella grow.

She was also tired from her nightly explorations. The castle might not have been as large in reality as it always had been in her imagination but she'd begun to realise it would take her several weeks to search every room. Often she couldn't escape from dinner until after eleven, and then had to go through the pretence of going to bed before sneaking out again. She was also surprised at how many people seemed to live here. Although she was light on her feet she often had to duck behind curtains or hide beneath tables as servants or soldiers toured the building checking it was safe. What surprised her more, however, was the discovery that she found her secret task quite exciting – far more than her new life as a princess – especially when she came close to getting caught. On those nights she would arrive at the kitchen door with her face flushed and so high on the thrill that the coach driver would laugh out loud; a rough, earthy sound, and she would laugh with him even though she had nothing to report.

One night her search brought her to the prince's apartments. That afternoon they had played chess together and she had won and he'd looked at her in such surprise, as if seeing beyond the *pretty little thing* she was to the woman beneath. The woman she was growing into. Her heart had surged with the possibility that he might love her after all.

As she stood outside his bedroom, the floor cold beneath her bare feet, she couldn't help but push the door open a little to look inside. She didn't want to wake him, just to see him sleeping and imagine herself next to him, their naked bodies entwined in life as they often were in her fantasies.

The bedroom was empty and the covers still perfectly made. She stared for a long moment, the cold from the floor suddenly nothing next to the chill in her heart. Where was he? It was nearly three in the morning and he'd said at dinner that he was tired.

Slowly, she closed the door. She tried to turn her mind from the only logical reason for his absence but she couldn't quite manage it. He was somewhere in the castle with another woman. She felt sick. Suddenly, she wanted her old bedroom with his picture on her wall where she could look at him and imagine him perfect. She'd been stupid. A stupid little girl. She turned and ran, her heart a little more broken.

'I still haven't found anything,' she snapped at the fairy godmother's man, waiting as he was for her by the kitchen door. 'But it would help if I knew what I was looking for.'

'Trust me,' he said. 'You'll know when you find it.'

'Trust you? I don't even know you.' She knew the words were harsh but she couldn't help it. She felt sick. Her prince was in another woman's bed. He hadn't even tried to get into hers – even after everything at the Bride Ball. She thought of the fairy godmother. What had she said? She'd make sure Cinderella got her prince, but she couldn't guarantee true love? How arrogant she'd been to think that love wouldn't be a problem. She thought of the third dark nut tucked into the folds of her dress. What would happen if she cracked it? Would life go back to as it was before? Her stomach tightened. Even if she really wanted to – and she wasn't sure she was ready yet – she couldn't escape before fulfilling the fairy godmother's commands. She'd made a promise to search the castle. She had to see that through.

'You know me well enough. As I know you.'

'That's not true. I don't know anything about you.'

'I'm a huntsman,' he said. 'One who is very tired of royal games. Will that do?' She felt his dark eyes studying her. 'Why did you fall in love with the prince?' he asked eventually.

The question came so far out of the blue and cut through the pain in her heart so suddenly that she found herself answering without any thought. 'He was so very beautiful.' She didn't think about the past tense. She didn't think about what that meant.

'I suppose he is, if you like that kind of thing,' the huntsman said. 'But tell me,' he leaned against the wall in his easy fashion, 'didn't you wonder for a moment how foolish and self-absorbed a man must be to only recognise the woman he claims to love from her foot fitting a shoe?'

'No,' she said, her face burning. 'No I didn't, because I'm a stupid, stupid girl. Is that what you want to hear?' She spat her anger at him with tears stinging her eyes, and she turned and ran back inside. She wouldn't cry in front of him. She wouldn't cry in front of anyone.

'Cinderella,' he called softly after her. She turned. He was merely a shadow in the night.

'I would have recognised you. I'd recognise you always.' The shadow moved and then he was gone, leaving Cinderella staring after him wondering what exactly he meant.

She was tucked up in her bed, her heart still heavy, when the interconnecting door opened and Rose came in, leaning on her stick.

'Where have you been?' she whispered. There was no accusation in the question, only curiosity. She walked towards the bed, and Cinderella noticed how elegantly she moved, even with her limp.

'I couldn't sleep.'

'Were you with the prince?'

The tears came then, she couldn't help it. She cried for all of them, but mainly for her and Rose and all the trouble her childish dreams had caused. 'He wasn't there,' she whispered.

She leaned against Rose who wrapped her arms around her and rocked her gently back and forth, just like she had done when they were both little girls and Cinderella couldn't sleep.

'You put too much importance on love, little sister.' Rose said. 'He is a prince and he will be a king and they always do as they please, even if they love their wives as he must love you. There are things you must learn to ignore. You will be the queen and that's what matters. You'll be the mother of his children. The rest, well, the rest of it won't really matter.' As Cinderella listened, she felt the walls of the castle close in around her. Rose made it sound so easy, this royal life. But how could you live without love? Without passion? She'd rather be dead.

'I don't know that I can,' she whispered.

'Of course you can. I'll help you.' Rose stroked Cinderella's hair as she talked, her hand running gently over the thick red curls. 'But it might do you well to love him just a little less. Life will be easier that way. You know, if you play it cleverly, you could do some good for the kingdom. Make life better for people.'

'I don't want to play anything,' Cinderella sobbed. 'I just wanted to fall in love and live in the castle.'

'Well, one out of two isn't that bad,' Rose said. 'Life isn't a fairy tale, Cinderella. I wish it was, but it isn't. And perhaps he will love you as you love him. Who can tell?"

Rose stayed in her room until she eventually fell

335

asleep, Cinderella relishing the contact and affection. She'd been so lonely. Rose must have been too.

'I love you, Rose,' she whispered, as the knot in her stomach finally unfurled and sleep claimed her.

'I love you too, Cinderella,' her sister said.

The prince continued to be attentive to her but she found it hard to maintain her facade of joy when he was clearly keeping a lover secret from her. She checked his room twice more in the following nights and neither time was he there. She'd asked him how he slept and whether his apartments were comfortable. He always replied yes, and she kept the smile on her face even though she wanted to shout at him and call him a liar. By the third day, she took refuge in her room claiming fatigue at all the wedding preparations and ordered the maids to fill her a hot bath.

It was only when they'd left did she notice the little brown mouse that had followed them in. A scar ran along its back and she was surprised at the sudden surge of affection she felt at the sight of the little familiar creature.

'How did you get in here?' she asked. She crouched and held her hand out to it and laughed delightedly as it ran onto her palm, its tiny feet tickling against her skin. 'You're quite the little adventurer, aren't you, Mr Mouse?' She placed him carefully on a cushion on her bed. 'Maybe you should be Mrs Mouse, actually,' she said, undoing the laces of her dress. 'Women are more reliable.'

Her dress slid away to the ground and as she peeled off her undergarments it was good to feel the air on her skin. Even though it was warm, she shivered slightly with the pleasant sensation. The mouse stood up on its hind legs, its dark eyes studying her. It was a strange little thing, but she was glad of its company.

'Where do you think he goes every night?' she said, softly, lowering her naked body into the hot bath, and closing her eyes. 'Am I so terribly unlovable?' She sighed and then opened her eyes to pick up the sponge and soap. The little mouse was sitting on the edge at the other end of the large tub. It really was a remarkable little thing. She soaped the sponge and ran it over her small firm breasts and flat stomach. Her skin tingled. The prince had awoken something in her at the ball and although she was realising that love was elusive, that fire of lust still burned. 'Was it all just the shoes? Really? Why would she do that to me?' Her voice grew softer as her body responded to her own touch. 'Some fairy godmother,' she murmured as she grew lost in her fantasy.

She closed her eyes and shut out the little mouse and the castle around her and she was back on the balcony at the Bride Ball and the prince's hands were exploring her. Her hands moved across her body. In her mind, his hands were tanned this time, however, and rougher, and when he kissed her she could feel rough stubble rubbing her cheeks. She gasped as her fingers worked, imagining his mouth down between her legs, and then him moving up and inside her, and as she moved towards a climax she was surrounded by the scents of the forest.

The shouts of 'Thief! Thief! The thief has been caught!' woke her suddenly from her fantasy and, barely noticing the mouse scurrying away, she got out of the bath and wrapped a robe around her wet body before padding to the window, pulling back the thick rich curtain and looking down on the courtyard below. Castle life was kept relatively quiet at the request of the queen who was always suffering from some headache or ailment or another. But this morning there was a huge amount of fuss outside as an Earl's carriage, identifiable by the blue flag hanging from the front, drew up and a fat man with impossibly thin stockinged legs climbed down awkwardly.

Behind the carriage was a cart carrying what looked like a wooden cage. Cinderella frowned. Was that the prisoner? She was sure there was someone inside it.

As the Earl was escorted inside, four footmen ran down the stairs and lifted the cage down. Several of the ordinary servants and merchants who had loitered nearby rushed forward as soon as the Earl had disappeared inside. 'Thief!' one shouted at whoever was locked in the box, jabbing a stick in between the bars. 'They'll send you to the Troll Road!' The footmen shooed them back, but still the jeers and catcalls continued.

Cold flooded Cinderella's stomach. A thief. Her nerves jangled. It couldn't be, could it? There must be hundreds of thieves in the city? She pushed the window open and leaned out into the cold morning air.

'Buttons?' she called down, not caring about the heads that all tilted upwards, staring at her in her clingy robe. 'Buttons? Is that you?'

From between two bars, a pale hand appeared and waved weakly.

'Oh no,' Cinderella muttered, stumbling backwards into her room. 'Oh, no.' She grabbed at her clothes. 'Rose!' she shouted. 'Rose! Something terrible's happened!'

8

'Take the Troll Road . . .'

The evidence against Buttons, or Robin as it turned out was his real name, was overwhelming. Caught red-handed stealing two of the earl's silver spoons – from a collection of one hundred and twenty three which should have been a collection of one hundred and thirty – it did not take long for the masters of various households to marry up visits from the castle boy with small items going missing. It was true in the castle itself, too, where the kitchen staff confirmed that there had been many instances of fresh loaves and cheeses vanishing along with occasional bottles of wine from the cellar. Even those items that had simply been mislaid were being added to the list of Buttons' crimes.

There was no trial to speak of. He was, after all,

accused of crimes against the king. Although judges did exist for the common people – albeit the trials were always a speedy and rather haphazard affair – in this instance Buttons was dealt with behind closed doors in the presence of the king, the prince and the council of nobles. It was no surprise when he was declared guilty and sentenced to take the Troll Road.

Cinderella and Rose had waited in the corridor outside, clasping each other's hands, until the nobles in all their fur-trimmed finery filed out, already discussing the fine lunch that awaited them and Buttons' fate forgotten. The two girls looked at each other and knew what had to be done. Rose would try and talk to the king; Cinderella would tackle the prince.

Cinderella's heart was beating fast when she knocked on the apartment door and stepped inside. She was used to seeing the main bedroom at night and in the dark, merely shapes in the gloom, but the vast space was beautifully decorated in creams and whites with trim in blues and purples. She noticed her diamond shoe had been tossed carelessly on top of a wardrobe so high that it could barely be seen. She wondered when it had no longer merited the velvet cushion.

'What are you doing here?' The prince asked, surprised to see her. He was changing out of his formal clothes, and was stripped to his waist. 'Excited about the Troll Road?' He clearly was, his eyes bright and face flushed. 'Have you ever been?'

Cinderella shook her head and stared at his chest; broad and smooth and exactly how she'd imagined it in her fantasies. A silver chain glinted against his skin. She swallowed and tried to focus her thoughts. 'No, I'm not excited. I'm here to plead for mercy for the servant boy.'

'What?' he frowned. 'You are joking, aren't you? He's a thief. What does he matter to you?

'He's just a boy,' she said. 'And he didn't steal anything too terrible.'

'How would you know?'

'I . . . well, I knew him. Sort of.' A flush crept up her face. 'He sometimes brought me things. Coal when it was cold. He gave other people things too.'

'I didn't realise your mother's marriage had taken her so low that you were relying on gifts from dishonest servants.'

'I don't think he thought he was doing any harm. He's a good . . .'

'Shut up.' The prince's face hardened as he cut her off, his mouth tightening into a thin line. He didn't look so handsome anymore. 'He stole from *us*. He will go to the Troll Road and you will sit beside me as he drops. And you will never say another word about him to me. Do you understand?'

'But—'

'You need to stop behaving like a commoner,' he muttered, pulling a fresh shirt over his head. 'And talking like one. Your voice – it's very coarse. Concentrate on the elocution lessons and leave matters of royal justice to my father and I.'

His words stung. She hadn't thought he could hurt her any more than his cooling affections had done, but seeing his avoidance of her writ large on his face and hearing his words made her want to weep all over again.

'Why are you marrying me?' she asked, quietly. 'You don't love me.'

'I have to.' He looked at her and she saw sadness in his eyes, and she wondered who exactly it was for. 'The whole kingdom is expecting it. If I put you aside now I will look heartless and fickle.'

'Maybe I should leave,' Cinderella said. She found that, after all her childish dreams of living in the castle, the idea of returning to her old home wasn't so terrible after all. Even with the cold and the meagre amounts of food.

'You can't. I'm the prince and you're a commoner.

How much more foolish would I look if you were to go?'

'I thought you wanted me,' she said, and a tear slipped down her cheek. She didn't know what to do. How was this going to be any kind of life?

'I don't know what happened on those nights of the Bride Ball.' The prince slumped into a chair as Cinderella sat on the edge of the bed and they looked at each other, this time as honest strangers rather than supposed lovebirds. 'I wasn't looking for love. I was done with beauty. I wanted to find a practical wife; someone my father would approve of. Someone who understood what being a queen would entail.' He looked over at Cinderella. 'My mother was a noble and she still finds it difficult.'

Cinderella thought once again of Rose, her cool head and warm heart and sense of distance from the world. Rose had never talked of boys or crushes or hung the prince's picture on the wall.

'And then there you were,' he said, and shrugged. 'And from the moment I saw you until the moment they found you, I was driven with a desire I've never known. I thought I loved you. I would have died for you. But then when you arrived here, it was all different.'

'That . . .' Cinderella struggled to find the right

word, '. . . that passion we felt on the balcony, though, surely that's still there?'

'You're like a perfect copy of that girl. I *should* want you. You're beautiful. When I look at you I'm reminded of how I felt that night and yet none of it is there. I can't make myself want you.'

Cinderella stared down at her shoes; blue satin to match her dress, but no magic in them to light a fire in this man she'd been so convinced was her destiny.

'What will we do?' she asked.

'It will get better.' He leaned forward and squeezed her hand. 'You will want for nothing. You will have a good life.' With each sentence Cinderella could feel the walls of the castle tightening around her. His voice hardened and he straightened up, as if only by touching her, he'd felt repulsed. 'But you will behave like a queen and you will come to the Troll Road with me at dusk tomorrow.' Cinderella felt her insides crumble. She couldn't help Buttons. She had no power to.

Rose had no better luck with the king who wasn't even interested in Rose's point that perhaps he had been doing some good with the things he'd taken. A thief was a thief, and the earl was angry. The king would not take the side of a serving boy over a man he relied on for funds and bodies in times of battle.

Buttons was going to the Troll Road and there would be a royal procession there to remind the people that although he was a generous king, his justice was also to be feared.

That night, Cinderella's search was half-hearted. She looked through libraries and studies, filled with books on law and science, where the kings' secretaries drafted new laws and old. She went down to the kitchens and wine cellars but people were still working there, the heart of the castle never really slept, but while she looked she figured that if there were something strange hidden here that her wicked fairy godmother – as she'd come to think of her – was so keen on having, it wouldn't be kept in a place where all and sundry passed by. Her head and heart were filled with thoughts of poor Buttons, locked up in the dungeons with no chance of mercy. He had been so kind to her and others and yet none would step forward to save him. How could they if even Cinderella and Rose couldn't get the king or the prince to intervene. The castle sank into slumber as three o'clock rolled around again and she crept through the narrow corridors at the back of the kitchens until she reached the small back door.

The huntsman was waiting, as he always was. Cinderella was surprised at how relieved she was to see him, and he listened as she blurted out Buttons' fate. He didn't speak until she was finished and then stared into the night, where somewhere an owl hooted.

'The Troll Road,' he said, thoughtfully.

'He'll never survive. No one ever does.' Cinderella thought of all the gifts Buttons had brought. Gifts she'd taken so lightly, without seeing this eventual consequence in the cheeky young man's future. She'd wanted his stories and the game he played for her and hadn't paid attention to the risks he'd been taking. How stupid had she been? Her old life was only a few weeks gone at most, but it felt like a lifetime ago. 'We need to help him.' She looked at the strange man who'd become her nightly companion. 'Surely you can help him? Could we break him out of the dungeons? Give him some money and food and send him to the forest? We'd need a distraction, of course, and maybe some more people to help, but if you have friends . . .'

'The mouse,' he said, cutting her off. His voice was low and his eyes thoughtful as the winter wind lifted his dark hair. 'Get the mouse to him and tell him to keep it in his pocket until they drop him from the bridge.'

'What mouse?' Cinderella frowned. What was he talking about? 'Can't *you* do something?'

'The mouse that's been following you around. *That* mouse. And I am doing something.' He leaned into the doorway, standing close to her. 'You just have to trust me.'

And she found, much as it irked her, that she did.

Dusk was falling as Cinderella picked up the little mouse and tucked him into the bodice of her dress along with a purple silk handkerchief as Rose looked on horrified, leaning on her walking stick. 'What on earth are you doing?'

'I'm not entirely sure.' The mouse wriggled against her breast and Cinderella loosened the ribbons at the front of her dress just in case he was suffocating. He was tickling, that was for sure. 'I'm going to give it to Buttons. Apparently it might help him.'

Rose picked up her heavy fur coat and slid her arms inside. 'You do know what a troll is, don't you? I don't think it's going to be scared of a mouse. Who told you that anyway?'

'A friend.' She tried to be nonchalant but it didn't work. Rose paused and then picked up Cinderella's own pale fur and wrapped it around her shoulders.

'Darling Cinderella, we don't have any friends.'

349

She smiled. 'But I hope whoever this person is, they know something we don't.'

'Me too.' She looked out of the window to the procession gathering below. It was going to be a fine affair, she thought. If only the purpose wasn't so deadly. Beyond the castle walls she could see the route to the bridge lit up by great torches which sank the rest of the city into shade. The route would be lined by smiling people too, caught up in the excitement of seeing royalty and feeding the frenzy. Beautiful and terrifying, that's how the lights looked to her. She wondered how poor Buttons was coping.

'We need to go,' Rose said, pulling open the bedroom door. 'They'll be waiting for you.'

Out in the courtyard Rose found their parents alongside Ivy and the Viscount in the throng and stood with them, and Cinderella was pleased to see that they looked sombre and clearly were not caught up in the excitement of it as so many others were. Side by side, her step-mother and Rose looked elegantly aloof, as she imagined all noble women should, and even her father had taken on an air of sophistication. His back was straighter too, now he had a newspaper to run again. She wondered how he'd report this?

She nodded and gave them a small smile and they smiled back and for the thousandth time she wished she'd realised how lucky she was to have her family at all instead of living in her fantasies about a dead mother and having a royal lover.

A hush fell across the gathering as chains creaked and cogs ground against each and as the prisoner was brought up in the lift from the dungeons so far below. Cinderella didn't know if it was her imagination but the night seemed to fill with a stench of rot and damp as if the air coming up with the cage hadn't been fresh in a long, long time. Ahead she could see her grey pony, a gift from her fiancé, waiting to be mounted, and as the torch bearers and servants pulled back, she found she was almost alone when the gate opened. Buttons stood there, squinting even though it was nearly dark, with a fearsome, chain-mailed guard on either side of him. They pushed him forward. His hands were tied in front of him and he stumbled but didn't fall. The crowd jeered slightly.

'Wait!' Cinderella called, as they were about to haul him onto the back of a cart for the cold journey to his fate. All eyes turned to her. The prince, already on horseback, started to call something out to her, but the king grabbed his arm. To reprimand his bride-to-be in public would not be chivalrous.

She drew herself up tall and walked towards Buttons. As she reached him, she pulled the mouse and silk handkerchief from their spot, nestled against her thumping heart.

'A king must be just, and justice must be served,' she said, her voice ringing loud and clear across the impatient crowd in the courtyard, whinnying horses and stamping boots. 'But a princess must be gentle and kind. And so, to honour my husband to be and his majesty the king, I offer this traitor a good luck token' – she held her hand up for a moment and then thrust the contents into Buttons' pocket – 'and wish him a swift and painless end.' She held Buttons' gaze for a moment before whispering in a rush, 'Keep it with you.' He gave her the tiniest nod in reply.

The mouse delivered, Cinderella turned back to face the king and fell into a low curtsey, before walking towards her waiting pony.

'Your gesture is most becoming of a royal princess,' the king nodded at her. Even the prince gave her a half-smile. She reserved her own for a glance at Rose, standing at the castle wall to see the procession off, who beamed approvingly back. Cinderella was definitely getting better at the game.

She didn't look at Buttons once during the procession through the streets, and pulled her fur-lined hood over her head so no one could see she didn't share the excitement of the rest of the parade. People jeered as the cart went by and every now and then something rotten was thrown his way, hitting the poor, cold boy. Even though he was on his way to his death they seemed to want to punish him more. She scanned the crowds, lit up as they were by the high burning torches on the path, and wondered how many of them Buttons had helped with gifts of food or money when times were desperate. Perhaps they were the most aggressive in their shouting for fear that he might give up their names as the bridge grew closer.

Finally they reached the edge of the city and the bridge loomed ahead of them, the forest dark on the other side. Cinderella's stomach twisted as she saw the thick stone rising up from the overgrown banks of the dead river below. Her father and step-mother had never brought them here as children and neither had she been one of those who'd come to play at being prisoners and trolls near its edge before getting shooed away by the soldiers who guarded it. The bridge was wider than she'd expected, maybe twenty feet across, and as soon as the heavily armoured bridge-keeper leaned over the side and lit the torches that hung there, a fearsome growling rumbled from underneath, so deep and angry she was sure the ground beneath her horse's feet trembled with it.

They took Buttons down from the cart, and the royal procession watched in silence as he was delivered into the Bridge Guard's hands. He looked tiny between them. The Bridge Guard were known for their size and fearsome, silent natures, and all that could be seen below their helmets were their beards. Cinderella thought they looked like armoured bears, and she shivered seeing her friend between them. Buttons did not look her way, but she was proud to see that he wasn't crying nor begging for mercy. His eyes were defiant.

The troll roared again, knowing fresh meat was coming its way, and Cinderella flinched. What had the huntsman been thinking? How could a mouse be any use against such a creature.

The night was dark around them, dusk having been eaten up in the hour's walk to the bridge, and as Buttons, his hands untied, walked into the middle of the bridge, Cinderella wished all the torches would fail so she wouldn't have to watch.

'You have been found guilty of theft and treason,' the crier called out to him. 'Do you have anything to say before the sentence is carried out?'

In the flickering light, Buttons simply smiled. It was his cheeky grin, the one she'd taken so much for granted in their friendship. A brave smile. He'd known what risks he was taking all along and it hadn't stopped him. She hadn't paid attention to his words of warning about castle life but now she understood. She'd only seen him as a boy, but he'd been far more grown up than she was.

'I'll be back for more silver,' Buttons said. 'There's plenty to go round and people are hungry.' He looked down at his feet. 'Not as hungry as the troll sounds, mind you, but maybe I won't be to his taste.'

'Do it,' the king growled, unimpressed by this lack of repentance from his subject.

Buttons pulled the handkerchief and the mouse out of his pocket and his smile fell as he looked down confused. Cinderella strained to see. Something was happening there – something was changing.

The largest of the Bridge Guard tugged at a heavy wooden lever at the edge of the bank, and it squealed at being forced out of winter's grip and into use. The trapdoor opened and Buttons fell, vanishing from sight to the dead riverbed below. The troll roared. And then roared some more.

'Please,' Cinderella rested her hand on the prince's arm. 'Can we leave now?' If she was forced to hear poor Buttons screaming then it would tear her heart apart.

'Of course we're leaving,' the prince said, already

turning his horse around. 'We're not barbaric.' Cinderella looked into his perfectly beautiful face and wondered if he had any idea how ridiculous that sounded after what they'd just done.

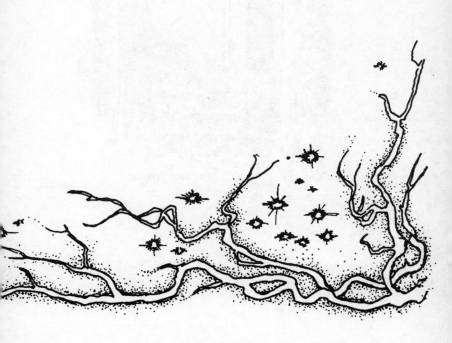

9

'A secret'

Dinner was waiting for them at the castle, but Cinderella couldn't eat. Instead she pushed her food around her plate until it made a heap at one side that wasn't fooling anyone, but unlike when she was a child and food was scarce, no one told her off or forced her to eat it. She wondered perhaps if it was simply that no one noticed. The prince and the king were talking and laughing and the queen just smiled occasionally and commented on the fine quality of the venison and how she hoped the weather would break soon and they could all get back to the hunt.

Cinderella's insides churned as a servant took her plate away. She itched to see the huntsman and hear about his plan to save Buttons. Had it even been possible? There were always rumours of people surviving taking the Troll Road and escaping to the forest, but as far as she knew none of them had ever returned to the city, so it was all just myth and legend. The huntsman wouldn't come until three and that was four long hours away. Time that she should spend searching the castle for whatever it was the fairy godmother was so keen for her to find. She'd been through so many of the rooms she was sure she'd never find whatever it was, and what then? Would the fairy godmother transport *her* to the Troll Road for her uselessness? The way their bargain had turned out she wouldn't be surprised. She looked across the mahogany table to the prince whose face was ever more handsome in the candlelight.

She also wanted to know where he disappeared to every night. Was it something as simple as a serving girl? Or one of the other ladies of the court? She wondered why she cared – for all her worry about his feelings towards her, she hadn't really taken much time to think about how her feelings for him had changed. Had it ever been more than a childish crush? She'd fallen in love with a picture and a dream. The reality was different. Still, the image of his empty bedroom stuck in her mind and her curiosity was beginning to overwhelm her.

She'd follow him, she decided, as the apple pie arrived laced with Chantilly cream. The scent of sweet apples was like perfume in the air and her mouth suddenly watered. Following the prince and searching the castle weren't necessarily different things — especially if he was going somewhere she hadn't yet explored. She bit into the pie and the pastry melted on her tongue and cinnamon apple exploded sharply on her tongue. That's what she'd do. She'd follow him.

After dinner, while the king and the prince drank brandy and discussed whatever it was men talked about when women weren't present, Cinderella ran back to her room and breathlessly changed out of her stiff formal dress into a looser, lighter one that she could move quickly and quietly in. Barefoot, she made her way back to the drawing room and hid behind a thick curtain, peering through the gap at the double doors. She didn't have to wait long before the prince came out, nodding a polite goodnight to his father and leaving the king to the fire and the quiet and his thoughts.

Cinderella saw his shoulders slump as soon as the door closed and he paused for a moment before walking away. She gave him a head start and then crept out from between the curtains and followed, staying close to the walls. It was late and most of the castle was sleeping or in their rooms; the only sound was the click of his heels on marble echoing as she snuck along behind him.

Her heart sank as they reached his apartments, Cinderella still on the stairs, peering with one eye round the wall to watch him. He'd stopped outside his door. Was this going to be the first night he actually went to bed? Surely it couldn't be? Surely—

The prince leaned his forehead against the closed door and took a deep breath as if battling some internal dilemma. Cinderella's heart raced as his jaw clenched and he stood up tall. What was plaguing him? Surely if he was just sleeping with a serving girl that wouldn't cause any inner crisis. Unless he was beginning to fall in love with Cinderella, of course. Her heart leapt slightly at that. Even if she wasn't sure that she loved him, she wanted him to love her. He sighed again, tapped his head gently against the wood two times and then turned away. Cinderella crept after him.

The servants' quarters – with the exception of the king and queen's personal maids and footmen

– were mainly located in the lower levels of the castle, and that was where Cinderella had expected them to head. The prince, however, didn't lead her down into that hubbub of warmth and life. Instead, he walked steadily, with a sense of purpose rather than urgency, along several corridors that twisted and turned and then led into the heart of the building. It seemed far from the places that Cinderella knew, where windows let in so much light. This part of the castle she'd never seen before. She wondered how many months she'd have taken to find it herself.

The corridors were darker, only occasional lamps lit on the walls, and here and there statues and pictures had been covered to protect them from dust. The air was cold and smelt slightly of damp as if no fires had been lit in the surrounding rooms for years. The prince's shadow stretched long behind him and Cinderella let it guide her in his wake. She wondered for a moment what would happen if she lost him? Would she ever find her way back to the castle that she knew? Or would she wander these rooms screaming until she died? She wished she'd taken a hunk of bread from dinner and left a trail of breadcrumbs to follow should she need to. She shivered and crept closer. She wouldn't lose him. She didn't have a choice.

Finally they came to a spiral stone stairwell and the prince began to climb it, Cinderella behind him. They climbed for several minutes and Cinderella hoped the prince wouldn't hear her breathing as it became more laboured. There were no lights here, but a cold breeze zigzagged in the small space, and here and there tiny holes had been cut into the thick stone, perhaps for bowmen to shoot through a long time ago when the kingdoms were still to learn to keep their battles away from their capitals. Through them, shards of moonlight landed on patches of stone and Cinderella caught glimpses of abstract parts of the prince's body; a leg, a shoe, a slice of torso, as the air grew colder and the stairs turned into a level floor.

She'd thought they must be in one of the turrets, but instead it was another corridor. There was no pretence at decoration here, however, the walls only hung with cobwebs that extended from their corners, covered in dust. Grit dug into her bare feet as she hid in the shadows and watched the prince as he finally came to a halt outside a door. Unlike the others they'd passed this one had been polished recently, the dark wood shining and the iron that studded it black and gleaming. The prince reached around his neck and undid a chain. A gold key glinted in the gloom and Cinderella pressed herself against the wall as he glanced around before sliding it into the lock.

The door swung open and then he was gone. Cinderella scurried forward in time to hear the grating of metal on metal as he locked the room once again from the inside. Her heart thumped and she pressed her eye to the tiny gaps where the hinges sat. What was he doing in there? What did he have in there that was so precious he'd locked it up so far from the central hub of the castle? He was the prince – surely he didn't have to worry about anything being stolen? Why hide whatever it was? And why only visit in the middle of the night when everyone was asleep? She could see nothing through the tiny gap and pressed her ear against it instead. She could hear something; the scrape of a chair, and then his voice. He was talking, but she couldn't make out his words. She frowned and listened harder, holding her breath. There was only one voice: his. Who or what was he talking to?

She stared at the door wishing she could see through the wood. What was in there that was making him so secretive?

A secret.

That's why he kept the key around his neck. That's why he only came in the middle of the night. And that was why he kept whatever it was in this forgotten part of the castle. The king didn't know about it. No one did. Her face flushed with excitement. Could this be what the fairy godmother had wanted her to find?

She shivered in the quiet and the cold for an hour, listening to his voice burbling through the wood and then, when the key turned in the lock again, she darted back to the shadows, this time on the far side. Her hiding place didn't matter. He was lost in his own thoughts when he emerged, and as soon as he'd secured the room he placed the key on its chain back round his neck and tucked it under his shirt before heading back towards the stairs, oblivious of Cinderella behind him.

This time she paid attention to the journey. Her searching of the castle had honed her directional skills and at every turning they made she logged some small landmark, whether it be a covered picture or a crack in the paintwork on the walls. Finally, the lights grew brighter and she recognised her surroundings.

She stopped and allowed the prince to slip away from her, knowing that he would be going back to his bedroom. Whatever need had driven him was sated by the secret contents of that locked room.

A secret

Somewhere a clock chimed as if to welcome her back to the world of warmth and light and beauty. It struck three times. The huntsman would be waiting. Her heart leapt and she raced down the stairs, red hair flying out behind her, flames against the wall. Perhaps he'd have good news of Buttons. And she had news of her own.

She arrived at the back door breathless and yanked it open. He was leaning against the wall, just as he always was.

'I think I've found something! There's a room! Somewhere forgotten! And he keeps the key around his neck. The prince! It's where he goes at night. Do you think that's what she wants?'

She was dancing from foot to foot with excitement and it took a moment for her to realise something was wrong. The huntsman was leaning against the wall, that was true, but not with his normal laconic elegance. His head was down and one arm clutched against his side where a dark stain was spreading through his clothes. Her stomach shrank into the pit of her belly.

'What happened?' She stepped outside, not caring about the icy cold that stung her bare feet. 'You're hurt.' Finally, he looked up.

'I'll be okay.'

His eyes were black with pain and his mouth pressed tight. Blood stained the side of his face.

'No, you won't.' Without thinking she pulled one of his arms around her shoulder. 'Come on.' He was heavy against her, using all his strength to stay on his feet, and she tried to murmur encouragement to him as they negotiated the route back up to her bedroom. In the light she could see that half of his tunic was sodden with blood and his tanned skin was pale. She choked back tears that suddenly sprang hot in the back of her eyes. The huntsman was always *there*. He couldn't die. He just couldn't.

Thankful it was the dead of night, they finally made it to her apartments and once inside she locked the door behind them.

'I shouldn't be here,' he muttered.

'Shut up,' she said. 'And take your shirt off.'

He gave her a half-smile and raised an eyebrow. 'You might not get my best performance but I'm willing to give it a shot.'

'Just do it.' She flashed him an angry look, but inside her heart leapt. He wasn't dying at least. Badly injured perhaps, but not dying.

She filled a pan of water from the large jug on her table and hung it over the fire to warm, before turning the lights down and creeping through the connecting door into Rose's room.

Rose rolled over and murmured, but didn't wake, and Cinderella checked her drawers as quietly as possible until she found the box of bandages and salves she knew Rose would have, exactly as she always had in their old house for every time Cinderella fell or scraped her knee or banged her head while playing. She silently thanked her step-sister and crept back to her own room, closing the door behind her.

She left the lighting soft in case it would creep under the door and wake Rose and fetched the warm water. The huntsman had peeled his filthy shirt off and she could see the gash that ran up his side, his skin pulled apart and his flesh exposed. Thankfully it didn't look too deep. She took a soft towel from the table and dipped it in the water, carefully starting to wipe the blood from his chest. His skin was tanned and the muscles in his stomach twitched as the cloth touched him. The prince's chest was pale and smooth. The huntsman's was tanned and scarred and dark hair curled across his sternum. She wondered what it would be like to run her fingers through it and feel the strong muscles underneath, and she swallowed involuntarily as a heat flooded through her body that had nothing to do with the fire. She could feel him watching her as she washed the edges of his wound, the atmosphere between them suddenly electric.

'What happened?' she asked, desperate to break it. She dipped her fingers in the pot of salve and smoothed it over the long cut. His skin was warm beneath her touch and he gasped and swore under his breath.

'Don't be a child,' she said, and smiled up at him from her place on the floor and for the first time she realised how very handsome he was. She didn't know what she felt about him, this stranger. Sometimes she was sure she didn't like him very much at all, and yet her heart was beating so fast she thought it would burst out of her chest. Her skin tingled with a sudden urge to feel his hands on her. 'Tell me what happened,' she said again, wiping her hands.

'It doesn't matter.' The huntsman pressed a pad against his wound and held the end of the bandage against his stomach as she passed it round his back and wound it tight against the dressed wound. 'All that matters is that your friend is safe. He's in the woods.'

'Buttons?' Cinderella looked up. 'But how . . .' The questioned drained away as she thought of the gash on his side. It hadn't been from a knife or a sword, it was too ragged at the edges. A claw, however . . .

'*You* fought the troll?' She got to her feet and

stared at him as he tucked the end of the abandoned bandage away and stood up.

'Sadly I didn't kill it.'

'But I don't understand. How did you get past the guards? How did you—?'

'It doesn't matter,' he said.

He stood up, and they were so close the bodice of her dress was nearly brushing his bare skin.

'You saved him?' she said. She was breathless. She couldn't help it. She felt like she had on the balcony at the Bride Ball but this time there were no charmed slippers to encourage the heat.

'You wanted me to.' His voice was cracked slightly and as his eyes travelled over her face she knew he felt the same passion she did. He reached for her, one hand sliding round her neck, the touch of his rough fingers sending sparks through her whole body, and he wrapped them in her hair. He spun her round so quickly she gasped. They were facing the large, ornate mirror that hung almost the length of the wall.

'I want to watch you,' he breathed into her neck. He held her tight against him and she was sure if he'd let go, her legs would give way beneath her. 'I want *you* to watch you. See the woman you are.' Their eyes locked in the mirror and he lowered his mouth, tracing his lips against her neck as one hand undid the laces at the front of her dress. She moaned and her head tilted sideways, as he breathed on her, barely touching her with his lips and tongue, as his fingers expertly sought out her nipple, teasing it, all the time his dark eyes watching her reactions from beneath the hood of his soft, dark hair. She pressed back into him feeling the hardness there and she reached a hand behind her to touch him. He grabbed her wrist firmly and stopped her, smiling at her reflection.

'Slowly, princess,' he whispered.

'I want you to kiss me,' she said, breaking his hold and twisting round to face him. Her dress was falling free, and he stared at her for a moment and then pushed her up against the mirror. Her arms slid round his waist and she ran her fingers up his naked spine. She could feel scar tissue breaking the smoothness of his skin and her stomach tingled all the more for it. This was no spoilt prince. This was a man who'd fought a monster because she asked him for help. He ran one hand up over her breast and to her neck, pinning her firmly against the glass. As their lips moved so close together she could feel the warmth of his breath and the strength of his hand and she thought she would explode. She gripped his back, the strange skin of the long scar on his back heightening her excitement and then, out of no-where, her head was filled with the image of brown fur. A twitching nose.

Scar tissue. On his back. The troll.

Oh no. Oh no, it couldn't be. Could it?

'Wait just one minute.' Just as his lips had been about to brush hers, she pushed him away, the pres-sure of her hand touching his bandaged side enough to make him gasp and pull back.

'What? What's the matter?'

She stared at him as the realisation dawned on her. 'You've got a scar on your back.'

'So what?'

'Just like the mouse. The one you insisted I give Buttons.' Surely it couldn't be? But the mouse had always been so odd, following first Buttons and then her. What kind of field mouse did that? She raised one shaking finger at him. 'You're the mouse, aren't you? That's how you got to the troll.'

He stared at her and then shrugged. 'She cursed me. And then when she needed me, she half-lifted it. Man by night, mouse by day.'

'The fairy godmother?' Cinderella's eyes widened.

'If that's what you want to call her. She's a queen, and she can be a bitch.'

373

'But why? I mean . . . what did you do? And . . .' Her head was filled with questions which were abruptly crushed by the sudden weight of memories. 'Oh god,' she wheezed, suddenly almost unable to breathe with the horror of it. 'You've seen me naked. You watched me in the bath.' Her eyes widened. 'I put you down my top!' She stared at him. 'You bastard.'

She turned away and covered her mouth as another memory dawned. Buttons. The mouse had been there when Buttons . . . . 'My kitchen. You *saw* . . . you watched . . .'

'What was I supposed to do?' he said, the start of a smile twinkling in his eyes.

'Close your eyes at least? Run away.'

'I'm a hot blooded man,' he grinned, a lop-sided, infuriatingly handsome expression. 'To be fair, inside your dress it was too dark to see anything. But the bath, and Buttons well, that was amazing . . . what could I do?'

She let out some sound halfway between a growl and a shriek and slapped him hard across the face. He was unbelievable! How could she even have thought about kissing him? Had she forgotten how much he irritated her? She stormed to the door and unlocked it with shaking hands. 'Get out,' she said. 'And get me the other slipper back from that witch.'

'What do you need the slipper for?' He frowned slightly.

'Just get it. Then she can have her prize and then we can both be free of that woman's meddling.' She glowered at him. 'And of each other.'

'Fine,' he strode towards her, his jaw locked. She wasn't sure if it was in pain or anger or lust and she didn't care. He was impossible. He was uncouth. What had she been thinking? She had almost kissed him! He stopped before her, in the doorway, and her heart started racing again despite herself. 'If that's what you want,' he said. 'Next time you need someone saving from a troll do it yourself.'

She pushed him out of the door and locked it again, her breathing loud and angry, before throwing herself down on the bed like she used to as a teenager. She wanted to cry with the shame of it. How could he have just sat on the side of the bath and watched her doing *that*? He must have been laughing at her. God, she'd been so stupid. She punched the pillow and then buried her face in it. She hated him. She really, really did.

10

'She'd finish it once and for all . . .'

She'd covered the mirrors over, for once wanting some complete quiet so she could think. There was nothing to see anyway. Black ice and slush filling the roads. The occasional tradesman heading to work early; bakers and butchers determined to catch what trade they could. She needed to lift the winter spell soon, but it came from a dark place in her soul that had a life of its own and was difficult to manage. But the people would need to eat and there was only so much ore the exhausted dwarves could mine in order to trade for grain. The kingdom – her kingdom – needed to thrive again and she had to make it happen. Yet she couldn't make the ice inside herself melt, so how was she supposed to save the land?

But maybe things would change soon. Perhaps they already were. Outside, the sky was turning from black to blue with hints of purple as dawn bruised the horizon. For once there were no heavy clouds gathering at the start of a new day, as if the shivers of excitement she'd felt had swept them away. She drank more wine and stared out at nothing. She knew she should steel herself for disappointment but she couldn't help the warmth in the pit of her stomach. Her heart thumped hard against her ribs. It had been doing so for hours, ever since the huntsman arrived, frozen and exhausted, and asked for the slipper. He'd been wounded but wouldn't say how, and refused help from her medical men. He'd been bandaged well enough, he said. By better hands than anything she could offer. She didn't argue with him. It would take far more than a flesh wound to kill off the huntsman.

The slipper.

The girl wanted the slipper. Lilith had frozen at that and for a moment all the servants in the castle had inadvertently shivered as if someone had walked over their graves. The huntsman said Cinderella hadn't told him what her plan was, only that she'd found a secret room and the prince had the key to it. She'd smiled at that. It hadn't taken the girl too long to realise that if you're going to hunt for something hidden, you first look for some-one who's hiding something. Her charming prince hadn't managed to love her for long, it seemed.

She gave the huntsman the slipper and lifted the curse for long enough to send him back with it. He'd get twenty-four hours as a man; then he'd turn back into a mouse again forever. That, however, was his problem not hers.

The minutes were ticking by eternally slowly. She wondered how far he'd got on his journey. She wondered what would happen when he gave her the slipper and Cinderella got into the locked room. Mainly she wondered if this could really be it. The end of her long search. Restless, she got to her feet and wandered into the warmer ante-chamber where all her treasures were laid out. She hoped for the comfort they normally brought her but felt nothing. In the far corner the cabinet door creaked open.

'She truly is the most beautiful in all the land . . .'

She didn't bother trying to shut the thing up. It was pointless. Instead, she put down her wine glass and walked with more purpose than she had in a long time to the stairs leading down to the heart of the castle. She would wait for them at the edge of the kingdom. It would be safer that way, depending on the outcome, and it was time she got out into the world. And if the huntsman's girl really had found the prize after all this time then she'd finish it once and for all.

It was cold and crisp but, for the first time in a long time, the sun shone over the kingdom that day as the queen with no mercy rode into the forest.

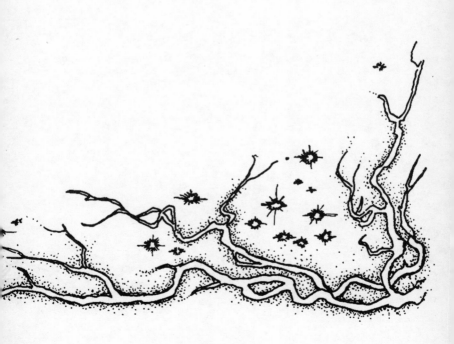

11
'I can take care of myself ...'

It was late afternoon and Cinderella had just finished retracing her steps of the previous night,
making small marks on the walls with a piece of
chalk at regular intervals just to make sure she didn't
take a wrong turn later, when she bumped into Rose
in the corridor at the base of the stairs.

'I've been looking for you everywhere,' Rose said,
frowning. 'You missed lunch with father and mother.
They're worried about you.' The wooden cane she'd
been using had been replaced by a slender silver one
but she was barely leaning on it at all. The king had
sent for the finest shoe makers in the land and they
had worked tirelessly to make her beautiful shoes
that helped her balance. It didn't stop Cinderella feeling guilty whenever she saw her. If she hadn't been

so selfish and stupid then it would be Rose preparing for a royal wedding, her family would be financially secure, and she herself would be free.

'Sorry,' she said, trying to nonchalantly edge Rose away from the stairwell. 'I forgot. How are they?'

'They're fine. Surprisingly so. I think what happened with my foot . . . well, it sobered mother up.' She smiled. 'Don't get me wrong, she's happy to be back at court, but I think she's more excited about father setting up the newspaper again.'

Cinderella smiled absently, but her mind was already racing ahead. What time would the huntsman be back? Would he have the slipper? But more and more her thoughts were filled with wanting to know exactly what the prince kept behind that locked door. 'Oh,' she said, her voice dropping to a whisper. 'I think Buttons is safe. He's in the woods.'

'How do you know?' Rose's eyes widened. 'Are you sure?'

'Yes, my friend told me.' Some kind of friend, Cinderella thought. She could still die of shame when she thought about what she'd done so brazenly in front of him. She could only hope that mice didn't have very good eyesight. She began to walk away knowing that whatever secrets she was involved in she still had a teacher waiting for her in the music room who was determined to force a delicate melody from her fingers, which were proving remarkably defiant. After that it would be poetry recital practice. Both, she'd discovered, bored her to tears. Being a noble woman wasn't quite the life of love and laughter she'd fantasised about.

'Cinderella,' Rose called after her, and she stopped and turned.

'What?'

'What is going on? I know all this wedding planning must be overwhelming for you, but what are you hiding from me?' Rose had one hand on the hip of her plum dress. 'I went into your room to find you and there was some blood on your rug. And you've been in my medical kit.'

'Don't go in my room!' Cinderella snapped. Her skin burned. She hadn't even checked the carpets for drops of the huntsman's blood – she'd been too angry with him to think so practically. She'd need to find time to clean that up. The servants wouldn't say anything, but it was better to be safe than sorry.

'I'm just worried,' Rose recoiled slightly. 'That's all.'

'I'm sorry,' Cinderella said. She didn't want to upset Rose. She'd done her enough harm already which she would never be able to put right. 'I didn't mean to sound so harsh. I'm fine. I really am.'

Rose said nothing but she still looked suspicious. Cinderella turned and headed fast down the corridor before any more questions came. She didn't want to lie, not if she didn't have to, but she didn't want to involve Rose either. This was her problem, she was going to deal with it by herself and she'd do whatever it took to get into that room. She was marrying the man anyway, so she would have to do it at some point, and it wasn't that long ago that she'd been desperate to be alone with him. Still, her stomach twisted nervously. It all sounded good in theory. But how would it go in practice? She pushed the worry out of her head. If the huntsman didn't come back with the slipper then it would all amount to nothing in the end.

He came as she was dressing for dinner. She'd styled her hair as she'd worn it for the Bride Ball, her face was powdered and painted and she was perfuming her skin when the knock on the door came. She pulled a robe on and opened it. There he was. Heat rushed to her face and her heart thumped. She lifted her chin. She had nothing to be ashamed of. He was the one who should be embarrassed.

'Where did you get that?' she asked, looking at the footman livery he was wearing.

'Don't worry, no one got hurt,' he answered, stepping inside. 'Men in taverns, however, should be more careful where they leave their uniforms when they get distracted by a warm body,'

'Have you got it?' she asked.

He held up a small brown bag and flinched slightly. His injury was clearly still causing him a lot of pain and her heart softened slightly. 'Why don't you sit down?' she nodded towards the chair. He did as he was told and she opened the bag and pulled the diamond shoe out.

'You look like you're getting ready to go into battle,' he said, his eyes studying her.

'Battle?'

'All the war paint.'

'Are you trying to insult me?' Anger flared up in her stomach again. Why did she find him so confusing? He'd risked his life to save Buttons because she'd asked him to, and yet he could be so infuriating. She always felt so uncomfortable under his gaze. Why was that?

'No, you look beautiful,' he said. 'I'm just curious about all this effort for dinner. And what you're planning to do with that slipper.'

Cinderella sat at her dressing table with her back to him. It was just easier that way.

'I know where the second slipper is,' she said, fixing a diamond necklace around her neck. 'And I need to get the key.'

'Which he keeps on a chain under his shirt,' the huntsman said dryly.

Cinderella's back stiffened slightly. 'That's right.'

There was a long pause. 'I see,' he said.

'I'll wait until he's asleep and then steal it. We can get whatever's in there and then we're done.' She skipped over the meat of her plan. Why did she suddenly feel awkward? And – if she was honest with herself – more than a little bit scared?

'You've got it all figured out then,' the huntsman said.

'Yes.' She swallowed hard. 'Anyway, you should go. I need to get dressed.'

Behind her, he pulled himself to his feet. 'Why bother?' he asked. 'Clothes don't seem to be part of your plan.'

His words stung but she didn't turn round as he limped towards the door.

'But as long as you know what you're doing,' he said. 'It's not my business.'

'I can take care of myself,' she snapped. Tears

sprung to the back of her eyes suddenly and out of nowhere. How else did he expect her to get the key from
the prince and then return it without it being noticed?
And he was her husband-to-be. It was hardly . . . well,
hardly like the things the girls in the taverns – girls
the huntsman no doubt spent all his time with – did.

'I'll take your word for it,' he said, and then the
door closed behind him and he was gone. Cinderella
stared at her reflection and her whole body trembled
for several minutes; anger, unhappiness and something else she couldn't quite figure out all roiling
into a storm of emotion inside her.

War paint. Maybe it was. She certainly didn't
recognise the woman staring back at her from the
mirror. A lady of the court with tamed and lacquered
hair and painted features. Still, she thought. Perhaps
it was best to think of herself as someone else for this
evening. It might work better that way. She peeled
off her robe and pulled on a long green dress with
a hem which reached the ground. It was perfect for
disguising the fact that she would be wearing two
different shoes.

The warm slipper fitted her perfectly, just as she'd
expected, and on her other foot she wore another
with a similar heel. She was ready. Her heart beat
fast in her chest. There was no going back now.

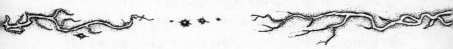

Even though she was only wearing one magic slipper, she could see the effect over dinner. Instead of simply casting a bored eye over her before sitting down, this time the prince frowned slightly and then smiled, before coming round to her side of the table and pulling her chair out for her.

'Thank you,' she said.

He leaned down and spoke softly into her ear, his breath tickling the back of her neck. 'You look beautiful tonight.'

She smiled and, when he sat down, lifted her glass to click against his but she only sipped at her drink, even though she longed for the bravery that came with wine. She needed to keep her wits about her for later. The prince, however, drank his.

All through the meal he talked to her, attentive to her every need, asking about how her music lessons were coming and telling her how excited he was for the wedding to come quickly. It was all the conversation Cinderella had wished for when she first came to the castle but now, somehow, although she smiled and laughed in all the right places, it bored her. *He* bored her. She thought of the picture she'd kept on her wall in their old house, how she'd dreamed of meeting her handsome prince and falling in love, and now, as he talked of the hunt and his friends and various balls that were being arranged in their honour, she realised that his personality had about as much depth as that picture.

The king and queen smiled approvingly – if not without a little surprise – at how engaged their son was with his ill-chosen bride and when the meal finally drew to a close the king suggested that perhaps the prince should walk Cinderella back to her apartments. The prince didn't argue and the young couple left the dining room arm in arm.

'I was wondering, your highness,' Cinderella started, her heart racing so hard in her chest that she was sure he must be able to hear it, 'if you still had my other shoe from the ball. I want to wear them with a new dress.'

'Yes, of course I do,' he said, looking down and smiling at her. 'It's in my apartments. We can go there now if you'd like.'

Her stomach came up to her throat as she nodded. There was no turning back now. Why was she suddenly so nervous? He was handsome. She'd wanted him for such a long time. Maybe when she had the other shoe on, all the passion she'd felt at the ball would come back. Maybe if she *kept* the shoes on, he'd love her forever and she'd live happily ever after with a husband who adored her. It was an empty thought. Who really wanted an enchanted love? She hadn't, even before the ball. She'd just presumed they'd fall in love if given the opportunity, as if love was something easy and took nothing but a pretty face and a longing for it to achieve. She realised she felt nothing for him and, in a way, that was worse than if she hated him.

Her mismatched heels clicked down the corridor below her dress as they drew closer and closer to his rooms. His arm pulled her tighter to him; a rare gesture of affection. He was talking softly to her of their future, but it was drowned out by the hum of blood and the thumping of her heart.

A footman with his back to them was polishing the silver arms of a decorative chair just past the prince's door and she suddenly felt an overwhelming urge to talk to him if just to delay stepping inside. She bit the inside of her cheek instead. There was no point in delaying. She needed to get the key and discover the contents of that room. Delaying now wouldn't prevent the inevitable. At least the prince was a little hazy from wine and if everything went well would soon be asleep.

She took a deep breath and stood tall. She was no longer a foolish little girl. She was a woman and it was time to start behaving like one. She'd got herself into this – it was her responsibility to see it through.

The effect was almost instant. He'd retrieved the shoe from the top of the wardrobe and as soon as she'd slipped it onto her other foot she saw the change in his expression. The lights were low in the room and his eyes glazed as he looked at her.

'How could I have forgotten how beautiful you are?' he said softly, more to himself than her as he walked towards her. Her heart thumped as his hand slid round her waist, his arm pulling her tight. She felt as if she couldn't breathe. She lifted one hand and rested it on his arm. It was muscular and firm and his chest was broad and strong. He smelled of light cologne and body heat. His white shirt was un-buttoned at the collar and the patch of skin she could see was pale and hair-free. Suddenly, she felt as if she might cry.

'Oh, Cinderella,' he breathed as he slid one hand into her hair and tilted her head back, exactly as the huntsman had done, but this time she felt nothing.

His lips lowered to hers and kissed her, gently at first and then, as she felt him becoming aroused and pressing against her, with more urgency.

Her spine stiffened. She waited for the rush of passion she'd felt before, but none came. Instead, she began to squirm in his arms, trying to twist her head away and break their embrace. He held her tighter, mistaking her movements for excitement. His breathing was coming hard and he was lost in his lust.

'No, look . . .' she started to say as he broke away for air, but then his mouth was on hers again, and one of his hands was tugging at the laces of her dress as he turned her around, moving them towards the bed.

'No, we shouldn't . . . I don't—'

He wasn't listening to her as he pushed her backwards and started tugging at his trousers. He was murmuring under his breath, no doubt sweet nothings, but Cinderella didn't want to hear them. She no longer cared about the key or the room upstairs, she just wanted to be free of his grip so she could run away and keep on running. She tried to push him off her but he grabbed her arms and held them down with one hand as his mouth moved down her neck and towards her breasts. His other hand reached under her skirt, and he groaned as his fingers felt their way up her leg.

'No, please stop . . .' Cinderella said again, aware that sobs were beginning to choke her throat. This wasn't what she wanted. This wasn't how she'd thought it would be. She desperately tried to free herself of the charmed shoes, but they were fixed tightly to her feet. She closed her eyes and tried to withdraw into herself as her body continued to struggle against him. His hand reached higher and higher, pushing her skirt up and . . .

. . . and then the weight of him was gone as someone hauled him off the bed with a grunt and the prince cried out in surprise. Cinderella looked up dazed, her vision bleary.

'How dare you!' the prince hissed at the footman as the two men faced each other at the end of the bed.

The footman punched him hard, sending the prince reeling.

'Shit,' the attacker said and winced, touching his side, before punching the recovering prince again and sending him to the floor clutching his mouth.

Cinderella's eyes widened. This was no ordinary footman. It was the huntsman. *Her* huntsman. She scrabbled to her feet and without even straightening her dress ran to him and flung her arms round his neck. He reeled back slightly and put one hand around her.

'Thank you,' she said, looking up at him. His skin was rough and he smelt of the forest and she felt a rush of warmth tingling through her body.

'You're welcome.' He looked down at her. 'But just so you know, this plan stank.'

'You!' The prince was on his feet, his bottom lip was bleeding. 'I thought you were dead.' His face flushed as his passion mixed with anger.

'You never bothered to find out,' the huntsman said.

Cinderella looked from one to the other. 'You know each other?'

'That's a story for another time,' the huntsman said. He pulled a knife out from under his jacket. 'And now I think we'll take that key around your neck.'

'You'll never get away with this,' the prince hissed. He looked at Cinderella. 'My darling, step away from him. I love you. I—'

'Oh, take those bloody shoes off, woman,' the huntsman cut in. 'We'll never get any sense out of him until you do.' Cinderella did as she was told and the prince's face immediately fell, confused. He stared at her as if he was looking at a stranger.

'What do you want?' he asked. 'What's going on here?'

'You tell us,' the huntsman said, nodding at Cinderella to tie the prince's hands behind his back. She rummaged in the wardrobe and found a grey silk necktie and used that, pulling the a tight knot around his wrists. Then she reached around his neck and undid the chain. The gold key hanging there shone brightly.

'Got it,' she said, smiling.

'You can't go into that room,' the prince growled, his face darkening. 'No one knows what's in there. It's mine. It's private.'

'Oh, I think I have a pretty good idea,' the huntsman said, grabbing the prince by his arm and holding him close, the knife pressed under his ribs. 'And private it might be, but it doesn't belong to you.'

'You'll take the Troll Road for this,' the prince snarled. 'You'll—'

Cinderella thrust a screwed-up flannel into his mouth turning his words into muted grunts.

'That's better,' she said, and then smiled at the huntsman. 'Shall we?' She picked up the diamond slippers and crept to the door. She peered out. The corridor was empty.

With the knife held firmly so close to his vital organs, the prince didn't struggle but let the huntsman and Cinderella lead him. They crept past her

397

apartments into the darker, quieter core of the castle and then started up the cool winding stairs. The moon was in hiding and the steps were simply ghosts in the darkness beneath her feet. Cinderella's heart thumped in her chest. There was so much she didn't understand. How did the huntsman and the prince know each other? How much did the huntsman know about what was hidden in the room, and why did the fairy godmother want it so badly? And she couldn't help but wonder how to get herself out of a lifetime married to the odious man now snivelling behind his gag, snot running from his nose.

All her wondering stopped as the huntsman froze just as they rounded last corner. He raised his hand and she stopped where she stood. Her scalp prickled as she stared into the black musty space. She didn't need to ask him what was wrong. She could sense it herself. They weren't alone up here. Beside her, the huntsman was tense, ready to spring into attack, and then, from deep within the gloom came the delicate tap of silver on stone.

'I wondered when you'd get here.'

'Rose?' Cinderella said, incredulous as her step-sister came into view. 'What are you doing here?'

'I followed your markings. I thought something strange was going on and you might need my help.'

She rested her cane against the wall and lit the small lamp in her hand. As she held it up, casting yellow light on the three figures in front of her, she raised an eyebrow. 'I was right on the first count at least.' She dropped into a slight curtsey. 'Your highness.' She looked at Cinderella. 'What the hell is going on?'

The prince was staring at her and his mewling grew louder and more indignant.

'It's a long story,' Cinderella said. 'He's got something secret in that room. And we need it.'

'Come on,' the huntsman pushed the prince forward. 'Let's get this done, shall we?'

Rose held the light up and Cinderella darted forward with the key.

'Are you sure you want to do this, little sister?' Rose asked. 'You're going to be a royal princess. Sometimes you have to look the other way.'

'I can't do that.' Cinderella shook her head. 'And I'm not sure I'm going to be a royal princess either.' Just saying the words aloud made her feel better, as if a weight had been pressing down on her, pushing her into the very foundations of the castle, and she'd suddenly been freed.

'Oh, Cinders,' Rose said. 'You do like to make life difficult. Go on, then. Unlock the door.'

And Cinderella did.

12

"There has to be a wedding . . ."

For a moment Cinderella couldn't breathe. She had expected the room to be as dusty and dirty as the rest of this part of the castle, but instead everything shone. The polished floor was inlaid with mosaics of dragons dancing in the summer sky. Overhead a chandelier glittered brightly, rubies and emeralds and diamonds sparkling with the light within. Heavy red velvet drapes hung over the windows and in the corner a table was laden with bottles of wine and a silver goblet. A chaise-longue of gold and blue was on the far side of the room, matching cushions at its head and feet as if someone spent a lot of time on it and wanted to be comfortable.

But it was the centrepiece she couldn't tear her eyes from.

'I had no idea what to expect,' Rose said, softly. 'But it wasn't that.'

The glass coffin sat on a raised dais in the middle of the room. Inside it, a beautiful dark-haired girl in a pink dress lay perfectly still. Her cheeks had a dusky rose tint and her lips were cherry red. Cinderella peered in. The girl had the most extraordinary violet eyes. They stared, empty of expression, at the ceiling.

'Snow White,' the huntsman said. 'I knew it.'

Cinderella looked at him. 'You know her?'

'We . . . we've met.'

'Met?' There was something in his voice that sent a flare of jealousy through her. 'What do you mean, *met*?'

'Her step-mother too as it happens.' He smiled at her, his eyes twinkling and she realised he was enjoying her reaction. 'I was feeling lucky to be alive. And they were hard to resist.' He winked at her and she almost growled again, but swallowed it down. He was *still* infuriating. Was that all their moment had been? Another notch nearly carved on his bedstead?

'You slept with her?' The prince spat his gag out and glared. '*You?*' He looked from the huntsman to Cinderella and back again. 'And her?'

'Not yet. I'm working on it.'

'Don't hold your breath,' Cinderella muttered. The girl in the casket was truly beautiful. She almost looked as if she was just sleeping, but that couldn't be possible.

'If perhaps we could worry less about who's been sleeping with whom, and focus on what's going on here, I think we might make more progress towards a solution.' Rose said, pouring herself a glass of wine. 'I take it this is something to do with how you managed to get to those Bride Balls in dresses you certainly couldn't afford.'

'I made this stupid deal . . .' Cinderella started. 'I'm so sorry, she gave me these slippers . . .'

'There's this queen,' the huntsman said, over Cinderella, 'and after he abandoned me she wanted me to kill this girl and I didn't so she cursed me but now . . .'

'I can explain' the prince joined in.

'Okay, enough!' Rose held her hand up and Cinderella fell silent. She was surprised to see that the huntsman did too. Rose had always been good at being in charge. 'I don't want to get lost in the details. I'm not sure I even want to hear the details.' She looked at the prince.

'Is she dead?'

'No,' he shook his head like a berated child,

and Cinderella wondered how she could have ever thought he would be the one for her. He was charming and handsome, but so weak. She looked at the girl in the box. And clearly damaged.

'She's just enchanted.'

'Just,' the huntsman muttered.

'And I take it the king doesn't know she's here?' Rose continued. The prince shook his head.

'He wouldn't understand. I don't *do* anything. I just like to talk to her,' he said, as if it was the most reasonable thing in the world. 'She's so perfect like this. She listens.' He looked at Rose as if she of all of them would understand. 'I wasn't hurting anyone. Not until *he* came back.' He glared at the huntsman. 'I'll have you arrested for this. The Troll Road is too good for you. I'll hang you from the castle walls to rot!' His face had twisted into a sneer and his eyes were cold and ugly.

'And I in turn,' the huntsman leaned casually against the wall, 'will tell your father and anyone who'll listen exactly what happened with that *other* beauty of yours.'

The prince's eyes widened. Cinderella wished she knew what they were talking about. What other beauty? A different girl to the one trapped in the glass box? She stared at her again. Who was this

Snow White? She frowned as a glint of gold caught her eye.

'She's wearing a wedding ring,' she said, staring at the frozen girl's left hand. 'She's married.' The truth hit her like a blast of the winter wind and she turned to the prince, her mouth half-open. 'She's your *wife*?'

'But that can't be right,' the huntsman said. 'No priest would marry a girl in this condition. No matter who wanted . . .' his sentence drifted away. 'You bastard,' he said, eventually. 'I knew you were spoilt and pathetic, but this?' His words contained the growl of every predator in the forest, and as he stepped forward the prince cowered backwards, seeking protection from Rose. 'You married her and then did this to her?'

'It wasn't like that,' the prince said, although from the tone of his voice Cinderella was pretty sure it was something close. 'I just . . . she was just . . .' his shoulders slumped and whatever energy he had for the fight left him in a heavy sigh. 'I just don't understand beautiful women. They're so much . . .' he glanced at the glass coffin and then at Cinderella. 'Trouble.'

'I think this cancels our engagement,' Cinderella said.

'But there has to be a wedding! My father will insist on it. All the preparations have been made! I can't tell him about this. I can't . . .'

'No one's going to tell him about this.' Rose laid a gentle hand on the prince's arm. 'But nor can this continue. It's time to let the past go.' She looked at the huntsman. 'You have someone waiting for this girl?'

He nodded. 'Yes.'

'I'll go with him,' Cinderella blurted out. 'I don't want to live here. And I want to see this queen who's messed with us all so much. And . . .' she closed her mouth. And what? What had she been about to say? And she couldn't imagine never seeing the hunts-man again? She could feel him looking at her and her face burned.

'But there has to be a wedding,' the prince mut-tered. 'There has to be.'

'And there will be,' Rose said. 'You'll marry me. I'll smooth all this over and the kingdom will carry on happily.'

'Marry you?' He frowned slightly.

'I'll be a good queen,' she said firmly. 'I can guide you through the parts of ruling that you'll find dull. And I won't care when you take mistresses so long as you treat me with the respect a queen deserves.' She held his face until his eyes focused on her. 'It could be a good partnership.'

Slowly, the prince nodded. 'Yes,' he said. 'Thank you.'

'Are you sure?' Cinderella looked at Rose, even though she could feel the rightness of the match in her stomach. Things were as they would have been if she hadn't turned up with her enchanted slippers and wrecked it all.

'Certain,' her step-sister – her *sister* – said. 'I'll explain to mother and father. But you'd better stay in touch. Come and visit when things have calmed down.' She clapped her hands together and smiled. 'Now, we'd better organise you two a cart of some kind. You'll want to be gone before everyone wakes up. And you'll need to dress down.' She lifted her chin and as she walked away, leaning so carefully on her cane, Cinderella thought Rose looked every inch the queen already. Cinderella rummaged in the pockets of her dress and pulled out the final nut the fairy godmother had given her. Escape, that's what she'd said, and Cinderella knew this was exactly the moment she had meant.

13

'Of course it's love . . .'

R
ose was ruthlessly efficient and, by her side, the prince did exactly what he was told. Horses were saddled and a donkey brought out of the stables and attached to the cart.

'He looks old and tired,' the prince muttered. 'But he'll walk steadily and for as long as you need him to.' He looked at the girl in the glass coffin on the back of the cart. 'If she wakes up, she'll know who he belongs to.' He didn't look at Cinderella as she flung a small bag of possessions alongside it, and she didn't care. She had nothing to say to him. Neither did the huntsman, or so it seemed. He looked pained. 'Hurry up,' he told her. 'I haven't . . . we haven't got a lot of time.'

She nodded. Rose came alongside her and pushed a

small bag in her hand. It was heavy with coins.

'I can't take that,' Cinderella protested. 'Not after everything. I'm so sorry. You were right. I was spoilt. Stupid.'

Rose pulled her in tight and hugged her. 'No. Everything is as it should be. And all will be well.' She stroked Cinderella's face and smiled. 'You'll see. Now go before I get too emotional.'

The moon broke through the heavy clouds as they slipped away but when Cinderella looked back Rose was still standing by the gates. She raised her hand, and Cinderella did the same, just before cracking the nut and letting the dust settle over her and the huntsman. She breathed in, and her fine court gown turned into a dusty green dress. It was the colour of the forest and she loved it. Once her sister was out of sight, she kept her head down. This city held nothing for her anymore.

They travelled in relative silence until they reached the edge of the sleeping city and the border of the snowy forest, disappearing under its canopy and being embraced by the trees. The huntsman led them to a track and gave her his jacket to keep warm. Slowly dawn was edging into the sky, bringing a strange light with it that found gaps in the branches and cut strange shapes around them. Cinderella noticed that the huntsman was pale and trembling. Was it his injuries? Or was he about to transform back into the tiny mouse? She touched his arm. 'Are you all right?' she asked.

He nodded, but his face was drawn and his eyes were filled with sadness. 'You might have to finish this journey alone,' he said, and glanced up at the sky, his handsome face furrowing.

'Well, only until tonight,' Cinderella said. 'I'll keep you warm until you become a man again.'

He shook his head. 'I don't think it will be that way this time. The deal changed.'

'What do you mean?' Cinderella stared at him. He had to be joking. 'She can't do that.'

'Have you got the slippers? She'll want them back.'

'Yes,' Cinderella was still staring at him. 'They're in my bag.' She thought of all the times they'd laughed in the doorway by the kitchen. She thought of how he'd saved her from the prince. She thought— suddenly a whole new thought struck her. The slippers.

'Why didn't the slippers work on you?' she said. 'When you came in the prince's room? They didn't affect you at all.'

He smiled, creases forming around his eyes, and he looked at her. His dark hair hung over one eye, but she could still see all the kindness and strength and warmth that lay beneath his humour and roughness. 'They didn't work on me because I dreamt of you before we met,' he said simply. 'And there's no magic stronger than that.' He looked away and moved his horse forward.

'You love me?' she said. The cold was forgotten. Her head was in a whirl. Love? Is that what this was? All this irritation? All this infuriating anger?

You're on a dirt track in the freezing forest at dawn. You've left your family behind without a second thought.

Of course it's love.

'Wait,' she called after him, jumping down from her horse, her heart racing with joy. He turned and looked at her. His trembling was getting worse. He was changing and she couldn't allow that to happen, not without letting him know. She ran to him and he slid from his saddle, his legs almost buckling under him as he stood.

'Don't watch this,' he said. He gasped and bent over a little. 'Please.'

Cinderella took his face in her hands. Her whole body tingled just from touching him.

'I love you too,' she whispered. And then she kissed him.

She wasn't sure if it was just inside her head, but

she was sure that as he held her, the stars danced around their heads and lights twinkled in a whirl-wind of fireflies that warmed their hands. She was lost in the moment and so was he.

'The curse,' he said, pulling back slightly. 'You broke the curse.'

'I don't care what I did,' Cinderella murmured. 'Just kiss me again.'

His lips met hers and as their tongues danced to-gether, their bodies wound around each other's, he pulled her down to the forest floor. For a moment, caught up by the magic of true love, the forest created a space of warmth for them. The ice evap-orated and the earth welcomed them. Cinderella ran her fingers through his dark hair and this time there were no comparisons with the prince's blond good looks. They were sterile. This man was all pas-sion and nature. Panting as his hands pulled at her clothes, she reached between them and tugged at his belt. This time he didn't stop her, pushing her dress upwards and groaning slightly as her hand found him. Cinderella thrust her hips up to him, aching to finally feel him inside her, already warm and wet and wanting. There would be time for exploring each other later. There would be time for everything later. For now there was only urgency, all of the delayed need between them. He pushed inside her and she gasped, wrapping her legs around his hips, pulling him in further as he moved, one hand touching the roughness of his face and the other sliding down between them and touching herself. She didn't care about princes and shoes or fairy godmothers and curses. This was all the magic they needed.

When they were done they lay there for a while, talking quietly and laughing and kissing until need overwhelmed them again, but this time it was slow and controlled and their mouths went where their hands had been before and when the gentleness was done and she was sure they were both going to explode from it, they took each other again.

It was late afternoon when they reached the boundary between kingdoms and found the fairy godmother waiting for them. Her long blonde hair hung loose around her shoulders and she wore riding breeches under her thick fur coat. A carriage sat patiently in the road further back.

She turned to Cinderella, her expression hard to read in the encroaching gloom. 'I see you realised the prince wasn't the hero of your dreams after all.'

She smiled, and it was almost gentle. 'I think you made the better choice.' She walked round to the back of the cart, pausing to pat the donkey's neck.

The sun broke through in streaks of reds and pinks leaving the sky stained as if with blood as the queen or fairy godmother or whoever she was stared into the back of the cart.

'I'll take it from here,' she said.

With her hair loose around her pale cat-like features, Cinderella didn't think the woman looked like a queen or a fairy godmother at all. She looked like a water witch from the legends her step-mother used to read to her, tales from the days of the dragons. She didn't know whether to be afraid or in awe. Probably both.

'And it will be as you said?' the huntsman asked.

The queen nodded.

'Let's go,' the huntsman muttered. 'I'm done here.'

Cinderella thought of her huntsman cursed to become a mouse. She thought of the girl in the box and wondered how that story would end. She turned her horse around though, and as they rode away, leaving the icy queen and the frozen girl behind, she decided that for her that story was done. She had her own story to live. She looked at the handsome man beside her and smiled, before spurring her horse into a canter and heading into the woods.

14
'Is that a spindle . . . ?'

Rose had dyed her hair red for the wedding, and she found it suited her as well as fooling just about everyone that the prince was still marrying the same girl. After all, who had really paid any attention to Cinderella? The people had only seen her from a distance, and anyone in the court who might have realised something rather strange had gone on – that the girl walking down the aisle was taller and more buxom than the curly haired beauty they'd trained to walk and dance – knew well enough to keep their mouths firmly shut. The prince was married and that was all anyone needed to know.

She was content. She had never wanted love in the way that other girls sought it out. For some, love was needed for life; it kept their hearts racing with its ups and downs and desire for one person to make you complete. Rose had always felt complete, and what she wanted was to shape things. To make the kingdom better. The prince would be a good husband in his own way and as time passed she knew she would come to make most of the important decisions. It would work better for them both that way.

She looked out of the window and down to the courtyard below where lights still glittered in the trees and in the bushes of the maze beyond. There had been a sudden thaw, and although it was only just approaching the New Year spring had been in the air for the three days of festivities that had accompanied the royal wedding.

A figure standing in one of the maze paths caught her eye. He stood perfectly still, wearing a bright crimson jacket, and staring up at their bedroom window as if he could see her looking back, which she was sure was impossible. She frowned. What a strange man.

'Darling,' she murmured to the prince, who was changing his shirt for their dinner with the high council and king, 'come and look at this. There's a man in the maze.' She squinted, trying to focus more closely. 'What's that on his back?' He was carrying some kind of knapsack, but there was something sticking out of it. 'Is that a spindle?'

The prince came alongside her.

'Oh no,' he said, his reflection in the glass pale as his eyes widened. 'I didn't think he'd find me.'

Rose's heart sank a little. 'What did you do?'

'I made a deal,' the prince said.

He was still talking but Rose wasn't listening. She stared at the stranger, who stared directly back. She drew herself up tall and then took her handsome husband's hand.

'We'll take care of it, dear,' she said. 'The thing about deals, you see, is that they can always be renegotiated.'

Perhaps her married life was going to be more interesting than she'd thought.

'Why don't you tell me what happened?'

Epilogue

'*rue love's kiss . . .*'

When the sound of hooves had faded the queen climbed up on to the cart and stared at the silent girl on the other side of the glass. 'I just need to know,' she whispered, before carefully opening the glass lid.

The forest was eerily still around them, as if even the winter wolves were holding their breaths.

Her heart raced as she leaned over the thin glass edge and pressed her lips against Snow White's. They were warm and soft, and Lilith thought her heart might stop in that instant of sweetness. She thought of the cabinet where her own face would stare back from the enchanted mirror. She thought of the words it used to speak, tormenting her with the honesty of her innermost truths, ones she'd fought to deny for so long. She'd fought them for so long she'd confused love for hate.

'Snow White, the fairest in all the lands.'

And she was. Beautiful, kind and desirable.

The girl in the box gasped, life flooding back to her violet eyes, and the sun burst through the clouds creating a rainbow above their heads. The queen sat back on her heels as the girl slowly took in her surroundings and sat up.

'I'm so sorry,' Lilith said, eventually. They were inadequate words. But what else could she say. Her heart raced. She had her answer and it was one she should have seen so long ago.

'I thought you hated me,' Snow White said. 'I only ever wanted you to love me.'

They stared at each other for a long moment, and then Snow White reached out and pulled the queen forwards, kissing her again.

When they finally broke for air, they sat and smiled and Lilith thought of the wisdom of her great-grandmother's curses. True love was the only true magic. The huntsman had earned his happiness. Just as she hoped they had earned theirs.

'Let's go home,' she said, taking Snow White by

the hand and helping her down from the dwarves' cart.

The dark-haired beauty paused and smiled. 'Are you wearing riding breeches?' She slid her arm around the woman's waist and they were a vision of light and dark and winter melted around them.

'How did you wake me?' she said.

'True love's kiss,' the queen answered and the two beautiful women smiled at each other. 'We should go home. We'll pick up my great-grandmother on the way. I think she's been causing a bit of trouble. She can go without children for a while.'

'Children?' Snow White asked.

'Oh, you'll understand when you see her house,' the queen said. 'But I should probably apologise for her in advance.'

'I'm sure I'll love her.'

And then they kissed again.

THE END

Beauty

Sarah Pinborough

GOLLANCZ
LONDON

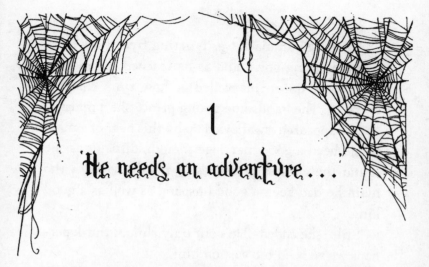

1

'He needs an adventure...'

It was a warm spring and the king and queen took their breakfast on the balcony outside their private apartments, enjoying the fresh air without the burden of any sort of protocol. The sun was warm without burning and the sky was bright without making them squint. For the queen it was almost perfect. The only thing spoiling the moment was the subject of their conversation. It was, however, a talk they both knew was overdue.

'He needs to grow up,' she said, sipping her tea. 'We've spoiled him, I fear.'

'It's very hard not to spoil a prince,' her husband, the king replied gruffly. 'No doubt my father spoiled me. A prince must feel superior. How else can they ever become a good king?'

Beauty

The king's stomach was bursting free of his thick white dressing-gown and as he reached for another pastry the queen marvelled at how time changed them all. The handsome young prince she'd married had disappeared, swallowed up by this bear of a man. It had been a good marriage though, difficult as she found the endless pressures of royalty, and in the main he had been a good husband as well as a good king.

'Still,' she added. 'He's our only child. I think perhaps we've been too soft on him.'

'Perhaps you're right,' he grunted. 'He must soon marry and start a family of his own. He should attend more council meetings. Undertake more training with the generals for when he must lead the army. Learn to understand the revenue as he promised to.' He paused and frowned. 'What does he do with his time anyway?'

The conversation wouldn't have started if they hadn't seen their only child, the hope of the kingdom, their handsome golden boy, staggering up the castle steps in a wine soaked shirt as they'd taken their seats on the balcony that morning. It had become something of a habit, as a quick chat with the servants had revealed. Being out all night at inns and houses of ill-repute with various other young men of noble birth, then sleeping most of the day away. Occasionally riding out with the hunt, but too often not.

It was all, perhaps, to be expected of a young man, but it was becoming a lifestyle and that would not do. Their boy was going to be a king one day, and that would require a level of gravitas and respect that he currently did not have. The queen looked at her husband again. He was no longer a fit ox of a man. His face was red and veins had burst on his cheeks. He was carrying far too much weight. Her son's destiny might be closer to hand than any of them liked to think – and although no parent liked to think it of their own flesh and blood, the queen had become concerned of late that her boy would not rise to the challenge.

'We need to find him a good woman,' she said. 'Someone with a calm temperament and a clever brain.' It was easier to consider the qualities of a future wife than to discuss the flaws in the prince.

'He'll want a pretty wife,' the king muttered and then smiled at his queen. 'I was lucky. I found that truly rare creature: a woman with both beauty and brains.'

The queen said nothing but shared a contented

moment with him, knowing that the king too felt they had spent their years together well. Yes, she suffered from terrible headaches and various forms of anxiety, but she had been a good advisor to him behind the closed doors of their rooms and when he'd strayed, as kings, the most spoiled of all men, were wont to do, she had shrugged it away and known that he would be back in her bed before long. It was a royal marriage after all, and she'd had romance before it, a long time ago. Romance and—

'He needs an adventure,' she said, the words out before she'd really thought it through. 'All these wild nights; they're not good for him. He needs a proper adventure.'

'Hmmm,' the king said. 'The thought had occurred to me. But to send him from the kingdom? Our only son?'

'A king needs to know the outside world,' the queen said. 'He needs to understand how the nine kingdoms are different. Why they are at war. Perhaps find a way to make peace with an enemy. He can't do any of that here.'

The king knew the wisdom of his wife's words and somewhere in the recesses of his mind a memory stirred. 'My grandfather had such adventures, you know. When I was a child he told stories of visiting a faraway land and rescuing a girl from a tower by climbing her hair.'

They both laughed at that and the queen's eyes twinkled. 'I hope he was a slim man at the time.'

'I'd break your neck before I'd got one foot on the wall, wouldn't I?' The king shook his head. 'A crazy story from a crazy old man. But still, I think there is something to this adventure idea.'

The queen watched as her husband slipped off into his own thoughts. His eyes were narrowed and she knew better than to speak and interrupt him. Her seed was sown and now he'd be trying to determine the best kind of adventure for their son to have. One that was important enough, not too dangerous, but which might benefit the kingdom. After all, the kingdom was the only thing that mattered when everything was said and done.

She sipped her tea and leaned back in her chair, gazing up at the turrets far above her and the many, many windows that glinted brightly in the sunshine. Her head was mercifully free of pain and today there were no official engagements or lunches with noble women for her to attend. Birds sang in the trees. Below them the city rumbled into life. She felt content with her lot.

'I think I have it,' her husband said eventually. 'I think I have the very thing.'

The king spoke to his son about it over dinner. Being a relatively wise king he invited several influential noblemen to dine with them, along with their sons. A prince was as likely to bow to peer pressure as any other young man, and now that the king and queen had made their decision he would brook no arguments from his son about the task he was about to set him.

'Plague?' the prince said after his father had started speaking. 'What kind of plague?'

'I don't know,' the king answered. 'It might just be a legend. All anyone knows is that deep in the heart of the forest, near the base of the Far Mountain, there was once a wealthy city. A tenth kingdom. The story goes that nearly a hundred years ago a terrible plague struck the city. The forest, rich with magic so close to the mountain's edge, closed in around it, the trees and brambles growing so high and thick that the city and all its people were sealed off and lost forever.'

'And no one looked for them?' the prince asked.

His venison sat untouched on his plate and the king was pleased to see the story had his son's attention. But then the boy had always chosen romanticism over practicality.

'Perhaps they did, but the forest didn't allow them to be found.'

'Surely they could have cut themselves free from the other side?'

'But they didn't. Which leads me to believe that the entire population died very quickly.' The king paused. 'But of course, all the treasures will still be there. And if the city could be found, it would make a welcome addition to our kingdom. A lucrative discovery, a useful outpost for keeping an eye on our enemies or a perfect place to host peace talks between warring kings.'

'And you want to find it?' the prince asked.

The king smiled and sipped his wine. 'No, my son. I want *you* to find it. Every prince should go out into the world and have an adventure before settling down. This will be yours.'

Several of the young men around the table burst into excited chatter and the prince, the jewel at their centre, grinned. 'Then I shall find it for you, father! I promise you I shall!'

Beauty

The huntsman had been lost in the dream when his father woke him. It was the same dream he'd had for several nights and it was so powerful that the echo of it stayed with him during the days. There was a girl with hair that tumbled in thick curls down her back, as red as autumn leaves. She was running through the forest and he was chasing her, following the flashes of her hair and the echo of her laughter, but all the time her face was out of sight. He ran as he had as a child, with no sense of awareness of the changing shape of the forest around him and without the tracking skills that had become second nature to him as a man. Nature didn't matter. The beasts that lived around him didn't matter. The forest itself, so much a part of him, no longer mattered in his dream. All he cared about was finding the girl who stayed so elusive ahead of him. His breath rushed in his ears and his heart raced.

He sat up with a start, for a moment confused by his surroundings. His father grinned at him. 'The girl again?'

He nodded.

'I told you. She's your true love. You're lucky; not many get the dreams. But if you do, you have to find her.'

'Well, she's not in the village, that's for sure.' The huntsman stretched and yawned.

'And a good thing too. You've had most of the girls here. Or they've had you.'

They smiled at each other, good-natured, easy with the natural way of men and women, and how frequently they tumbled into bed with each other until wedding vows claimed them. Men and women both were just animals after all, and life in the forest could be hard. Comforts had to be taken where you could get them.

'Why did you wake me?' The huntsman, said as he shook away his sleepiness and pulled on his shirt. Beyond the glow of his father's torch, he could tell it was still dark outside and the air held the crisp scent of a chill spring night. It wasn't dawn, but maybe two or three in the morning.

'The king's men want you.' His father held up a hand. 'It's nothing bad. They want the best young huntsman and the elders have all chosen you.'

'I *am* the best,' the huntsman muttered. 'But what do they want me to hunt?'

He peered out the window and saw several soldiers

in shining uniforms, sitting high on thoroughbred horses.

'They want you to babysit the prince. Be his companion on a trip to the edge of the Far Mountain.'

The huntsman's heart fell. He had no time for kings or princes. From what he'd heard around the campfires on the long winter hunts, nothing good ever came from their company. 'Can't he take care of himself?' he asked.

His father snorted with laughter. 'He's a prince. He's no match for the forest. He'll be lost within a day. Starving within two—'

'—and eaten within three,' the huntsman finished.

The horses outside pawed at the ground, picking up on their riders' impatience.

'I don't have a choice, do I?' he said, reaching for his knife and his axe and his old leather bag for carrying food and water.

'No, son, you don't. The king's decided his boy needs an adventure.' His father's tanned, wrinkled face looked like a craggy rock face in the gloomy light. 'But maybe you do too.' He smiled. 'Maybe you'll find that redhead of yours out there.'

'The girl of my dreams?' the huntsman said, wryly.

'Stranger things have happened.'

'If this prince doesn't get me killed first,' he said and stepped out into the night. He didn't look back at his father, or at any of the huntsmen and women who had gathered in front of their small cottages and huts to watch him leave. Long farewells weren't their way. He'd either come home or he wouldn't. Huntsmen knew each other well enough to know the things that were so often said by other men – and to know how rarely they were meant. He climbed up on the back of a waiting horse and patted its neck. The beast whinnied as nature recognised nature, and then they were gone, leaving the the village behind in the pale pre-dawn light.

he huntsman had been to the city before but had only visited the markets on its edges. The castle at its heart glittered like a diamond when the sun hit the banks of sparkling windows, but it had always seemed like an illusion in the distance. It was beyond him how men could build such edifices and he wondered how many ordinary people had died cutting, dragging and lifting the thousands of quarried stones that made up its smooth, perfect surface. He wondered if the king ever wondered that.

Now that he was standing in front of the man, he doubted it. Gruff and ageing as the king was, he had sharp, cool eyes within his fattening face.

'They say you're the best of the huntsmen,' the king said as he studied the man before him. 'That no one knows the forest as well as you.'

'I know the forest, that's true,' the huntsman answered. He had no intention of expounding upon his own skills. The king had already formed his opinion, otherwise they wouldn't be face to face. Boasting just set a man up for a fall, and the only reason to boast would be to somehow ingratiate himself with the king for personal favour or political gain. The huntsman wanted nothing from the king for, unlike so many, the glittering life did not appeal to him. He neither understood nor trusted it.

'And you're good with a knife? And a bow?'

The huntsman shrugged. 'I'm a huntsman. Those are my tools.'

'You don't say much,' the king said, smiling as he leaned back in his vast, ornate throne, inlaid with rubies and emeralds so large that the huntsman could almost see his reflection in them. 'I like that.' He waited for a moment as if expecting the huntsman to respond to his praise, and then his smile fell to seriousness and he continued.

438

'The prince is my only son. He needs an adventure. He also needs to come back alive. He is my heir and the kingdom needs him.'

'I'll do my best,' the huntsman said. 'But I am only one man.'

'If you were to return without him, it would not end well for you.' Any pretence at warmth had vanished from the king's face. 'Or for your village.'

His father, not without an adventure or two of his own below his belt, had warned him about the merciless ways of the rich and royal, and the king's threat came as no surprise. 'As I said: I'll do my best, your majesty. My best is all I have to offer.'

The king frowned for a moment as he tried to work out whether the huntsman was being ignorant, obtuse or just speaking plainly in a place where every sentence was normally laden with subtext, but eventually nodded and grunted.

'Good.' He ran thick fingers over his ruddy cheek. 'The prince must never know about this conversation. He knows you are to be his guide, and that your skills will be needed to pass through the forest, but he must believe that he's the hero in this tale, do you understand? Your role in protecting him must never be spoken of.'

The huntsman nodded. He had no time for heroes or stories or tales of true love, despite his own dreams.

'Good,' the king said again. 'Good.'

The huntsman met the prince down by the stables where he was choosing their horses, fine steeds whose muscles rippled under their glossy dark hides. The prince was as blond as the huntsman was dark and his easy smile charmed all those around him. At least he looked fit, the huntsman thought, and they were of a similar age. Perhaps it wouldn't be such a bad journey. The prince shook his hand vigorously and then pulled him close, patting the huntsman heartily on the back.

'We leave at first light,' he said and then winked. 'Which gives us all night in the taverns to give this city – and its maidens – our farewells! There will be wine and women for us, my new friend, before we leave to find a new castle for the kingdom!'

The huntsman forced a smile as his heart sank. He had no problem with wine and women – especially not with the women – but it appeared the prince was in danger of believing the legends of his princely deeds even before he had done any. That was never good. When huntsmen got too cocky they normally ended up gored. What would happen to this fine, handsome prince, he wondered. And how on earth was he going to save him from it?

2

'Bloody bastard wolves...'

She hadn't meant to come back this way but when her feet had turned her down the path she had followed them. Her basket was full and heavy and she should have gone straight to granny's cottage, but the forest came alive in the spring and nowhere were the scents more alive than at the edge of the impenetrable wall of briars and bushes and, as usual, she couldn't resist their lure.

None of the villagers ever came here. They spoke in whispers about it and the noises that could sometimes be heard in the night, and children stayed away, but Petra had always been drawn to it. She placed her basket on the rich long grass and pushed back the hood of her red cape so that she could gaze upwards. The dark green wall stretched up as high as she could see, blocking out any sight of the mountain, coloured here and there by small bursts of flowers poking through the brambles.

As she did every time, she wrapped her hands in her cloak to protect her from hidden thorns and tried to pull a few branches apart to see what lay on the other side, but it was a fruitless task and all she could make out were more twigs and vines, all locking together. She held her breath and listened, but there was only birdsong and the rustle of the forest. That was *all* there ever was in the daylight and she couldn't fight the disappointment she felt. Perhaps she'd sneak out again tonight and see if she could hear the plaintive howling that sometimes carried quietly over the briar wall on the breeze. The sound might have terrified men and children alike, but something in it called to Petra and made her heart ache. For a while she had just listened, but then one night she'd thrown her hood back and howled in response and the forest wall itself had trembled as their two voices became one. It had become a song between them, a delicious, private secret that made her shiver in ways she didn't really understand. But she longed to see beyond the wall and find the other half of her duet. What manner of beast was trapped there? Why did it sound so lonely? And what had made the forest create such a daunting, impenetrable fortress that no man had tried to break through it?

'I thought I'd find you here.'

Petra jumped slightly at the soft voice and turned. 'Sorry, granny. I just ...'

'I know,' her grandmother said. 'You just wandered here by accident.' She was a short, stout woman whose face was rosy with both good humour and good nature. Here and there a grey curl sprung out from under her cap. Petra loved her very, very much. 'The forest can be like that with places and people. When your mother, may she rest in peace, was little she was always up at the emerald pond. She'd stare into it for hours, hoping to see a water witch or some such foolishness.' She smiled and Petra smiled back, picking up her basket and turning her back on the lush vegetation that grew so unnaturally and fascinated her. She'd heard her mother's story many times before but she never tired of it and she knew it cheered her grandmother, although by nature a happy soul, to talk about her.

'I've put some soup on for lunch,' her granny said. 'Let's go home.'

They chatted about their mornings as they walked, the route second nature to them both even though the tiny paths that cut through the dense woodland would barely be noticeable to a stranger. The stream somewhere to their left finally joined them, babbling into their conversation as they walked alongside the flowing water, and finally came to the clearing where granny's cottage sat. Smoke rose from the chimney and flowers were starting to bloom in the borders that ran in front of the small house. It should have been a beautiful sight but today, as had happened on too many days recently, it was marred by a bloody trail of innards that emerged from behind the house and vanished at the edge of the forest.

'Oh, not again!' Granny gasped and the two women, age being no impediment to panic, ran to the small enclosure behind the cottage where granny kept her precious goats. It was as Petra feared. The gate had been broken through yet again. From somewhere deep in the trees a low howl of victory drifted towards them. It had none of the plaintive texture of the sound that drew Petra to the mysterious forest wall; this was all animal, fierce and hungry.

'Bloody wolves,' her granny swore. 'Bloody bastard wolves.'

'I'll mend it again,' she said, quietly. 'Make it stronger.'

Her grandmother was moving through the rest of

the scared goats who had huddled at the far corner of the pen. 'Adolpho. It's taken Adolpho.'

Petra had never tried to persuade her grandmother to move to one of the houses in the village as she grew older – she knew how much the old lady loved the peace and quiet of the forest – but recently she'd started to think it might be a good idea. It had been a hard winter and the wolves, normally a rarity in this part of the forest, had arrived as a hungry pack and, when the weather broke, they'd stayed. Where foxes were a menace they'd learned to deal with, the winter wolves were braver and stronger. Men in the village talked of cattle lost in the night to the wolves working in twos and threes, and although they had tried to hunt them, the pack was elusive.

'Go inside, Granny,' Petra said, knowing that the old woman would want a quiet moment to mourn the loss of the animal. 'I'll clean up out here.' The wolves would be back, that she knew for certain, and she couldn't help but wonder how long it would be before they saw the stout old woman as an easy meal. Especially if they couldn't get to the goats. She needed a fence as high as that wall of greenery around her granny's cottage. She needed to protect her. The wolf's gruff howl was joined by another and she was sure they were mocking her. She cursed them silently, then went to the shed and pulled out more planks of wood and rolls of wire. She would not give up. The wolves would not win. Her hair fell into her eyes as she worked, angrily focused on her task and wishing that the wolf from far away would come and scare these rough relatives away for her. At least then her fingers wouldn't be full of splinters and her skin slick with sweat.

She was halfway through the job when there was a crash from inside the cottage, a scream, and the sound of plates being dropped.

'Granny!' Her heart in her mouth, she turned and ran.

They had been travelling through the forest for several days before the two men eased into a comfortable silence. The first day, once out of sight of the fanfare and grand send-off the king had arranged for his son, had been a relatively slow one given the prince's hangover. The huntsman's own head was clear having been on the outskirts of the group for the night, gritting his teeth every time the prince introduced him to some new dandy as his servant. Huntsmen served no one but nature. He'd drunk one or two cups of beer but the group of rowdy young men hadn't impressed him and neither had they particularly encouraged him to join them, which suited him just fine. He was glad when dawn broke and he could wake the prince and prepare to get out of the city. He'd had enough. He wanted their 'adventure' over so he could return to his people, and at least in the forest he would feel that he was almost home.

By the time they'd made camp, the fresh air had revived the prince's spirits enough for him to make a fire while the huntsman fetched water and killed a rabbit for their dinner. At first the prince had been determined to prove his superiority by trying to impress the huntsman with tales of castle living, but after a while he'd become curious about his companion's way of life. The huntsman answered his questions as best he could as he skinned and cooked the animal, and it was clear that the prince, away from the peer pressure of his cohort, was begrudgingly beginning to admire his companion. The huntsman relaxed his own judgement on the royal in return.

The next few days passed well and they even laughed together occasionally at some joke or story one or other would tell. They might not have been a natural pairing for a friendship, but it wasn't the prince's fault that the king had dragged the huntsman from his home and rested this burden – and the fate of his village – on his shoulders. He would make the best of it and perhaps they would both come out of the experience better and wiser men.

After ten days of travelling the Far Mountain had grown taller in the skyline and the forest thicker; green and lush and rich with life. The light scent of spring in the air became tinged with something heavier, and when they finally found a large pond to drink from the water was bitter and they had to spit it out. The prince declared it was magic they could taste and shuddered slightly, afraid. The huntsman pointed out that magic was simply nature in another guise and nothing to be either feared or courted, but before they could get into an argument about it he saw chimney smoke drifting up from behind some trees to their right.

'They'll know where there's good water,' the huntsman said.

'Isn't it your job to find it?' the prince shot back.

The huntsman ignored him and found an almost invisible path through the trees that led to a small clearing at the heart of which sat a cottage surrounded by pretty flowers ... and by the faintest blood-stained trail through the grass that none other than an animal or a huntsman would be likely to spot. He frowned slightly; there had been trouble here. He paused and looked up. The door was open and from inside came the crashing of plates and a short scream. He gripped the hilt of his knife and ran forward.

'Granny!' A girl's shout came from somewhere behind the cottage but the huntsman and the prince didn't pause. They ran straight inside.

A low growl came from beyond the cosy main room and the two men knocked over a side table as they followed it, the prince with his sword drawn and the huntsman with his knife.

A large grey wolf, teeth bared, was scrabbling and scratching at a tall cupboard door in the corner. It suddenly jerked open an inch and a broom handle poked out sharply and jabbed at the beast. 'Shoo! Shoo!'

The prince, clearly nervous, was waving his sword so high in the small room that the huntsman had to duck to avoid losing an ear.

'Watch what you're doing with that thing,' he muttered, as the wolf turned to face them. It snarled, ready to pounce. Faced with the full sight of its bloody mouth and sharp teeth, the prince paled. 'Perhaps we should run.'

'We can't outrun it,' the huntsman said, his voice

low. The wolf growled again, and the prince trembled slightly, grabbing at the huntsman's arm and tugging him backwards – and off balance – ruining any chance he had of defending them.

Sensing their fear, the wolf leapt, across the table at them, all raging heat and hunger. The huntsman shoved the clinging prince away, sending him flying into a dresser and breaking more crockery, but as the beast loomed over him his own balance was gone and he cursed under his breath, preparing to feel the sharp thick claws and heavy teeth tearing into his skin.

An arrow whistled past him, straight and true, and struck firmly lodging several inches deep in the wolf's chest. All momentum suddenly lost, it mewled and dropped, crashing onto the table. It shuddered for a second and then was gone. As the prince got to his feet, the huntsman stared at the dead beast, and then turned to look behind him at the girl holding the bow.

'You can come out now, Granny,' she said, softly. 'It's dead.'

The girl stared at the wolf with a mixture of loathing and sadness and then turned her eyes to the men; one dressed in the finest clothes with royal insignia on his red cloak and sword, and the other in the rough green fabrics and tan leathers of a working huntsman.

'Can I help you?' she asked.

'We heard the scream,' the huntsman said. 'And came to help. But it seems you had it all under control.'

'We were hoping you could direct us to the nearest stream,' the prince said, as if he hadn't been trembling in fear only seconds before and there was no dead wolf bleeding over the kitchen table. 'We've been travelling for days and this part of the forest is strange to us. We found a pond, but the water was undrinkable. And then we heard the crash and saw the door was open, and came inside.'

'Oh, they say that pond's cursed. But that can wait until we've had our somewhat late lunch. The wolves have ruined our day.'

A small, stout woman with a cheerful face lent character by a life in the forest, stepped out of the cupboard, put the broom she was holding away, and then smiled at them. 'You will be staying for some food, I presume? The stew's nearly done and there's plenty to go round.'

The girl sighed and put her hands on her hips. 'We don't know them, granny. They could be anyone.'

Her grandmother peered over her glasses and looked the men up and down.

'Everyone's someone, Petra dear, and that one has the manners of royalty about him, and the other looks like a huntsman to me. You can always trust a huntsman, that's what my mother told me. Now, come on, having visitors will be nice.' She smiled warmly. 'I'm always curious when strangers from distant places turn up at my door, and so should you be.'

'They can help me clear up first then.' The girl didn't look as convinced as her grandmother.

'We'll be more than happy to help,' the prince said, and gave the girl a curt bow. She didn't look too impressed, but instead grabbed the wolf's forelegs. 'Then one of you give me a hand getting this outside.'

A s Petra and her granny cleaned the cottage, the huntsman and the prince worked hard to make the goat pen secure. When they were done, the huntsman smeared the wolf's blood on all the posts until they looked almost painted red. The goats shuffled nervously inside.

'It'll help keep the wolves away,' he said, as Petra came and inspected their work. 'And better the goats are nervous than dead.' She didn't disagree, and he saw a little of the tension escaping her shoulders. They might not be friends yet, but perhaps they were no longer irritating strangers.

The cottage was warm and cosy and it was good to spend a night inside. Petra fetched them some wine and there was bread and stew enough for them all to be full and have some left over. The huntsman was pleased when he saw the young prince leave a few gold coins on the dresser when he thought no one was looking. By the time they'd eaten night had fallen and they sat gathered round the comforting warmth and light of the large fire in the grate.

'So,' Granny said, her knitting needles clicking together and her chair rocking slightly under her. 'What brings you to this corner of the kingdoms?'

'We're in search of a legend,' the prince said. 'My father has sent me to find a lost castle, vanished for nearly a hundred years. Apparently it's hidden behind a forest wall of some kind—'

'A wall of forest?' Petra sat upright in her chair. 'I know where—'

'Shhh dear,' her granny patted her knee. 'All in good time.'

It was the most animated the girl had been since their arrival, and that intrigued the huntsman. Unlike the city girls she seemed unimpressed by the handsome prince, and he liked her all the more for that.

'Why does your father send you to find it?' the old lady asked.

'He thinks all young men should have an adventure,' the huntsman cut in, before the prince could muddy the waters of their travel with talk of outposts and amassing land.

'And that's a good enough reason,' Granny said and she smiled, nodded and put down her knitting.

'Have you heard of this place?' the prince asked.

'Oh yes.' Granny's eyes twinkled. 'My mother would speak of it sometimes. Mainly when she was older than I am now, and her mind was not always as it should have been. It sounded a strange place, from her tales. But then most cities are strange and, to be fair, she was always full of fancy stories which no one knew the truth of.'

'I go to the wall,' Petra said suddenly. Her face was flushed and alive. 'Sometimes I hear a sound from the other side. A lonely, echoing cry. It haunts me.'

'I think it's more than that, dear,' her grandmother's

eyes twinkled fondly as she looked at her. 'You should go with them.'

'Oh no,' Petra said, holding her granny's arm. 'I'll stay here with you. I need to keep you safe.'

'Don't be silly, dear. It's not just men who need adventures, you know. Everyone has their own destiny to find. And if there's something over that wall that's calling to you, you have to find it. That's the way of things.'

'No,' Petra said, although it was clear in her eyes that she was desperate to go. 'There are still too many wolves in the forest. If the pen holds and they can't get to the goats, what if they come for you again? Like today?'

The huntsman looked thoughtfully at the two women and then left them by the fire with the prince and went outside. He dragged the wolf's body into the forest to work on it and then took the result to the pond to wash it clean, relying on his forest instincts to lead him where he needed to go. By the time he was done he was sweating but pleased.

'Here,' he said, and held up his completed work. 'This will keep them away. They'll smell one of their own instead of you.'

'What *is* that?' Petra asked.

'A wolf wrap,' the huntsman said. He helped the old lady put the wolf's skin on, and then wrapped her own blanket round her shoulders and placed her cap back on top.

'It's lovely and cosy,' she said from somewhere under the wolf's snout. Her hands, under the wolf's claws, looked strange as she continued her knitting.

'You look so peculiar,' Petra giggled. 'Like a wolf has dressed up in your clothes!' They all laughed aloud as the old lady rocked her chair backwards and forwards. 'Well, I quite like it,' she said. 'I can save on wood for the fire if I have this keeping me toasty. And you,' she turned to her grand-daughter and lifted her head so her own face was visible beneath the wolf's, 'Can now go on your adventure.'

And so it was decided. They would leave their horses in Granny's care and Petra would join them.

The next morning they ate a hearty breakfast of eggs and bacon and forest mushrooms, and Petra's granny packed some bread and cheese for them which she loaded up in the huntsman's knapsack, before fixing Petra's red cloak over her shoulders. She smiled and her eyes twinkled but the girl looked as if she was about to burst into tears.

'I love you, Granny,' she said.

'I love you too, Petra.' She squeezed the girl tight.

'But your life is out there, not here with me. And I shall be just fine.'

She waved them off from the doorway, and then the girl led them towards the forest wall and whatever lay beyond it.

3

'Once upon a time...'

Once upon a time a young king was out hunting in the forest that lay at the edge of his city. He had not long come to the throne, but he was a good man and was mourning the loss of his father rather than relishing his new power and preferred to hunt alone as it gave him some private time away from the rigours of court life and kingship.

It was a warm day and, with his enthusiasm to chase and kill a living creature dampened by his recent loss, he dismounted and walked his horse to a large pond of sparkling blue water that was so cold and deep that it must have been home to a natural spring beneath its bed.

The young king sat by the pool as his mount drank

and stared into the surface of the water, lost in his own thoughts. Now it is said that deep in the heart of the pond that rarest of creatures, a water witch, sensed the young king's distress and looked up. She saw his handsome face, so weighed down with grief and responsibility, and it touched something inside her. She immediately came to the surface, unable to stop herself.

The young king and the young water witch fell almost instantly in love and in order to be wed she sacrificed her watery home and went back to the city to become his queen.

At first the king's advisors and, indeed, many of the ordinary people, had reservations about their match, but the new queen kept her magic locked away inside her and she was always so kind and ethereal that soon, despite her icy beauty and eyes that changed colour as water does when the sun hits it, they grew to love her almost as much as the king himself did and the kingdom was content.

For the queen's part, sometimes the wild call of the water and the pull of her old solitary life tugged at her, but she hid that longing away with her magic because in the main she was happy and she loved her king so very, very much. Occasionally, when the yearning became too great, she would return *and secretly allow her magic a release, diving deep into the water and feeling the cool aching caress on her skin. But the visits were not often, and she never looked back when she walked away from the pool. Her husband was waiting for her, after all.*

Only one thing blighted their bliss. The lack of a son or daughter to make their union complete and secure the future of their kingdom. Eventually, as months passed and no sign of a child was to be had, the king, sensing his beautiful wife's growing sadness, asked the advice of a witch who lived in a tower far, far away. He begged her to help them and, after a few minutes reflection, she smiled and said she would. She told the king that he would be blessed with a daughter. She would be graceful, she would be intelligent and she would be kind. The king smiled and laughed and offered the witch gold and jewels in reward, but she shook her head and raised her hand and said she hadn't finished. There was something more. He should know that the princess would be happy, but one day she would prick herself on a spindle and would sleep for a hundred years. The king was aghast at her words and demanded that it not be so, but the witch disappeared in a cloud of sparkling dust and his words were spoken to an empty room.

Within a year, they learned that the queen was with child. There was much pageantry and the kingdom celebrated. The queen went to the pond to tell the spirits of all the water witches who had lived there before her, whose magic ran in every drop of its clear water, of her great joy, and to ask their advice on how to manage her child, who would no doubt find it hard to be of two such different peoples. The only answer she received was the ripple of the surface and silence from the spirits. She took that to mean she should not be concerned. She chose to read it that way. She would not allow any concern to spoil her happiness.

The sun shone on the kingdom and, as she bloomed, everything was perfect. The king, remembering the witch's words, sent his men throughout the kingdom and all the spindles in the land were destroyed. He would keep his child safe. Whatever it took.

Finally, the queen's time arrived. The birth was difficult, and a storm raged over the kingdom, heavy rain flooding the streets. For nearly two days and nights she struggled and sweated and bled and finally, in the wreck of her bed, the tiny healthy baby girl was delivered. The best efforts of all the king's physicians, however, could not save the beautiful queen. She died in her devastated husband's arms. The magical pond in the forest turned bitter overnight. In tucked-away corners, the king's advisors muttered that they could have predicted this. Happy as they had been, such a union was never meant to be.

Eventually after a month spent locked away in his apartments, the heartbroken king took his baby daughter in his arms, and as she gurgled up at him, pure white streaks in her soft dark hair, he finally spoke.

'Beauty,' he said. 'We shall call her Beauty.'

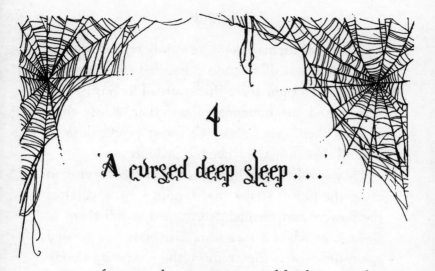

4

'A cursed deep sleep...'

After two hours or more of hacking at the thick branches and vines, the tangle of which made up the thick wall, it was clear to all three of the travellers that there was nothing natural about this occurrence. It was also slow, hard work. As the huntsman cut with his axe, the prince and Petra would hold the space he made open and they would all edge forward and beat at the next section. When the branches behind them were released, they would close up again, the splintered wood and severed vines re-linking and entwining so tightly that no break in the join was visible.

They had started the day bantering lightly – especially the prince and Petra, whose excitement was greater than the huntsman's – but soon the only words any of them spoke were purely related to their task. They were all hot and exhausted and crammed together in a tight space that shuffled forwards very slowly, and the huntsman knew that should they stop, or their axes break, the forest would close in around them and they'd be trapped forever.

They tied handkerchiefs over their faces trying to avoid the heady scents that sprang from several of the flowers and seemed determined to lull them to sleep. Even when Petra's slim, firm body was pressed again his own as they moved, the huntsman's body didn't respond. This forest was dangerous and the trees were clearly against them in their work. The huntsman had always trusted the forest. Nature was honest ... and nature was very keen to keep them away from whatever lay beyond this wall.

Finally, however, the pig-headedness of men prevailed and they tumbled, gasping and free, from the grip of the wood. The spring sunshine was bright and warm, and they sat on the grass for a moment, laughing and sharing some water and regaining their strength. It was a few seconds before the eerie quiet around them became too much to ignore.

'I can't even hear any birds singing,' Petra said softly as their moods and laughter quietened. 'On a beautiful day like this they should be everywhere.'

She frowned up at the empty sky. Ahead of them lay a small city and in the distance, as was the way with all the kingdoms, there sat a castle at its heart.

'It's not just the birds,' the prince said. 'I can't hear anything. No noise at all.'

He was right. Even the trees dotted along the edges of the narrow road didn't rustle as the warm breeze moved through them. The hairs on the back of the huntsman's neck prickled and he kept one hand on the hilt of his hunting knife as they began to walk, once again cursing the king and the prince and the royal necessity for adventures. As if life wasn't adventure enough.

The cart was just over the other side of the slight hill from the forest's edge and Petra gasped when it came into view. The huntsman didn't blame her. It was a strange sight, that was for sure, stopped as it was in the middle of the road with the shire horse laying down in front of it. Around it were a dozen thick-wooled sheep with a dog lying in their midst He wasn't sure what he'd been expecting, but this wasn't it.

As the prince clambered onto the cart, the huntsman crouched and touched the horse. It was warm and blood pumped in a steady rhythm through its body.

469

'Hey,' the prince said. 'I think he's still alive.' Up on the cart, a fat man's head lolled forward, the reins having slipped from his hands. The prince tried to straighten him up, but the man's weight slid sideways and he lay across the seat. The prince shook him. 'Hey!' he said, loudly, the word a stranger in the eerie silence around them. 'Hey, wake up! Wake up!' The fat man didn't move. He didn't even snore or grunt or shuffle as the prince wobbled him.

The huntsman looked at the animals around him; not one of them dead and rotten as he'd been expecting to find in this lost kingdom. The prince had struck on it without thinking.

'They're asleep,' he muttered. 'They're all asleep.'

'That can't be right.' Petra dropped to her knees and stroked the sheepdog. 'They can't have been asleep all this time. Not for a hundred years. It isn't possible.'

But it appeared, as they moved on, that it was entirely possible. Every living creature they passed was lost in slumber, apparently having fallen asleep in the same instant. There was a soldiers' outpost as they walked into the first main streets of the city, and two were asleep face down on a chess board. Others had crumpled in a heap at their sentry posts.

The huntsman counted about fifteen. 'That's a lot of soldiers,' he said.

'Maybe they were at war,' the prince answered. 'The kingdoms are always at war.'

It was an apparently affluent city and there were some beautiful mansions set back in their own grounds, again with sleeping soldiers guarding the high gates, but even the ordinary cottages closer to the castle were well maintained, even though the flower-beds were overgrown with weeds. Here and there long grasses had sprung up everywhere between cobbles and flagstones. Animal life might be slumbering but the plant life still grew, although not to the proportions expected. 'Whatever this is, it's affected every living thing,' Petra said, stooping to examine the flowers.

As they moved closer to the centre of the pretty town the huntsman noticed that some houses had the windows roughly boarded up and when he prised the wood from one they saw that the glass behind was smashed and the contents of the house were either broken or ruined in some way. This had clearly been done before the city fell asleep, and he could find no rhyme or reason to the house that had been wrecked. They were ordinary people's homes. What had happened to the people who had lived in them?

After a while they split up to explore more thoroughly, and everything they found was the same. Men, women and children, all asleep in a variety of strange places. One woman's face was badly burned where she'd been making soup on a stove, now a long time cold, and as she slipped to the floor she'd pulled the pan down over her.

Only in one cottage did the huntsman find anyone in their bed. Whoever it was they must have died before whatever happened to send the city to sleep, and all that remained was a skeleton in a nightdress with wisps of thin hair poking out from beneath a black nightcap. A knife stuck through the thin fabric of her dress and now that her flesh had rotted away, it leaned loose against her ribs where some unknown assailant had stabbed it into her breathing body. It was a strange cottage, with none of the bright colours found in so many of the others, and there was a cold, stale dampness hanging in the air as if none of the outside warmth had crept in during the long years that had passed. He looked in the small cupboards and found jars of herbs and bottle of potions with words he didn't understand on the labels. It was a witch's cottage, he was sure. He shivered and was about to leave when the small stove in the tiny main room caught his eye. The door was open a tiny

fraction and something glittered inside. He crouched
and pulled the black iron door open.

Inside, sitting on a pile of soot, were a pair of
sparkling slippers. He reached in and took them out.
They were light and warm in his hands. Diamonds,
he thought. They were made of diamonds, not glass
at all. Why would someone have been trying to burn
them? Was this the work of whoever had killed her?
Were the two deeds linked in the strange history of
this kingdom? He stared at them for several seconds
until he heard Petra and the prince calling for him.
The woman upstairs was long gone. She would not
miss them, and he and his companions might need
something to barter with at some point. He slipped
the shoes into his bag and got to his feet. If the city
were to somehow wake and the shoes were declared
missing he would return them. For now, he'd consider them his fee for this babysitting task the king
had set him.

'What do you think they are?' the prince asked, as
he and Petra climbed the stone steps and examined the lines on the base of the statue more closely.
'These can't be old, can they?'

'No.' The huntsman frowned. Even though it was clear that the whole city was in some kind of a cursed deep sleep, now they were closer to the castle he couldn't shake the feeling that they were being watched. It was an instinct he was trained not to ignore. 'Look at those ones round the other side. That chalk is fresh.' The lines grew more ragged, but they were definitely some form of counting. Were they charting days? Or months? It was hard to tell. There were a lot of them, whichever it was.

'You mean someone's still awake?' Petra asked.

'That can't be right,' the prince said. 'Even if they hadn't fallen asleep, they'd surely be dead by now.'

'Maybe, maybe not,' Petra said cheerily. 'None of this is normal, after all. And I used to hear howling sometimes. Through the wall. Something's alive in here.'

The huntsman wasn't listening to her. A noise, faint and far to his left had caught his attention. Someone was following them. He was sure of it.

'Hello?' he called. 'Anyone there?' There was no answer but a return to silence. 'Come on,' he muttered. 'Let's get to the castle. If there are any answers, we'll find them there.' The prince nodded, not picking up on the huntsman's point. Trouble, when it came to ordinary people, was normally delivered to them by royalty. Whatever had made this city silent, it had started in the castle.

Petra had never seen anything like it. Even as they'd walked through the city she'd felt slightly overwhelmed by the looming building that rose so high above the ordinary houses she wondered if in the right light it would engulf them all with its shadow, but as they walked through the open gates, carefully stepping over the crumpled heap of soldiers, for the first time in her life she felt small and insignificant. The village, the forest and her grandmother's cottage had been her world, and all the time this whole city had been sleeping so close by. How much more was there that she would never see, even if she spent a lifetime exploring?

'Heavily guarded,' the huntsman said.

Petra glanced at him. His dark eyes scanned the heavily armed men at their feet and she could see the sight bothered him.

'Perhaps they had more to worry about than my father does,' the prince said. 'Who knows what lies on the other side of this kingdom?'

The huntsman nodded but said nothing more.

They were a strange pair, this prince and his companion. One so full of charm and courtly grace, the other quiet and hardy. Petra liked them both, but she knew which one she trusted the most. A man of the forest would always win her vote if it came to her own survival. The prince might be good with a sword but she imagined that he'd learned to duel with rules. Killing something living was very different to courtly sword play – the prince had discovered as much in Granny's kitchen when faced by the winter wolf. There were no rules when it came to fighting for your very existence. They were both handsome, though, she'd give them that.

Vines and ivy had crept up the high stone walls, clinging to the mortar between the heavy rocks as if trying to suffocate the life out of the building itself. In the courtyard men and women slept where they'd stood, one still holding a saddle that was no doubt meant for the horse that slept beside him. Another was surrounded by loaves of bread that had tumbled from his basket.

The huntsman pushed a door open and the hinges shrieked, shocked at the movement after so long. The sound echoed as they stepped inside. Dust danced upwards as they moved, suddenly disturbed from its own slumber on the marble floor. Unlike the smaller houses in the city, no passing wind or weather had been able to penetrate the thick wall and Petra felt as if she had truly walked into a forgotten tomb. Her heart thumped as they walked, leaving footprints in the dirt behind them.

'We should split up,' the prince said. His voice was loud and confident. Petra wondered why he didn't find the castle as eerie as she did but then, she supposed, he was used to castles. He was not in awe of the wealth or beauty that lay under the dust of years passed. 'I'll take upstairs. Petra, you stay on this floor.'

'I'll search the lower levels and dungeons,' the huntsman finished. 'But don't touch anyone. If you find anything then shout and wait.'

'Just what I was going to say,' the prince said.

Petra nodded. The idea of searching alone made her shiver but she wasn't going to admit her fear to the two men. If they were happy to do it then she would be too.

'If we can't find the source of this curse by tomorrow,' the huntsman said, 'then we load some riches onto a cart for your father and try and cut our way back out. Agreed?'

The huntsman had barely smiled since they'd found the city. Petra was sure that if it was up to him they'd be leaving it by now. Whatever had brought him here it wasn't thrill-seeking or adventure, but Petra couldn't help feeling a little of those things herself. She couldn't imagine turning her back on this place and not knowing how the story had begun, or how it ended.

'And mark your path on the walls or in the dust,' he said. 'So you can see where you've been and find your way back here.' This time he did give her a small smile and she liked the creases that formed in his cheeks, as if in his normal life he smiled a lot. The instruction was for her alone. The prince might be used to finding his way round castles, but she most definitely wasn't.

The ground floor of a castle, she'd decided within an hour or so, was a very strange affair. There were three ballrooms; two light and airy and with ceilings painted with beautiful dancing couples, and another further back – which could only be accessed through a library and then a small annexed corridor – that was painted red and decorated with ornate gold and heavy black curtains. It was an odd contrast with the other two and she decided she didn't like it very much at all. The air had a metallic tang to it and, although she was technically trespassing wherever she went, this was the only room in which she felt she'd invaded something secret. No one was sleeping in any of the main function rooms, all of which were breath-taking and yet slightly impersonal and as she explored them she decided that royal residences were clearly as much about the visitors as they were about the family that lived there. It was clearly a strange thing to be a royal.

In some kind of meeting room, several grey-haired men in sombre robes were asleep on thick documents and open books and more soldiers slept in the door-ways. A jug of wine had been knocked across the table and where it had soaked into the polished wood and scattered papers, the stains looked like blood on the large table.

She felt happier when she found the smaller, more ordinary rooms where servants were working. In one long corridor boot boys slept over pots of polish, and in the kitchens the tables were full of half-made pies and pastries, the cooks and maids crumpled on the cold stone floor. Despite the huntsman's orders not to touch anyone or anything, Petra dipped her finger in an open apple pie and then tasted it. The filling was sweet and fresh as if the mixture had

479

been placed inside only minutes before. She ate some more. At least they wouldn't starve while they were here. There would be enough food in the city to keep them going for several hundred years.

An echo of a shout carried its way to her and she frowned, abandoning the pie and running back towards the centre of the building, her shoes slapping against the floor and raising dust in her wake. Was that danger? The shout came again. Closer this time.

'I've found something. I need help!'

She almost collided with the huntsman as she rounded a corner into the central hallway and without pausing they both ran up the sweeping staircase, taking the steps two at a time, following the prince's shouts until they found him in a set of luxurious apartments in the middle of the castle.

Petra stood in the bedroom doorway and her mouth dropped open.

'We've got to do something,' the prince said. 'We've got to help.'

Petra cautiously followed the huntsman inside the vast room. At its centre was a large four poster bed, covered in sheets and blankets of pure, soft white. Sheer linen curtains hung around it, tied back to the posts with ribbons like curtains. In a glass by the bed, a single red rose sat in water, all of its petals scattered around the glass save the last one which drooped low but still clung to the stem. A beautiful young woman lay sleeping on the bed. She was fully dressed in a blue silk gown and jewels sparkled at her neck. Her full lips were parted slightly as if something had just surprised her, and her hair, jet black apart from two thick blonde streaks on either side, spread out across the pillow in glossy waves. She was beautiful, but she was also incredibly pale. Given the state of the floor around the bed, that wasn't a surprise to Petra.

Blood. It was everywhere. A pool of it, thick and crimson, had spread beneath her and now almost circled the large bed. The girl's right hand hung over the side of the bed and as Petra stared at it a single tiny drop of blood fell from her forefinger to the floor.

'It's her finger,' she whispered. 'Look. She must have pricked her finger.'

'Have you got any bandages?' the huntsman asked. 'Any salve?'

'Maybe.' Petra yanked the small bag her granny had packed from her shoulder and tipped the contents out over the end of the bed, taking a careful step to avoid the blood. 'Is she still alive? She must have lost nearly all her blood.'

The prince leaned over the bed and placed one hand on the girl's chest. 'Yes!' he exclaimed, smiling. 'She's breathing. Just.' He didn't lift his hand though, but ran it up the sleeping beauty's body. 'I've never seen a girl like her,' he whispered. 'She's perfect.'

'I don't think you should be touching her like that,' Petra said as she handed the huntsman a small jar of her granny's natural antiseptic. 'She's asleep. You can't go around touching girls when they're asleep.'

The prince either wasn't listening or chose to ignore her, because as the huntsman cut a strip of sheet from the bed, the prince stroked the girl's face. 'I should kiss her,' he murmured.

'No you really shouldn't.' Petra glared at him. 'That would be all manner of wrong. If someone kissed me without my permission – handsome travelling prince or not – I'd punch them.'

The huntsman laughed. 'She has a point.'

'She's a princess. I'm a prince. I'm *supposed* to kiss her.'

'We need to talk about the dungeons—' the huntsman started.

Two things happened at once. The huntsman wrapped the strip of cloth tightly around the tiny salved cut and stopped the next tiny droplet from escaping the wound; the prince ignored Petra's warning, lowered his mouth to the sleeping princess's and kissed her.

A sudden tremble ran through every stone in the building, and then, as the prince lifted his lips from hers, the girl on the bed gasped and then coughed, and then her eyes opened.

'She's waking up,' Petra whispered. In the glass by the bed, the rose came into full, beautiful bloom.

A clattering noise came from somewhere close by, followed by a brief exclamation. Outside, a horse whinnied.

'Not only her,' the huntsman said, getting to his feet. 'They're *all* waking up.'

'We've lifted the curse,' the prince said, his hand still holding the princess's.

As the city came alive around them, all three travellers stared at the beautiful girl on the bed who was slowly easing herself into a sitting position. Colour was rushing back into her face as if with the curse lifted her body was restoring itself to perfect health. She looked at them, her eyes bleary.

'Who are you?' her voice was soft and sweet. 'What happened?' She looked down at her bandaged finger and the blood on the floor below and her eyes widened, her confusion gone. 'There was a spindle! Rumplestiltskin!'

'I'm a prince from a faraway kingdom,' the prince said. 'My father had heard legends of your city's plight and we came to save you.' Petra could clearly see that the young prince was in the process of falling head over heels in love. 'I woke you with a kiss,' he finished.

The woman on the bed smiled at him and either chose to ignore the fact that the bandage was more likely to have saved her than a stolen kiss, or wasn't awake enough to think it through properly.

'How long have I been asleep?' she asked.

Petra thought of the lines that had been scratched into the statue at the centre of the sleeping city.

'We think nearly a hundred years,' she said softly.

The princess said nothing for a long moment and then, just before the soldiers burst into the room, she muttered that one word again.

'Rumplestiltskin.'

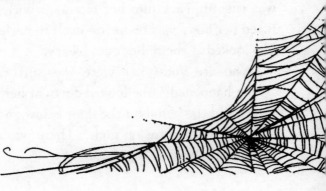

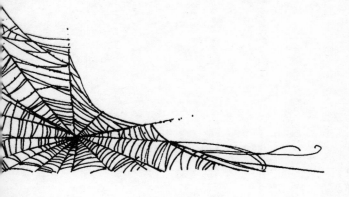

5

'Tonight is for celebration'

As it turned out the princess wasn't a princess at all but a queen, and her name was Beauty. As the city woke from its slumber she declared the day a holiday and ordered the kitchens to prepare a great feast to celebrate. She was a whirlwind of light and laughter and the huntsman saw that the prince was dazzled by her. She, in turn, seemed quite taken with him, and she kept her arm linked with his as she walked through the castle with her guests.

'My poor father, the king, has only been gone six months,' she said. 'We were a city in mourning but now we must put that behind us and look to the future.' She looked up at the prince and smiled. 'And I can't thank you enough for saving all of us from this terrible curse.'

'We— I –' the prince said, '– am your humble servant. I would have slain a dragon to save you.'

'But why would anyone want to curse you?' Petra asked.

'I don't know,' Beauty answered. She frowned. 'I can't remember. I just know that it was Rumplestilt-skin.' Her voice was soft and her frown deepened into puzzlement. 'Uncle Rumple.'

'Your uncle?' the prince said. 'But that's terrible. He must want the crown for himself.'

'I called him my uncle,' Beauty said, 'but he wasn't a blood relative. He was my father's closest advisor.' Her frown dissolved into sadness. 'I thought he loved me.'

'Everyone loves you, your majesty.' A middle-aged man dressed in heavy, fur-lined robes swept along the corridor towards them. 'You must never forget that.' When he reached them, he bowed deeply. His dark eyes were sharp under his bushy eyebrows. 'Let your faithful advisors worry about such things. He will not get close to you again, that much I person-ally guarantee. For now, you should put it out of your head and be glad that such a dashing prince has restored all to order.'

He smiled at the prince who beamed back, happy to be at the centre of such adulation, but the huntsman caught the sharp edge to the older man's smile and the hint of nervous energy escaping from him.

'Thank you, First Minister.' Beauty said. 'You have always been so very good to me.'

'That's because I know and understand you, your majesty. Let your council worry about such things; you should all be bathing and preparing for the feast,' her advisor continued. 'Tonight is for celebration!'

'You're right.' The queen rose up on tip toes and gave the man a kiss on his bearded cheek. 'You are so often right. I just wish I could remember. There are always so many things I can't remember.' She clapped her hands together, her smile restored. 'But let us retire to our rooms and prepare. Later there shall be music and dancing and everything will be well in the world again.'

The huntsman let the small group walk ahead and hung back with the advisor. 'What does she mean when she says there are things she can't remember?' he asked. 'Is she ill?'

'No, no,' the first minister said smoothly, picking up his pace to return the huntsman to the group. 'She has had occasional small memory blackouts since she was a child. They are nothing unusual. Nothing to concern you.'

The huntsman smiled and followed him, but his skin prickled. He might not be a man of court, but he was pretty sure that whenever someone said there was nothing to concern him, it meant exactly the opposite.

The huntsman did not take much time preparing for the dinner, choosing to keep his own clothes on after washing rather than wear the fancy shirt and trousers left for him in his room. These people were not his people and while he would be polite and respectful, he had no desire or need to impress them. As far as he could tell his job was nearly done. He just needed to get the prince safely home again.

He catnapped for half an hour or so and then wandered the castle and grounds for an hour. After the stillness and silence of their arrival it was strange to see the people suddenly active, like dolls brought back to life. Did they even know how long they had slept, he wondered, as women scrubbed dust from the floors and men polished windows. Most were laughing and talking excitedly, but here and there some cast suspicious looks his way and kept their heads down as they scurried to their next task.

In the central corridors of the castle he passed groups of gentlemen and ministers, each dressed like the first minister but with perhaps less fur and finery on their robes. A few were huddled in deep conversation, only breaking away and pretending mirth and laughter as he went by. Were they plotters, he wondered. The young queen was sweet and kind; were these old men trying to take her kingdom from her? He tried to push the thought from his mind. This was not what he was here for. This kingdom's problems were none of his business.

He climbed high up into one of the turrets, wanting to get a view of what lay to each side of them, but as he reached the summit he was stopped by two soldiers. They were not boys, but men; thick set and gruff. Beyond them, a large black bell hung in a recess.

'You're not allowed up here,' the largest of the two men said. 'Everyone knows that.' His hand was on his sword, and the huntsman raised his hands slightly.

'I'm just a visitor,' he said. 'I wanted to see the view.'

'Then use the windows. This tower is out of bounds. Only the ministers are allowed up here.'

They took a step forward and the huntsman retreated back down the stone stairs. Why would a bell need guarding? Why did he get the feeling that this castle was filled with secrets? There was only one person who could give him the answers: the traitor Rumplestiltskin, wherever he was.

The moon was full that night and the windows were wide open to let the light shine through; the feast was a merry affair. The sumptuous banqueting hall had been decorated with flowers and candles and every table was filled with more food than the guests could possibly eat. The huntsman and Petra sat to either side of Beauty and the prince, who really only had eyes for each other and spent most of the evening holding each other's hands and feeding each other sweetmeats.

Petra, dressed in a beautiful red gown and looking every inch the court lady, was talking to a minister seated on the other side of her while the huntsman, not one for small talk at the best of times, ate and drank while quietly watching the gathered guests. They were mainly older men and women and although they smiled and laughed, he noticed that they did not look often to the main table where their queen sat.

'Some more wine, sir?'

The huntsman looked up to see a pretty serving girl smiling at him. He nodded and she leaned forward to refill his glass, angling her body so that her ample cleavage was clearly on display should he choose to look. Being a hot-blooded man of the forest, he did. 'Tell me,' he said. 'Who are all these guests?'

'Ministers and their wives mainly,' she answered. 'Friends of the old king. Why do you ask, sir?' She continued to lean forward intimately and he could smell her clean warmth and her young skin was clear and bright.

'They just all seem a little old for the queen. Where are all the young men of the court?'

'Oh, they don't come to these dinners, sir. They come to the balls. I don't serve at the balls so I can't tell you about them.'

The flirtation in her voice was replaced with a

slightly defensive edge, but the huntsman squeezed her hand and winked and the blush returned to her face. Suddenly he felt the need for something simple and uncomplicated and this girl was clear about her attraction to him.

'Perhaps, after the feast,' he said, 'we could drink some wine and I could tell you a few things about my homeland.'

'I'd like that.' The girl grinned. 'I'll find my way to your rooms then.' She turned and bustled away and the huntsman smiled after her. Courtly intrigue he could live without.

'Hey.' A finger tapped his shoulder and Petra snuck into the seat beside him. 'The forest hasn't opened up.'

'What?' The huntsman was still wondering how the serving girl would feel beneath him. Petra nudged him again.

'The minister I was talking to. He said that the forest wall is still there. The curse or whatever it is can't have been broken fully.' She paused. 'Is it just me, or does everything seem a bit odd? Bits of this castle just don't make sense.'

'It's not just you,' the huntsman muttered. 'I saw the dungeons—' But before he could say any more the prince got to his feet, tapping the side of his crystal wine glass with a small spoon. His face was flushed and his eyes sparkled.

'Firstly, I would like to thank you all for this wonderful hospitality you have shown me and my travelling companions. We are honoured and humbled at the kindness you have shown us.'

There was a smattering of applause and the huntsman nodded awkwardly at the guests who caught his eye.

'But my biggest thanks must be for the beauty that you have brought into my life.' The prince looked down at the smiling woman beside him and suddenly the huntsman knew where this speech was going. The prince was headstrong and impulsive, he'd already known that, but foolish was about to be added to the list.

'From the moment I saw her asleep on her bed, I knew I would love her forever. I had never seen anyone so perfect,' he said. 'I have asked her if she will marry me,' he smiled at the guests, 'and she has said yes.'

A few gasps ran round the room and then the assembled ministers burst into applause. The huntsman watched as a few of the men exchanged glances as they clapped. Behind their smiles, they weren't entirely happy with the news.

'And so,' the queen got to her feet, 'let there be music and dancing!'

It was when the young couple were on their third dance that the first minister signalled the huntsman and Petra to follow him to an ante-chamber and closed the door behind them. He poured them each a glass of red wine and then sat behind a heavily inlaid desk. The huntsman wondered if the young prince realised who really ran this kingdom. It wasn't the pretty girl he was dancing with, that was for certain.

'I want you to undertake a task for me,' he said. 'Your prince has said I may count on your agreement.'

For the thousandth time since leaving his home, the huntsman once again silently cursed the prince.

'My job,' he said, leaning against the wall and sipping his wine, 'is to protect the prince and ensure his safe return. Nothing more.'

'Then you will do as I ask. For I imagine his safety depends on it: you must find Rumplestiltskin and bring him to me.'

'Don't you have soldiers who can do that?' Petra

asked. 'You do seem to have a lot of soldiers here.'

'The soldiers are looking for him too. But I have my reasons for wanting you to find him rather than them.'

'Why?' the huntsman asked. He thought of the dungeons but didn't mention that he'd seen them. Somehow he thought that might blacken his card and, as Petra had pointed out, there were a *lot* of soldiers in the city. It wouldn't be difficult for the first minister to dispose of a travelling huntsman. And nor did he want to end up on the wrong side of one of those cell doors.

'Just to be certain,' the first minister smiled, hiding an impatient flash of an expression behind it.

'You don't think he was working alone,' Petra said. 'You want names from him.'

'My reasons are none of your concern. Suffice to say that I want him brought to me and the spindle he carries destroyed.' He took a thick piece of parchment from the desk and handed it to the huntsman. 'Those are the addresses of his home and other places he frequents. Perhaps you'll find clues to his whereabouts there.'

The huntsman took it and tucked it into his belt. 'We'll try, but we don't know your city or its people. The soldiers will have more luck.'

'You're a huntsman,' the first minister purred. 'Hunt.'

'We'll wait until the city is asleep,' he said, 'and go then.' He opened the door for Petra and they left the minister behind.

'He thinks there are other conspirators,' Petra said. 'Why would anyone conspire against Beauty? She seems the kindest and gentlest of creatures.'

Without consultation, neither of them headed back to the banqueting room from which music and laughter drifted towards them, but took the central staircase up to their rooms.

'Who knows?' the huntsman said. As they turned onto a vast landing the curtains billowed in the evening breeze coming through the open veranda doorways. Petra paused and her gaze drifted, as if their current conversation was suddenly forgotten. 'Did you hear that?' she asked.

'What?' the huntsman frowned. His hearing, trained by years of tracking, was excellent but aside from the revellers below and the breeze the air was empty.

'Oh nothing,' Petra said softly, heading towards the balcony doors. 'Just something I've heard before. From the other side of the wall.' She pulled the curtains back and stood in the open doorway.

Outside the moon shone full and low in the dark sky. 'I think I'll sit out here for a while. Get some fresh air.'

'You don't have to come with me tonight,' the huntsman said. 'You may be safer in the castle.'

'I want to come,' she answered. 'There's something in this city I need to find too.' She glanced back at him over her delicate shoulder, her eyes dark in the gloom. 'And I'm not at all sure how safe this castle is.'

He couldn't argue with that. His own senses had been humming ever since the queen woke up and the first minister's request made his nerves jangle. He was already a pawn in one royal court's game, and now he was embroiled in another. As Petra wandered out towards the edge of the balcony, he left her and took the stairs two at a time, needing to release some energy.

A figure waited outside his bedroom door. He frowned and then smiled. It was the serving girl. She dropped into a slight curtsey.

'I wondered where you'd gone.' She looked up, her eyes sparkling mischievously. 'I thought p'raps you might like something brought to your room.' She held up a jug of wine. 'I thought I could serve it to you. Personally.'

The huntsman laughed and swung open the door to his room. He bowed. 'Ladies first.'

'Oh,' the girl giggled as she passed him. 'I'm no lady.'

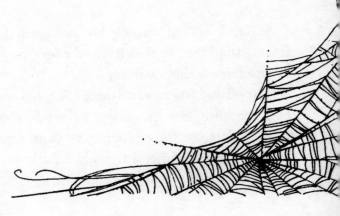

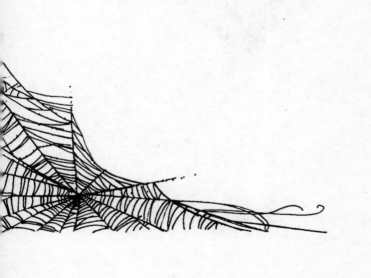

6

'The dark days...'

'Perhaps all this was just fate,' Beauty murmured into his chest as the prince held her close and they danced. 'If Rumplestiltskin hadn't ... done whatever he did, if I hadn't slept, then we'd have never met.' She looked up at him and smiled. It was the sweetest expression he'd ever seen and his heart melted all over again just looking at her exquisite face. Her eyes were the colour of clear water in a summer stream and he wanted to dive into them. To know her completely. 'I would have been long dead before you were born,' she continued. 'You would never have woken me.'

'Then yes, my love.' He kissed her forehead. Her skin was soft and her hair smelled of spring flowers. He was completely enchanted by her. 'It must be fate.'

'You saved me,' she tilted her face up to him, the two blonde streaks in her perfectly black hair hanging loose in styled curls to either side of her pale cheeks. His lips met hers and they kissed again. She was soft in his arms and the feel of her tongue touching his was electric. He *had* saved her. Already, in his mind, he had pushed aside the image of the huntsman bandaging her finger and stemming her dripping blood at the moment she woke. That was simply coincidence.

'True love's kiss is the only way to break a curse,' she said, her mouth only parted from his by a breath. 'Everyone knows that.'

'And I love you truly,' he whispered back, his voice raw. He did love her. It had gripped him from the moment he'd touched her, a wave of wonder and awe and passion that he'd never felt before. It was almost like magic. He pulled her closer to feel the swell of her bosom against his shirt. His mouth dried slightly as he fought the urge to run his hands over her body.

'Let's get married quickly,' he said. His desire for her was so great he wasn't sure he could wait any longer. Everything else had faded away; his father's wishes for an expansion to his kingdom, the desire to return home laden with treasure and be treated like a hero, even his normal lust for drinking and

wenching had gone. Home was a distant memory.
All that mattered was this girl and possessing her
completely.

'Yes,' she said, as breathless as he was. Her eyes
sparkled in the light from the glittering chandeliers
above. 'I will announce it to the city tomorrow and
we shall wed the next day. We'll have a family and
live happily ever after. I shall give everyone in the
city a gold coin as a wedding gift to show my happiness. And there will be days of feasting. I want my
people to be as happy as I am. It's all I ever want.'

The prince was sure his heart would explode. Not
only was she beautiful, she was kind and gentle and
generous too. 'I can't believe that you weren't betrothed already,' he said. 'What is wrong with the
noblemen of this kingdom? Or the princes close by?'

'My father was very protective of me,' she said,
quietly, a slight shadow darkening her face and her
eyes glancing away. She must have loved him very
much, the prince thought. 'Well, now I'll protect
you,' he said. 'My huntsman will find the traitor and
all will be well.'

'And we'll live happily ever after,' Beauty murmured again, her smile returning. They kissed once
more and the music played on. Around them, aware
that the young couple had eyes for none but each

other, the ministers and their wives quietly slipped away. They were no longer young and neither was the night, and despite having spent a century sleeping their bodies were tired and their feet ached and they wanted to let their smiles drop.

A few paused at the door and glanced back with a mixture of nerves and heart-ache. She was so very beautiful, and so very sweet. And then they shuddered slightly, unable to stop themselves, before heading to their rooms in the castle.

It was a cool spring night, but Petra didn't care. The castle, exquisite as so much of it was, felt claustrophobic, and she couldn't shake the unsettled feeling that had plagued her since Beauty had woken. The prince was blind to it – blind to everything but his sudden love – and even that she found strange. She knew men could be fools where women were concerned, and although the prince was too spoiled and arrogant for her to find him attractive he hadn't struck her as stupid. Her great-grandmother had passed down many tales of handsome princes – stories that were no doubt just flights of fancy – but they had ingrained in her the truth that royals were invariably only true to themselves. This one was suddenly a changed man, if that were the case.

The forest wall was still thick around them. The garish ballroom she'd found while the city slept was now firmly locked. Things were not well in this kingdom. She leaned on the smooth white marble of the balcony and tilted her head back. Above, the moon was full and heavy in the sky, shining its cool light over the darkness of the city below. Music drifted up from the ballroom as the party endlessly continued and she frowned as she tried to listen *beyond* it. It was an irritating distraction from the sound her ears sought. The counterpart to her soulful duet that had drawn her here even before the prince and the huntsman had arrived in her life. She didn't care about castles and sleeping beauties. She didn't even care about curses. These things were best left to run their course. It was the haunting song which had found her through the thick forest wall that held her here.

There it was. She almost gasped as she heard it; a faint low howl. It sang to her, so full of melancholy and yet so strong. Her heart fluttered. Her skin tingled. She stared out into the night. 'Where are you?' she whispered. '*What* are you?' The howl came again. Animal and human rolled into one. Without a thought to anyone who might hear her, she tilted her head back and answered the call. The creature, wherever it was, let its voice join hers, and she was sure she could hear her own excitement in the sound as their cries mingled in the night. Her feet yearned to run down the stairs and out into the strange city night. The huntsman could find this Rumplestilt-skin. She would be on a different search.

The sheets were a tangled mess around their legs and the serving girl, whose name it turned out was Nell, lay on her side next to the huntsman, her hair tumbling over one shoulder. She took a sip of wine and then handed him the glass. 'You must be thirsty.'

He laughed a little and drank, enjoying the sweat cooling on his body and then leaned forward and kissed her. She had an earthy beauty and a full vol-uptuous body that might one day swell into fat but for now was young and firm. She smiled and then settled down against his chest, both of them content in the enjoyment they'd taken from each other. They hadn't done much talking, their needs too urgent, but now they were sated they shared that comfort-able space that only exists between two strangers who'd just had good enough sex to be at ease in each other's company. Their bubble of intimacy and affection might not last, but it would at least remain as long as their nudity did.

'How long have you worked at the castle?' the huntsman asked, his fingers trailing through her hair and running down the soft skin of her back. She had been no virgin, her forward behaviour had made that clear before anything she'd done, but she was young – no more than seventeen or eighteen – and a bright enthusiasm shone in her eyes.

'Only two weeks.' Her warm breath tickled the hairs on his chest. 'I used to work at the dairy out on the edge of the city. Been there since I was twelve, when my parents were taken by the flu.'

'I'm sorry,' the huntsman said.

'Don't be. It was years ago and the women at the dairy were good to me. I can't complain. Lots of girls there had no families for one reason or another. I wasn't alone in that and it was a good place. The work wasn't too hard once you knew what you were doing, and they weren't too strict.' She giggled a little and then glanced up at him, her eyes full of remembered mischief. 'I used to sleep in a dorm with six other milkmaids. Some nights there were as many men in our room as maids. Some times *more*.'

Beauty

'I thought you'd learned a few tricks from somewhere.' The huntsman pulled her closer, enjoying her
uncomplicated warmth. Her past sexual encounters
didn't bother him – and wouldn't have even if he had
loved her. He had no time for bedroom double standards. It didn't fit with his internal logic and just struck
him as stupidity. They were all just animals, after
all, and why should a woman deny herself pleasure
simply because an insecure man might think less of
her? If no women gave in to their lusts then his own
life would have been much duller – women were by
far the more sensuous sex but most men didn't know
how to keep those feelings alive in them. Most men
made them feel ashamed of their desires rather than
delighting in them and then wondered why everything died and dried up between them. It would not
be like that for him, should he ever find the girl in
his dreams.

'From the dairy to the castle seems a big leap for
an orphan girl,' he said. He was probing her but he
couldn't help it. Ever since he'd got here his hackles
had been up and soon he would have to go and hunt
a traitor – a job he didn't relish if he was working in
a situation where he felt blinkered. He was no soldier
who could simply obey orders. 'How did you manage
that?'

'A few of the dairy girls have come to the castle over the years,' she said. 'The first minister visited and he chose me himself. So I packed up my things and here I am. I sometimes miss the dairy though. Even though life is easier, everything's so much stricter here.'

'You still seem to manage to find your fun, it seems,' he said.

'Well when a handsome stranger comes visiting I have to make the most of it.'

'So life in the kingdom is good then?' he asked, sipping wine thoughtfully.

'Yes, why?'

'There are so many soldiers everywhere. The castle is so heavily guarded. I thought you must have recently been attacked by another kingdom. They're always fighting, after all.' He paused. 'When we arrived and you were all sleeping, I saw the dungeons. Some of the equipment in there is . . .' It was hard to find an appropriate word for it. He hunted and killed as a way of life, but he made every death as swift and as painless as possible. The things he'd seen here were designed, as far as he could make out, to cause the maximum agony while keeping someone alive. It was the dungeon of a tyrant king, not of a beautiful, happy queen. 'Barbaric,' he said in the end.

'I wouldn't know about that.' She tensed slightly in his arms. 'And there's been no fighting. I think there are so many soldiers because of the dark days. We haven't had one for a month or so. There must be one due.'

'Dark days?' he asked.

'We're not meant to speak of them. No one is. It might upset the queen and no one wants that. She's such a gentle soul.' She sat up, crossing her legs and wrapping the sheet around her for warmth now that their sweat had cooled and heat faded. She took the wine glass from him and sipped. He didn't press her with another question but waited as she drank.

'They say that the queen was one of twins, but her sister was born mad and cruel, and lives locked up in apartments high in the castle. She's been there ever since her father locked her away for the safety of all. Sometimes at the queen's insistence, because she is fair and good and kind and loves her sister despite her wickedness, they change places. The queen locks herself in the apartments and her sister takes control of the castle. A bell rings out over the city and we are all to lock ourselves away until it's over.'

'And what does this other queen do during her time free?' The huntsman was troubled and intrigued in equal measure.

'No one really knows. There are always huge thunderstorms overhead that turn the roads to rivers. They say the other sister has her mother's magic. Sometimes there are parties at the castle.' Her face was animated but not without fear. 'I've heard carriages pass through the streets on those nights. But soon enough the sky clears and the bell sounds again and life carries on as normal.'

'How often do these days happen?' he asked.

'It depends. Although I'm sure they happen more often than they used to.' Nell shrugged. 'Like I said, we don't talk about them. No one would want the queen to know, and she's so kind to everyone. Perhaps there are so many soldiers because the ministers worry that someone might try and hurt her sister?'

It was the same thought the huntsman had. Nell was earthy but she wasn't stupid. A voice cut across the room.

'Well, my dear, now that you've given our visitor a potted history of our city's ridiculous rumours, perhaps you could get back to work?'

The huntsman had reached across the bed for his hunting knife before he realised that the speaker was the first minister. He stood in the corner of the room, his mouth tight with disdain. How long had he been there? It wasn't like the huntsman not to sense a stranger nearby. Maybe they hadn't closed the door to his room properly as they'd tumbled inside.

'I'm sorry, sir.' Nell leapt from the bed, her head down, the sheet wrapped round her as she dropped into a clumsy curtsey.

'She didn't do anything wrong,' the huntsman said, still lounging on the bed, forcing his body to relax so as not to give the statesman any clue how much his sudden interruption without knocking had irritated him. 'I didn't really give her any choice.'

The first minister looked at Nell who, having gathered her clothes, was shuffling to the bathroom door in order to dress with some modicum of modesty. 'Yes. I'm sure,' he said, his tone heavy with irony. 'She looked entirely *coerced* when I came in.'

'I have very strong powers of persuasion.'

'I'm sure you do.' The minister drew himself up tall. 'I hope your hunting skills are as impressive. It's time for you to go and find Rumplestiltskin. Remember, I need him alive.' He paused. 'And remember that your prince is still in the castle.'

The huntsman got up and stretched, enjoying the minister's discomfort at being presented with his nudity, before reaching for his trousers. 'Was that a threat?' he asked. 'When he is so beloved of the queen?'

A sneer crossed the minister's lips. 'Her safety is more important than her happiness. Sweet she might be, but I know her better than she knows herself.'

'But it's still a threat.' The huntsman smiled, his eyes twinkling. He had no time for anything other than plain speaking. The first minister shrugged. 'I prefer to think of it as a reminder of the balance of our relationship.'

'Don't worry,' the huntsman said, pulling his rough shirt over his head. 'I'll do my best.' He tucked his knife into the sheath on his belt and picked up his bag. He wasn't leaving the diamond shoes behind: there was no one here he trusted not to go through his things, not even the prince. He headed towards the door, deliberately brushing past the older man's slight frame. Not enough to nudge him, but just enough to let him know he wasn't intimidated by him. The huntsman might not have been educated in castle politics but he understood that power play amongst men worked in many different ways, and being the stronger of two was a primal strength.

'One more thing,' the first minister called after him. 'The soldiers.'

'What about them?'

'Don't assume they are friendly.'

The huntsman frowned. 'What do you mean?'

'I can't guarantee they are all loyal to the queen.' The minister steepled his fingers together under his chin. 'Let's just say that there may be some amongst my number who are my enemies. The soldiers are ordered to deliver the traitor to the whole council. There are some there who would use him to try and discredit me. That would not be good for the safety of our queen.' His eyes darkened. 'Or, by extension, of your young prince. I think we can both agree that the boy is too blinded by love to see anything other than wonder in the world at the moment.'

'That will be no problem,' the huntsman said. 'I've yet to meet someone here I trust. If I find your Rumplestiltskin alive, I'll bring him back to the castle. You have my word.'

He turned his back and strode through the door. He'd be glad to get back in the fresh air, even if he was to be confined by the city. At least most of the population would be asleep and he and Petra would have some peace from the wily ways of the strangers they had awoken.

Plus, despite the addresses and maps the first minister had so thoughtfully provided for them, the
huntsman had a pretty good idea where to look.

7
'The Beast is coming...'

As they walked through the silent streets Petra could almost convince herself that the city was enchanted again. She wondered how the residents could bear to sleep after their hundred year slumber, but it seemed the whole kingdom had fallen straight back into their daily routine. For them, after all, only a moment had passed.

Night was not that far from day and the sky was shifting to a midnight blue from black above them. Never having been in a city so big before, Petra felt as if she was in a maze. Only the castle dominating the skyline behind them giving her any sense of direction. The huntsman, however, was moving confidently.

'Are we going to this Rumplestiltskin's house?'

she whispered. She was back in her own clothes, and she pulled the hood of her red cape over her head as a sudden sharp breeze cut through an alleyway. For the first time she wished her beloved coat was black or grey or some colour that would blend into the buildings around her. In the dawn, with all the colour stripped from the air, she wouldn't escape attention, no matter if a soldier or the traitor they hunted only caught a glimpse of her from the corner of his eye. Not to mentioned drawing attention from the creature whose howls danced with her soul. Fascinated as she was to discover it, her heart raced with the danger. She knew only too well how wolves could rip weaker animals apart. Perhaps the colour of her coat was prophetic.

'Would you be in your house if you were him?' The huntsman answered quietly. 'I think not.'

His tanned face and dark eyes were lost to her as he kept in the shadows, but his feet moved with purpose. Petra trusted him. They made a strange trio – the prince with his adventure and need for a fairy tale ending, the huntsman who was clearly with him under duress, and then her, the forest girl, drawn by a rare sound that should terrify rather than attract her. Three outsiders with no common aim and only their need to get home uniting them.

'But we might find a clue there. To where he's hiding.'

'Soldiers will have searched it already, and no doubt wrecked anything of any use. They're rarely the most subtle of men.' They turned a corner and suddenly Petra recognised where they were: the large market square that sat at the heart of the common people's part of the city. The huntsman led them towards the monument in the middle. 'And I might not know where he's been hiding, but I have a good idea where we'll find him.' He pointed at the lines scratched into its surface. 'Someone was alive all this time. If it was him then the best hunter in the world won't find him. He's had a hundred years to explore this city. He'll know every nook and cranny and secret space in it. But people can't hide forever and this Rumplestiltskin must know that at some point he will be spotted by someone. What would you do if you were him?'

Petra looked at the lines which grew more unsteady with each marker of time. 'I would want to get away. Before the queen got too organised again.' She pulled her cloak tightly round her. 'But where could he go?'

'We got in. I imagine he saw us. If I was him I'd try that spot in the forest wall first.'

'But the forest closed up again behind us,' she said.

'Which is why we have a chance to catch him. And then maybe the forest wall will be kind enough to let us out again.'

'Good luck getting the prince to leave,' she muttered under her breath as they moved on again, at a faster pace this time. 'He's completely under her spell.'

Petra was out of breath and slightly sweaty by the time they'd followed the road to the city's edge. Here and there they'd ducked out of sight from passing groups of soldiers, but none noticed them, and they made so much noise as they approached that there was plenty of time to find a good corner or shadows to hide in. The huntsman studied the high matted wall of the forest and then smiled. 'Look,' he whispered. Petra followed his gaze. A bronze coin sat in the thick grass. 'A marker. He must have left it here after we came through. Remind him where the place was.' He looked around, scanning the area in the gloom. 'Over there,' he said, nodding towards a cluster of weeds and overhanging branches. 'We'll hide there until he comes.'

She had no real desire to press herself against the forest wall again – the memory of how it had tried to suffocate them on their way in was still fresh in her mind – but she stood behind the huntsman and did as he did. The perfume which enveloped them from behind was almost overwhelming, as if every plant and flower had a place in the wall. There was oak and sandalwood, lilies, lilac and apple blossom mixed with blackberry and the crisp scent of thick green leaves. For a moment, it almost made Petra giddy.

'When will he come?' she whispered.

'Dawn, I think. He'll want more light.'

As it turned out, it was not a long wait. After twenty minutes or so a dark silhouette scurried into view and, peering out between the branches, Petra knew it was the man they sought. He was tall and perhaps fifty years of age, and wore a crimson jacket that had seen better days. He had a heavy-looking knapsack on his back from the top of which the tip of a spindle poked out. Petra held her breath as he came closer to them, muttering under his breath and scanning the ground until he reached down and picked up the coin. In his other hand he carried a small axe and, after slipping the coin into his pocket, he began to hack at the thick greenery in front of him.

Petra barely felt the huntsman move. He dropped

to a crouch, below Rumplestiltskin's sightline, and moved silently out from their hiding place, working his way in a circle so he came up behind the man. The trees rustled as the axe beat into them, and with the sky slowly lightening a flurry of leaves danced around Rumplestiltskin while he tore at the wall, focused entirely on his task. Behind him the huntsman came closer, slowly and steadily, no sudden movements to alert his prey, until, with only two or three feet separating them, he lunged forward, fluid and agile.

It happened so quickly that Petra barely had time to gasp before the huntsman had spun Rumplestiltskin around and in his moment of shock, taken the axe from him. The man let out a low moan and slumped against the forest wall. Petra stepped out from her hiding place.

'You,' Rumplestiltskin said, his voice clear in the still dawn as he looked from the huntsman to her and back again. His eyes glistened and shone with despair. 'What did you do? Why did you wake her?'

'We need to take you back to the castle,' the huntsman said. 'This is not our business. You and your peers can resolve it.' Petra was surprised by the kindness of his tone.

'You've made it your business,' Rumplestiltskin

wailed. '*You* woke her. It was so close. After all this time, so long a time, a hundred years of waiting. It was so close. And then you woke her.'

Petra kept her distance. She wasn't sure what she'd been expecting but this complete emotional desolation wasn't it. Not after what she'd seen of the other ministers. But then, this man had been awake for the hundred years they'd all slept. What would that do to a person?

'After everything I lost,' he whispered, his eyes filling with tears. 'Everything I foolishly gave up. And then you *woke* her. And now everything is just as it was before.' He looked up at the huntsman. 'You stupid, stupid strangers.'

And then he broke. His shoulders slumped further and as he wept a low moan erupted from him carrying in it a hundred years of loneliness and despair. It was a terrible sight. She'd thought he would beg them to let him go, plead for his life, ask to be saved from whatever punishment awaited him at the castle, but instead he was resigned to it. Looking at the small axe he'd brought with him, that was now tucked into the huntsman's belt, perhaps he had never truly believed he could cut his way free.

The huntsman, clearly moved by the man's plight, stepped forward to put an arm around his shoulders, and Petra was so focused on the scene in front of her she didn't hear the footsteps rushing up behind her until it was too late.

Suddenly, she was jerked backwards by her red coat, and as strong arms roughly held her she felt cold, sharp steel against her throat. She let out a short yelp and the huntsman turned, Rumplestiltskin forgotten.

'You'll give him to me now.' The voice was gruff and the breath that hit her cheek was stale. She could feel a metal breastplate against her back and she wriggled slightly to try and break free but his arms were strong. He stank of sweat.

'Why don't you release the girl then, soldier?' the huntsman said. 'We're all on the same side here. We were bringing him back as instructed.'

'He's not going anywhere. I've got my orders. There are more men behind me.' His grip on Petra tightened and she struggled to breathe. 'Kill him now and we might let you both live.'

'Let the girl go. She's done nothing.' The huntsman took a small step forward and held up his hands. 'You do what you have to. But I'm not killing a man in cold blood.'

'Stay back.' The soldier – Petra guessed from the tension in his body that he was young and nervous under his bluster – pressed the knife harder against her neck. Too hard. A sharp pain upon her skin and she yelped again, knowing the knife had nicked her. Warmth trickled down her neck. Blood.

The huntsman froze. And then, from nowhere, it came, bounding over the huntsman and leaping towards Petra with a terrifying, angry growl.

The wolf.

It filled her vision. Thick blue-grey fur over a vast, muscular frame. This was no ordinary wolf, like those who scavenged her grandmother's goats. This was ethereal and earthy at once. It was twice the size and its fur shone so brightly that even in the dead light of dawn it seemed to glow. It flew through the air before her. Eyes that burned yellow and sharp teeth behind bared black lips. Claws extending from enormous paws. It was rage. It was fury.

Just before it hit her, Petra thought it was the most beautiful creature she had ever seen. And then the air was gone from her lungs and she was on the ground.

The ball had finished an hour or so before, but the prince and Beauty couldn't bear to part company just yet. The prince was sure he should be tired, but the sheer elation of having found love kept him wide awake. Although they had kissed, many times now, there was an innocence about her that stopped him suggesting they go to her rooms despite the throbbing desire he felt for her. He'd wait for their wedding night and then he'd take her gently and sweetly and their love would not be sullied by haste. She was so pure. After all the serving girls and wenches he'd shared his time with he was now almost ashamed of his past earthy encounters. Perhaps he should have kept himself pure for her. But then princes were supposed to be men of the world, and it was right that he should have experience: she was queen, but he would be master of their bedroom.

As night inched towards day they walked arm in arm, pausing here and there as she pointed out paintings she loved, or pieces of ornate sculpture she had commissioned, and slowly she showed him around her vast home; a castle equal to his father's own in wealth and lavishness. They paused in the kitchens where the night bakers had made fresh bread for the morning, and Beauty's kind words to them made the men blush as she praised them in their work.

Nibbling on hot croissants they wandered back into the heart of the castle and through the ballroom that had so recently been full of music and dancing. He pulled her close and they spun, laughing like children, across the floor until they reached the far door and paused to kiss. She was so natural in his arms and he ran his fingers down her face, brushing them across the tops of her breasts and listening to her sigh and shudder slightly with pleasure. She wanted him too, he could see it in the slight parting of her perfect lips and the haze in her eyes.

'I love you,' she said softly and then smiled.

'I love you too.' And he did. She was perfect.

From the ballroom, she led him into the library, all the walls lined with thousands of books which filled polished mahogany and oak shelves. As shafts of sunlight cut through the windows, Beauty ran from one shelf to another pointing out her favourite stories from childhood; princes who slayed dragons on the Far Mountain, pirate tales from the eastern seas and other tales of love, magic and adventure. As she giggled and promised him that they would read these stories together one day, to their own children, the prince spied a small door in the corner, virtually unnoticeable among the beauty and colour of the books around it. It was wooden, mahogany like the shelves, and as he opened it he was sure he heard the tinkling of distant bells. He looked up to see wires running from the hinges and up into the ceiling. A servants' bell? But why here? This was an in-between place, nowhere you would stop and require refreshments or a fire lit. Why would you? It was simply a narrow corridor. Was the door left over from some conversion years ago? Had the corridor once been part of a different room? He stepped forward, curious.

'Beauty,' he called back to her. 'What's down here?' The corridor was unadorned with any portraits and there was only a plain oak door at the other end. He walked towards it, not waiting for her, and lifted the heavy iron ring handle. He turned it and pushed, but nothing happened. The door was locked.

'I never come down here.' Beauty's voice sounded small, all humour gone from it, and he looked back to see her frowning slightly at the other end of the corridor. 'Why don't we go now? I'm tired. We should go to bed.'

The prince crouched slightly and peered through the keyhole. It was dark but he could just about make out the red of the walls and what looked like heavy black curtains. Gold glinted here and there. 'I think it's another ballroom,' he muttered, before straightening up and turning back to her. 'And you've never seen it? How can that be?'

She had started to tremble a little and her mouth tightened. 'I don't want to be here.'

'But aren't you curious? Surely you should know all the parts of your castle. You are the queen, after all.'

'I said I don't want to be here.' The trembling was becoming more visible and as Beauty backed away from him, she tugged at her hair, pulling strands free from the carefully arranged curls piled on her head.

'What's the matter?' What was suddenly upsetting her? Had someone died in this room? One of her parents perhaps? 'I'm sorry,' he said, rushing towards her. 'I didn't mean to upset you.'

He reached for her, but she stepped away from him. Her eyes had glazed slightly and he wondered if she even knew he was there. 'Beauty?' he said.

'I don't like it here,' she muttered, and then, without warning, she slapped herself hard across the face.

The prince was so shocked that for a moment he couldn't react at all. Bright red finger marks stained her smooth skin. Only when she lifted her hand to do it again did he reach forward and grab her wrist to stop her.

'What's the matter with you? What is it?'

She hissed at him and struggled to pull away, the trembling turning to shuddering so strong that the prince thought she might be about to have a fit. Perhaps that was it. Her breathing was coming faster and she hugged herself.

Rapid footsteps came across the library, and the first minister rushed towards them, his robes flowing behind him. 'What are you doing here? Why did you open the door?'

'I didn't ... I just ...' the prince didn't know what to say. The older man pushed him aside and wrapped his arm around Beauty. 'Is she okay?' the prince finished, feeling helpless. She clearly wasn't okay. Not only was she having the strange physical symptoms but something was happening to her hair. The two blonde streaks at the front were darkening and the rest was somehow getting lighter.

'I'll look after her.' The first minister blocked the prince's view. 'Go back to your apartment. Stay there.' He spoke sharply, his words cutting through the prince's shock. The only man who'd ever spoken to him like that was his father. 'Do not come out until I come and say you can. Do you understand me?'

'What's happening?' the prince asked. He felt like a child again.

'The Beast is coming,' the first minister said quietly. 'Now go.'

The prince did as he was told.

8

'Some Kind of terrible magic...'

They left the soldier where he lay, his throat ripped out and his eyes forever staring shocked and surprised at the greying sky, and moved quickly. The man might have been lying that there were others close by but dawn was breaking and soon the city would be alive again. It wouldn't be long before the body was found.

The wolf immediately calmed after its swift attack, standing by the dead man and letting out a long sorrowful howl before padding to Rumplestilt-skin's side, its eyes fixed on Petra. The man patted the fierce beast's head and then led the small group away. Petra was staring at the wolf, stunned, and the huntsman grabbed her arm and pulled her along. They had no choice now. He couldn't take the huge wolf on – and nor did he want to. There was something almost noble about its grace and ferocity. Had Rumplestiltskin tamed it? It didn't matter; the wolf had saved Petra, and he trusted animals more than men. Where the wolf went, he would follow.

Rumplestiltskin led them to a large oak tree and crouched to pull up a wooden hatch hidden beneath grass and leaves. 'Get in,' he hissed urgently. The wolf bounded through the dark hole first, and the rest followed. Only once they were sealed up in the dank earth did Rumplestiltskin take a torch from a slot on the rough wall, and light it. Ahead of them was a low tunnel, wooden struts here and there propping up the ceiling. It didn't look overly safe to the huntsman, but he followed anyway, holding Petra's hand in the gloom.

They walked, hunched over so far they might have been better off crawling, for several minutes, until the tunnel opened out into a man-made cave, with a door at the far end and a small hole in the ceiling that let in a shard of natural light from the surface several feet above them.

Rumplestiltskin had clearly tried to make it home and as well as two beds and piles of books there was a table holding a jug of wine, some fresh bread, cheese and a leg of roasted pork.

'If you're hungry, take something,' he muttered, clearing some papers from a chair so Petra, still slightly winded from the weight of the wolf, could sit down. The wolf's arrival and their subsequent flight had calmed him.

'You dug this place out? Yourself?' Petra asked, dabbing a piece of cloth over the cut on her neck to stem the blood.

'We had nearly a hundred years.' Rumplestiltskin put his knapsack down and sat on the bed. 'Relatively, it didn't take very long.'

'We?' the huntsman asked, and then just as the first ray of sunlight pierced through the narrow skylight, the wolf began to change.

His fur glittered a thousand colours and his yellow eyes widened as he whimpered. Myriad lights lifted from his coat and spun in a whirlwind around him until they were so bright the huntsman had to close his eyes. Even then the brightness made him flinch. The beast let out half a howl and then there was silence.

When the huntsman risked looking again the room was back to normal. The light was gone. So was the wolf. In its place, a man lay on the rough ground. He coughed twice and then sat up.

'That never gets any easier,' he groaned, and sat

up, dusting off his white shirt and black jacket. His hair was thick and dirty blond and his eyes were green with yellow flecks.

'You're a man,' Petra said quietly. She stared at him. 'I knew you weren't just a wolf. I knew it. All those times I listened through the wall it was you.' She smiled, and the man smiled back, and the huntsman felt the magic between them. It hummed in the room far greater than the glittering lights had shone.

'You're the girl who howls back.' The two stared at each other with the kind of recognition only people who have never met and yet are destined to be together could share.

'You saved my life,' Petra said.

The man nodded, but his jaw clenched with shame at his deed. 'I'm sorry I killed him,' he said. 'Things are different when I'm the wolf. There are no grey areas. I act on instinct.'

'I'm not sorry you killed him,' Petra said. 'He was going to kill us, after all.' Her elfin face glowed slightly and she trembled.

'Then you're welcome.' Rumplestiltskin had poured the man some water and he drank it and then got to his feet. He bowed to Petra. 'My name is Toby.'

'You've been awake all this time too?' The huntsman asked.

'Yes.' The gregarious grin left Toby's face. 'I was cursed. There was a witch in the city, an older woman, and she fell in love with me. She was a beautiful woman, famed for the diamond slippers that had enchanted many men before me into her bed, and she pursued me relentlessly. But I did not love her and she did not take my rejection well. One night she saw me with a lady of the court and her jealousy overwhelmed her. She cursed me. Every full moon I would spend the nights as a wolf. The first time it happened, my family were terrified. Rumours spread of a wolfman, and I was hunted. I hid in the forest and would only creep back into the city to forage for food and drink. It was on one such trip that the forest formed a wall behind me and the city fell asleep. I can only presume that because I was already cursed, the second curse didn't affect me.'

'Was she sleeping?' Petra asked. 'Will she be awake now?'

'No, I went to her house. She was dead in her bed. Murdered. I wonder if she had picked a man to lure to her bed whose wife's jealousy overwhelmed her fear.' Toby shrugged. 'The city will be better without her. She brought her fate on herself.'

'And I am forever grateful for that, despite your being trapped in this ageless time with me,' Rumplestiltskin squeezed Toby's shoulder. 'I would have gone mad without you.'

'Why didn't you sleep?' Petra asked the old man.

'I caused the curse. The magic doesn't affect he who carries it. Time froze for me, but I did not sleep.' He poured himself some wine and the huntsman noticed his hand was trembling. It had been a long hundred years. But why had he brought it on himself? He seemed a harmless man, unless some natural viciousness had been beaten out of him over the century. It was unlikely. Viciousness grew with bitterness and a hundred years alone would make any man bitter.

'Did you curse the wrong sister?' he asked. 'Surely you didn't mean to attack Beauty.'

'The wrong sister?' the old man smiled, wistfully. 'It was so easy for people to believe that story. The dark days. The second sister. The evil twin. One dark with hints of blonde, one blonde with hints of dark. One so kind and gentle and pure, the other wild and wicked and filled with her mother's magic.'

Somewhere overhead a flash of blue lightning crossed the sky and lit up their cave, and thunder rumbled so hard that the ground around them shook.

Rumplestiltskin looked at the huntsman, his eyes tired. 'There was only one child. They named her Beauty. And beautiful she was. But she was more than that: she was Beauty *and* the Beast.

𝕿*he young king and his people grieved for their beautiful queen and returned her body to the waters from whence she'd come, but still they stayed bitter, and the king did not blame the spirits of her ancestors for their anger. Being a kind and optimistic man he hoped that one day, when his daughter was grown, they would forgive him for his selfish act of loving the water witch and see that something beautiful could come from the union of earth and magic.*

He took great comfort in the infant Beauty for she was a good-natured baby and rarely cried. She smiled and gurgled in her father's arms and soon, although his heart would never truly mend, the cracks began to heal and he poured his love into his little girl, just as his dead wife would have wanted him to.

All the kingdom loved Beauty. It was impossible not to. Even the old and cynical ministers' hearts warmed at the sight of her. Goodness shone brightly from her every pore and she loved them all in return. It was her nature to love. For her fourth birthday there was a feast and the whole city rejoiced. She was showered with gifts, given not for political advantage, which was so often the case with royal children, but from the heart. She received so many that she insisted on sharing them with the poorer children of the city, and that just made the people love her more.

The only present she didn't give away was the one that made her eyes sparkle more than any other: a black and white kitten she called Domino, a present from her father's best friend and closest advisor, Rumplestiltskin. Domino was just like her, she said, his hair was black with some blond bits too. She smiled and cuddled him and all was well.

Beauty loved Domino and the cat loved her back. Unlike most felines he did not crave his independence but, like a puppy, would follow the little girl wherever she went and slept curled up on her pillow. Some said – or whispered – it was because Beauty came from witch's blood and all witches had a way with animals, but even those who found the kitten's behaviour odd couldn't bring themselves to think badly of the little princess who was always so full of kindness and love.

Domino died three years later on the first dark day. They did not call them dark days then, and none had any idea how dark they would become, but it was the first time that Beauty changed. There was no trigger for it. Perhaps if her mother had still been alive, she would have known what to do with her child to make it better. But the water witch was dead, and the half-child princess was alone in the world of men.

It was a perfect day and the princess had finished her music and dance lessons and returned to her rooms to play. Thankfully, her servants were dismissed and she was alone.

It was the king and Rumplestiltskin who found her and for a while it would be their secret to bear. They had planned to take Beauty riding, but the clear summer day had suddenly grown cloudy and rain had burst from the sky. The king, perhaps because of the loss of his beloved wife, was protective of Beauty's health and decided that they would stay inside and play cards instead. The two men were laughing together when they opened the doors to her apartment.

The laughter stopped immediately.

All the king could see was blood.

At first he thought the blood was Beauty's and he ran towards her in panic, ordering Rumplestiltskin to fetch the doctors. But then, as he got closer, he saw the bloody sewing scissors and Domino's glassy eyes staring up from the mess in his daughter's lap.

'His fur wouldn't change,' Beauty snapped, her voice sharp and irritated. *'His fur wouldn't change. And he scratched me.'* She was indignant and her normally beautiful face was screwed up so tightly it was ugly. *'He scratched me.'*

'What have you done, Beauty?' the king asked in horror, unable to absorb what was so clearly in front of him. He crouched and took the wrecked, lifeless body of the beloved cat from her.

'Look at her hair,' Rumplestiltskin said, having closed the door and locked it to prevent any passing servants from seeing the awful sight within. *'What's happened to her hair?'*

'His hair didn't match mine,' Beauty muttered, although she now sounded slightly confused. With bloody fingers she pulled at her own locks. *'He wouldn't change it. Why wouldn't he change it? Why did he scratch me?'*

Her hair, which was normally black with two

blonde streaks of her mother's colouring, had re-
versed, leaving her head a cool blonde with midnight stripes on each side of her cherubic face.

'This isn't right,' Rumplestiltskin said, grabbing a
towel and wrapping the dead cat up in it. 'This isn't
our Beauty.' For she was more than just the king's
daughter, she was loved by them all. 'Is this some
kind of terrible magic?'

'Daddy?' Beauty was frowning now, looking up.
'Daddy, what are you doing here?'

Her hair began to change again, returning to its
natural state, the two opposing colours bleeding
into each other, and through the window the first
shard of sunlight cut through the rain, the weather
changing with her.

The king swept his daughter up and took her
into the bathroom. 'Get rid of that cat,' he growled.
'Where no one can find it.'

Rumplestiltskin did as he was told. There were
plenty of places he could have thrown the stabbed
and half-skinned animal, but he found a quiet place
in the orchard and buried Domino. He had been a
good cat and he had loved the young princess well,
and Rumplestiltskin, a kind man with a daughter
of his own, felt responsible for the animal's fate. A
little sweat was not too much to give him. That and

a grave where the foxes couldn't scavenge his corpse in the night.

By the time he got back to the princess's apartments, she was washed and changed and sitting on the bed playing cards with the king. She looked up and smiled, all light and laughter again.

'Have you seen Domino?' she asked. 'I don't know where he is.'

From where he stood in the doorway, Rumplestiltskin could see that the king had hastily rolled up the bloody rug and shoved it under the bed.

'He's probably gone to the kitchens,' the king said. His face was a picture of forced normality, his smile stretched across his face as if it were on a rack. 'Maybe he wanted some milk.'

'That's probably it,' Beauty said, but Rumplestiltskin could see the worry on her pretty face for her missing pet. 'I just wish I knew where he was. I don't remember him leaving.'

'He'll be back,' Rumplestiltskin said cheerily as he sat on the bed. 'I'm sure of it.' Inside, he felt a small part of him die with the lie, the first of what he feared would be many, many lies, and life in the castle had changed that day. Of course the change in her had been magic. But it was a magic that she held. This was nothing to do with the witch and her talk of spindles. Beauty was cursed from within.

Beauty was inconsolable for weeks when Domino, rotting in the orchard, failed to return to her. Everyone searched for him, but the little cat was of course not found, and although she missed him terribly Beauty had the resilience of a child and her nature was too full of joy to hold onto her sadness. Eventually she stopped asking after him and life moved on.

The king and Rumplestiltskin remained watchful and stayed close to the princess as best they could to watch for the signs of change. The instances were at first so rare that, for a few years, they did not cause too much consternation, the two men simply sweeping up the child and locking her in her rooms until the skies outside cleared of rain and they'd know that their good girl had returned to them.

They chose her maids carefully but even so, after a while, there were rumours that another child was in the castle, a blonde girl uncannily like Beauty but who huffed and puffed and stamped her foot.

Being a wise man, and knowing in his heart that now that a door had unlocked inside Beauty it would stay that way, Rumplestiltskin didn't try to quell the rumours. Instead, he added one to circulation – that there had been two babies born to the

*king and queen. Twins. But the second girl was a
difficult child who needed special care and the king
had chosen, for her own sake, to keep her out of
the limelight that came with being part of the royal
family. When the rumour was whispered back to
him he knew he'd been successful. Should anything
untoward be seen then Beauty would not be blamed
and that was all that mattered.*

*The king hoped that as Beauty grew her changes
would become less frequent, but it was a false hope.
The princess reached puberty late, but as soon as
she woke, bloody, just after her fifteenth birthday,
things grew worse.*

*The changes became more frequent. And when
the other girl was in charge, she now had all her
mother's repressed magic at her fingertips. It was
no longer possible to lock her away in a room until
the moment passed, and instead of simple thunder-
clouds in the sky, blue lightning would crack across
the city and rain would flash-flood the streets.
She was wild, this blonde girl who ran, laughing
and dancing wantonly through the castle corridors, tipping trays of food from servants' hands as
she went.*

*She whipped the stable boy to within an inch of
his life for not polishing her saddle well enough,*

and the king caught her half-naked with one of his ministers.

The man went to the dungeons for that.

That was a mistake.

The princess followed. Not to save him, but to watch the punishment.

She liked blood.

Rumplestiltskin caught her once in the butcher's yard at the back of the castle, her hands buried in the hot entrails of a freshly killed deer. Her eyes were glazed, and as he pulled her away she licked her fingers. He didn't tell the king that. His precious Beauty, Rumplestiltskin feared, was also a monster.

The changes did not last long, a day or two at the very most, but they were impossible to hide. Rumplestiltskin amended his rumour to say that Beauty insisted her sister had the run of the castle in her stead for a few days here and there, and although some in the kingdom believed that, the king could not keep the secret from his ministers any longer. But there was no other heir, and for all her wildness and streak of cruelty, the Beast, as she became known on those days, still loved her father, and was always affectionate towards him and Rumplestiltskin as if Beauty, locked inside her, had that much control over both of them.

The king had a bell installed high in the castle roof, and proclamations were sent out around the kingdom that when it rang all the people should go to their houses and stay inside until it was rung again. The criers claimed it was to protect them from the terrible blue lightning that spat at the ground during these times, and the dangerous floods, and although it was the nature of the people to do as they were told, rumours were still rumours and there was talk of a monster in the castle and magic at play.

It worked for a while. Several years passed and the kingdom and the castle settled into their new routine. Beauty became a young woman her father could be proud of and everyone continued to love her. She was still kind and thoughtful and full of joy. Young men came to court her. One kissed her and fell so passionately in love that when she told her father she didn't love him the boy hanged himself.

When a second kissed her and also fell completely in love with her – although with less disastrous consequences when she rejected him – Rumplestiltskin and the first minister broached the subject of magic once again to the king. Her mother's magic was not just contained within the Beast. Her kisses put men

550

under a spell, and perhaps, although none could argue that she was not the sweetest of girls, there was a little magic involved in the unconditional love everyone who met her felt.

They decided this was a good thing. It would protect the princess from any who might harm her because of the Beast, and the king took to touring the city with her to ensure that she had all of their subjects' love. There was, he reminded them all, no other heir for the kingdom, and the king refused to even consider marrying again. Things continued in their strange new normality.

But as with all things that we pretend are not so bad as they seem, there comes, for each man or woman, a breaking point.

For Rumplestiltskin it was the poisoning of the king.

He had been growing sicker for a while. At first the changes were not noticeable; just a day or two of feeling off colour, a general tiredness, a reluctance to ride. These times came and went and none of the ministers thought anything of it. He grew thinner. Rumplestiltskin and the first minister noticed that the Beast, when she was in residence, was more affectionate towards her father and this caused them both to be suspicious. They kept her from the kitchens when his food was being prepared and she was followed at all times to ensure she did not go near his wine or water.

They saw nothing suspicious. Perhaps the king was just going through a bout of ill-health.

It was a summer's day when Rumplestiltskin found Beauty in the orchard picking apples from a tree. He did not look down at the flattened piece of earth close by where her forgotten childhood companion lay buried. She smiled at him as he asked her why she needed so many as she carried in her basket, and said she was baking apple cakes for her father and had been doing so for weeks. He liked them and that made her happy. Her eyes were clear and her face shone. She was innocent. She was sweet.

Rumplestiltskin was suspicious. For if Beauty lurked within to protect her father and Rumplestiltskin when the Beast was in charge, logic dictated that the Beast likewise lurked within Beauty.

He watched her from the shadows beyond the kitchen door as she baked. She sang sweetly to herself as she peeled and cored the ripe fruit and prepared the dough. He chided himself for his dark thoughts. There was nothing amiss here – she was still entirely their Beauty. He lingered though, for he was a thorough man, and as he loved Beauty he also loved his best friend, the king.

Just as the cakes were ready to go into the oven, with Beauty's face covered in an endearing dusting of flour and sugar, a dark cloud passed across sky and the room darkened. Beauty frowned, suddenly confused. She had opened the heavy oven doors and had the tray in her hand, but she paused. She turned, returned to the table and put it down. Her eyes were glazed and lost as she reached into her pocket and pulled out a small vial of liquid, tipping a tiny drop of brightness onto each cake. Once the vial was again out of sight, she picked up the tray again.

The cloud passed and life returned to Beauty and she began to hum once more, closing the door and letting the cakes bake. She smiled, content in her work.

Rumplestiltskin slipped silently away, shivering in horror, his worst fears confirmed. He did not blame Beauty. She didn't know what she had done. But still, the danger was there. As she grew, who would win the battle there? Beauty or the Beast? He could not watch her forever. One day he would not be able to foil her efforts.

Separate batches of apple cakes were made that

the king could eat in front of his daughter to keep her happy without being poisoned, and when the bell rang and the Beast came, he would walk a little hunched over and feign some illness.

But the king was troubled. He had grown into a wise king and he knew that above all else his loyalty should lie with his people. There were talks long into the night of what should be done. The Beast grew wilder and less controllable, and her visits more frequent. The king knew that she went to the dungeons and arranged terrible punishments for the prisoners there, then bribed the guards not to speak of it. None would argue with her. It only took one guard to be punished to show the rest that she was not to be disagreed with. She had magic, after all. Worse, there were those among the nobles, Rumplestiltskin could see it, who almost admired her ruthless nature and brought their sons and daughters in to be her companions, and curry her favour. As Beauty herself was divided, she was also dividing those around her. The good and bad in people became more pronounced and factions grew in the court where there had been harmony before.

The king loved Beauty, but he could not love the Beast. He wept for the water witch and for what their love, which should never have been, had created. When his tears were dry he summoned Rumplestiltskin, his most trusted friend, and asked him to go to the witch in the tower and beg her to help Beauty. Perhaps magic could fight the dark magic in his daughter – perhaps the witch would have a power to ensure that the dark days ended. He told Rumplestiltskin to give her whatever she demanded in return, if she could find a way to free his daughter from the curse of her nature.

It was the end of summer when Rumplestiltskin left, taking his own daughter with him. She was uncomfortable in court life and although she had been friends with Beauty when she had been little, after Domino's death Rumplestiltskin had slowly removed her from the princess's company and sent her to a school on the far side of the city. Now she was grown she was out of place amid the stylish confidence of the nobles, and he feared this would mark her as a victim for the Beast while he was away as she took great pleasure in taunting those whom she perceived to be weak.

It was a long journey to the white tower that rose above the trees in the distance, one not without its own adventures, and as they drew closer both Rumplestiltskin and his daughter were in awe of the height of the edifice. There were only two windows they could see, one halfway up and another far away at the very top that would no doubt be lost from sight in the misty days of winter.

There was no visible door and after exploring the perimeter and seeing no way in Rumplestiltskin called up to the window in the hope that the witch would hear him and come down. He shouted himself hoarse, but there was no response. He began to think that perhaps this was a wild goose chase and the witch was long gone or dead within the impenetrable walls. He sat on a rock, ready to give up, and then his daughter shouted for him, begging the witch to show them mercy and hear their plight.

A door, previously invisible, swung open in the smooth curved wall. The witch smiled and invited them in. Rumplestiltskin was not sure what he had been expecting, but she was unchanged – an ordinary middle-aged woman. As they followed her up the winding stairs inside, however, he caught glimpses of artefacts and objects that were hundreds of years old. She noticed his glance and smiled.

'A witch's years are different to a man's. I've stopped counting them.'

She fed them a hearty broth, settled Rumplestiltskin's daughter down on a soft couch to sleep, and then listened to his tale of Beauty and the Beast. The witch was thoughtful after that. She hadn't been out in the world since the king had summoned her, before Beauty's birth, and after hearing his tale she was glad of it.

'A water witch's daughter,' she mused, 'should only be born from a water bed. This trouble is one anyone could have seen coming.'

She sat by the fire for a while and watched Rumplestiltskin's daughter sleep, as if that sight brought her some clarity or peace, and then made her decision.

'Can you help?' Rumplestiltskin asked. 'I fear for our land if the Beast can't be controlled.'

'Come with me,' she told him. They climbed two more flights of stairs until they came to a room with several locks. 'I have something for you.'

It was full of spinning wheels and spindles of different shapes and sizes and Rumplestiltskin's eyes widened. 'Spindles. Beauty's curse.' The witch smiled. 'They are each bewitched or blessed or cursed, depending on how you use them.' She walked between them, her fingers lovingly caressing the wood of each until her hand settled on one. 'I cannot change her nature,' she said, eventually. 'She is who she is, and no magic is strong enough to change that. But I can save your kingdom from her inevitable tyranny.'

Rumplestiltskin stared at her. 'How?' he asked, his mouth drying. He knew the answer before she spoke and his heart was heavy with the decision he would have to make.

'I can give you something which will kill her, should you feel that is your only recourse.' She turned to Rumplestiltskin and in the candlelight he was sure he could see hundreds of years of life in her eyes and a dead heart beating inside her. No good came from magic, his conscience screamed, and he trembled slightly. She looked so very ordinary but in her soul she was a crone. No good could come from a crone. 'This,' she said, and lifted one of her precious spindles.

'How does it work?' he asked, after swallowing hard. Ever since Domino he had known that one day a decision would have to be made about Beauty. And somewhere in his soul, and in his love for the king, he'd known it would be his decision to make. 'And will it be painless?' He paused. 'We all love her, you see.' He wondered if he was justifying his actions to himself or to her. 'Hopefully, I will never have to use it.'

'I will need it returning,' she said. 'Especially if

you decide some less extreme action is called for.'
She carefully lifted it and handed it to him. 'One
prick of her finger and she will die,' she said, her
voice devoid of emotion. 'And it will be painless.
Like going to sleep.' She smiled at that.

'It's poison then,' Rumplestiltskin said.

'She'll bleed to death,' the witch replied. 'But I
assure you she won't feel a thing.'

His hands trembled as he took it. 'I must be sure
not to prick myself on the way back then.'

'I've given you this magic,' she said, leading him
out of the room and locking it with the keys that
hung from a chain around her neck. 'It can't hurt
you. A curse cannot touch the one who wields it.'

'And what do you want in return?' he asked.

'You will leave your daughter with me until you
bring my spindle back,' she said, softly.

Rumplestiltskin felt as if all the air had been
sucked from his lungs. His daughter? His only child.

The witch squeezed his hand. He was surprised
at the warmth of her fingers. He'd expected them
to feel like the touch of a dead thing. 'She will want
for nothing and I shall teach her many things. She
will be happy here and I am lonely. I have been
lonely for a long, long time.' She smiled again.
Her lips were thin. 'And when you return you may

reclaim her if you so wish. This I promise you.' She shrugged. 'Perhaps she will also be safer here. Dangerous times lie ahead.'

Rumplestiltskin felt the weight of all his responsibility to the kingdom settle on his shoulders and his heart grew heavy. He had no choice.

'I will come back for her,' he said.

'I'm sure you will,' the witch replied.

He did not wait for his daughter to wake because he knew he would not have the strength to say goodbye, but left her a letter telling her he loved her very much and that he would return soon to take her home. He kissed her forehead and left his darling daughter, Rapunzel, there where she slept.

By the time he got back to the kingdom two months had passed and much had already changed. The king was dead; killed in a riding accident while out with the princess a mere day after Rumplestiltskin had left. While Beauty mourned for her father, the Beast revelled in her new power. She held masked balls for the wild young things of the city and took her vicarious pleasure not only from their bodies, but also from torturing those unfortunate enough to be in the dungeons. If there were no prisoners there, they were brought in, innocents chosen at random to feed her blood lust, their houses wrecked and looted by the soldiers knowing they would not return.

She redecorated the third ballroom to suit her tastes; decadent red and black and gold, and music played long and loud as the young people danced and enjoyed each other, and girls from the dairy came and never left again alive.

The ministers kept these secrets and managed the kingdom around her as best they could until the bell rang once again and they could let out a collective sigh of relief. None challenged her because her mother's magic was at her fingertips, and they had seen the unrecognisable bodies that left the dungeons. They kept their own counsel and shuffled around the castle trying to look invisible as they did exactly as they were told. With the king gone and Rumplestiltskin away, only the first minister had the true affection of their queen and they left the management of the Beast to him.

It could not go on, Rumplestiltskin thought, as he held Beauty's hand beside her father's grave and cried with her for his oldest friend. It just could not go on.

Whispers of murders and torture, wild parties and patricide; that was only two months into the new reign and it would only get worse. Beauty was sweet and kind, but the Beast was stronger, he was sure of that. That Beauty had unknowingly killed the king, he had no doubt. He'd spoken to the terrified stable boy who whispered that the girth on the king's saddle had been nearly cut through and that it had been the princess herself who had prepared his horse for him. Who would be next? Her father's friends?

He sat up late into the night, turning the spindle in his hands. One prick, the witch had said, and that would be that. He wished it could be done while she was the Beast. Somehow that would feel easier. But the Beast rarely slept and her magic would protect her from danger. It had to be Beauty he murdered.

He went to her rooms the next afternoon. It was a beautiful day. The city was full of life. A rose, Beauty's favourite flower, sat in a glass on the window sill. She sat on the edge of her bed and laughed with delight as she reached for the spinning wheel, happy that he'd thought to bring her a gift from his travels, especially a thing she had never seen before in her life, and in that moment where she was joyous he saw her delicate finger touch the spindle.

It was done.

Her eyes widened for the merest moment and

then the spinning wheel slid from her hands to the floor and she fell backwards onto her bed. Rumplestiltskin stood and cried, silently begging her forgiveness, for what seemed like forever, before he laid her out on the bed. He was so absorbed in his grief and guilt he failed to notice the sudden unnatural silence around him.

He did, however, notice that the princess, one arm flopped over the side of the bed, a tiny drop of blood striking the floor from her pricked finger, was still breathing.

It didn't make sense. Not at first. Not until he'd been outside and to the forest's edge and seen the wall that had grown there. And even then it had taken weeks, maybe even months, for the terrible truth to sink in.

'**T**he witch lied,' Petra said, softly.

'Oh no.' Rumplestiltskin shook his head. 'Witches never lie. But they do speak in riddles. The queen *would* die. She would bleed to death and it would be painless. But she would bleed to death one drop at a time.' He shuddered and sipped his wine. 'Before Beauty's birth, the witch told the king that a spindle would send his daughter to sleep for a hundred years. Her prophesy was not destroyed by my deeds. I brought the spindle. I sent her to sleep as I killed her. She would sleep the hundred years it took her blood to drain from her body and then she'd be gone. A hundred years of waiting. And we were so nearly there, when you woke her.'

'Your daughter?' the huntsman said.

'Long dead now. After a life abandoned and locked away in a witch's tower.'

'Locked in a tower,' Petra repeated, her gaze misty as if she was lost in a different story.

'So why is the first minister so keen that we find you and take you to him? You were doing something that surely they all wanted?'

'If I had succeeded, of course. But I failed. The queen is awake, and there's only one other person who knew of my plan and my visit to the witch.'

'Him?' Petra said.

'Exactly. If I'm captured and the Beast tortures me, he knows I'll have no choice but to give up his name. It's better for everyone if she thinks I acted alone.'

'Shhh.' Toby tilted his head and frowned.

'What?'

'The bell,' Toby said. 'The bell is ringing. A dark day has come.'

Rumplestiltskin looked up at the huntsman. 'The Beast is awake.'

'But what about the prince?' Petra asked. 'He's with her!'

'Hopefully the first minister will look after him,' the old man muttered. 'But I fear he's about to have a very rude awakening about his sweet queen.'

9

'Perhaps he was in a dream...'

The bell rang out from somewhere at the top of the castle, a steady heavy knell, and as the prince stared up at the ceiling of his apartments he shivered slightly while his heart raced. Whatever affliction had struck poor Beauty the first minister had not been surprised by it, but the prince had also seen that he was afraid and that in turn frightened the prince. Much to his own chagrin, he wished the huntsman were here. Surrounded as he was by the kind of luxury he was used to, he still suddenly felt very alone and far from home. He loved Beauty, he knew that to his very core, but he was unimportant here. The way the minister had spoken to him made that abundantly clear.

Blue lightning flashed in jagged lines beyond the

window and a moment later an almighty rumble of thunder shook the sky. He was sure the castle walls trembled. He was about to go to the window to look when the door to his rooms opened and the first minister entered carrying a silver tray.

'I know it is early, but you have had a long night and I thought you might like something to eat,' he said smoothly, placing it on the table against the wall. 'And a hot drink to help you sleep.' His smile was tight. 'I'm very sorry to have rushed you away like that, but our beloved queen has occasional fits.' He nodded towards the window. 'They come with the bad weather.' The minister had regained his usual poise, but the prince remembered all too well the urgency with which he'd spoken earlier, insisting that the prince leave. What was he hiding? 'It's unlikely she will be well again today, so eat now and then sleep as long as you wish. Take time to recover from your long journey.'

'I should be with her while she's sick. I am her husband to be, after all. It's my job to look after her.'

'And when you are married of course you shall. But the queen requires privacy at these times – the fits are quite traumatic for her – and you can understand why she might want to keep them private from you at this early stage. She is young and easily embarrassed. Anyway,' he clasped his hands in front of him and they were lost in the sleeves and folds of his robes, 'once this one has passed, which I'm sure it shall quickly, I shall teach you how best to deal with them. But for now she is well cared for, so eat, drink and sleep. Then you have a wedding to plan.'

His eyes lingered a moment too long on the tray and there was a flash of intensity, almost hidden under the first minister's hooded brows, as he turned his gaze back to the prince.

'Of course,' the prince said, his mouth drying. 'You are right. I was simply worried.' He lifted the goblet and pretended to take a sip. 'I shall see her tomorrow. Perhaps, if she is unwell, we should delay the wedding for a day. We can plan it together so it can be perfect.'

The first minister smiled. 'Perhaps that is wise.'

The prince felt the red wine touch his lips but refused to let it pass. Why would the first minister bring him his food and not send a servant? He was a proud man – the prince had known enough counsellors and politicians to know they did nothing to diminish their status in the eyes of others. The minister must have wanted to ensure the prince received it and was going to consume it, and that meant he had probably added an extra ingredient between the kitchen and his rooms. The prince was spoiled and could be selfish but he wasn't stupid. All castles housed ruthless men with their own personal agendas – what if the first minister had decided that Beauty marrying a royal was not in his best interest? She was sweet and gentle – her husband might not be. Who would wield the power then?

He looked down at the silver plate containing half a roast chicken covered in gravy and surrounded by potatoes and vegetables. 'That looks delicious. Thank you once again. I think I'll read while I eat it and then sleep if you think that's for the best. But please,' he knew he had to keep some of his urgency. 'Tell Beauty I love her and am thinking of her.'

'I will.' The first minister's eyes twinkled and he bowed before he backed away. 'Remember to stay in these rooms. We like to keep the castle peaceful for the queen while she's unwell.'

'Thank you,' the prince said, and sat at the table, picking up his knife and fork and cutting a piece of the succulent chicken. The first minister paused in the doorway and watched as the prince put the food into his mouth and then quietly closed the door behind him.

As soon as he was gone, the prince spat the meat out and ran to the water jug to rinse his mouth out.

He picked up the plate and wine glass and went to the window. Outside it was dark as night and the storm was raging. As soon as he lifted the catch the glass flew back, propelled by the wind that sent the curtains billowing up around him as if they were suddenly enchanted. He flinched against the torrential icy rain that blasted into his face, and tipped away the food and wine. It fell into the gloomy grey street below as more streaks of blue cracked the sky and stabbed at the city. He pulled the window shut and put the empty plate and goblet back, before closing the curtains and turning out all but one lamp.

There were several old books on a shelf in the corner and he took one and opened it somewhere near the beginning and then lay on the bed, placing the book at an angle across his chest as if he had dropped it there. He closed his eyes. Now all he had to do was wait.

His heart thumped in his chest as the minutes ticked by and the fire in the grate slowly burned down. After a while he thought he might have drifted to the edge of sleep, but was woken by the sound of carriages arriving below. He opened his eyes and where daylight should have been creeping through the gaps in the curtains, instead there was a strange darkness, as if the raging storm had created an artificial night. There was something unnatural about it, and he shivered. Shrieks of laughter carried on the wind as carriage doors closed and people ran inside and away from the rain. The prince was suddenly alert again. Who were these people and why were they arriving? There had been a formal ball the night before and if the queen was ill, and the first minister insistent on peace and quiet, surely none would disobey him? So what was really going on? Did he take advantage of the queen's fits to stage entertainments of his own? Maybe that was it.

He was just about losing patience with lying still when he heard the quiet click of the door opening. He forced his body to relax and dropped his mouth open slightly, taking long, deep breaths. Feet padded softly across the carpet. The prince's eyelids twitched, but he remained motionless. After a moment the feet moved away, and the door clicked shut.

The room once again in silence, the prince kept his eyes shut for several seconds longer, afraid that perhaps it was a trick and the minister was still watching him, but eventually he opened them and let out a sigh of relief that he was once again alone.

Back at the window he looked out at the storm. In the courtyard below sat several carriages made of gold and silver and sparkling with jewels. Noblemen's

carriages, he was certain of it. Perhaps the first minister was trying to claim the throne for himself and
had called some kind of meeting while Beauty was
ill? The question was, what could he do about it?
What did he really know about this kingdom?

He turned away and glanced at himself in the
mirror. He was tall, and blond and handsome; everything a prince should be. Princes should also be brave
and honourable. Princes, he reminded himself, did
not sit back politely if they thought the security of
the one they loved was threatened. And if there was
one thing which was beyond doubt, it was that he
loved Beauty with every inch of his body. Being apart
from her was a physical ache that he almost couldn't
bear. He pulled back his broad shoulders. If nothing
else, he was going to explore and see what was going
on, and he would talk to her about it when she was
better. It wasn't as if the first minister could do anything to him. He was betrothed to their queen. Soon
he would be their king and he would not be manipu-
lated by old men, even if his sweet-natured beloved
was.

He waited another thirty minutes before creeping
out into the silent hallway. He stayed close to the
walls and followed the wide corridor until he reached
the central staircase. He paused and strained his ears

to hear. At first there was nothing, but then he was sure he caught the faintest tinkling of music. Two kitchen hands crossed the central atrium below, their heads huddled together and whispering, and then they disappeared from sight. In their wake, the air carried the hint of roasted meat. They'd delivered food somewhere, but where?

When he was certain there was no one else about, he went quickly down the stairs and headed towards the main ballroom where he and Beauty had danced before. He opened the door a fraction but the space beyond was quiet and empty. He stepped inside. The music was definitely louder here. He jogged across the vast space, his footsteps echoing eerily around him.

The second ballroom was empty too, and he frowned for a moment, before the thought struck him. There was the third ballroom. The locked-up room beyond the library that Beauty had known nothing about. Was that where the first minister was entertaining his guests?

He'd passed through the library and reached the door to the small corridor. He opened it a fraction and slid his hand up to keep the bellwire steady before squeezing the rest of his body in. He was in the right place. The music, slightly discordant and darker than any of the jolly tunes that he and Beauty had danced to, was much louder, and above the notes he heard the occasional laugh.

With sweaty palms and a racing heart, he crept forward and lowered his eye to the keyhole but couldn't get a clear view of what was happening inside. The chandeliers were giving off a muted light rather than glittering brightness, and he saw flashes of the red walls and movement of clothes and bodies. From the other side of the thick wood, a woman laughed, a tinkling sound like breaking ice.

His curiosity overwhelmed his fear, and he carefully twisted the handle and quietly pulled the heavy door open an inch to see inside. As his eyes widened, so did the door. All sensible thought tumbled from his mind, and he stared, for a moment completely astonished, at the tableaux that faced him.

The room was smaller than the other ballrooms and with the heavy red and gold decoration and the thick black drapes that covered the windows it seemed to shrink further. A fire blazed in the vast ornamental grate and large candles flickered in sconces decorated with gargoyles that cast strange shadows across the floor. Along one side was a table laden with food; roasted chickens and hares, piles of fruit, and all manner of exotic dishes, but instead of using plates and knives the food had been torn apart by hand and gnawed bones littered the floor around it. Silver jugs of wine were scattered everywhere and the thick rug that covered most of the central area was splashed with red where glasses had been carelessly knocked over. Even without the people, it was a decadent sight. With them, the scene was one of flagrantly wild abandon. Men and women in beautiful expensive gowns laughed and talked in groups, some dancing together, some eating or drinking, but all with a lack of formality unlike any royal ball he'd ever attended. All the guests wore elegant masks across their eyes; some black, some ornate bird feathers, some with beaks and all fitting closely to their young features. None were over thirty, he was sure of that, and whereas they were all handsome and beautiful people, the dark shadows they cut in the candlelight across the floor and on the red walls were strange and gothic, the women flirtatiously and confidently moving among the men; no standing on ceremony or waiting to be approached.

There was more though, and from his place in the doorway the prince felt both aroused and revolted as his eyes moved to the others who were lost in their actions, oblivious to the party around them.

On the low stage angled from a corner, three men

dressed in black screeched out the strange fiddle music. Two women danced in front of them; but this was no courtly waltz. They swayed slightly, their slim hips gyrating against each other's as they kissed, their eyes half-closed and lost in the pleasures of their soft mouths. The taller of the two, a brunette whose hair had fallen free and hung down her back, ran one hand down her partner's body stroking the bodice of her dress, freeing her breast and teasing the nipple between her fingers before lowering her head and flicking her tongue across it. The other girl tipped her head back and gasped.

A little further away, a full-figured woman was bent over a chaise-longue by the wall. The skirt of her ballgown had been pushed up over her hips and the pale skin of her thighs was visible above the tops of her stockings. She moaned as a man behind her gripped her buttocks and thrust into her, panting loudly with each of his movements and lifting herself up to meet him. After a moment another man, a gold mask across his face, joined them and slid his hard cock into her mouth as he leant backwards and drained his wine. The woman sucked greedily, matching her movements with those of the man behind her.

On the thick fur rug two women straddled a naked

577

man and faced each other, one spreading her thighs across his face, the other his pelvis, and as they ground themselves into him for their pleasure, they leaned forward and kissed between their moans.

Other pairings and groups were dotted here and there, all in some stage of undress as they pleasured each other with wanton abandon. As well as their lust, they were feeling love for each other, these people hidden behind their masks. It was strange and unnatural, but despite his revulsion the prince was throbbing.

One woman was alone in midst of the party, and she moved among the people smiling, pausing to laugh with those still dressed, and trailing one hand gently across the skin of the naked as she passed and when she did so the whole group would shudder with pleasure. She wore a dress so sheer the firm curves of her body were clearly visible beneath it, but none of the revellers made her part of their depravity.

When her tour was complete she stood in the centre of the room and turned slowly, her arms out-stretched, sparks of gold flying from the tips of her fingers. The air instantly grew heavier and a wave of something warm and sweet hit the prince where he stood. His head spun as if he'd drunk too much wine too quickly. Suddenly he wanted to be in the room, to be part of this madness that was taking place before him. Unable to stop himself, he pushed the door further open, and the woman at the centre of it all looked up. She smiled.

The prince's heart stopped. How hadn't he recognised her before? It was Beauty. *His* Beauty. Except for her hair – her hair was the wrong colour. What was this? How could his sweet fiancée be part of this? Was it really her? Was it a different girl? The last sober shred of his mind knew he should turn and run, but the strange intoxication that tingled in his blood refused to let him move. He remembered her in the corridor behind him. Her confusion. Her trembling. *Her hair had been changing colour.*

She walked towards him, lithe and supple, her movements like a cat, and her eyes sparkled. His eyes drank in the outline of her breasts, the dark circles of her nipples visible through the sheer cream fabric that floated around her as she moved.

'My darling,' she purred as she reached him. 'I knew you'd find me.' She took his hand and his arm shuddered with sharp sparks of something between pain and pleasure. As he crossed the threshold she closed the door behind him and any resistance he might have had was gone. The air was heavy and filled with a musky scent of sex and magic and he longed to tear himself free of his clothes and tumble to the floor with Beauty, not caring who might see their act of love. He pulled her towards him and kissed her. The surge of passion he felt was greater than any that had come before. What was this? Was she enchanting him? She pressed her body confidently against his, teasing him, and then drew back, wriggling free of his grasp.

'Not until our wedding night.' Her voice was slightly deeper than normal, and although he was sure that this was his Beauty, she was, at the same time, a completely different woman. 'Not for me.' She ran her fingers down his shirt, teasing some of the buttons free as she went. 'I have different lusts to fulfil tonight.'

'What is this?' he whispered, as she led him over to the two dancing women who were now writhing with each other on the floor. 'What are you doing?' Warm hands reached up and tugged him down. He didn't resist. The women made space for him between them and, as Beauty smiled at him, they slid their fingers and tongues under his clothes and his head whirled and he gasped.

'Sometimes,' Beauty said softly, sipping from her silver goblet, 'everyone needs to let the beast inside them out for a while.' She laughed, a sound like a waterfall meeting the sea and more glitter escaped from her fingertips. 'I like to see it. We all have our dark lusts. We should enjoy them.' Somewhere inside him a voice screamed witchcraft and then he was lost in sensation as his hands found firm breasts, and a soft mouth touched his as another explored a far more intimate part of him. And for a while, even his love for Beauty was forgotten.

Time meant nothing as the groups of bodies moved and merged and created new formations, but by the time the first minister brought the serving girl into the room, the prince was covered in sweat and his body ached from both desire and the desire to be free of it. The world was a bleary haze and he felt as if perhaps he was in a dream.

The minister walked, his back stiff, without look-ing at any of the decadence that surrounded him, until he reached Beauty, who was sitting on a throne from which she could survey all around her. She clapped her hands together in delight as she saw the blindfolded girl he'd led inside.

'A special night!' she cried. 'I shall drink!' From his place on the floor, the prince watched as she leapt to her feet and embraced the man before her. He flinched. 'Her name is Nell,' he said. 'She was talking to the huntsman.'

'Why do you tell me the names?' Beauty frowned, cross. 'I don't care for the names. My guests have had their pleasure and now I shall have mine!'

The first minister nodded. His face was tight, as if he dare not show any emotion he might have. 'I shall wait outside,' he said. 'Your guest's carriages are prepared. I suggest you dismiss them before . . .'

'Yes, yes,' she snapped, and the first minister took his leave. She clapped her hands together again, louder this time, gathering the attention of the revellers.

'Ladies and gentlemen,' she said, addressing them as if this were any normal ball. 'It has been wonderful to see you all again. A *pleasure*.' The guests laughed at that as they re-clothed themselves where necessary, and smiled while seeking out their original partners and preparing to leave. 'We shall have another such evening soon. But for now it's time for you to return home and continue your delights at your leisure.'

The room cleared relatively quickly, as if they were used to the parties ending abruptly, and while many came to say their goodbyes to Beauty and thank her for her hospitality, none paid any attention to the blindfolded girl who was swaying slightly in the middle of the room. Beauty held the prince back with her and when the musicians scurried out, the doors clicked shut and the three of them were alone.

'And now for my pleasure,' Beauty said, smiling at him, her eyes dancing with excitement. Her face was flushed and the prince thought, in that moment, he'd never seen her so aptly named.

She circled the girl, an earthy-looking buxom wench, one hand trailing around her waist and the servant gasped but didn't speak. Was she drugged? What did Beauty want with her? The expression on the first minister's face when he'd brought her in flashed before the prince's mind's eye. He'd looked like a tortured man.

'Pretty Nell,' Beauty said softly. 'They're always so pretty.' She reached down to the silver jug on the table and refilled her goblet and then poured a second for the prince. The red wine looked thick and dark and he stared into it as she drank hers.

'Drink,' she said. Her eyes had hardened and the prince suddenly felt unsettled. He lifted the cup and sipped. The taste was metallic and the substance too thick to swallow easily without gagging, as if his body recognised it before his brain had time to.

'Is this ... blood?' he asked, as the awful truth dawned on him.

She smiled at him and he could see where the

crimson liquid clung to her teeth. 'This is cold, but soon we'll have warm. Fresh and warm and so full of life.' She clung to him and pulled him close and kissed him, seeking him out with her tongue. The prince's stomach churned. *Blood*. His princess, his Beauty, was drinking blood. *He'd* drunk blood.

Beauty broke away, breathless, and laughed, tipping her head back and then pouring the glass of blood over her, coating herself in it, the sheer material of her dress clinging to her every curve with the weight of the liquid. She dropped the empty goblet and the sound of the metal hitting the ground echoed loudly in the empty room and the serving girl — Nell, the prince reminded himself; she had a name — flinched.

Beauty stroked her face and hushed her, kissing her cheek and leaving bloody marks on her pale skin. She looked at the prince. 'Are you ready?' she whispered, and pulled something from a hidey hole in the side of her throne. The prince nodded, despite his need to run far from this place and vomit. He shivered as she nodded at him to drink more from his cup. Cursing his own weakness, he did. He thought it couldn't get much worse than this. He thought she would want him to have blood-drenched sex with the poor girl before him.

It was only when he saw the knife in Beauty's hand and she folded his own over it and they both held the cold blade to the girl's warm neck, that he realise it was all going to get much, much worse before it got better.

Too late he remembered what the first minister had said before sending him to his room.

The Beast is coming.

The prince's mind had cracked a little by the time it was done and the first minister was leaning over him, his eyes wide with anger and hissing, 'I told you to stay in your room! I tried to ensure you would, you stupid, stupid boy.' The prince cried after that, rocking backwards and forwards as the old man put his arm awkwardly round him and tried to pull him to his feet. His feet slipped under him on the blood and he fell back down.

He couldn't get rid of the taste. He didn't think he'd ever be able to get rid of the taste, or of the images that were burned into his mind. The things the Beast had done to the poor, dead girl.

'Why?' he whispered. 'Why would she do that?'

Beauty and the knife. Watching as she . . . as *they*

... and then her terrible dancing in the warm blood, smearing it over herself and him, filling wine glasses with it. Forcing him to drink. Being too weak and afraid to stop her doing any of the terrible things she did.

He groaned and, trying to preserve his sanity, he curled up in a small ball in the corner of his mind. He needed to forget. He *had* to forget.

'Get up,' the first minister hissed again. 'Get back to your room. The bell will ring soon and then the castle will be busy again. You can't be seen like this.'

'The bell?' the prince croaked.

'The Beast will leave now.' The minister forced him to his feet. 'The blood precipitates the change. Our queen will return to herself and she can't see you like this.' He glanced at the blood-soaked woman who was starting to tremble. 'She can't see herself like this. Now go. Burn your clothes. Wash and sleep. Forget this ever happened.'

The prince didn't know whether to laugh or cry at the ridiculousness of the suggestion that this could ever be forgotten. That he could ever be normal again. As if he'd heard the prince's thoughts spoken aloud, the first minister gripped his wrist tightly, his thin fingers digging into his skin. 'You will forget it.

Or change it in your mind. It's all you can do.' He glared at the prince. 'Now go.'

This time the broken prince did not hesitate.

10

'A deal like that is worse than a witch's curse...'

It was early evening when the skies cleared and the bell rang out again over the city. The group hidden in the hideaway beneath the tree had slept for a while and then eaten. Petra and Toby escaped to the surface to walk in the fresh air, leaving the huntsman and Rumplestiltskin to talk.

After the fierceness of the storm damp lingered on every surface and the trees glistened green as water dripped from their branches, but although there was a light breeze it was not cold.

'Do you think Rumplestiltskin's story of his daughter and the witch is true?' Petra asked as they walked. 'Or in his fragile state of mind did he just make it up?'

'It's the story he's always told,' Toby slid his arm

589

around her waist as if it was the most natural thing in the world, and Petra believed that it might be. 'I think it's true. Why do you ask?'

'Oh, no reason. No reason that matters right now, anyway. Will you change again tonight?' Petra asked, as Toby glanced up at the sinking sun.

'Yes,' he said. 'There's two more nights of the full moon.' He smiled at her. 'But I've got an hour or so before it'll come on me.'

The city sparkled ahead of them, clean and bright, and Petra stared at it, still fascinated by a sight so different from any she'd experienced before. 'It's very beautiful,' she said quietly. 'But it must have been so very lonely for you with only Rumplestiltskin for company.'

'Yes, it was lonely,' Toby said. 'But it was good to be free. To not have to hide for several days a month and to not have to lie to people. They would have killed me, I'm sure of it, had the curse not come.'

'I don't understand how anyone who heard your howl could hunt you. I found it beautiful.' Petra blushed slightly.

'I'll never forget the first time I heard you howl back to me. It was like seeing a light in the darkness.' Toby said. 'When you called to me from the castle, I knew I had to find you. And I knew when I saw the soldier with his knife at your throat that I had to save you.' He stopped walking and looked at her. 'I'd happily die to save you.'

She smiled at him, warmth rushing through her body. The howl beyond the forest wall had drawn her to it, and this was why. Toby leaned forward and kissed her and for a moment after his lips left hers she was breathless with the rightness of it all.

'I thought the prince was a fool with his love for Beauty,' she whispered. 'Do you think this is what he feels?' She slid her arms around Toby's waist and rested her head on his chest as he held her. His laughter vibrated through his shirt.

'No, you can't blame the prince for his stupidity. He kissed her and that was his downfall. The water witches are famous for their allure. Their sisters, who live in the Eastern Seas, are called Sirens. They lure men to their deaths on the rocks because the sailors can't resist getting closer to them. Your prince may be a fool in many ways – I can't judge him on that – but where our queen is involved, it is hard to not love her. Her blood dictates that we do.'

He kissed her forehead and she liked the feel of his stubble against her skin. 'This, however,' he said. 'This is a different kind of magic altogether.'

She didn't need to ask what he meant. She felt it

inside her. They were made for each other and were destined to be together. Was that why the wolves had come to her grandmother's house so often? Had her longing for him been what had drawn them?

'You should go back,' Toby said softly. 'I can feel it coming and I would rather change alone.'

In his last sentence she could feel the weight of shame he felt about his curse, the loneliness and dread it brought with it, and as she headed back to the oak tree she vowed that, whatever it took, she would break *that* part of the curse – he would never be lonely again.

He joined them ten minutes later, padded over to Petra, curled up beside her on the floor and rested his heavy head in her lap, one ear cocked as the huntsman and Rumplestiltskin continued to talk.

'I won't do it again,' the old man said. 'Everyone I love is dead. My child is dead. Let the city live with the Beast until we're all dead and rotting behind the forest wall.'

'I don't care about your curses or your Beast,' the huntsman countered. 'My responsibility is towards the prince. We cut our way in through the forest, and we can get out again the same way. We don't belong here, it will let us pass. But I need to get to the castle and force him to come with me, and do it without the first minister seeing me. Once we've gone you can do what you like. Hide and die in here, or destroy the spindle and free the city.'

'I will never release them while she lives.'

'Then you should do what you promised your friend the king you would do,' Petra said softly. 'Prick her finger again.'

'And wait another hundred years alone?' Rumplestiltskin's voice trembled with horror at the thought. 'A hundred years, only for someone like you to come along and ruin it again?' He shook his head. 'I could not. I could not. No good comes from curses.'

Petra stroked the wolf's head and thought that Toby should have been dead for decades before she was born. 'Sometimes it can,' she said.

'Just tell me how I can get to the prince without being seen,' the huntsman said. 'I have no loyalty to your first minister and I have no desire to see you dead. But I do have to see the prince and if you can't give me another way in then I'll have no choice but to walk through the castle doors, and then he'll want to know whether I found you. If what you say about the dungeons is true then I will have no choice but to tell him.'

'This isn't my only hiding place,' Rumplestiltskin said roughly, but the huntsman's words had clearly caused him alarm. 'But I will give you a way in. Our tunnels go everywhere.' His untrusting eyes flashed darkly. 'But I will go with you, to be sure you don't betray me. And I will not bring the spindle.'

The network of tunnels that Rumplestiltskin had built was extraordinary, and even with his natural sense of direction and eye for remembering details of a path, the huntsman knew that he would never find his way back without the old man. They'd left Petra sleeping and the wolf had slunk out, no doubt to feed on nearby chickens or other domestic animals. He pitied the cursed man, wondering how terrible a thing it must be to spend part of your life trapped in an animal's body with all the cravings that came with it. He made a quiet vow to himself never to cross a witch if he could avoid it.

They eventually came up into the dark castle through a fireplace in what appeared to be an empty set of apartments. Rumplestiltskin lowered the hatch back down and stretched as he straightened up.

'How did you know it would be empty?' the huntsman asked, his hand on the hilt of his knife.

'These are my apartments. I doubt anyone is keen

to take a traitor's rooms just yet.' It was the dead of night and the castle, the tension eased now that the Beast had left them for a while, slept soundly. They crept through it undisturbed. Under the prince's door, however, a strip of light shone out.

He almost shrieked when he saw them, leaping from his bed and grabbing at an ornament to use it as a weapon. The huntsman rushed over to quieten him as Rumplestiltskin secured the door.

'What did we do?' the prince said, trembling. 'We should never have woken her. We should never have touched her.' He gripped the huntsman's arm. 'I can't get rid of the *taste* of it.'

'You've met the Beast then,' Rumplestiltskin said and the prince shuddered again.

'We need to put everything back as it was,' he said quietly. 'We need to put them all back to sleep.'

'Forget about that,' the huntsman said. 'That's not our business. We need to escape. Cut through the forest as we did before and return to your father.'

'I can't forget it. You didn't see. You didn't see what she did to that serving girl.' The prince frowned slightly and his pale face turned to the huntsman. 'I'll never be able to forget. Not while she's awake.' He paused in his mutterings. 'You *knew* her. That's what he said. He brought her because she'd been talking to you. And then she ... and then she ...'

'Nell?' the huntsman's blood cooled. 'What did she do to Nell?'

The prince's mouth opened as he worked to force out some words, and then he simply burst into tears.

'Blood,' Rumplestiltskin said, quietly. 'She'd have taken her blood. The Beast has a blood lust and the orphaned servants feed it. When the lust is satisfied, the Beast often leaves. It's a price the kingdom must pay.'

'Beauty killed her?' The huntsman was stunned. Even after hearing Rumplestiltskin's tale he found it hard to equate the pretty, kind queen with cruelty. And Nell? She killed Nell?

'She danced in her blood,' the prince moaned. 'She made me ... she made me drink it with her. I couldn't stop her. I couldn't ...' He looked from one man to the other. 'I was too scared. Can't you see? Can't you understand? I couldn't do anything.' He stared into space. 'She was so beautiful when she was sleeping. How could we have known?'

The horror of his words hung in the air.

'And you want to let her live?' the huntsman rounded on Rumplestiltskin as he thought of poor Nell. The feel of her soft skin and the sound of her easy warm laugh were fresh to him. She had been a sweet girl who'd done nothing wrong and he loathed himself for falling prey to his nature and taking his pleasure with her – especially when he had inadvertently drawn her towards her death. His anger raged. 'Then you let her live. But give me the spindle. You go with the others and cut through the forest. I'll stay behind and curse her again.' He gritted his teeth knowing what he was subjecting himself to. A hundred long years alone. But if it wasn't for him Nell would still be alive. If they hadn't woken Beauty then she would have been sleeping peacefully, her whole life waiting for her when the Beast was dead. He would do it. He had to do it.

'No,' Rumplestiltskin said. 'Why should I? No one cares that my daughter spent her life trapped in that witch's tower. No one cares that I will never look on her face again. So what do I care of the fate of the city?'

'What if you could have another child?' the prince blurted out. There was a mania in his eyes and the huntsman knew that if Beauty wasn't returned to her long dying sleep then the prince would never feel free of her. His terror would drive him mad; if it hadn't a little already. The young man had endured far more adventure than he'd bargained for.

'My wife is dead,' Rumplestiltskin spat bitterly. 'I will not take another.'

'I will give you my child. My first born.' He grabbed the man's arm, his whole body trembling.

'What?' The huntsman turned, his anger over Nell's death sideswiped by shock. 'You can't make a deal like that!'

'I can.' The prince didn't take his eyes from Rumplestiltskin. 'My first child. I promise you. You shall have the first child from my marriage bed to raise as your own.'

'A child?' Rumplestiltskin sat on the edge of the bed and stared at the fireplace. 'A child to raise as my own. Away from court. Away from the games of others. A child to love and never leave.'

'Yes!' the prince nodded, enthusiastically. 'Yes! You have my word.'

'Don't do this,' the huntsman growled. 'This kind of deal is worse than a witch's curse.'

'I have your word?' Rumplestiltskin reached out his hand to the fevered prince.

'You do.'

The two men shook and the deal was done. Watching them, aghast, the huntsman wondered how much madness could be held in one kingdom. Suddenly a hundred years alone did not seem too terrible a fate to be waiting for him.

'Let's go,' the prince said. 'The huntsman can come

back with the spindle while we're cutting through the forest. We could be gone by morning.'

'No,' the huntsman gritted his teeth and tried his best to ignore the prince's indifference to his sacrifice of a hundred years. 'The castle will be waking soon and there won't be enough time. If you're not here then the first minister will know we're escaping and the forest wall will have soldiers along every inch. You have to stay here and act normally. Plan the wedding. Lull them into thinking all is well. Tell them you want another party to celebrate your bride. Make sure all the ministers – and Beauty – drink heavily. Tell her she must sleep well before the wedding and make sure she's in bed by midnight. We will meet you back here and you will leave. I'll give you four hours from then. If you haven't cut through the forest wall, then you will be trapped in slumber with the rest of the city until she is dead.'

'But I can't!' The prince looked horrified. 'How can I pretend everything is fine? With her? How? Surely the ministers will be suspicious?'

'The mind is capable of many things,' Rumplestiltskin said, 'when exposed to true horror. It will protect itself. You should put the day's events down to a dream. A nightmare. They will think you have chosen to forget.'

'I don't know—'

'You have to,' the huntsman snapped. He was tired of the prince's weakness. He was tired of these royals who wrecked ordinary people's lives. 'It's the only way.'

Finally, the prince nodded and straightened up. 'I'll do it.'

He made it sound like a noble sacrifice in the way that only a prince could when surrounded by the sacrifices of others on his behalf.

'Good,' the huntsman said, and nodded to Rumplestiltskin. 'Let's go.'

'I will hold you to your promise, young prince,' the old man said. 'First, I will go to the witch, and then I will come to you. Do not forget me.'

'You have my word,' the prince repeated.

When Petra woke, a small streak of light was cutting through the earthy ceiling. Rumplestiltskin was asleep in the chair and the huntsman had made a place for himself on the floor. There was no sign of the prince. Of Toby. Not wanting to wake them, she crept quietly along the narrow tunnel and up the ladder into the fresh air.

Toby was sitting under a tree in the morning

sunshine and he smiled at her. 'They still asleep?'

'Like babies.'

'What a beautiful day.' She sat beside him, the grass dry even though it was only just past dawn. 'Warm too.' He was staring out at the slowly-waking city and Petra thought she'd never seen anyone more handsome in her whole life, and nor was she likely to. She reached up and turned his face to hers and slowly kissed him. Despite the stubble on his face his lips were soft as they met hers, his tongue and hers entwining until the heat inside her was too much and she fell backwards, pulling him with her. She slid her hands under his shirt and felt him quiver as she traced her fingers over his flat stomach, teasing the line of hair that ran down from his chest to beyond his belly button.

He groaned and wrapped one hand firmly in her hair as her own moved lower, her breath coming harder as he pushed up her dress. She reached for him through his trousers and he paused and gripped her wrist. His face was flushed and the yellow flecks in his green eyes had brightened with his lust.

'Are you sure?'

She answered by smiling and wrapping her legs around his hips, pulling him towards her.

'I'll take that as a yes,' he managed, before their

passion overwhelmed them and any words were lost in mouths and hands and movement and love.

When they were done, they lay together and looked at the sky and laughed and smiled in the way new lovers do, and then kissed some more. Soldiers could have stood over them and Petra wouldn't have noticed. This was true love. She'd realised it the first time she'd seen him, and her heart had known it the first time she'd heard his distant howl through the forest wall. He was for her, and she was for him. Petra and Toby. Petra and the wolf.

'Are you hungry?' he said eventually, gently pushing loose strands of hair out of her face. 'There's a bakery just down there. We could get some bread.'

'What about the first minister's men?' she asked.

'They're not looking for us, they're looking for Rumplestiltskin.' He grinned and got up before pulling her to her feet. 'And if he's not carrying a spindle I doubt very much they'd recognise him. Soldiers, as a rule, aren't the brightest boys. Not in this kingdom at any rate.'

'Then let's get some bread.' She linked her arm through his and they strolled down the path in the sunshine as if they had no cares in the world.

As soon as the waft of baking hit the light breeze, Petra realised just how hungry she was, and they joined the small crowd of early risers waiting for their turn at the baker's hatch. She was lost in her own thoughts of love and laughter, leaning her body into him, needing as much contact as possible, until she felt Toby's grip tighten slightly on her arm, and then the words of those around them became more than just background hubbub and her appetite vanished.

'I just saw the blacksmith's wife. It came into their house through the back door last night. The blacksmith came down to catch it ripping a haunch of venison they'd been saving apart. He said he'd never seen such a beast. Its eyes glowed, that's what the blacksmith said.'

'It's not natural, everyone knows that. All that blue fur. And twice the size of a normal wolf.'

'Should be hunted down. Maybe then the forest will open up.'

'Maybe the wolf's what's cursed us.'

Toby mumbled at the baker who presented him with four large freshly baked rolls, and then he tugged Petra away.

'We'll go to the queen and she'll send soldiers to find it. Nowhere to hide with the forest closed round us. They'll hack it to death. Before it starts coming for the children.'

She kept her arm in his and kept their pace slow

as they walked back up the path and the voices faded behind them. Their sentiment echoed loudly in the silence though, Toby's jaw stayed tight and all smiles were gone.

'Don't listen to them,' Petra said. 'They're just stupid gossips.'

'I would never attack children,' he said, through gritted teeth.

'I know,' Petra said. 'Forget about them.' It was easier said than done, and she knew it. 'Come on, let's see if the others are awake. Find out where the prince has gone.'

Beautiful as the day was, she couldn't help but feel a wave of relief when they were underground again. Whatever she'd said to try and make him feel better, Toby was right to worry. Petra might know very little about court life, but she understood village gossips. It didn't take much for a few exaggerated words to become blazing torches and pitchforks, and the idea of a mob coming for Toby made her stomach lurch up to her heart and vice versa.

'**N**o,' Toby said, when they'd heard the huntsman's plan. 'You don't have to do that.'

'Yes, I do.' The huntsman glowered up back from beneath his dark hair. 'That girl's dead because I bandaged Beauty's finger and woke her. I have to put it right.'

'It has to be put right, yes. But not by you.'

Most of the bread lay half-eaten on their plates, any hunger forgotten after hearing of what the Beast had done, and of the prince's deal with Rumplestiltskin. Petra felt quite sick. But nothing could prepare her for what came next.

'I'll do it.' Toby said simply. 'You can all go back to the forest and I'll stay.'

'No,' Petra gasped. 'That's stupid. You have to come too.'

'Why?' He looked at her, his eyes flashing bitterly. 'You've heard what they said. Why would it be different anywhere else? Wherever I go, I'll be hunted. At least here I'll be free.'

'You can't!' Tears sprung to Petra's eyes. 'We can't be apart. I won't leave you!'

'You're better off without me,' he said. 'Safer too. When the mob comes, which they eventually will, they won't take kindly to anyone who's protected me.'

'You can't do it anyway,' the huntsman sighed. 'It must happen tonight. You'll be a wolf.'

'Wait until the morning,' Toby said. 'I can do it then.'

Petra stared at him. The idea of living without him – of knowing that he was just the other side of the wall, living on, young and healthy, as she grew old and died with only the sound of his distant howling drifting through the wood to haunt her – was too much to bear. For a moment she couldn't breathe.

'We can't wait until morning,' Rumplestiltskin said. 'It will be too dangerous; the Beast will be too alert. The plan is set for tonight.'

Petra's head spun. She could see Toby's distress. He didn't want to leave her, but neither did he want to spend his life as an outcast. Always lying to people. Always hiding.

'Wait,' she said, suddenly. 'Wait.' As the perfect thought struck her, she smiled. 'The curse doesn't affect the one who wields it?'

Rumplestiltskin nodded.

'Then I'll do it,' she said. 'Toby can guard the room and I'll prick her finger.'

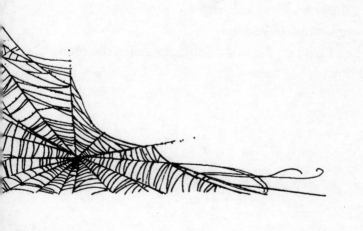

11
'I give you this magic . . .'

he prince was surprised that after the huntsman and Rumplestiltskin had left he did
manage to fall asleep for a fitful few hours
although he had left all the lamps burning. He met
Beauty on the terrace for breakfast and she rose from
her chair and dashed towards him, a sweet smile
making her face glow.

'I missed you,' she whispered, reaching up on her
tiptoes to kiss him. She tasted of the sweet apple she'd
been eating, but still his stomach flipped and churned
as their lips touched. He focused on the darkness of
her hair, so different to the blood-streaked blonde of
the Beast who'd tormented him the previous day. He
forced the memory away, doing his best to lock it in
a far corner of his mind.

'I missed you too,' he answered weakly. 'I barely slept.' The last part wasn't a lie. He wondered if she had realised an entire day was missing from her memory. She took his hand and they sat in the sunshine and she talked merrily about their wedding plans as he forced a pastry and some juice inside him. In the bright daylight, and in the presence of her gentleness, it was almost possible to think that all that had happened had been with someone else completely. The girl was good-natured and lovely. She didn't even sound the same as the other.

'And how are you both this morning?'

The prince turned to see the first minister standing in the shadow of the awning.

'Wonderful, thank you,' Beauty answered, gracing him with an affectionate smile. 'And what a glorious day.'

'Just the man,' the prince said, happy to hear how confident his voice sounded. He may have had a moment of weakness when he failed to defend the servant girl – he knew from the huntsman's expression that he thought him a coward – but he was brave. How could the huntsman know what it had been like in there? Would he have behaved any differently? Probably not. The prince could be brave. And he would play his part well today. 'I wanted to have a private dinner tonight. Just Beauty and all her ministers. I'd like to get to know them better – and for them to get to know me – before we have our wedding.' He smiled at Beauty. 'I don't want them to worry that perhaps she's made a bad choice.'

'What a lovely idea,' Beauty exclaimed. 'But how could they think that?'

The prince stood up and went to kiss her. 'I would like to make sure. I want you to be proud of me.'

She wrapped her arms round his neck and laughed and then he spun her off the ground and kissed her. More passionately this time. It was strange this allure she had. He ached for her beauty even as he was re-volted by the knowledge of the dormant woman who shared her body.

'This shirt is too hot,' he said. 'I need to change. Shall I meet you by the maze?' he asked her. 'We could walk and make our plans together.'

She nodded, her face shining with love, and he turned away. The first minister followed him back into the castle, his face thoughtful.

'How are you feeling this morning, your highness?'

'Oh, I'm fine.' The prince smiled. 'Tired but fine. I had some terrible dreams. I think I might have had a fever. Or too much wine. And that terrible storm raged all night.' He shuddered as memories of blood and the Beast and the knife rose up unwelcome. 'But now the sun is shining and all is well.'

He knew he wasn't looking entirely normal. He could feel himself trembling and there was an entirely surreal quality to the day, as if perhaps this was the dream and all the horrors he'd experienced were the reality that was waiting for him to wake. But perhaps that would help the first minister to believe him.

'Dreams can be strange things,' the first minister said reassuringly. 'I find it best to keep busy and then they fade quickly.'

'Exactly,' the prince flashed him a smile. 'So will you organise the dinner?'

'Certainly,' he said. 'Hopefully your friends will have returned to us by then.'

'My huntsman is thorough,' the prince said, balling his hands into fists to stop them trembling. 'He will return when he has your traitor and not before. Unless your soldiers find him first, of course.'

'Of course,' the first minister agreed.

'And then we can all live happily ever after.'

The prince had never been so happy to close a door behind him. This was going to be a long day.

e did, in part, take the first minister's advice and kept busy. His stomach was in a knot that somehow the huntsman's and Rumplestiltskin's plan would be found out, and then the full wrath of both queen and ministers would land on him. He wasn't afraid of the dungeons, although he was sure that were he dragged there that would change, but he was afraid of anything that might bring the Beast back. As he walked through the maze with Beauty, pretending to be enthused about finding the right path through it and laughing loudly when they found themselves in yet another dead end, he fought back images of the writhing couples and the extraordinary pleasure he'd felt before the horrors of the serving girl's death. How could Beauty have wrought it all?

Finally, they found the centre of the maze, a circular space with a waterfall and a stone bench decorated with woodland creatures, and Beauty pulled him towards her and kissed him again, and despite his inner torment he felt himself responding to her. He remembered the full curves of her firm body under the sheer dress the Beast had worn and he felt a sudden urge to rip her clothes from her and take her rough and fast over the bench.

'I can't wait until our wedding night,' she said, softly, her own eyes glazed with longing. 'When at last we can love each other properly.'

A part of his heart broke then. He couldn't help it. He had thought she was so perfect – and, here in the maze, she *was* so perfect – that he wondered if he was still, after everything, a little in love with her. That thought revolted him and instantly all he could see behind his eyes was blood, and the heat of the sun was the feel of it on his skin, and the rush of the waterfall was the sound of her mad laughter as she revelled in death, but still he wanted her. Was that her magic at work, he wondered? How could he tell? If he ever loved a princess again, he decided as they finally strolled back out and towards the castle, he would make sure she was as beautiful on the inside as out before he kissed her. Whatever spell Beauty held over him would soon be over, he comforted himself with that. And when he was gone from here, he would think of her and the Beast no more.

Dinner finally came around and the prince was the perfect host, ensuring everyone's glasses were constantly full and regaling them with tales of his life back at his father's castle. He took time to question all the ministers about their families and their roles in the queen's cabinet and they in turn, as the wine flowed, told him tales of their city that clearly filled them with pride. In the main, he was surprised to re-alise, they were good men. How much did they love Beauty that they could cope with the Beast? Or were they simply too afraid of her to act? Once again, he felt proud of his own bravery and vital role in the plan to return them to the safety of their slumber. He sipped his wine, careful not to drink too much, and reflected on the huntsman. It was good that he would stay behind and put her back to sleep; that would ensure that when the prince returned home he could tell the story as he wished, with whatever small adjustments were required. This was his ad-venture; it would be told his way.

'Goodnight, my love,' the prince said, about to leave a swaying and giggly Beauty at her bedroom door. 'Until tomorrow. Until our wedding day.'

Even though his sane mind was desperate to get away from both her and the castle, his heart ached with the knowledge that if all went well, he would never see her face again.

'I love you so much,' she said, squeezing him tightly. 'Tonight, I will go to sleep the happiest girl in the world knowing that you are to be my husband.

I'll be dreaming of you and our happiness until I wake, of how perfect our life will be together.'

He was glad her face was pressed against his chest, because although the prince could be weak and selfish and part of his mind and heart had been more damaged than he could yet imagine by his experiences with the Beast, he did not consider himself a cruel man. The knowledge that he was sending her to her death ached inside him in the echo of her happiness. He did care for her – for this sweet girl – how could anyone not? He felt every one of his flaws like knives in his skin, and for a moment she was only Beauty; there was no Beast.

'Dream of us forever,' he whispered. 'And may your dreams be wonderful.'

'Oh, they will be,' she said, squeezing him tighter. 'My sleep will be wonderful because tomorrow we wed.'

When the prince finally walked away, he did not look back. He couldn't bring himself to, and then there was the click of a handle turning and she was gone.

'So, you're not staying?' he said, slightly dismayed, when he heard the new plan. They'd arrived together an hour or so after the prince had returned to his room, the wolf – a part of the story that the prince felt he could wait until later to hear about – guarding the room outside while they fetched him. He'd changed back into the clothes he'd arrived in, his royal cloak freshly cleaned, and bundled towels arranged under his sheets to look like someone was sleeping there. With the arrangements made and his things gathered and ready to go, a little of his confidence had returned.

'It's better this way,' Petra said. 'And he knows the forest and the forest knows him. If anyone has a chance of cutting you out, it's the huntsman.'

'Yes,' the prince said. 'Yes, I suppose it is.' He smiled at the huntsman. 'It will be good to return together.' In many ways, on reflection, it would be. The prince wasn't entirely sure he could find his way through the forest on his own, and he'd had enough adventures for a lifetime. As for how the story was relayed to the king, he doubted the huntsman would care. He was a rough sort, but he wasn't stupid. He'd know not to contradict the prince. 'And I shall make sure you are rewarded for your noble offer anyway,' he finished.

The huntsman simply nodded, but the prince shook the slight away. They were leaving and that was all that mattered.

'Do you want to stand here all night talking about it, or shall we get on?' Petra asked. The huntsman grabbed her arm, as she turned towards the door.

'I'm still not happy about this,' he said.

'Well, I am.' She smiled and her elfin face was transformed into something beautiful. 'We'll have a hundred years together, and then after that we'll get to grow old. What other lovers have had that opportunity?'

Rumplestiltskin was carefully pulling the spindle from his knapsack and the girl looked at him with a strange affection as she opened the bedroom door and led them back out into the corridor, the wolf immediately rubbing itself against her leg. She stepped closer to the huntsman so the old man was out of earshot. 'When you get back to the forest, tell him he must go to my grandmother's house and tell her his story. '

'Why?'

'Just make sure he does. It's important. Also, have him tell her to listen for me at the forest wall.' She reached up and kissed the huntsman on the cheek, and then did the same to the prince before taking the spindle from Rumplestiltskin. 'Now go.'

'I give you this magic,' Rumplestiltskin said. 'I hope it brings you better luck than it did me.'

Petra smiled at the old man. 'It will. And we'll make sure it works this time.'

'Good luck.' The prince said, his feet itching to be gone. Every second they loitered was another moment they could be caught.

'Three hours, remember,' Petra said. She smiled once more, and then with her red cloak flowing behind her and the blue wolf leading her, she turned and ran down the corridor towards the queen's apartments.

12
'See to the queen!'

The forest wall was battling them every inch of the way as the three men hacked and squeezed their way through the branches and vines, repeating the method the huntsman, Petra and the prince had used, holding a small space open while they cut through to the next. None spoke as they worked, all three aware that they weren't going fast enough. The forest had been tough before but this time the branches seemed aggressive. Even before they'd travelled the first foot, the prince's shirt had been torn, leaving a small piece of cloth flapping on a thorn behind them.

The enchanted kingdom was still visible through the gaps and they must have been working at it for more than an hour. Even in the dead of night it was hot, sweaty work and they gasped and cursed quietly with every tiny step forward.

'Will we make it?' the prince asked, breathless.

'Maybe,' the huntsman grunted, hacking at a thick branch with his small axe. 'Maybe not. 'If we wake up in a hundred years with trees growing out of our arses, then I'd say we didn't make it.'

'*Hey!*'

Light from a flaming torch swept over them, and a horse whinnied as the patrol came to a halt.

'*Sir, look! There's someone cutting through the wall!*' The light pressed against the branches and for a second the three men froze, but it didn't help. They'd been seen.

'*It's him! Rumplestiltskin! Get after him!*'

'*You! Get back to the castle! Quickly! Tell the ministers!*'

Suddenly, the greenery behind them was being vigorously attacked by swords and a group of soldiers was following them into the wall.

The huntsman beat at the wood faster, painfully aware that there was only three or four feet between them and that the soldiers would be stronger.

'Come on, come on,' the prince muttered, pressing his weight against the resistant hedge so the huntsman could move further.

'I'm doing my best,' the huntsman growled.

'I can see them. The bastards! I can see them!'

There was a flash of steel as the men behind them lunged forwards, thrusting their blades through the gaps.

The prince cried out as the tip of a sword slashed into his side.

The huntsman found he could work quicker after that.

Petra had pulled a chair close to the queen's bed, and with the wolf beside her, occasionally licking her hand, she'd held the spindle on her lap and watched Beauty sleep as the quiet minutes passed. The prince had done his job well and she was dead to the world. The phrase hurt Petra's heart with the truth in it. If everything went according to plan, she'd never wake again.

She couldn't help but feel sorry for her. Despite the Beast who resided inside her she was the sweetest of girls and, water witch magic or not, Petra felt a pull towards her. The terrible things that were her nature were also not her fault. Petra imagined that if Beauty knew the suffering she'd inflicted on her subjects, or what she'd done to her poor father, she would prick her finger herself. Still, lying there so still, she looked perfect.

Petra wondered how many more hours in the decades to come she would sit in this chair and wonder about the girl who would sleep until her last drop of blood had fallen. She ran her fingers through the wolf's rough fur, taking comfort from the heat of his head.

Suddenly, the wolf's ears pricked up and he let out a low growl. All thoughts of the queen's tragic life vanished as Petra sat up straight, her nerves jangling.

'What is it, Toby?' she whispered, but within a second she had her answer. There was movement in the corridors. From outside, the sound of people urgently calling to each other drifted up to them. Despite the urge to get up and look, Petra stayed by the bed, her hand hovering over Beauty's delicate, pale fingers. Her heart raced as the noise in the corridors grew louder, footsteps dashing this way and that, and men barking commands.

Her heart raced, and the wolf's hackles rose, his fur puffing out so much that he truly looked like a magnificent unnatural beast. She needed to give the huntsman and Rumplestiltskin the longest time possible to get away. They did not deserve a hundred years sleep, or to wake to find everyone they loved lost. And her grandmother did not deserve to die without knowing Petra's choice or meeting Rumple-stiltskin. She gritted her teeth. She was ready to do it, but not until the very last minute.

As the noise grew around them, Beauty stirred but she did not wake. The wolf was ready to pounce and pin her down should she try and run, but Petra hoped beyond hope it wouldn't come to that. What if the Beast woke when she was terrified? What would happen to them all then?

'The prince is gone!' a voice shouted. 'He's tricked us!'

'See to the queen! Check her majesty is safe!'

Petra was staring so fixedly at the main doors to the queen's bedroom that the secret side entrance, hidden in a panel in the wall next to the wardrobe, slid open and the first minister was inside before she could react. She almost dropped the spindle in surprise and with a growl, the wolf prepared to spring.

For a moment, amidst all the commotion outside, the old man said nothing. He stared at Petra and the spindle and then at the girl in the bed.

'Stay quiet,' he said and then strode to the doors.

Petra's mind was racing and she kept one hand firmly on the wolf who she could feel was ready to spring and rip the minister's throat out to protect her. She still had time to do it. Even if he screamed blue murder into the corridor. There was no need for more bloodshed than necessary but the wolf, although still Toby, thought in more black and white terms than that.

The first minister opened the door a fraction. 'Her majesty is sleeping. She's fine,' he said quietly. 'Now find that prince!'

He closed the door again and leant against it. For a long moment he stared at Petra and she saw the conflict in his face, and then the tired sadness that he carried for his own complicity with the Beast.

'They will come back,' he said quietly. 'And she will wake. The Beast will sense the trouble.' He walked over to the window and stared out at the peaceful kingdom for a moment, before sitting down on the window seat with a heavy sigh.

'If you're going to do it,' he stretched his legs out and leant his head back on the soft cushions, 'then do it now.'

Petra looked out at the sky that was streaking with purple dawn and hoped that she'd given them enough time, and then, with a deep breath, she carefully lifted the girl's slim forefinger and jabbed the sharp spindle into it.

The huntsman and Rumplestiltskin pulled the bleeding prince through the last of the branches just as the air around them trembled and a wave of heat rushed through the tightening branches, filling the air with the scent of a thousand types of bark and leaf and flower. The wall shimmered momentarily and sparkled in the breaking dawn.

The three men stared as they panted, the prince hunched over slightly as his side bled. If they had thought the wall was dense before, it was now completely impenetrable.

'Well, that answers that then,' the huntsman said, nodding at the men who had been so close behind them. The soldiers had fallen instantly asleep and, held up by the branches, vines were now curling up around their limbs. After a few seconds they were no longer visible.

They all stared at the wall as the relief of their freedom sank in, along with the exhaustion in their limbs.

'I want to go home,' the prince said, weakly.

Rumplestiltskin looked around him, scanning the horizon for something familiar.

'What now for you?' the huntsman asked.

'The tower.' There was no hesitation. 'I will have my revenge on that witch, and I will see my daughter's grave.' His freedom from the city and the return of Beauty to her sleeping death had not eased his bitterness. He looked at the pale prince, who was examining his flesh wound with more than a touch of horror. 'And then I shall be back to hold you to your word.'

The prince nodded but said nothing.

'There was something else,' the huntsman added, as he slung his bag back over his shoulder and prepared to move on. 'Something Petra made me promise to tell you. She said it was important. About visiting her grandmother ...'

Dawn claimed the silent city as the first drop of blood hit the floor beside the sleeping Beauty's bed. In the glass by her bed, the rose drooped ever so slightly. Petra gave Beauty one last look and then went out into the corridor to join Toby who smiled at her and her heart sang.

'No more wolf for a month,' he said.

'Shame,' she said, taking his arm. 'He's a good

looking creature. I guess I'll have to make do with you at night until then.' They stepped carefully over the sleeping bodies and their shoes tapped out against the marble, the only feet that would walk these corridors for a long, long time. 'Let's get some breakfast. I'm starving.'

'Do you think they made it?' Toby asked as they turned onto the sweeping staircase.

'I think so,' she answered. 'This adventure deserves a happy ending.' She rested her head on his arm. 'Other than ours.'

'What was all that about your grandmother?' he asked. 'And Rumplestiltskin.'

Her smile stretched wider as she thought of how happy those two would be when they met. 'I couldn't tell him. I don't think he'd have let me stay here if I had. My great-grandmother made me this cloak, you know. Well, she made it for my grandmother. She said it was her favourite colour because it reminded her of her father.'

'I'm not following,' Toby said. 'What's that got to do with Rumplestiltskin?'

'She was a strange woman,' Petra said. 'She arrived in the village out of nowhere when she was twenty-two. When my grandmother was little she told her stories of her childhood, of being trapped in a tower by a witch until one day a handsome prince rescued her.' She paused. 'It clearly didn't work out, but she left my grandmother and then my mother and then me, with a healthy cynicism about Prince Charmings that stuck, even though we never really believed her stories.'

Toby turned and stared at her. 'You think your great-grandmother was Rumplestiltskin's daughter?'

Sunlight burst through the castle windows and Petra knew it was going to be a beautiful day.

'Her name was Rapunzel,' she said. 'So yes, I think she was.'

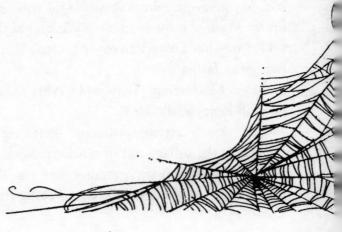

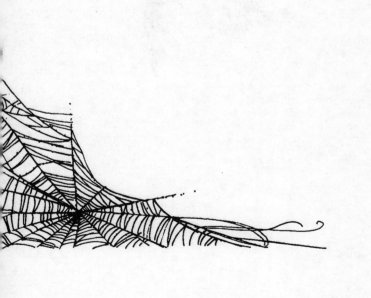

Epilogue

'You stay here,' the huntsman said, after carefully bandaging the prince's wound and setting a fire. 'We'll make camp for the night and then tomorrow we'll figure out where we are.'

Somehow, and he wondered if it was the forest's wiles at work, they had lost their bearings and even the huntsman thought they might have strayed into a separate kingdom rather than the prince's own. Still, what more could happen to them? They'd have a good rest and then they'd be on their way. The prince's wound would not kill him and a few extra days in the forest would do neither of them any harm.

'Don't be too long,' the prince said, a sorry sight

with his royal cape wrapped round him and his face pale and sweating. 'I don't want to be alone. I keep thinking about her. About Beauty.' The huntsman slapped him gently on his shoulder.

'These woods are rich. There'll be food a plenty and I'll be back soon enough.' He picked up his bag and carried it with him, even though he only needed his knife. He'd earned the diamond shoes, but if the prince found them he would have to give them up, and something raw and animal in his soul told him that he could not let that happen.

He left the prince staring into the fire torn between grief and celebration – Beauty and the Beast – and headed out of the clearing.

It was a warm day in the forest and even though it made the hair on his chest tickle with sweat as he moved through the trees, that pleased the huntsman. Heat slowed animals as much as men and although his skills were such he had no doubt meat would roast over the fire tonight, the task was going to be easier than expected. He could counter the laziness that came with the sun and force himself to be alert. It was unlikely to be the same for the animals in this dense woodland. So far, apart from an old crone scurrying between the trees just before he'd spied the stag, he'd seen little sign of human habitation and he'd heard no horn blowing for a Royal hunt. It was wild here. He liked that ...

THE END

The end ...
or is it just the beginning?

High in her tower the clever witch smiled,
the spindles around her so many beguiled.

How easy it was to riddle with men,
and now Beauty was deep in her death-sleep again.

The princess was cursed, both without and within,
Yet one thing could save her: a love free from sin.

The Kingdoms would change; there would be war
    and fear,
And Beauty would sleep for a full hundred years,

What happened then was a mystery, she knew,
But she had great faith in kisses that were true ...

Acknowledgements

First off, I have to thank my editor Gillian Redfearn who started this fairy tale with me, and without whose input they would not be so magical. Secondly – or in fact, on a par, as I'm sure Gillian would agree – I owe a massive debt to Les Edwards whose beautiful illustrations really bring the stories to life and also to those in the cover department at Gollancz who make the books a joy to hold and look at. A big thanks to Simon Spanton, Jon Weir and the rest of the Gollancz posse for all their hard work, and invariably, their drinking companionship. Also thanks Jon and Genn for their hard work promoting these, and to my agent Veronique for always being there when I need her.

On a more personal note, thanks to Lou Abercrombie and Muriel Gray for their kind words

Acknowledgements

on the books, and to my flatmate Lee Thompson for putting up with boxes of books arriving, paper everywhere and my general writer stresses. And for buying me wine when required.

SARAH PINBOROUGH was born in 1972 in Buckinghamshire, and now lives just a few miles away after a childhood spent travelling all over the world (her father, now retired, was a diplomat). When she was eight she packed her trunk and left the Middle East for a ten-year stretch in boarding school. The memories provide her with much material for her horror and supernatural thrillers . . .

• • •

Find out more by following
@SarahPinborough on Twitter.

More from Sarah Pinborough . . .

• • •

THE DEATH HOUSE

This is an exceptional, contemporary heart-breaking novel

Toby's life was perfectly normal . . . until it was unravelled
by something as simple as a blood test.

Taken from his family, Toby now lives in the Death House,
an out-of-time existence far from the modern world, where
he, and the others who live there, are studied by Matron and
her team of nurses. They're looking for any sign of sickness.
Any sign of their charges changing. Any sign that it's
time to take them to the sanatorium.

No one returns from the sanatorium.

Withdrawn from his house-mates, and living in his memories of
the past, Toby spends his days fighting his fear and wondering
how much time he has left. But then a new arrival in the house
shatters the fragile peace, and everything changes.

Because everybody dies.
It's how you choose to live that counts.

• • •

'A beautiful story, honestly told' Neil Gaiman

'Moving and totally involving. I couldn't put it down'
Stephen King

**'Shocking and gripping, albeit
ultimately hopeful and utterly
moving, and it's Sarah Pinborough's
finest novel to date' *Sci-Fi Now***

'Compelling, heart breaking, yet
sinister this novel is beautifully
written and thought-provoking'
Telegraph and Argus

13 MINUTES

I was dead for 13 minutes.

I don't remember how I ended up in the icy water but I do know this - it wasn't an accident and I wasn't suicidal.

They say you should keep your friends close and your enemies closer, but when you're a teenage girl, it's hard to tell them apart. My friends love me, I'm sure of it. But that doesn't mean they didn't try to kill me. Does it?

13 MINUTES by Sarah Pinborough is a gripping psychological thriller about people, fears, manuiplation and the power of the truth. A stunning read, it questions our relationships - and what we really know about the people closest to us . . .

• • •

'The most exciting premise of the year surely belongs to Sarah Pinborough's *13 Minutes*'
The Express

'A must-read for fans of Megan Abbott, and fans of TV shows like *Broadchurch*. Very highly recommended, this is an addictive, must-read. Excellent. I can't wait for Pinborough's next novel'
Civilian Reader

THE DOG-FACED GODS TRILOGY

*A world in recession, a shadowy secret organisation,
terrorist attacks . . . and one DI who must unravel it all*

Recession has gripped the world, leaving it deep in debt
to The Bank, a secretive company run by the world's
wealthiest men. Pulling the strings in the background,
they answer to no-one and do as they please.

Meanwhile the sinister Man of Flies, spreader of a lethal virus,
has come to London and it's up to DI Cass Jones to catch him.
But he is already burdened by visions of his dead brother, and
a personal investigation to save his nephew . . . and has no
idea he is heading into conflict with The Bank . . .

• • •

**'Those who like their fantasy dark should grab
Sarah Pinborough's *A Matter of Blood*' *The Times***

'Pinborough's fiction moves at a breakneck pace. Once
you start you can't stop . . . she understands how people
tick. I always trust the ride, because I know I'll wind
up some place good' Sarah Lagan

**'A pitch black thriller with a fierce emotional payload – gritty,
authentic and compelling' Michael Marshall**

'A gnarly, involving and atmospheric mystery that
explores some very dark territory. Uncomfortable
timely, exceptionally well-written' *SFX*

ABOUT GOLLANCZ

Gollancz is the oldest SF publishing imprint in the world. Since being founded in 1927 Gollancz has continued to publish a focused selection of bestselling and award-winning authors. The front-list includes **Ben Aaronovitch**, **Joe Abercrombie**, **Charlaine Harris**, **Joanne Harris**, **Joe Hill**, **Alastair Reynolds**, **Patrick Rothfuss**, **Nalini Singh** and **Brandon Sanderson**.

As one of the largest Science Fiction and Fantasy imprints in the UK it is no surprise we have one of the most extensive backlists in the world. Find high quality SF on Gateway written by such authors as **Philip K. Dick**, **Ursula Le Guin**, **Connie Willis**, **Sir Arthur C. Clarke**, **Pat Cadigan**, **Michael Moorcock** and **George R.R. Martin**.

We also have a strand of publishing in translation, which includes French, Polish and Russian authors. Gollancz is home to more award-winning authors than any other imprint, with names including **Aliette de Bodard**, **M. John Harrison**, **Paul McAuley**, **Sarah Pinborough**, **Pierre Pevel**, **Justina Robson** and many more.

The SF Gateway
More than 3,000 classic, rare and previously out-of-print SF novels at your fingertips.
www.sfgateway.com

The Gollancz Blog
Bringing you news from our worlds to yours. Stories, interviews, articles and exclusive extracts just for you!
www.gollancz.co.uk

GOLLANCZ
LONDON